E

William Gill was b
He trained as an a
Great Britain in 1:
London.

By the same author

SUGAR AND SPICE
FORTUNE'S CHILD
UNFORGETTABLE

WILLIAM GILL

Eyes of Jade

HarperCollins*Publishers*

HarperCollins*Publishers*
77–85 Fulham Palace Road,
Hammersmith, London W6 8JB

This paperback edition 1995
1 3 5 7 9 8 6 4 2

First published in Great Britain by
HarperCollins*Publishers* 1994

Copyright © William Gill 1994

The Author asserts the moral right to
be identified as the author of this work

ISBN 0 00 649015 8

Set in Sabon

Printed in Great Britain by
HarperCollinsManufacturing Glasgow

All rights reserved. No part of this publication may be
reproduced, stored in a retrieval system, or transmitted,
in any form or by any means, electronic, mechanical,
photocopying, recording or otherwise, without the prior
permission of the publishers.

This book is sold subject to the condition that it shall not,
by way of trade or otherwise, be lent, re-sold, hired out or
otherwise circulated without the publisher's prior consent
in any form of binding or cover other than that in which it
is published and without a similar condition including this
condition being imposed on the subsequent purchaser.

For Eliza and Bruno

ACKNOWLEDGEMENTS

I am very grateful to Dr Robert Hancock and Christopher Chope for their help with my research.

It takes only one lie
to change the history of the universe
Jorge Luis Borges

PROLOGUE

'Peter, we *must* go! We're going to be late!'

Frances Fellowes rarely raised her voice, but now it was imperative if she was going to make herself heard over the racket of skateboarders in the echoing space of Spitalfields Market on a Sunday morning. Her son had been ignoring her efforts to stop him for the last five minutes, and she stood in irritated impatience by the edge of the track as he zoomed past. Peter had heard her, she was sure, but he was enjoying his moment of glory with the all-excluding determination of a ten-year-old having fun – and being envied. He was one of the very few people on roller-blades, and none of the others was as impressive ('cool', he would say) as his own pair, recently sent from America by his godmother.

Frances watched him rush away towards the bend until he disappeared from sight, before he came racing back towards her again. His skill, his obvious enjoyment and her pride in his good looks made it hard for her to be *really* upset by his equally obvious disobedience.

'We'll never come back here unless you stop *now*!' she warned him none the less as he launched into yet another lap. The threat registered because she saw him slow down and turn back.

'That was great. *Please* can I stay for another five minutes?' he begged as soon as he joined her among the shivering bystanders.

'We must go. I told your father we'd be in Swanton by lunchtime, but we won't get there by tea at this rate,' Frances countered, helping him to undo his laces. 'We could come

I

back next Sunday,' she added enticingly as Peter put his trainers on, although she knew it was extremely unlikely. The election campaign had started three days ago; Norman would want to spend as much time as possible in his constituency, and he would want Peter and her there at weekends. The display of happy family life had become as large a part of electioneering as the promise of infallible policies, and Norman Fellowes was a worried man. He was fighting a marginal seat; much depended on the outcome, although he remained as unflappable as ever in public. Too astute a politician to own up to his great ambition, he seemed dismissive and amused whenever journalists pressed him on the strong possibility of his promotion to the Cabinet after the election, but Frances knew better.

'You must write to Donna to thank her for her present,' she reminded Peter as they left the market through the Commercial Street entrance. It was a dull, late March morning; even in the open air, the light had a similar greyish tint to the ghostly clarity under the market's glass roof. They turned left, walking alongside the piles of empty cardboard boxes and crates.

'I will, Mummy. You've already told me,' Peter replied. The edge of vagueness in his voice betrayed his lack of enthusiasm at the prospect, reminding Frances that she herself didn't contact Donna as often as she should. Guilt, a frequent experience in her life, flashed through her mind at the most unexpected moments, like a beam of light bouncing off a mirrored ball. It wasn't Donna's fault that she was Frances's last link with the past.

'You could write to her from school this week,' she suggested. 'I'm sure you have time in the evenings.'

'I don't want to go back to school,' Peter grumbled.

'That's nonsense. Why?'

'Because they all keep teasing me about my picture in that bloody magazine.'

'Mind your language,' Frances admonished him, but less sternly than she should have, because she shared his feeling. She had made a point of keeping herself and Peter out of the public eye, on the grounds that she wanted him to have the same life as any other boy his age. It had been easy during the early stages of Norman's political career, but he had started putting pressure on her when he became a Minister of State a year ago, and the pressure increased as soon as the election was a firm prospect. Eventually Frances agreed to an interview with *Hello!*, arranged through the Communications department at Central Office. The gushing copy of the published article made her cringe, as the spread of photographs of her, including one with Peter, had made her uneasy.

'That was nearly two weeks ago. They'll have forgotten by now. Anyway, there's nothing to be ashamed of, darling. They're just being silly,' she said as they walked into Folgate Street. Her car was parked about a hundred yards ahead, and she started to walk faster, anxious to get going.

'This place is really creepy,' Peter commented, looking around at the empty street. Frances took in the shuttered brick sheds and the Georgian houses, the eerie stillness of the scene, and silently concurred. There would have been something quaintly picturesque about the setting, if it hadn't been so lifeless.

'*You* found out about the track, and *you* were desperate to come here. Every bit of London doesn't look like Knightsbridge, you know,' she said lightly. A small white van drove slowly past, and stopped about twenty yards ahead of them. Two men got out and stood on the pavement, leaning against the van, and stared at her, so Frances made a point of looking the other way. Expecting some nasty comment from them, she took Peter's hand and increased her pace, but the men remained silent, unnaturally still; only when Frances had her back to them did she hear something. Not words, but the rush of swift movement, and then she felt an arm around her, a hand at her throat. She struggled as she saw the other man grabbing Peter.

'I'll give you whatever you want, but please don't hurt my son,' she managed to cry out before a cosh smashed against the side of her head. Almost unconscious, she felt her knees give, her body slumping in the man's grip.

Peter tried to scream, but he was too frightened. No sound came out of his throat. He kicked as his captor raised him from the ground, attempting to break free. The man had dragged him for a couple of yards when a calm male voice spoke.

'Let them go, or I'll blow your heads off. Now.'

Peter fell to his knees as his attacker dropped him. He stayed absolutely still, not daring to look back.

'Keep your hands up. Don't move,' the voice said. A moment later, Peter heard the clang of metal hitting the paving stones, then he saw a knife and a gun on the ground.

'Get away before I change my mind,' the voice said. The thugs scrambled into the van; a second later, they were speeding off, and Peter felt a hand on his shoulder.

'Don't worry, it's all over now,' the voice said. Peter turned and looked up at the tall, dark man who had saved them. He could not get a clear view, because the man leaned towards Frances, who was lying unconscious on the ground, then pulled a portable phone from his pocket.

'Mummy, please answer me. Are you all right?' Peter pleaded, kneeling by his mother's side.

'An ambulance will be here in no time. Your mummy will be fine, I assure you, but I can't stay with you. I'll see you again,' the man said. The boy watched him walk away, his pace increasing as the sound of an approaching siren filled the air. Only when the man had turned the corner, vanishing as suddenly as he had appeared, did Peter wonder if he should have asked him his name.

4

PART ONE

ONE

Melanie Clark had no reason to believe this morning would be different from usual. It was early January, the weather was cold and grey, and by now the only reminder of the Christmas break was the occasional mistake when she dated correspondence '1978' rather than '1979'. Just another morning: she had opened the mail, made coffee, placed or answered calls for her boss, and even done some filing before she sat at her desk, switched on her typewriter, put on her headphones and began to tackle the day's paperwork.

Melanie had worked as a secretary ever since she left high school; two years ago she had joined the Unity Investment Bank as secretary to Ted White, one of the Portfolio Managers in the Private Clients section. Now she was also training to become a Sales Assistant, the first real step towards a career in Asset Management. She didn't want to be a secretary for ever, and she looked forward to her eventual promotion. So far, though, life didn't seem to have changed much.

Her intercom buzzed.

'Mr Santos is here, Melanie,' the receptionist's voice crackled over the speaker.

Melanie liked to guess what new clients would look like on her way to meet them. Some features were common to all of them: they were rich, and middle-aged or old. Many were foreigners, as she guessed Diego Santos was, although Spanish names were common in New York, and clearly he didn't belong to either of the two distinctive groups among their clientele: the Widows and the Arabs. Melanie decided that Mr Santos would be in his late forties or early fifties, not very tall and rather stocky; his thinning grey-black hair would be slicked back, and he would probably have a moustache. It was more than likely that he would be wearing a gold Rolex.

Melanie approached a man sitting in one of the leather armchairs in reception, his face invisible behind an open *Wall Street Journal* he held in his tanned hands. His watch was very simple, as discreetly expensive as the rest of his clothes.

'Mr Santos?' she asked. He put down the paper and stood up, towering over her; middle age was a long way ahead of him. All her other guesses were wrong too.

Diego Santos was the most attractive man she had seen in her life.

'But what does this guy *look* like then?' Donna sank her teeth into a tuna and cottage cheese bagel as she waited for her friend's answer.

'Like heaven,' Melanie replied.

'Cut the poetry and give me the lowdown, will you? Is he tall?'

'About six two, I guess . . . He's got wonderful eyes. And a great nose. A bit Roman, but very sharp . . .'

'Big nose?' Donna interrupted.

'It's not small. Just right. Why?'

'You know what they say. Big nose, big dick,' Donna laughed.

Donna Campbell was a secretary in the Legal Department. They had met not long after Melanie joined the bank, and had become friends. Donna was good company; her stories were as entertaining as her life was eventful, if a little one-dimensional. The New York Health and Racket Club served a double purpose for her: it kept Donna trim

8

and lithe, and it supplied her with a never-ending supply of equally well-toned males. Donna wasn't very beautiful, but she listened to men as if spellbound by their brilliance, spoke to them in a special low, breathy voice, her lips writhing like a couple of snakes in warm sand, and few men could resist her. Melanie found her friend's performance laughably obvious, but there was no doubt that it was effective.

'I wouldn't know. "Size of dick" is not one of the questions on the client's Fact Sheet,' Melanie replied.

'How rich is he?'

'Not *that* rich. He valued his business in Argentina at two million dollars.'

'You *are* dumb,' Donna sighed. 'All these foreigners lie like married men when it comes to their assets. He must have zillions if he mentioned millions. You ought to give him some encouragement.'

'Oh, sure,' Melanie said. 'I've only got to whistle, and he'll be at my door. The fact that he didn't say a word to me is just a detail.'

Donna raised her hands in mock despair.

'You're blonde, gorgeous, and your legs are longer than an evening alone. You underrate yourself, sweetheart. Just give him a long sizzling look next time he's around, that's all.'

'You're better at that than I am,' Melanie smiled. 'He'll be back here next year, if I'm lucky. Foreign clients don't show up that often, unless they're losing money.'

'Then think of him as just another man,' Donna offered as consolation. 'Anyway, so far you haven't told me what's so special about him. There are plenty of good-looking guys around.'

Melanie thought for a moment.

'He's got class,' she replied. 'Real class.'

'He's probably just some smartass,' Donna said, 'and

9

I'm the world's greatest expert on smartasses. Maybe *I* should meet Mr Santos, and find out. It would save you a lot of time and hassle.'

Melanie knew that, given the opportunity, Donna would be only too willing to 'help'. It had happened before, but luckily always when it didn't matter very much to her.

'Ted White's office,' Melanie said briskly.

'Could I speak to Mr White, please?'

'He's in LA today. Can I help you?'

'I'm sorry. How stupid of me. He told me yesterday he would be away, but I forgot . . .' the man said, and Melanie's fingers clutched the receiver as she recognized the accent. She was sure it was Diego Santos. 'Perhaps you can do something for me,' the man said tentatively. 'I've filled in the form Mr White gave me, and I'm leaving tomorrow morning. I would like to show it to you, to make sure I haven't made a mistake . . .'

'Why don't you . . .' Melanie didn't complete the standard suggestion that she might be able to help him over the phone. Diego Santos was giving her a chance to see him again. 'I'd be very happy to help you, if I can,' she said instead.

'Oh, that's great. Now, let me look at my diary . . . I have so many things to do. The last day is always the worst . . .' He sighed in frustration. 'Would you mind meeting me for a drink after work? I don't have a moment until then . . .' he said apologetically.

Melanie felt as if her lottery number had just come up.

'Yes, sure,' she replied, trying to sound business-like and failing.

'I really appreciate your help. Can you meet me at the St Regis at six? I'll wait for you at the bar.' *He* sounded very business-like, and Melanie tried to make sense of the conversation once she'd put down the phone. Diego Santos didn't need to meet her. A ten-year-old would have no trouble filling in the form; even if he'd had any genuine queries, he could have cleared them up over the phone. He had gone through this childish fabrication because he wanted to see her, and Melanie couldn't help smiling at his diffidence.

Then she remembered something else. He hadn't told her his name once during the conversation. Diego Santos took it for granted she would know. His pretended shyness and the business excuse were all for her sake, to make it easy for her to accept his invitation.

Diego Santos certainly had class.

'. . . So I finished high school and moved to New York. My mother was about to remarry then. It was . . .' Melanie heard herself, and stopped. Her answer to Diego's standard question about whether she had been born in New York or not had evolved into the story of her life, prompted by his further questions, as if he was trying to find a pigeon-hole for her.

'What did your father do?' He *was* trying to place her, and Melanie wondered if she should lie. Diego hadn't told her much about his own background, but he had made passing references to yachts, country houses and polo ponies. Not exactly her scene. What the hell, she thought. It was his problem, not hers.

'He's a plumber. Or at least that's what he was doing when he left us. I haven't seen him since I was fifteen,' Melanie replied. 'I must be the first plumber's daughter you've ever had a drink with.' Diego smiled. There were tiny laugh lines at the corners of his eyes, leaving white, feather-like traces amidst the tan, the perennial tan of those who can afford to do much more interesting things than merely sunbathe when they get the chance.

'I wouldn't know. Most people lie about themselves, but

11

you don't. I like that.' He was staring at her now, and Melanie looked away, noticing the clock on the wall. They had been talking for well over an hour. She was happy to sit there, watching his handsome face, but she was supposed to have come here because of work.

'Do you have the form?' she forced herself to ask. Diego pulled out a folded piece of paper from his breast pocket and gave it to her. Melanie checked it. She saw that he was twenty-eight, and her eyes skimmed to the 'Next of kin' box, where she read 'Amilcar Santos (father)/ María Torres Castillo de Santos (mother)'. He wasn't married.

'Everything seems to be in order,' she said, putting it away in her bag.

'I know,' Diego replied with a mischievous gleam in his eye. 'I've investments with four other New York banks.' He seemed slightly embarrassed now. 'I hope you don't mind my stupid excuse. I very much wanted to ask you to have dinner with me, but I thought it would be easier if we had a drink first. Are you free tonight? We could go to La Côte Basque; it's just across the road,' he explained, as if the restaurant's proximity would be a decisive factor in Melanie's decision.

'You mean *now*?' She sounded shocked.

'I'm sorry. It's very short notice, I know. It can only be tonight though. I'm going back tomorrow morning.'

Melanie's shock had nothing to do with the immediacy of his invitation, and she would have dropped dinner at the White House for him if necessary. She had never been to La Côte Basque in her life, but she booked tables there for her boss when a *really* important client was in town. Her shock was at the thought of having to make an entrance in her imitation Calvin Klein dress, bought at a discount store and now in the twilight stages of its office life. What the hell, she thought again. It should be her motto for the evening.

'I'd love to have dinner with you,' Melanie said, and all her worries vanished immediately. There was such genuine, delighted admiration in his eyes that she felt as if the Fairy Godmother had just waved her wand, turning tired wool jersey into beautiful new, rustling silk.

Later, when Melanie left La Côte Basque, she was relieved to be outside.

It had been different earlier in the evening. She had savoured every second, every detail: the fawning of the waiters, the surreptitious glances cast at Diego by some of the women, the polished silver on the table, the brittle glow of expensive glass, the esoteric menu full of promise of marvels to come. Then the food arrived: crisp, golden pastry light as tissue, the succulent pale flesh of lobster, vivid red tomatoes and the velvet green of tiny beans, lamb glistening with juices and smelling of thyme, wildly expensive wines the colour of summer sunlight or old velvet, lustrous domed dishes uncovered to reveal more wonders of colour and smell, and there she was with the handsomest man in the world.

Melanie said how delicious it all was, Diego apologized for the food not being quite what it used to be. It was a brief, isolated difference of opinion. Otherwise they talked and laughed about everything and nothing in particular; they covered fears and dislikes, trivial pleasures and private dreams. Conversation soon became total agreement, their delight in coincidence as strong as their wish to please the other, to find accord.

At some point, Melanie realized that they would sleep together. Nothing was said; their eyes did not meet across the table, nor did Diego's hand close over hers. On the contrary. She knew it because they self-consciously avoided any of the possibilities of physical contact available to them: their fingers didn't brush over the butter dish, their legs kept their distance under the tablecloth. To touch here would be frustrating, unfulfilling.

The waiter arrived with their brandies. By now Melanie wasn't really listening; Diego's words were just an excuse for her to focus on his lips, on the occasional glimpse of his white teeth, his tongue. Her mouth felt dry, hungry, and her gaze shifted to his hand, moving towards his drink. His long fingers cupped the smooth roundness of the glass in an easy, well-rehearsed gesture, gently swaying it in a slow circular motion, the honey-coloured liquid rippling inside. He raised it to his lips, his fingers apart, their skin pressed against the glass, the inside of his hand amber gold in the light filtering through the brandy.

Melanie wanted him now. She had never wanted a man so soon, so strongly. She didn't know him, it couldn't work, she might be drunk, she might be mad; she didn't care. She wanted him.

'Melanie?'

She shook her head. The din around them, the elegant bustle of the expensive restaurant reached her again. She saw her untouched brandy, then the pretty flowers in the middle of the table, and Diego, in his chair, very still. Looking at her.

'We ought to go. Now,' he said. They headed for the door, Diego handing a bundle of notes to the maître d'. Outside they faced each other, their breath mingling in the dim street light, and then, at last, he kissed her.

They kissed until they were both gasping for air. Diego took her hand and they ran across the street, into his hotel.

Melanie let herself into her building, and opened her mailbox. It was empty, as she knew it would be. Diego had left that morning, so she wouldn't find any letter from him until tomorrow morning. If there were a letter.

She headed for the elevator, and reality hit her at last.

14

Until then the day had been painful, as she had left Diego asleep in his hotel room early in the morning, or numbing as she went through the office routine, typing letters to people she didn't know about things that meant nothing to her, fighting to keep out of her mind the image of Diego's face, the memory of his hands, the touch of his skin. Now life became real, and dull; dull as the greeny-grey paint on the walls, the tacky carpet, the row of steel doors along the corridor. Everything that had seemed so normal yesterday was dismal now.

The sight of her own apartment only made her feel worse. Her whole life was there, and what did it amount to? A few shelves with books and records, a round table with four old chairs salvaged from the street, a convertible sofa shrouded in a patchwork quilt, and three plants, all of them sickly. The air felt hot and stale. Melanie walked across the room and opened the window just a crack. A blade of cold came in but she stayed where she was, vacantly looking out at the rear windows of the buildings on 88th Street. 'The apartment has a great view of Riverside Park,' the realtor had told her before she saw it for the first time, five years ago, when Melanie could hardly believe her luck at finding a place to live in Manhattan. It cost twice as much in rent as she could afford, but she never wanted to commute from Jersey City again.

There *had* been a view of the park through a gap between buildings, from the fire escape outside the window. Then a great white brick box of a building went up on the other side of West End Avenue, obliterating the glimpse of greenery for ever.

'Now, come on, tell me. How many times? Three, four?' Her eyebrows raised in expectation, Donna leaned across the table towards her friend, waiting for a full account. Melanie said nothing.

'What, *five* times?' Donna insisted in breathless astonishment, and Melanie regretted telling her about her night with Diego. She should have remembered Donna's cross-examinations.

'Oh, shut up, Donna!' she snapped.

'I know you, sweetheart. That's embarrassment, not anger . . .' Donna sat back and whistled softly. 'He must have screwed you six times then. No wonder you looked a bit wobbly yesterday. Did he call you?'

'No.'

'When are you seeing him again, then?'

Melanie stirred her coffee.

'I don't know. He went back to Buenos Aires yesterday morning.'

'And you're here . . .' Donna sighed. Melanie was stung by the implicit sarcasm, because it touched on her own fears.

'What do you want me to do, run after him?'

'No. You only needed to tell him that you've always been dying to see Buenos Aires. If the guy's rich, unmarried, and you've been screwing each other until the sheets catch fire, he would have agreed to take you there on the spot. Wouldn't you rather be smooching with him on the plane now?'

'He flies his own plane, so he'd better keep his hands on the controls,' Melanie replied.

'Wow,' Donna said admiringly. 'You shouldn't let this one out of your sight then. Go to Buenos Aires.'

Melanie stared at her friend.

'You must be nuts,' she said. 'I'd have a great time there, then he'd take me to the airport, send me home and when I got back I'd be out of a job.'

'Or you walk off into the sunset together. Listen, Melanie, you can find ten jobs like ours in the *New York Times* every day. This guy looks like a million bucks, he even *has* a million bucks, and you're crazy about him. If I were you, I would take that plane tomorrow, and just see what happens.' Donna put some money on the counter and stood up.

'We're going to Discorama tomorrow evening. You can come with us if you want,' she said.

'Thank you, but I don't feel like doing much. You have a nice weekend,' Melanie said quietly. Donna shook her head in disapproval.

'Chin up, honey. I'll call you on Sunday, to make sure you're not putting your head in the oven.'

On Saturday morning Melanie got up, made herself a cup of coffee, and went jogging in the park. Back in the apartment, she showered, got dressed, took the week's laundry to the basement and dumped it in one of the washing machines, then left the building, bought the *New York Times* and had breakfast at Romeo's Café on Amsterdam Avenue. Her eyes moved over the front page without really reading it; neither the flight of the Shah nor the release of John Mitchell on parole succeeded in focusing her attention.

Back at home again, she put the damp load of washing in the drier, went upstairs, and gave the place a perfunctory going-over with the vacuum cleaner. For once, Melanie had had no inclination to organize anything for the day, but now she realized her mistake, and began to call friends. It was too late. They were all out, or had made other arrangements.

She left the building just before noon. An hour later, she walked into the Frick Collection. She had been there once or twice before, and enjoyed the opulent quiet of the place; now it seemed solemnly gloomy to her. Bloomingdale's was a livelier choice in which to kill time, but after five minutes she couldn't stand the Saturday crowd. At two

17

o'clock or thereabouts Melanie decided to treat herself to lunch, although she wasn't hungry, and go to a movie afterwards. She found a nice, old-fashioned French restaurant nearby; it was a bit expensive, but she was in no mood to be cautious. Half an hour later, self-conscious about being alone, she finished lunch and left, and went back to her apartment instead; an empty cinema would make her feel lonelier, and a full house would be worse.

As she approached her front door, a fresh, delicate scent reached her, and then she saw the vivid patch of white at her doorstep. It was made of lilies of the valley, tightly packed into a perfect rectangle. She leaned down and picked up the small white envelope stuck in a corner. 'Missing you', read the unsigned card. Some men had given her flowers in the past, but none had laid them at her feet.

Melanie went in, and looked up Pan Am's number. Fifteen minutes later, she had packed a bag and set off for Kennedy Airport.

Alone in the middle of the huge hall, Melanie saw the counters ahead of her, and paused. I must be crazy, she thought. She was about to fly to the other end of the world without an invitation, at a cost she couldn't really afford, to find someone who might not even be there. All she had were her hopes and Diego's address and phone number, which she had managed to get out of the client's file at the bank. She had hesitated to call him before in fear of being given a polite brush-off, but now it could save her a lot of time and money.

She headed for the telephones. Her heart jumped as she heard the phone ringing at the other end.

'*Hola . . .*' It was a woman's voice.

'Could I speak to Diego, please.'

'*Con quién quiere hablar?*'

'*Señor Santos, por favor . . .*' That was all the Spanish

Melanie could summon up. 'I'm calling from New York,' she pleaded.

'*Un momento, no corte.*' The line seemed to go dead, but Melanie didn't hang up. Her persistence was rewarded a moment later.

'Hello. Who's calling, please?' A woman's voice again, but it was an educated voice this time, with an edge of refined petulance.

'I would like to speak to Mr Santos. My name is Melanie Clark.'

'Mr Santos is not available at the moment. Would you like to leave a message?'

'Who am I speaking to?' Melanie asked in turn.

'I'm Mrs Santos . . .'

Melanie dropped the receiver.

Some days it was in the mornings, when Melanie got out of bed, but it might not happen until later, on her way to work. Other days she would be able to carry on as usual, and then it would hit her at lunchtime. Or in the evenings. It could make her feel sick, or almost jubilant. Her feelings about how she would deal with Diego Santos if he ever reappeared in her life ranged from the murderous to the dismissive, as changeable as the persona she would adopt for each imagined occasion. She could be *Cosmo* girl, brisk, flippant, dealing with him between her work-out and meeting some exciting new man for dinner; or she could be vintage Joan Crawford, ignoring his pleas of innocence as he trailed her along the bank's corridors, while she ignored him. She might pretend nothing had happened . . . No, that she couldn't do. She was in love with a man she knew was a shit.

A week went past, then another one, and by the third she wasn't thinking about Diego all the time. Only most of it.

* * *

Melanie was startled awake by the entry phone. She stumbled in the dark to answer it.

'Melanie? It's me, Diego. Let me in, please. I'm dying to see you.'

She squinted at the clock on the table. It was two o'clock in the morning. She pressed the button before she had time to think about it, then rushed to the bathroom. Her face in the mirror confirmed that she had been dragged out of bed in the middle of a bad dream. She only had time to brush her hair before the bell rang. She pulled the door open.

'Look . . .' she started to say, and then stopped because there he was, clearly so pleased to see her.

'I've been thinking about you all the time. All the time . . .' Diego said, dropping his small suitcase on the floor. His arms were around her, and he kissed her. Melanie stepped back, and Diego kicked the door shut behind them. Soon his clothes were a jumbled pile on the floor, next to Melanie's crumpled T-shirt, and they fell together on the bed.

Melanie turned her head on the pillow and looked at Diego, the beautiful line of his profile outlined by the early morning light. He was awake too.

'I spoke to your wife ten days ago,' she said. There was no bitterness in her voice. Melanie had realized she wanted Diego, on whatever terms she could have him. All those sad tales and warning articles stored in her memory about the dangers of getting involved with married men meant nothing when *this* man was naked beside her. She wanted to tell him that she knew, to make everything as simple as possible for them.

Diego chuckled.

'Nice try,' he replied, 'but you have nothing to worry about. I'm not married.'

Melanie felt angry. He didn't need to lie to her.

'Then there must be a mad woman in Buenos Aires, who is claiming to be your wife. She answers the phone at the number you left with the bank.'

Diego sat up.

'Tell me exactly what happened,' he said. Melanie explained, and Diego laughed.

'That was my mother! If you hadn't hung up in a rage, she would have told you. She always assumes that anyone asking for Mr Santos must mean my father. I suppose I'm still her baby in that respect.'

'Do you live with your parents?' Melanie was astonished.

'It's a big house,' Diego replied rather sheepishly. 'I know it sounds odd to you, but it's pretty usual over there to live with your parents until you marry.' He pushed Melanie gently until she was on her back, his weight on top of her.

'So there you are, I'm not married. So stop thinking about it,' he murmured, his hand gently stroking her breast. Melanie found she wasn't thinking about anything.

The following morning, they made slow, languorous love before breakfast, followed by hot, slippery sex in the shower. When they finally came out of the bathroom, Melanie phoned her office and said she had flu. She had decided to treat herself to the best day of her life, footloose in town, with Diego.

Their first stop was practical. Diego said that he had flown directly from Punta del Este – a beach in Uruguay where his parents had a holiday house – on the spur of the moment, and to fetch winter clothes from his home in Buenos Aires would have delayed his departure.

'I need to buy something to wear, before we do anything else. I'll freeze otherwise,' Diego said. Melanie thought he was asking for guidance about where to go.

'Let's go to Bloomingdale's,' she suggested, thinking as expensively as she could. Diego hailed a taxi.

'I can't stand big stores,' he replied. 'Saint Laurent on Madison Avenue,' he told the driver once they got in the car. Melanie felt Diego's hand on her shoulder, and she nestled up to him. As they cut across Central Park, she looked at the snow on the ground, gilded by the morning sun, at the feather-light tracery of the bare trees against the bright sky, felt the warmth of his chest against her cheek, and she was momentarily terrified by the thought that this could be the best moment of her life, only to become a receding memory.

'When are you going back?' she asked, trying to sound casual.

'Why, are you bored already?' he smiled.

'Don't be an ass. You know why I'm asking,' she said.

'Then you know why I don't want to tell you. We have plenty of time.'

The taxi stopped, and they got out. As soon as they were inside the shop, Melanie tried to look studiously casual, as if this was her usual element. A slim, elegant woman dressed in expensive black, her hair pulled back in a chignon, approached them.

'*Ah, Monsieur Santos, je suis enchantée de vous voir! . . .*' She kept on gushing in French. Diego replied, also in French; it became clear to Melanie that he did not need any advice about shopping in New York. Eventually, the woman beckoned a languid male assistant, also formidably well-dressed, who led them towards the men's section of the shop.

'I want a blue overcoat, a blue blazer, two pairs of grey flannels, and some dark-coloured rollnecks . . .' Diego disappeared into a changing room; the assistant came back after a while, holding a pile of clothes in his arms. Melanie wandered aimlessly around the shop, looking without really seeing, until she came across the most stunning black leather coat, the hide as supple as silk, extravagantly full and lined in some lustrous black fur. Melanie stroked the lining, and noticed the price tag discreetly hidden inside. It was four thousand dollars.

'Try it on, if you like it.'

She turned round. Diego was standing there, in his new clothes, making the models in the display photographs look like second-rate wimps. Melanie removed her hand swiftly, as if she had been caught shoplifting.

'Try it on,' he insisted. The woman in black appeared instantly, like a genie, and unlocked the steel wire running inside the coat's sleeve. She held it up in front of Diego and Melanie.

'It's just perfect for you, Madame,' she cooed. 'There's nothing more beautiful than a green-eyed blonde in black leather.'

'I agree,' Diego said. He moved forward and helped Melanie out of her cheap coat, disregarding her objections. She felt the weight on her shoulders, the warmth of the fur and the smell of new leather surrounding her, and she almost shivered in delight in front of the mirror. She saw a gorgeous, self-assured woman, surrounded by admiring faces, as if the Melanie she knew had crystallized into somebody utterly different – her true self at last. Eventually she slipped the coat off; it didn't feel that dissimilar to being skinned alive.

'Thank you. We should go now,' she said to Diego.

'We'll take the coat. Please send all the other clothes to the St Regis,' he told the woman, who took the gold credit card from him and busied herself at the till. Diego dumped Melanie's old coat on top of the counter, and helped her to slip back into the new one.

'You can't give me something as expensive as this. You're crazy,' Melanie said. Diego kissed her.

'I'm not crazy, I'm rich,' he smiled. 'It's not quite the same thing.'

Simultaneously enjoying the cool feel of linen sheets and the warmth of Diego's body next to her, Melanie helped herself to another piece of toast and dipped her knife into the bowl of caviar on the tray. It hadn't taken her long to appreciate the difference between this lustrous grey beauty and the Danish stuff from the deli which she bought for truly special occasions. Only Diego's bedside light was on, its soft glow reflected on the polished mahogany furniture.

'This is heaven,' she said, cuddling up to him, their backs resting against a pile of feather pillows. Diego took her hand.

'Would you like me the same if I didn't have any money?' he asked.

'I'd like you even if you didn't own the clothes on your back. I like you better without them anyway,' Melanie replied. 'But it's true that it doesn't make me like you less.'

'Sometimes things are not quite what they seem. It's not really my money,' he said.

'You could have fooled me,' Melanie teased him.

'I mean it. My father is rich, not me. I work for him.'

'You sound as if it you don't like it.'

'I don't mind. It's the family business, and one day I will be in charge. I shouldn't complain in the meantime.'

'Are you an only child?' Melanie asked.

'I have a sister, but she doesn't live with us any more.'

'What's her name?'

'Marina.'

'Do you like her?'

'Not very much. More than she liked us though. She didn't bother to tell us where she was going when she left us.'

'Us, us, us . . .' Melanie chided him gently. 'You sound

24

as if you and your parents are one and the same.'

'Sometimes it feels like that,' Diego agreed. 'But we are always talking about my family, never yours. Tell me about them.'

'Who?' She knew perfectly well who he meant, as she knew that evasions would not be enough after her insistent questions. It was her turn to repay confidence with confidence, and she regretted it.

'Don't be dumb. Your parents, who else?' Diego said.

'I don't know what they're *really* like. They argued all the time about money when I was a child, and then my father left. I've never seen him since.'

'Who do you like better of the two?' he insisted.

'My father, I suppose, because he never moaned about my mother to us, and he was always nice to me. Then I thought he was a shit, because that's what my mother told us. By the time I changed my mind about him again, I didn't know where he was. I couldn't tell him.'

'He couldn't have been *that* nice if he left you for good,' Diego commented.

'He tried to contact me a few times, but I didn't want to talk to him, or see him. I wanted so much to please my mother, you see. She made you feel that you didn't care enough for her, so I always felt I had to prove I loved her, until I realized it was her way to keep me jumping through hoops. I tried to trace my father three years later, after I left home myself, but he had moved. It was very expensive to hire someone to find him, so we lost touch.'

Diego pulled her close to him.

'You might come across him when you least expect it,' he said. They remained silent for a while, then Diego moved the tray to the floor.

'You don't have to worry about me. I will never leave you,' he murmured before kissing her.

* * *

Melanie was fixing her face when she saw Donna's reflection in the mirror, coming into the restroom. Donna's mouth opened in astonishment.

'Don't tell me you collected Kellogg's coupons to get *that*!' she gasped, pointing at Melanie's leather coat.

'Nope,' Melanie replied, retouching her lipstick.

'I thought your gaucho must be in town. I tried to call you yesterday, when I was told you had flu, but there was no reply from your apartment. I guessed you weren't in hospital.' Donna came closer and stroked the coat as if it was a favourite pet.

'You cheat at work, and he gives you something like this on your second date? It must be love.'

It was what Melanie thought too, but she didn't dare to say it aloud.

'I wish you hadn't gone to the office today,' Diego said. 'My business meeting finished early, and we could have done something together this afternoon.'

'I missed you too,' she replied.

'You should have missed work instead.'

'I can't pretend to be ill two days running. I might end up losing my job, and anyway I don't like lying.'

'So?'

'So what?' Melanie asked, annoyed by his flippancy. 'I might be the first person you ever met who has to work for a living, but . . .'

'Please forgive me,' he said, reaching for her hand. 'I'm an arrogant bastard sometimes. It's just that I want you to myself when I'm here.'

Melanie was touched by his obvious contrition.

'You can have me all to yourself during the weekend,' she said. 'It's only one day away.'

Diego looked at her.

'I won't be here, Melanie. I have to go back tomorrow

morning. The flight is arranged, and I can't change it. It's my mother's birthday on Saturday. I *have* to be there . . .'

She wondered if he was protesting too much, if there *was* a Mrs Diego Santos after all.

'You could have told me you'd be here only two days,' she said.

'I didn't want to ruin the time we had together,' Diego replied. Melanie saw his point, but she felt cheated.

'When are you coming back?' she asked, trying to sound unperturbed.

'As soon as I can, I promise,' he replied, but his eyes avoided hers.

At least his words were something, but they were not enough.

TWO

'Welcome to Argentina! As famous for its beef as for tango, it has much, much more to offer to the keen visitor. The eighth largest country in the world, its geography encompasses every climate, with a breath-taking wealth of scenery and fauna . . .' Melanie flicked through the travel guidebook she had bought at Barnes & Noble that lunchtime. The pictures showed a great variety of beautiful landscapes, in the heightened colours of all promotional photographs, alternating with shots of tango dancers; in most cases their corpulent waistlines revealed that the photographer had been more selective about the landscapes. She read at random, jumping from 'The Spanish Conquest' to 'Dining Out in Buenos Aires' to 'The Legend of Eva Peron'. After an hour, she closed the book and put it aside. It answered all the questions about Argentina except for the one that she really cared about: when would she hear from Diego?

He had been away for nearly a month now, but he had called her many times. Melanie had no complaints on that score, other than the unpredictable pattern of his calls. Sometimes Diego phoned her several times a day, at home and at work, then three or four days would pass without hearing from him. Some degree of certainty was all she wanted in their relationship.

Or whatever the word was for what they had. Three nights and two days together was really all it amounted to. They had been magical times for her, because of Diego – and because she had entered a lifestyle she had only read about before. But it was everyday life for Diego, and she couldn't help worrying if the same difference applied to their perceptions of each other, if she was 'just another girl' for him.

Melanie found it much easier to be objective about Diego when he hadn't called her for a while. They had great sex, they liked each other a lot – it was absurd to talk about love so soon – and the fact that he lived far away left them a lot of breathing space. It could be an ideal, enriching relationship between two independent adults.

The phone rang, and she rushed to answer it.

'I miss you,' he said at once.

'I miss you too.' To hell with enriching relationships between independent adults. She only needed to hear his voice to want him here, now, forever.

'Can you be in Miami tomorrow night? I've already booked a ticket for you, just in case, and you'll be back in New York on Monday evening. I thought it would be nice to have three days by the sea.'

It was Lincoln's Birthday, and Monday was a holiday.

'How did you manage that? My boss decided to go to Florida for the holiday at the last minute, but all the flights are booked.'

'I just killed somebody for their confirmed ticket,' Diego chuckled. 'Anything to have you here with me.'

'See you on Sunday then. I'll meet you at Penn Station at eleven o'clock,' Donna told Melanie as they came out of the building, into the great Friday night rush before the holiday.

'Damn, I forgot about Debbie's birthday,' Melanie replied. The wind swirled around them, and she raised her collar against the cold. 'I can't make it now.'

'Gaucho lover must be in town then,' Donna scoffed.

Melanie explained the arrangements. 'Don't give me that

29

look,' she said. 'What do you want me to do, cancel and go to Debbie instead?'

'No, but you *are* an idiot,' Donna said. 'You forgot about it, didn't you?'

'I'm sorry, I know that I shouldn't have . . .'

'You know nothing,' Donna sighed. 'I'd probably rush to Florida like Road Runner to meet Superdick rather than eat chicken drumsticks and rice in a stuffy room. But if you've forgotten about Debbie's birthday now, it means that you had forgotten when he called you yesterday, right?'

'OK, I forgot. What's the big deal?'

'You should have told him that you had made other plans, and you should have made it sound like Al Pacino had asked you out already. Then he'd beg you to change your mind, you'd let him stew for a bit, and at last you'd say, "OK". I bet you went all floppy as soon as you heard him, and accepted even before he asked you.'

'More or less,' Melanie admitted.

'You're making it too easy for him, honey. Believe me, I know about guys. Sure, you don't need to waste time if you want them for fun, but if you really care about a guy, make it hard for him. Then he'll appreciate you.'

Melanie opened her eyes. Diego's arm was just above her face, reaching for the icebox. She nibbled at his tanned flesh, and tasted the salt on his skin.

'Hey, that hurt,' Diego complained.

'Sorry, I couldn't resist,' she murmured, then closed her eyes and relaxed in the heat of the sun. A moment later she shrieked, shocked by the ice-cold liquid trickling into her navel.

'And I couldn't resist *that*,' he said, licking the champagne off her. Melanie saw a couple of gulls circling in the sky over them, two dots of white against the still blue.

Diego's lips moved downwards. She gripped his hair to stop him.

'I thought we were going to have a drink,' she said. Diego pulled two glasses out of the icebox, filled them and gave one to Melanie. He stood up and leaned on the taffrail, sipping champagne and looking out at the empty sea. Melanie stared at his naked back, the broad plane of his shoulders tapering into the small, firm roundness of his buttocks, a patch of white in the sweep of brown skin. She came up to him and rested her arms on the rail.

'What's that?' she asked, nodding towards the distant shore, barely visible in the heat haze. She hadn't noticed it when they dropped anchor.

'Cuba,' Diego replied. 'We must be inside their territorial waters.' He noticed the worry in her eyes and laughed.

'Don't worry, it's Great Abaco,' he said. 'The Reds are not about to throw us into prison. I could always tell them my mother is a cousin of Che Guevara.'

'I thought you only had grand relations,' Melanie said.

'He came from a very good family,' Diego retorted, sounding almost irritated – the first time she had ever heard him other than completely charming. 'And he was an eleventh cousin twice removed, or something like that. My mother has too many cousins for me to keep up with all the connections.'

'I have no cousins,' she said. 'At least if I do, I don't know anything about them.'

'You're very lucky, then, you can invent them. They're bound to be better than the real thing.' Diego put his arm around Melanie's shoulders, and pulled her towards him. She rested her head on Diego's shoulder, smelt the suntan oil on him, and stared at the huge sky and the sea in front of them. The gulls were still hovering over the boat.

'I want to stay here for ever.'

'I know what you mean, but we would starve in the end,' Diego smiled. 'Wish for something that wouldn't kill us.'

'I want to be with you. I wish I didn't have to go back,' she said.

'You don't have to go back to work. You could work for me instead.'

Melanie beamed. It was a most diplomatic way of asking her to go to Argentina with him. He was being tactful, she thought.

'That would be great,' she said enthusiastically, but then she paused. 'I'm not sure I'd find living in Argentina very easy though. I don't speak Spanish.'

'I'm sorry, I didn't mean that. Of course it would be impossible for you to move there. I was thinking about you working for me here.'

Melanie was puzzled.

'You have no office in New York. What would I be doing for you?' she asked.

'We'll find something,' he said blithely. 'I can buy an apartment, and you'd look after it. I might need you to do some shopping for me from time to time. There are plenty of things you can do . . .' He carried on with his suggestions, but Melanie stopped listening. First he had said he had never considered the possibility of her living in his country, and now he was offering to keep her.

'You can shove your job offer,' Melanie said, moving away from him. Diego took hold of her again. She tried to push him away, but he was too strong.

'I'm sorry,' he said over and over. 'I'm a fool. I didn't mean it like that, I was trying to find a way . . .' He held her face between his hands. 'I'll never make you cry again in my life, Melanie. I promise you that, even if there's nothing more beautiful in the world than tears in your eyes. It's like raindrops on jade . . .'

The hungry gulls circled over the stationary boat, waiting. The man lowered the woman on to a mattress on deck. His head sometimes covered her head, sometimes overshadowed her breast, and her face was contorted, as if in pain, but she didn't fight him. On the contrary, she held his head hard against her flesh. The man's arm moved in a slow, constant rhythm, his hand between the woman's legs, until she cried out as loudly as the gulls above them. The man raised himself slightly, then he pushed down, her legs gripping his hips.

The man's movements settled to a steady rhythm, and the gulls lost interest in the scene below. They glided away towards the infinite sea, in search of a flash of silver in the water, the couple and the bobbing boat getting smaller and smaller as they receded into the distance, until they became a speck in the ocean.

Spring was about to turn into summer, and Melanie was as happy as she had ever been. Or nearly. Diego came to New York two or three times a month now, never for long, but often enough. In April he bought an apartment in a gracious old building on Riverside Drive. It was luxury for her: doormen round the clock, a *real* view of Riverside Park and the Hudson, and it had a living room, a bedroom and an entrance hall. But she knew Diego thought it small, and the only reason for his choice of area, rather than the Upper East Side, was that her own apartment was a few minutes away. Melanie knew that, from his point of view, he was almost slumming for her sake. Since the boat trip in February, they had dined at nice restaurants, but not the kind where the waiters addressed the clientele in three languages, and his presents now were worth hundreds, not thousands. She loved him more for trying to live on her terms. It was safe for Melanie to use the word 'love' now. Diego had said 'I love you' during their first night in the

33

new apartment, and she said it back to him as if it was a revelation, not something she had known for months and kept in hiding for fear of losing it.

They lived together when Diego was in town, but he hadn't asked Melanie to move in. It bothered her, especially on occasions like this evening. Dinner was in the oven, the river was burnished by the setting sun, and they were lying on the big new sofa. Diego was watching motor racing on TV while Melanie flicked through *New York* magazine. Both were in their bathrobes after a long and eventful shower, the smell of soap and contentment about them. Diego reached for the remote control and switched off the TV set.

'When will dinner be ready? I'm hungry,' he said.

'It won't be long. There's no hurry.'

'You always say that,' he teased her, his hand sliding inside her robe and resting on her breast. Melanie felt his body against her, and let herself bask in her feeling of safety.

'Don't move. Just stay like that,' she murmured.

'I had a better idea,' he complained.

'No, this is heaven,' she insisted, and they remained still.

'I've been meaning to tell you something,' he said suddenly. It sounded like an announcement, and Melanie felt a flash of fear. He *was* married. Or he had found somebody else in Argentina perhaps. Or he was tired of her . . .

'Please don't say anything until I've finished,' he went on. 'I love you, Melanie. I've never been so happy in my life, and I don't want to lose you. Ever. I want to marry you . . .' He had to stop, because Melanie had flung her arms around his neck and was kissing him. She was exultant at first, but then she stopped because his reaction was not what she expected. Diego seemed strangely glum. 'I want to marry you,' he continued, 'but it won't be easy . . .'

'You need a divorce,' Melanie interrupted, impatient for him to get to the point.

'Here we go again,' he sighed. 'I've told you I'm not married. That's not the problem.'

'What the hell *is* the problem then?' Melanie couldn't make sense of the conversation.

'My family,' he mumbled.

'I can't believe it. I still can't believe it. It's like something out of *The Godfather*!' Melanie ranted.

'Worse,' Donna countered, licking her fingers. 'Snooty people kill you with kindness. Takes much longer.'

Donna busied herself over the table, inspecting the tin foil trays.

'It'll be OK in the end. Have some sweet and sour prawns, they're good,' she said, holding them out to her friend.

Melanie shook her head.

'I've had enough, thank you,' she said. She didn't like Chinese take-away food. It needed the chopsticks, the fringed pagoda lights, the dragons on the walls; on a dining table in an apartment it became an over-sweet, gelatinous morass. Some things only worked in their own context, and Melanie wondered if the same applied to her and Diego.

'It's not as bad as you think, honey,' Donna chirped reassuringly. 'He's made it difficult for himself to dump you. Once he's told you the problem is that his Mom and Dad won't like him marrying a nobody . . .'

'He didn't say that. He said "someone outside our milieu",' Melanie snapped.

'Same thing. He just used some fancy word for it, but at least he's owned up. He can't fool himself. If he lets you go, then he's tied to his Mom's apron strings, and guys don't like seeing the evidence. You just hang on, give him time, and it'll be all right.'

Melanie remained silent. Donna was at her agony-aunt best, and there could have been some truth in what she said, if it weren't for another factor, something much more relevant than amateur psychology: money. Melanie knew that Diego's money came from his father, as she guessed from his occasional comments on the subject that Mr Santos saw no difference between business and family; both were to be kept under his thumb. To displease his mother entailed emotional distress, but to oppose his father could mean Diego losing everything. Melanie wasn't sure she wanted to put him to the test. The result might not be to her liking.

She felt the familiar shadow of doubt. Too much had happened too quickly. In some ways she didn't know Diego at all. Maybe they had no future together.

'When is he coming back?' Donna asked.

'He said he'd be here next week.'

'You know something? We've talked about Diego for months, but I've never met him,' Donna said. 'It's time I did. Maybe you could bring him here one evening, and we go could out, the four of us . . .'

Whoever the fourth happened to be, Melanie thought. At first she had kept Diego away from Donna because she feared her friend would pounce on him. She had not even mentioned her, as she never mentioned other friends to him. They had their own, self-contained world. She couldn't bring Diego here, to this brickbox of a building in Queens, with its unimpeded view of the Super-Mart car park. Her own apartment was a couple of notches up the scale, no more, but was all she could afford, a place she had chosen because she had no better option, *faute de mieux*, as Diego often said. Friends were different, a free choice, and she didn't want Diego to judge her by Donna.

A few months ago, Melanie had had no trouble in telling Diego about her past, in teasing him about his affectations.

Now a mixture of fear and calculation made her ashamed of Donna, and the realization made her ashamed of herself.

'Sure,' Melanie agreed tepidly. 'Let's do something together sometime soon . . .'

Their heads on the pillow, they looked at each other and smiled.

'Hello,' Diego murmured.

'Better late than never,' Melanie smiled. They had jumped into bed as soon as he had opened the door and dropped his suitcase. He stared at the ceiling.

'My mother arrives the day after tomorrow. I've told my parents about you,' he said. 'My father can't fly, because of his health, but my mother wants to meet you.'

Melanie regretted ever doubting him. He was prepared to face his family with her. It was up to her now.

THREE

Melanie spun through the revolving door of the Pierre. A discreet brass sign announcing 'Rotunda Room' caught her eye; she smoothed down her skirt, wriggled her toes inside her new shoes, took a deep breath, and headed for it.

She hadn't expected a dinner invitation. It would have been both too formal and too intimate under the circumstances. Lunch was out of the question during her working day, so she assumed that Mrs Santos would ask her for a drink in the early evening. She was wrong. She had been asked to *tea*, an event that, until now, Melanie had believed only existed in old English movies.

At the end of a vista of old furniture, old waiters and old customers talking in hushed tones, she saw Diego stand up and come towards her. She would have liked him to kiss her, but he didn't. He took her arm instead, asked her if she had had any trouble getting there, and led her firmly towards their table.

'This is Melanie Clark,' Diego introduced her. 'Melanie, my mother . . .'

Mrs Santos was elegant. Very elegant, in fact, but not in a fashion goddess sense. She was immaculately turned out in a beige Chanel suit, the crisp blue silk of her shirt flattened by the weight of her triple strand of huge pearls; her dark hair was perfectly coiffed without giving the impression that she had left the hairdresser five minutes ago, and her nails were manicured, but her matt pink nail polish was so subdued it was almost unnoticeable. Her elegance was a combination of bearing, classic good taste, grooming and discreet money, as if to be well-dressed was more a question of manners than anything else.

Melanie guessed that she must have been very beautiful when she was young. It was possible to see the roots of Diego's stunning looks in his mother's, but the years, the lines, and the set of her mouth had overwritten their own message on her face.

'Please sit down, Miss Clark,' she said.

'I'm sorry I'm late,' Melanie apologized.

'Don't worry at all, we'd just arrived ourselves. We have been to see some friends in Sutton Place, and the traffic is terrible. Did you have to travel far?'

'No, my office is only a few blocks from here,' Melanie replied.

'What do you do, Miss Clark?' asked Mrs Santos, pouring her guest a cup of Earl Grey. Melanie was sure Diego must have told her.

'Please call me Melanie, Mrs Santos,' she suggested with a smile. 'I work at the Unity Investment Bank.' She expected some hint of recognition, but there was none. Probably she found it too demeaning to acknowledge that a secretary from their bank was at their table.

'I hope you like the hotel, *Mamá*,' Diego intervened.

'It's fine,' Mrs Santos replied.

'Is it your first time in New York?' Melanie asked her.

'Oh, no!' Mrs Santos sounded as if Melanie had asked her if she wore the same underwear for a whole week running. 'We used to come at least once a year, until my husband had to give up long flights . . .'

'My father has very bad sinusitis,' explained Diego, ignoring María's disapproving glance, as though any revelations were unacceptable. The woman had an excessive sense of privacy, Melanie decided.

'We always stayed at the Sherry-Netherland,' María went on, 'but on my last trip I thought it wasn't quite the same. My cousin Maneco used to have a permanent suite there,' she said to Diego, before she focused her attention on Melanie again.

'Do you have to do any travelling because of your work, Miss Clark?' María asked.

Melanie looked at Diego. His blank expression confirmed that he had said nothing about her work to his mother.

'Quite a lot,' she replied, unable to resist the opportunity to add some glamour to her life. After all, the coffee machine was at the other end of the floor, and her boss drank endless cups during the day.

'How fascinating. Here or abroad?'

'Er . . . both, in fact.'

'Do you go anywhere in particular abroad?'

The questioning made Melanie feel as if she was being interviewed for a job. In a way she was, so she ought to try to regain control of the conversation, and sound like one of those women in *Interview*. Or her boss's wife, which was as close to those sort of women as Melanie had ever come in real life.

'Paris, mainly. I *adore* Paris. It's divine.' Melanie heard herself, and feared that the effect was more hairdresser than socialite. She felt more confident about the statement itself: Paris was the only foreign place she had been to. It had been a Three Hundred and Eighty Dollars Pan Am Special Weekend, certainly not Mrs Santos's style of visit, but she had at least been there.

'It's my favourite city,' Mrs Santos agreed. 'Where do you stay?'

Melanie was intrigued by the aimless questioning. She had expected to be grilled about her family, her education, her past, but Mrs Santos seemed quite satisfied with drivel.

'The bank has a company apartment. It's near the Eiffel

Tower,' Melanie explained. By now she wished she hadn't lied originally.

'The *Septième* is such a beautiful *arrondissement*,' Mrs Santos said in urbane rapture. 'Aunt Meme's hotel was there, Diego.' She pronounced 'hotel' in the French manner, and Melanie imagined Donna hooting when she heard about it. She memorized the word: O–*tehl*, with the stress on the *l*.

'. . . I don't think you remember Aunt Meme, Diego,' Mrs Santos continued. 'She died long before you were born. She was Lulu's sister. Her O–*tehl* was really lovely.'

'Your family seem to live in hotels all the time,' Melanie said to Diego. Mrs Santos was nonplussed.

'What do you mean?' she asked.

'You said your cousin lived at the Sherry-Netherland, and your aunt lived in a hotel in Paris.'

'I meant her *hôtel particulier*. That's French for town house . . .' It wasn't the dismissive edge to Mrs Santos's voice that made Melanie hate her, nor her own embarrassment at having given the stupid woman the opportunity to feel superior to her. It was the slight, almost imperceptible flick of her hand, as if she was trying to wave away a small but rather unpleasant insect.

'But you must tell me about yourself, Miss Clark . . .'

'It's Melanie, *Mamá*,' Diego broke in.

'Melanie, of course . . .' She glanced at her watch. 'Oh dear, time goes so quickly. The Furtado da Silvas are picking me up in fifteen minutes. Now, you were saying . . .'

Melanie decided that nothing she could say would help her, as far as the insufferable Mrs Santos was concerned. Certainly not the truth.

Ten minutes later, Diego reminded her about their dinner reservation. Melanie Clark, daughter of Franklin Hopworth Clark, of the Mayflower Clarks, stood up and made her goodbyes. She had had just enough time to reminisce about her summers as a child at Cricklemount, her mother's family plantation. She would have loved to tell Mrs Santos about her great time at college, but it would have to wait for another occasion, perhaps when Mrs Santos was in New York again. Mrs Santos replied that she was delighted to have met Melanie, and she wouldn't hear of delaying their next meeting. She insisted that Melanie have dinner with her at the hotel, the following night, just the two of them. They had so much to talk about.

'I must confess that I didn't expect to enjoy our conversation so much, Melanie. You are a charming *raconteuse*,' Mrs Santos said, pouring herself more mint tea.

'Thank you,' replied Melanie, not sure about her precise meaning, but flattered to be praised. So far the evening had been far less awful than she'd expected, perhaps because Mrs Santos had tried hard to put her at ease, and Melanie guessed that Diego had said something to his mother after their frosty meeting the day before. Dinner had been light on both formality and calories. Mrs Santos insisted on eating in her suite, which suited Melanie better than the stiff surroundings of the restaurant downstairs, and Mrs Santos matched the relaxed mood – as far as she could. She was wearing her pearls again, but she was dressed in a blue pleated skirt and a cream silk short-sleeved top, which Melanie assumed was her version of informal wear, and she had listened attentively to Melanie's further embellishments on her invented life.

'Diego told me that you're going back to Buenos Aires tomorrow. Were you born there?' Melanie asked. She hoped it would be the final round of small talk that evening, before it was acceptably late for her to go home.

Mrs Santos put her cup aside.

'I think it's time we talked about what's really on our

minds, Melanie,' she said. 'I was intrigued to meet you. Diego had never asked us to meet any of his girlfriends before. Of course we have encountered many of them, especially if we know the parents, but never because he asked us to. You must be very special to him.'

Melanie should have been flattered by the last remark, but she wasn't. In some way, Diego's mother made it sound as if it was inexplicable; she was very good at amiable disdain.

'I don't want to jump to conclusions,' Mrs Santos went on. 'Diego hadn't told us anything other than that he wanted to introduce us. Is this because you've been making any plans?'

Melanie was annoyed by the fact that Diego had been so vague with his own parents. Or so scared of them. He had already upset her by insisting that Melanie should not mention their apartment to his mother at all, and his ludicrous attempts at propriety by pretending to stay at the Pierre. Diego would go back to the hotel early in the morning, so that his mother believed he had spent the night in his room. He mentioned his mother's stern Catholicism as a justification, but that wasn't a reason to hide discussions about getting married. On the contrary. Melanie decided to put the matter straight.

'Diego and I are in love, Mrs Santos. We want to get married,' she replied.

'It's time Diego settled down,' Mrs Santos agreed. 'My husband and I want grandchildren. Marriage is a very important step; I would say it is *the* most important thing in anybody's life. Or so it should be. It is crucial to find the right person, for the right reasons.' Mrs Santos took a sip of tea, then went on. 'We are a very close family, Melanie. We live together, and my husband and Diego work together. We have our own rules. It's not easy for an outsider to join us. To be candid with you, we wouldn't

43

like it.' Mrs Santos noticed Melanie's reaction. 'You may not care for my calling you an outsider, but that's what you are. We both know it. That's why you've been lying to me so imaginatively . . .'

'I haven't!' Melanie interrupted. She hoped that her blush would pass as anger, not embarrassment. Mrs Santos picked up a big white envelope from the table next to her sofa, and pulled out a typed sheet.

'Melanie Cheryl Clark, born 24 June 1954, in Hoppertown General Hospital, Illinois. Father: Gary Clark. Occupation: Janitor. Mother: Jane O'Reilly. Occupation: Salesgirl. Parents married at Hoppertown Town Hall on July 20th, 1954 . . .' Mrs Santos's eyes ran over the sheet. 'Your schools are listed here. No reference to college, I notice. Your parents divorced in 1970, and your brother Dan died the following year. An overdose of heroin, I'm sorry to see . . .'

Melanie would have cried in shame for her stupidity, if she hadn't felt so angry that Mrs Santos must have hired a private detective to find out all about her.

'You have no right to snoop on me!' she lashed out at María, who seemed to be rearranging some pleats in her skirt.

'Please don't raise your voice, Melanie,' she said. 'It's completely unnecessary. I just wanted to get some idea of your background, that's all. Otherwise we would have been talking under false pretences, and I'm sure we don't want that. It . . .'

Melanie felt like throwing her coffee all over Mrs Santos. Anything to shake the woman's smug condescension.

'What do *you* want then, Mrs Santos?' She cut her short. 'If the idea is that Diego and I should stop seeing each other, forget it. You are a dinosaur, you know, full of stupid prejudices nobody cares about any more . . .'

'I'm sure you don't want to say anything you'll regret

later, Melanie.' Mrs Santos's voice was very calm. 'And I don't want anything, other than that neither Diego *nor* you should make any decisions in a hurry. You have plenty of time to find out how you really feel about each other. I have no objections to you *per se*. Even if I had, there's very little my husband or I could do about it. Diego is nearly thirty. Like any other mother, all I want is to be sure that my son makes the right decision. You are very beautiful, you strike me as an intelligent girl, and you speak your mind. Those are important qualities, but I would be less than honest if I said you are the kind of girl I had in mind for Diego's wife. I think we all need a bit of time to get used to the idea. We won't put any obstacles in your way, but will you promise me you won't rush into anything either?'

Melanie was confused. She couldn't help disliking Mrs Santos; the woman had shown herself first as a snob who talked about *o—tehls*, then as a scheming bitch who hired private detectives. Suddenly she was all goodwill and common sense. Melanie hadn't expected to be welcomed immediately by Diego's family. To be acknowledged as his future wife was as good an outcome as she could hope for, and the request for a delay suited her. *She* had doubts herself. Diego had never concealed from her the influence of his parents on his life, but now she was confronting it directly. She would be marrying the family as well as the man.

'We are in no hurry, Mrs Santos,' she said. 'Neither Diego nor I would like to do anything until . . .' she was going to say 'we feel it's right', but changed her mind. 'Until we know you approve,' she finished, rather pleased with her diplomatic touch.

'You make me sound more important than I am in all this, Melanie. Diego is very much his own man,' Mrs Santos said.

At last they had found some common ground. Neither of them believed that the other was being honest.

'*Mamá* said you two got on very well tonight,' Diego beamed as soon as he walked into the room. Melanie was already in bed.

'We had a long talk, about this, that and the other. She's fine, your mother.'

Diego chuckled.

'She's my mother, but you don't have to be *that* diplomatic. What's next, then?'

'You tell me. They're your family, not mine,' Melanie replied.

Diego took off his shirt, and dropped it unceremoniously on to a chair.

'How about coming to Buenos Aires, and seeing if you like it?' he asked.

FOUR

After half an hour of flying over the toffee-coloured waters of the River Plate, Melanie saw the shore, and the jostle of high-rise buildings in central Buenos Aires. The relentless grid of the city sprawled away from the coast in every direction but then, like the tide rolling over sand, it began to falter, until it seeped into the ground and disappeared. In the distance, the airport runways drew grey lines deep into the green flatland.

The plane touched down, and Melanie heard the passengers in Economy burst into enthusiastic applause. Thanks to Diego, she was travelling first class, where the scene remained unchanged, the men reading their papers, the women flicking through magazines or looking out of the window, all pretending to ignore the commotion. The air hostess noticed Melanie's curiosity.

'Argentines are very effusive when the plane touches home ground. Sometimes they even sing the National Anthem,' she explained apologetically. Melanie smiled. She could hardly imagine Mrs Santos doing either. Obviously some Argentines were more effusive than others.

The usual announcement about smoking and hand luggage was made, and shortly afterwards the plane came to a halt. Melanie was eager to get out. She had been impatient to arrive ever since Diego had invited her seven weeks ago, but Melanie had agreed with her boss that she would take her summer vacation at the same time he did. Although at first she'd hated the self-imposed restriction, she came to think that it was better to let some time pass between her conversation with Diego's mother and her appearance in the family home as a guest. In spite of what she'd said to Mrs Santos, she wanted to marry Diego soon. A two-month gap would not dispel Mrs Santos's suspicions about Melanie's real timetable, but she supposed it would seem more leisurely than a couple of days.

Melanie returned the smiles of the crew flanking the exit, and stepped out into the bright winter sunshine. She was following the others towards the bus waiting on the tarmac when she felt a hand on her shoulder and turned around. It was Diego.

They kissed under the surprised glances of the other passengers, who were forced to alter their path like water around a rock in a stream. At last Diego released Melanie and led her towards a gleaming black Mercedes waiting nearby.

After a short drive, they reached the terminal buildings, and Diego asked her for her passport and luggage ticket. He got out of the car and talked to a man in uniform, then gave him the passport and the luggage tag. Melanie couldn't tell if the man was a policeman or a military officer. Diego came back to the car.

'That's it,' he said. 'They'll bring your luggage and your passport to the house later this morning. We don't have to wait now.'

Melanie wondered who Diego meant by 'they'.

'Did you have a good trip?' he asked before she could clarify the matter.

'It was great,' she replied. Certainly it had been the most luxuriously comfortable flight she had ever had, but she didn't say so. After several months with Diego, Melanie had noticed that luxury was the natural state of things for him, neither to be concealed nor mentioned. Behaving like a Santos could be a first step towards becoming one, certainly as far as his mother was concerned, and Melanie

48

was good at learning and paying attention to details.

'I'm glad you're here at last,' Diego said heartily.

'Keep your hands on the wheel, please,' Melanie said. 'And your eyes on the road.' She noticed the dark Ford Falcon on the side of the highway, two policemen with machine guns standing near the car, three men inside.

'What's going on?' Melanie asked.

'Nothing. It's just security,' Diego replied. 'Now, about your stay. We'll be in Buenos Aires for the first week, and then we'll go to the country. Do you ride?'

'No, I don't.'

'I'll teach you then. Paco and Dolores Larregui have asked us to stay at their *estancia* for the weekend. It's not far from ours. Paco and I play polo together, and you'll like Dolores . . .' Diego went on, running through a long list of parties they were supposed to attend, accompanied by an even longer list of names which meant nothing to Melanie, complicated by cross-references explaining who was a cousin of whom. Diego's last-minute present had annoyed her at first, but now she was glad of it. Her doorbell had rung yesterday morning; it was a delivery of an assortment of clothes from Saint Laurent Rive Gauche, including the sort of evening wear Melanie had never had need for. Until now.

'Thank you for your present,' she said. 'I love the clothes, but you shouldn't have.'

'I knew that you would turn it down if I told you about it beforehand, so I called Pauline and asked her to choose a few things for you. Appearances matter a lot here, Melanie. To me you're the best in the world even if you wear a paper bag, but by now you know what my parents are like, specially my mother . . .' Melanie didn't need to hear more. She could imagine the kind of comments from Mrs Santos that must have led Diego to order clothes for her in New York. She felt sorry for him, but she also felt

49

that no man his age should be so in awe of his parents.

But then very few men his age would be able to give her first-class tickets and a case of Saint Laurent's clothes as casual presents, let alone any of the men Melanie had met before him. She would have loved Diego as much if he wasn't rich, but it was impossible to remain indifferent to the fact that he was so *very* rich.

'Will your parents come to the country with us?' she asked.

'No, and thank God for that. We'll be on our own.'

Melanie wanted to know more.

'Because they don't like me, or because they don't like the country?'

'Because I don't want them there,' Diego snapped angrily, but immediately regained control of himself. 'My mother doesn't like the country in winter anyway. She says it reminds her of her childhood,' he said smoothly, going on to explain that they were driving along Palermo Park, built in the last century to replicate the Bois de Boulogne. 'The idea was to build a copy of Paris here. Once the houses along this avenue were all like that one. The American Ambassador lives there now,' he said, indicating a huge French-style stone house behind gilt and black railings. The wide avenue was flanked by a mixture of high-rise towers, elegant older apartment buildings, and the occasional very grand town house, usually bearing a crest and a foreign flag over the entrance. After a couple of miles they came to a junction, dominated by the heroic statue of a man on horseback, standing on a tower-like brick plinth, tops of palm trees bursting like green fireworks around the horse. Diego turned right. The road climbed a small hill through a park. Another turn, and they found themselves on another elegant avenue. Money was about.

The road narrowed, and they drove past yet more huge houses behind railings. 'That one belongs to Arianne de la

Force,' Diego said, pointing at a block-long pile. 'She's the richest woman in Argentina, but she lives abroad most of the time. She married my mother's half-uncle . . .' Diego gave Melanie some details about the connection, but she didn't really listen. She would have to hear enough about Mrs Santos's glorious relations from the lady herself.

The avenue led on to a plaza, almost triangular in plan, bordered by mansions and a few apartment buildings. They skirted the central island, where an ornate white marble and bronze monument stood in the middle of a large disc of grass. 'That's the Jockey Club . . . That used to be the Atucha's . . . That's the French Embassy . . . That's the Brazilian Embassy . . .' he explained as they drove past the *belle époque* façades. Diego turned into a car entrance and hooted in front of massive oak doors, so tall that Melanie was unable to see the top from the car. To the side, she noticed a succession of tall windows framed by pillars and mouldings in stone, but the gates swung open before she could take a really good look at the house. Once inside the vaulted foyer, the formal garden at the back was visible through wrought-iron gates at the far end. Diego got out and opened Melanie's door, then threw the car keys to a man in a pale blue waiter jacket.

'Welcome home,' he said to Melanie, opening the glazed main door and standing aside. She went in. Stone walls and the domed stone ceiling formed a pale, creamy-grey enclosure for the broad flight of white marble steps leading to the main floor, maroon carpet secured by thick, shining brass rods. At the top, Diego led her through the vast entrance hall, the main staircase of the house sweeping gracefully along two sides of the space. The soft light coming through the stained glass roof drifted down the old cut velvet lining the walls, as tall as a theatre curtain. Their steps echoed on the parquet floor, mixing with other faint, distant noises, the hum of a house where the owners are a small, pampered minority among servants.

'*Mamá* must be here,' Diego said, opening one of the doors. Melanie saw huge windows framed by rich curtains, the panelling on the walls carved into white planes and golden lines and curlicues, the patterned geometry of Persian carpets, the sheen of precious woods and brass on the antique furniture. They were impressions, glimpses, because almost immediately Melanie noticed María Santos by the fireplace at the far end of the room, and the house, the focus of her attention until now, took second place.

Mrs Santos was wearing Chanel as usual, in heavy blue wool, and her shirt was still silk, but pale pink this time. Her pearls and hairstyle remained unchanged, and her smile that contained no warmth was the same as the one bestowed on Melanie in New York. She was sitting on a Louis XVI armchair, her legs elegantly crossed, her left arm on her lap, resting on an open copy of *Hola!* The heavy gold chain around her wrist picked up reddish reflections from the burning logs in the fireplace.

'I'm so pleased to see you again, Melanie,' she said, holding her hand up to her guest, palm down.

If Melanie had been more familiar with the codes in Diego's world, she would have been flattered by the gesture, an improvement on the plain social kiss. She was supposed to squeeze Mrs Santos's hand briefly, while planting an equally brief kiss in the air next to her cheek, a combined kiss and handshake to confirm a certain degree of intimacy. But such subtleties were beyond Melanie as yet, and she thought that Mrs Santos was expecting her to kiss her hand instead. She didn't lean down, and Mrs Santos, after remaining in her slightly awkward position for a few seconds, returned her hand to her lap.

'Did you have a good trip?' she asked.

'Yes, it was a very good flight, thank you.'

'It's marvellous to be young, you look splendid even after a night on a plane,' Mrs Santos went on. It was flattery time, but Melanie found it hard to compliment Mrs Santos on her appearance in return. Neither did she want to praise the house; it made Melanie starkly aware of her problem. She settled for the biggest object in sight.

'That's a *really* beautiful picture,' she said, looking at the huge canvas in a gilded frame above the fireplace, a full-size portrait of a turn-of-the-century lady in an elaborate evening dress, a web of diamonds around her neck.

'Oh, that's Aunt Meme. Flameng painted her portrait in Paris. She built this house,' Mrs Santos replied casually. Melanie wished she had commented on the chair instead. Although it might have belonged to yet another aunt with a silly name, she thought.

They heard voices in the hall.

'That must be my husband,' said Mrs Santos. 'Amilcar likes to come home for lunch, if his work allows it,' she explained, politely quelling any possibility that it might be a special honour for Melanie's sake.

The door opened, and Amilcar Santos came in. He walked like a man who expected attention, and his physical presence compelled it, although not because he was striking in the conventional sense: he was neither tall nor handsome. But he was dark, and there was an aura of darkness about him, a general, unfocused animosity, as if he disliked everybody as a matter of principle. It was hard to imagine him smiling. If he ever did, it would be a lips-only gesture; nothing could illuminate those eyes, as impenetrable as dark glasses. The rest of the face was banal by comparison. He had a rich man's complexion, the kind of skin that is shaved by others and mollified by hot towels, and he wore clothes to match. But it seemed to Melanie that he didn't belong in the surroundings, probably because of his wife.

She belonged, or rather it was as if the surroundings belonged to her.

Amilcar Santos stared at Melanie.

'Do you have a good travel?' Mr Santos's English was not on a par with his wife's or Diego's, but that wasn't what Melanie found striking about his words. She had never heard a voice like it, a twangy, nasal sound, even more disturbing because he spoke so low.

'Yes, thank you, I'm so thrilled to be here. You have such a fabulous house,' she gushed, feeling as if her words bounced off him. Amilcar turned to María.

'Lunch ready?' he asked.

'Is she going to be trouble then?'

María Santos stopped patting her night cream on her cheeks, and gave her husband a sneering look.

'She's been trouble ever since Diego dropped Verónica because of her,' María replied.

'You should have offered her money,' Amilcar Santos countered.

'That's your way of dealing with everything,' María sighed. 'I have the feeling that money doesn't really matter to her, that's why she's dangerous, but we have to play for time.'

'You're wrong. The longer it goes on, the more difficult it will be to break them apart.'

María put the lid back on the jar, then blotted off the excess cream with a tissue.

'It's not like business, Amilcar. We can't lean too hard on Diego. She might do something to force him to marry her.'

Amilcar paced up and down the room.

'We should get rid of her. I can have that done tomorrow,' he said.

'Are you crazy? Diego is not stupid, and he adores her.

54

He could be very dangerous if he turns against us,' María retorted.

'You never agree with anything I say,' Amilcar hissed angrily.

María rubbed in her face cream, and said nothing.

During the following days, Melanie frequently heard about the link between a chair, an *objet d'art* or a tapestry in the house with some relation or other. Mrs Santos's blood network seemed to cover a prodigious number of individuals, and Melanie occasionally asked her hostess for clarification. It became apparent that the terms 'aunt' or 'uncle' were used to cover a multitude of family connections, some seemingly remote, but perhaps not since they had left María so many valuable objects in their wills.

It wasn't the kind of question Melanie would have concerned herself with a week ago, but after a few days in Buenos Aires, in close contact with Diego's world, it became inevitable. Money was a recurring subject: who had it or who was making it, how to invest it, *la bicicleta*, everybody's gratitude to Joe and his team. Melanie learned that 'the bicycle' was the process by which money was shifted from one *financiera* to the next, on a weekly or daily basis, chasing the best interest rate among an ever-growing number of investment houses. The man with the American nickname was the Minister of Economics, held to be a latter-day equivalent of Merlin on financial matters, architect of the boom – and 'one of us, at last', as many people told her with pride. Prosperity was flaunted like muscles on a beach, and the price of houses, boats or planes was invariably disclosed when mentioning their acquisition. Always in dollars, and frequently one or more *palo verde*, the proverbial million-dollar figure reduced to the trivial image of a 'green stick'. Millions were thrown about in conversation as if they were as light and easy to find as their metaphoric equivalent.

Melanie found her visit exhilarating. Everybody fêted her. She was blonde, green-eyed, and American, therefore triply exotic here; she was very beautiful, superbly dressed thanks to Diego, and – perhaps most important of all – his girlfriend. Or his future wife, for all they knew. She couldn't help feeling like a member of the club, and yet it was disquieting because she wasn't. She was still a secretary from New York, living in a one-room apartment, with four pairs of shoes and a few discounted dresses in her closet. Being with Diego here encouraged her to become the kind of person she had to be in order to marry him, but seeing his world close to made it painfully evident why a marriage was so unlikely.

The Santos family had been very much on her mind. After living in their house for a few days Melanie understood them better, or at least the mechanics of their relationship. Amilcar deferred only to his wife; he seemed to take the same pride in her as she did in her antique furniture. He seemed less proud of Diego. At best, his manner towards his son was condescendingly didactic, but more often it was just overbearing. As was María's, in a different way, as she fussed about Diego's eating habits or worried about his non-existent paleness.

Melanie had also discovered that she wasn't alone in finding Amilcar terrifying – it was a feeling that affected everyone who came across him, from servants to friends of the house, as indiscriminate as the curt manner in which he addressed everybody, other than Melanie, to whom he seldom said a word. Amilcar's animosity was a hurdle for her hopes, but at least it spared her the grinding sound of his voice.

Diego had explained to her that his father's voice was the result of chronic sinusitis, neglected in his youth and by now incurable, compounded by polyps on his vocal cords as a result of the infection. It made flying excruciatingly painful for him, which was the reason Diego had to look after their business affairs in New York on his own. 'If it weren't for his awful voice, we might have never met,' he laughed.

Now, sitting in the Santos' drawing room with a few other guests after dinner, the atmosphere had become more relaxed once Amilcar had made his excuses and gone to bed, but Melanie was glad it was her last evening in town, before she and Diego left for the country alone.

'That commode is splendid, María,' said one of the guests, a dapper man in his forties. 'Next time you're in Madrid I'll show you the pair. It belongs to the Duque de los Montes, a good friend of mine. He might sell it to you.'

María glanced at her Louis XV chest of drawers, ran her fingers over her pearls in a habitual gesture, and smiled.

'That's so sweet of you, Pancho. It belonged to Aunt Josefina. It's *signé* Dubois . . .' she said languidly, as if the subject was of little interest to her. 'I hear you're doing lots of work here these days,' she went on, her voice back to full vivacity.

'Oh, just a few things. I'm doing Fina's *estancia* and Baby's new house. And the Bravos' in Punta del Este . . .'

'It's marvellous to see people doing things again, confidence returning after those dreadful Peronistas,' María said enthusiastically. 'We owe a lot to this Government. We needed order, discipline, and the military have given it to us. Thank God for that.'

'They've also given us ten thousand people murdered, including my sister,' said a girl sitting near Diego. An instant chill descended on the room.

'You shouldn't repeat subversive nonsense, Inés,' María replied, a hint of overstretched patience in her voice. 'Nobody has been murdered. It's all terrorist propaganda.

They go into hiding, or they leave the country, and then they spread these rumours about people being killed in jails.'

There was anger in Inés's face and her voice when she replied, but Melanie was unable to understand her, because the girl spoke in Spanish now. She thought she heard the name 'Marina' a couple of times, and a word that sounded like 'assassins', and she remembered the occasional, small articles in the New York papers about alleged atrocities in Argentina. Melanie had glanced at the copy, or read the headlines only, and now she wished she had paid more attention to them. The argument went on. María didn't seem perturbed at all, but Inés clearly was. Her voice rose, her cheeks became red, her hands were clenched into fists, and eventually she stood up. 'Goodnight, everybody,' she said, leaving the room abruptly.

'Oh dear, look at how late it is! And I must get up at the crack of dawn,' moaned Pancho. He stood up among a chorus of assenting murmurs from the others, and they all gathered around María to say their goodbyes. After a few moments of last-minute gossip and compliments, everybody left the drawing room, accompanied by Diego. Melanie stayed in her seat. She didn't like being left alone with his mother after the argument, but she thought that if she followed Diego it could seem as though she were trying to play the role of mistress of the house. Amilcar Santos was a lost cause, but Melanie hadn't given up on María yet. There was no point in upsetting her unnecessarily.

'So, you are leaving for the country tomorrow,' María said, and Melanie admired her composure. Neither her voice, her face, nor her stance showed any hint of the confrontation a moment ago.

'I'm looking forward to it. Diego says it's very beautiful.' Melanie tried to think of something pleasant to say, and remembered her conversation with Diego in the car, on the way from the airport. 'I'm sorry to hear you won't be there. Diego says you don't like the place, because it reminds you of your childhood . . .'

For a second, Mrs Santos's glare seemed as terrifying to Melanie as her husband's, then her face returned to her usual, glassy smoothness.

Diego was tiptoeing back to his room from Melanie's when he heard a door open at the far end of the gallery.

'Diego, come here!' his mother whispered imperiously. He followed her into his parents' quarters, where she headed for Amilcar's bedroom. María was in her dressing gown, but his father was still fully dressed.

'I don't like to be kept waiting until you finish fucking,' Amilcar Santos said sharply. 'You know we don't like that girl, but you bring her here nevertheless, and you have the nerve to screw her under your mother's roof . . .' He was beginning to shout.

'Amilcar, please. There's no need to be rude,' María intervened, her eyes half-closed, her fingertips fluttering at her temples. 'Let's not get sidetracked, shall we? I wanted to talk to you earlier, Diego, but you weren't in your room. I can't believe you can be so reckless as to take that girl to San Matías, of all places. I *had* to tell your father.'

'We're going to Las Acacias, not San Matías. How could you think I'd be so stupid?'

'Because we know from experience that you can be very foolish, if we don't watch you,' Amilcar snapped.

'She said this evening that you're going there,' María insisted.

'Melanie doesn't even know that Salta exists, let alone San Matías,' Diego countered. 'What did she say to you exactly?'

'She said that you told her I don't like the place, because

it reminds me of my childhood. That could only be San Matías, Diego.' He thought for a second.

'Melanie asked me why you weren't coming to Las Acacias with us. I knew she was thinking that it was your way to spite her, and she's very touchy about that, so I told her you don't like the country because it reminds you of your childhood, which is what you always say . . .'

'About San Matías.' María finished the sentence for him. 'I'm glad it was a little misunderstanding, nothing else, and it's terribly late. Let's go to bed now.'

'No, we must deal with the rest as well,' Amilcar said. 'You asked us to have this *Melanie* of yours to stay here' – Amilcar made the name sound like a disease – 'because she was going to be in Buenos Aires for a couple of days, doing some work. Then it became a week, and now it's two. I thought your mother and I had been pretty clear, Diego. Fuck whoever you want abroad, but you're not going to marry someone like that. She's an outsider, and she has no place in our family.'

'And what are you going to do about it?' Diego asked acidly.

Amilcar stared at him.

'I don't think I need to tell you,' he replied.

'Now, now,' María said. 'We don't need to argue about this at two o'clock in the morning, do we? Diego is not getting married yet. I must say that I'm changing my mind about Melanie, Amilcar. She really is a lovely girl. I've always said that all we need is a little more time, that's all.' She took Diego's arm, and led him to the door.

'Goodnight, darling.' She kissed him. 'Go to bed now. You have a long journey tomorrow.' María closed the door behind her son and turned at once to Amilcar.

'There's no point in threats. It might make him do the

opposite of what we want. You don't want Diego to hate you, do you?' she said.

'He hates me already,' Amilcar replied.

'You see those trees on the horizon? That's the entrance to Las Acacias,' Diego announced, to Melanie's relief. She felt numb after nearly four hours in the car, not so much because of the length of the journey but because of the monotony of the landscape, the interminable prairie under the interminable sky, the wire fences running across the plain like stitching on a quilt. Diego stopped and opened a white timber gate splattered with mud, bearing a bronze plate with 'Las Acacias' cast in relief. The car rattled over the cattle grid, on to the long stretch of road ahead.

'There's something I want to ask you about last night,' Melanie said. 'What are these stories about people disappearing?'

'Nobody knows for sure. The terrorists were out of control five years ago, so the Government had to do something, and you can't be too polite if you're dealing with killers. They arrested a lot of people. Some say they only took people they knew were involved in terrorism, others say that just suspicion of involvement was enough. Some say a lot of them were tortured and killed, others say it's all a lie.'

'Someone must have asked the Government for an explanation. What do they say?' Melanie asked.

'That they don't know anything about people being taken, other than those who are arrested and charged under the law. Maybe it's true, maybe it's not. Everybody could be lying: the terrorists, the Government. You name them, they lie. It's better not to trust anyone, and just mind your own business. It's common sense.'

'That's not common sense, that's not giving a damn about anything!' For once, Melanie was truly shocked by Diego.

'I'm sorry, you're probably right,' he said apologetically. 'But we've gone through very difficult times here, and it makes me a bit cynical about everything.'

'What do you think, then?'

'About what?' Diego asked.

'About the disappeared. What do you think has happened to them?'

'Some might have died. There have been a lot of shootouts during arrests, things like that. Others are away, somewhere abroad. I know that for a fact.'

'How do you know?'

'Because of Marina, my sister.'

Melanie remembered the name from last night's argument between María and her young guest.

'Inés said her sister was murdered.'

'Maybe she was,' Diego said impatiently. 'But Marina is *my* sister, and she wasn't. She was involved in terrorism and the security services were after her, so she left the country.'

It was quite a different story from what she remembered him saying in New York, but Melanie could understand his reasons for hiding the truth. It was an obviously painful fact for the family, and he hadn't known her very well then.

'How do you know?'

'Because she phones my mother every now and then. Last time she called from India.' Diego seemed ill at ease suddenly. 'Can we talk about something else?' he asked.

'I'm sorry. I shouldn't have asked.'

'It's not your fault,' he said. 'These have been very difficult years for all of us. Here, this is Marina,' he said, pulling out his wallet. Melanie looked at the photograph, a snapshot of a smiling girl in her late teens or very early twenties, her long, auburn hair blowing in the wind. She looked pretty, and very vivacious, but nowhere near as stunningly good-looking as her brother. She returned the photograph, and they drove in silence for a while.

'There's the house,' Diego suddenly said in his usual, cheerful manner. 'I love Las Acacias. I feel as if nothing bad can happen here.'

Melanie looked at a sea of grass, a cluster of pink colonial buildings in the distance. The bright, early spring sunshine cast deep shadows in the arched galleries around the house, and a tower rose over the top of the trees that formed a thick screen behind. To one side, the ground rolled gently towards a lagoon with swans gliding on its surface.

Melanie loved it at once. She couldn't think of anything better than living there with Diego for the rest of her life.

FIVE

'I love you, Melanie. I'll never, ever, leave you.'

Her head resting on Diego's chest, Melanie closed her eyes and enjoyed the simple words that his voice turned into something dazzling, as unexpected as diamonds in a stream, but her enjoyment was short-lived; life with Diego had also developed Melanie's skill at reading between the lines.

'Does that mean you've been thinking about leaving me then?' she asked.

'You know I'll never do that,' Diego protested. Melanie believed him, but that wasn't the problem. The problem was that, after a glorious week together in the country in Argentina, she had expected to enter a new stage in their relationship. That had been five months ago, and nothing had changed. Diego kept appearing in New York a couple of times a month, he kept phoning her every day when he was in Buenos Aires, and they kept having a magical time when they were together. But it wasn't real. It was like a recurring wonderful dream from which she had to keep waking. Every now and then Melanie raised the question of marriage, and Diego changed the subject. It seemed to Melanie that they had settled into this pattern, which was much better than not having him at all, but was still not enough.

Diego reached across the table and took Melanie's hand.

'A whole year together, and you aren't bored with me yet. You *are* special,' he said.

Melanie smiled. They hadn't been to La Côte Basque

again since that first evening. Some things had changed: she was wearing one of her Buenos Aires dresses now, so she had no reason to envy the other women in the room, and she had become accustomed to expensive restaurants. After her visit to Buenos Aires, Diego had reverted to type, and given up on local bistros and hamburger joints. Other things hadn't changed. Dinner out was still a way to tease themselves, while they became more and more impatient to leave and go to bed as the evening went on, but tonight Diego lingered after coffee.

'I've got something for you,' he said, pulling out a small, square leather box from his pocket. Melanie opened it. There were earrings inside, a swirl of small diamonds. She kept her face down to hide her disappointment. They were very beautiful, surely very valuable, but not what she wanted. For a second, she had hoped it would be an engagement ring.

'What's wrong? Don't you like them?'

'Yes, I do. I like them a lot. They're beautiful, really gorgeous . . .' Melanie broke into hyperbole to make up for her initial lack of enthusiasm.

'Are you sure? I can change them for something you'd like better . . .'

Melanie had seen the jeweller's name on the white satin lining of the box. It was a Buenos Aires firm, so it made no difference. She couldn't go with Diego and choose something else, even if she had wanted to. He was saying all the right things, but they didn't mean anything.

'What are you so pensive about? You've gone very quiet,' he said.

'I was thinking about work,' she lied. 'I'll finish my training next month, and it will mean a lot of change. I'll become a Sales Assistant. I'll still be working for Ted, but I'll have more responsibility. I'll deal with clients myself now.'

'Then you'll know how much money I've got invested in the bank.' His concern was genuine, and he sensed Melanie's surprise. 'And everybody else, for that matter. You might come across someone much richer than me, and run away with him. I don't like it,' he went on, trying to slip into badinage.

'There are more interesting things about you than your money,' Melanie retorted, annoyed by his comment. She had never thought of checking his file.

'That's good news about your job, then. You always say how bored you are being a secretary, and now you've got what you wanted. Congratulations.' Diego raised his glass.

'Maybe it's not what I *really* want. I want a home, and I want children too.' Melanie thought she could hear her words land on the table with a thud, but Diego seemed completely unperturbed by them, as if she was discussing some interesting news item. 'It's a big commitment on my side, and I won't be able to take leave from my job as easily as now,' she added.

'But on the other hand you'll really enjoy your work. I don't think you should have any doubts. It'll be good experience for you. You should go for it,' Diego said.

For once, Melanie wished he wasn't quite so supportive.

'Get pregnant. It's an old trick, but it usually works.'

Startled by Donna's suggestion, Melanie relaxed, and her goggles fell off. They were stretched side by side, in the coffin-like privacy of two sunbeds at the Body Beautiful Tanning Salon, in an attempt to counteract the February gloom.

'I don't like pulling tricks like that, and I don't want to end up with a child on my own either,' Melanie said, putting her goggles back on.

'You'll have to do something, honey. I'm sure Diego's a

real nice guy, but he's been spoilt, like any rich kid . . .'

Very rich kid, Melanie thought. She had found out that Diego's investments with the bank had reached four million dollars in one year, and he had told her that they had money in other banks. '. . . And I told you that you make it too easy for him. Why should he marry you, when he has a nice set-up with you here? Why should he change anything? If you ask me,' Donna went on, without any need for the suggested encouragement, 'I'd say you should keep the honey pot out of his reach for a while. Tell him you need to think things over, and let him stew. He'll be back asking you to marry him pretty damn quickly.'

'What if he doesn't, and then he finds someone else?'

'Then he'll never ask you to marry you anyway, he'll dump you in the end, and you'll feel like killing yourself.'

'That's how I'd feel if he went now.'

'Sure. But if *you* freeze him out, it's your decision at least, you're in control,' Donna reasoned breezily. 'What other choice have you got? If you keep waiting, he'll find a nice Argentine princess sooner or later, Mom and Dad will love her, and by then you'll be good old Melanie in New York . . .'

Occasionally Melanie suspected that Donna's interpretation of the facts was coloured by envy, but now it coincided with her own reading of the situation. She wondered how much longer they had to stay on the sunbed. It had felt pleasantly warm at first, but now the heat of the lamps was becoming difficult to bear. She arched her back to let some air between her skin and the perspex, then lay flat again and waited for the buzzer.

'I told you I would arrive this afternoon. Why aren't you here?' Over the phone, Diego sounded more puzzled than angry.

'Because . . . I want to talk to you, Diego,' Melanie said.

'Come here quickly then, I miss you. I brought you *dulce de leche*.'

During her stay in Argentina, Melanie had developed a passion for the thick, wickedly sweet dessert. Diego's endearing childishness in mentioning it to hasten her arrival made her wonder if she was about to make the worst mistake in her life.

'I've been thinking a lot about us. I think it might be better not to see each other for a while,' she said, trying hard to sound more convinced than she felt.

'Are you seeing somebody else then? I'll kill you if you are . . .'

'No, I'm not seeing anybody else, and I don't want to. But we can't go on like this, Diego. I can't anyway.'

'Don't be silly, Melanie . . . I want to get married as much as you do. I need a bit of time, that's all. Don't do this to me. To us,' he pleaded.

'I'm not *doing* anything. I just want to have a break, to be able to think . . .' She heard herself waffling, but it was the best she could do. Melanie couldn't bring herself to give him an ultimatum, because she didn't dare to have her bluff called.

'That's the problem with you, you worry too much,' Diego said. 'It's no good sitting alone, chewing over your problems. You have to take life as you find it, make the best of what you've got . . .'

Melanie was enraged. It was easy for him to be pleased with things as they were.

'I wouldn't have to sit alone so much if you were here, you know. You only show up when it suits you . . .' She ran through her grievances one by one, airing frustrations large and small. Melanie had been pretending at the start of the conversation, but she didn't have to feign anger by the time she slammed the phone down.

* * *

Diego called her at home or at work, but Melanie refused to talk to him. He waited for her outside her apartment building in the morning, and outside her office in the evening. He apologized and lost his temper, sent her two-hundred-dollar floral arrangements and rambling letters, said he adored her in the same breath that he said she'd never see him again. After two days her phone stopped ringing, there were no more letters or sudden appearances in the street, and Melanie assumed he had gone back to Buenos Aires. She resisted an impulse to write or call him. If she weakened now, if she made the first move towards a reconciliation, everything would be as it was before, and Diego would have even less reason to risk a confrontation with his parents. She had made it plain that she would only see him again if they were to get married. Sometimes sure that she was doing the right thing, sometimes fearful of the consequences, Melanie carried on with her life, and waited.

María Santos walked into the library and closed the door. Diego was already there. She kissed his forehead, and sat at the other end of the old Chesterfield sofa. Diego had said he wanted to talk to her, and she had a pretty good idea what he wanted to discuss. María guessed that he had given up the American girl after Amilcar's explosion two months ago, before Diego's last trip to New York, but she also sensed that she hadn't heard the last of Melanie.

'Tito is not going to be in the Junta,' Diego said abruptly, catching María off-guard. She wasn't expecting a political discussion, no matter how relevant to the family business.

'I know. Your father told me last night, but it doesn't change anything. Tito is a clever man, you know. This way he keeps his power base, but he is not at risk. Once you are visibly at the top, you can only go down.'

'Maybe. But it could also be that he's losing power, *Mamá*.'

María guessed what he was aiming at.

'I'd rather you came to the point, Diego.'

'*Papá* and you have gone out of your way to get Verónica and me together over the last two months. If Tito is on his way out, then it wouldn't help us much if I were to marry his daughter, don't you think? Anyway, I don't want to marry her.'

'We've been over this a million times,' María sighed. 'I don't think Tito is on his way out, he is one of the most powerful men in the country. Business is one thing, but a family tie between us would make all the difference. Even if he were to lose his power, still Verónica would be an ideal wife for you. People like us can't marry just anyone, darling. You *have* to know that whoever you're marrying shares your interests, your beliefs, and that she won't let you down. We can trust Verónica. It would make us very happy if you were to marry her.'

Diego stood up and leaned against the fireplace.

'I told *Papá* I'll go to New York on Monday.'

'I'm so glad,' María said. 'You can't stay away from New York indefinitely, Diego. It's crazy to trust our money to others. It's a big place, you know,' she teased him. 'You're not going to bump into that girl so easily.'

'You don't understand,' he snapped. 'I'm going to see Melanie as soon as I get there. I'm going to marry her, and there's nothing *Papá* or you can do about it.'

María jumped to her feet, her languid calm quite gone.

'Now listen to me,' she said. 'I've done my best to restrain your father, but there's a limit to what I can do for you. He's told you how things stand. Marry that girl, and you're out on your own, as far as he is concerned. You won't see a cent from him again.'

'Then he won't see *me* again. And neither will you.'

70

'Don't be ridiculous, Diego. You're not going to live in poverty. You're not the type,' María replied. The thought was so improbable that she was almost amused by it, although she admired Diego's skill at bluffing. He sounded quite convincing for a change. Maybe he was growing up at last.

'Don't worry about that,' he said with a wry smile. 'There's plenty of money in New York. I don't have to be poor.'

María didn't like the turn of the conversation. Diego was her son, after all; he looked like her, thought like her, and most of the time the similarities between them made her proud. Better not to push him too far, María decided. Or to acknowledge his threat at all.

'Your father would be horrified if he heard this conversation,' she said.

'That's why you won't tell him about it. I don't want trouble, and neither do you, *Mamá*. I just want us all to be happy. *And* live together. I'm sure that in time, you'll love Melanie as if she were your own . . . as if you'd never had any doubts about her.' Diego avoided his mother's eyes for a moment.

María came up to him and embraced her son.

'I'm so happy for you, darling. Don't worry about your father. He loves you, in his way, and I'll make sure he understands. We must announce your engagement in *La Nación* as soon as possible. You'll get married here, of course . . .' María suddenly seemed too excited by the prospect. 'I'll pray for your happiness next Sunday. And Melanie's,' she added, quickly enough for it not to sound like an afterthought.

Melanie fed the coins into the slot, opened the small glass door and collected a copy of the *New York Times*, then walked towards the subway entrance. She was about to join the early morning crowd disappearing down the stairs, when she felt a hand over her mouth and an arm around her, gripping her from behind. Her first reaction was to scream, but the man's hand stifled any sound.

'Don't move,' he whispered hoarsely in her ear. Melanie struggled, frantically trying to break away.

'I'll kill you if you don't agree. I want to marry you. Now. As soon as you can get a wedding dress,' Diego said, no longer disguising his voice. He released her, and she didn't know whether to kiss him or hit him.

'I don't like any of them,' Diego said to the jeweller, his eyes scanning the black velvet tray. 'I want a green stone, but emeralds are a bit obvious. These look like the kind of ring my mother's friends wear.'

'Your mother must have very discerning friends, Mr Santos, but I have something else you might like better. Please excuse me,' the jeweller said. He came back a moment later, holding a small tray with a single ring on it.

'This is Imperial jade,' he explained. 'A perfect stone, like the one in this ring, is much rarer than emeralds. In China, only the Emperor wore it, because it was considered a gift of God. This piece dates from the Tang period. It belonged to the Empress Han-Shu.'

Diego slipped the ring on to Melanie's finger. She raised her hand and looked at the round, polished stone of a green so intense, so pure, it looked like solid light.

'Oh, Diego, I love it. It's so beautiful,' she said.

'It matches your eyes,' Diego said. 'We'll take it.'

'It is a unique piece, Mr Santos,' the jeweller murmured. 'Perhaps you'd care to know the price before making up your mind.'

'Not especially,' Diego said.

'It's two hundred thousand dollars,' the man whispered.

*   *   *

Melanie stood outside the church gates, waiting for the modiste to arrange the spectacular train of her wedding dress behind her. Like the dress, the woman had been sent to Buenos Aires by the Oscar de la Renta salon in New York, to supervise last-minute adjustments. Melanie had no idea how much the dress cost; nobody had mentioned anything during the fittings, and the bill, like all the others, had been sent directly to the Santos office in Buenos Aires. After six weeks of preparations for the wedding, money had stopped making sense to her.

It was late May, and winter was coming. The night was cold, but Melanie was too nervous to feel it. At last the modiste was pleased with her efforts, a signal was given, and the doors opened. As Melanie glimpsed the crowd inside, she wondered if she shouldn't have accepted María's insistent offer of some old friend of the Santos family to play the role of father of the bride. Melanie had been adamant about it; she had lived alone for many years, and she had no idea where her father was. He would probably have embarrassed her if he had been there in any case, a thought she found as upsetting as the idea of being walked into the church by some friend of Amilcar. After long analysis of Buenos Aires's social history, María found a couple of precedents of brides going into the church alone. In both cases, the girls' social standing was unimpeachable, so she came to terms with the fact that her daughter-in-law would walk up the aisle unescorted.

Now Melanie heard the organ music, smelt the flowers and the incense in the rush of warm air coming out of the open doors, and she was glad to be on her own. The moment was Diego's and hers alone, nobody else's.

Melanie swept along, her white satin shoes gliding over the white satin carpet, her long veil rustling behind, held in place by a pearl and diamond tiara lent to her by María, yet another of her mother-in-law's ancestral possessions.

She kept her eyes on the altar at the end, a coruscating mass of gilt, marble, flowers and candles soaring ever upwards, but all that she could see was Diego waiting in front of it. She ignored the congregation, the women's furs and jewels and the braiding on the occasional uniform among the men becoming more and more impressive as Melanie got closer to the altar. Neither did she notice Amilcar and María Santos standing on Diego's left, he fidgeting in his stiff white collar and silk cravat, she solemnly chic in a Paris couture masterpiece of dark grey velvet, nor the bishop in his ceremonial robes. Melanie saw only the masculine beauty of Diego's face, his skin golden in the light, the perfect cut of his morning suit flattering the width of his shoulders and the narrowness of his waist. He smiled, offering his hand to help her negotiate the altar steps.

The ceremony started. After the rehearsal the day before, Melanie had some idea of the ritual, but she could barely understand most of the priest's interminable words. At last he blessed the rings, and she smiled as she held up her left hand to Diego. Disapproval flickered briefly over María's face when she noticed her daughter-in-law's *faux pas*: Melanie was wearing her engagement ring. Imperial jade flashed in the light for a second, before his hand closed on hers.

SIX

'Now, let's try again, Mrs Santos ... *El ojo del amo
engorda el ganado* ...'

'*El ojo del amo engorda el ganado,*' Melanie repeated.
Or thought she did, until she saw her teacher shake her
head. A second later, Melanie could hear herself on the
tape.

'Can you hear the difference?' the teacher asked. 'It's a
firm, sharp O at the end, not *ojow* or *ganadow*. Once
more, please.'

Melanie tried again. Once she and Diego were back from
their honeymoon in Cancún, she had decided to learn
Spanish as fast as she could.

'St Matthew says that all virtues redeem us in the eyes of
God, Melanie, but it is Charity, first and foremost, that He
considers above all others, *mater pulchrae dilectionis*. It is
through our love of our fellow man that we can best
express our love of God ...'

Melanie closed her eyes, partly as an attempt to concentrate on Padre Angelotti's words, and partly because of the
torpor overcoming her from listening to him for so long.
She and Diego had attended a few meetings in church
before their marriage, in preparation for the ceremony, and
she was forced to consider what role religion played in her
life, if any. Her parents had not been religious, at least
during Melanie's early years. Her mother had started going
to church only after the death of Melanie's brother. She
lived in Los Angeles now, with her new husband, and

during one of their biannual chats on the phone, she had tried to convince Melanie to have her name engraved (at considerable expense) on a glass star that would dangle from the ceiling, among thousands of others, in the Glass Cathedral, a magnificent edifice built by a preacher through whom Melanie's mother had found the way of God. It wasn't even necessary to go into the new church, she explained. She and Bud, her new husband, would be able to drive there and worship from their car. Melanie had no reason to dispute her mother's new-found beliefs, although the idea of the word of God being relayed into a car through a speaker failed to fire her own.

Because religion mattered to the Santos, and certainly to María, Melanie felt obliged to attend Mass with them on Sundays. When she said she wanted to learn more about Catholicism, María Santos had been pleased and suggested Padre Angelotti, her own spiritual adviser. After a few meetings with the priest, Melanie wondered if a loud-speaker on a pole would be very different, but she persevered in her intention to adopt Catholicism. She wished to belong in Diego's world, to *understand* it, and María's approval was also an important consideration in her decision. Whether religious or temporal, neither reason was reproachable in itself, but Melanie felt uneasy about it.

'It can't go on, Diego. Banks are failing, two billion dollars left the country in June, and Sasetru collapsed last month. Have you seen grain exporters go bust in Argentina before?'

'They don't know how to run their business,' Diego sneered. 'The old ways are over, Juanjo. This is 1980. We need an efficient economy, open to world competition . . .' He carried on, explaining the virtues of free trade, and Melanie looked away, over the floodlit park outside the windows, the lights of the occasional ship on the River Plate in the distant darkness, like the signal from a failing heart on a monitor screen. They were at yet another party, in yet another elegant house, everybody dressed in European designer clothes and discussing impending catastrophe, as usual. Or at least the men were. Melanie noticed Zou-Zou Lobos, a recent acquaintance, talking to a strikingly beautiful woman nearby, and moved over to join them, in search of another topic of conversation.

'Melanie darling, how lovely to see you! You look absolutely gorgeous,' the ultra-chic Zou-Zou complimented her in her perfect English. 'Do you know Teresa de Tannerie? Melanie Santos. Melanie just married Diego,' explained Zou-Zou, then turned towards Melanie. 'Teresa lives in Paris most of the time. She arrived in Buenos Aires yesterday.'

'Are you French then?' Melanie asked.

'My husband is, but I lived in Buenos Aires until I married,' explained Mme de Tannerie.

'Teresa is as Argentine as one can be, Melanie. Her family is among the oldest in the country.'

'I'm not *so* Argentine, Zou-Zou. My mother is half-Scottish,' said Teresa, in gracious self-deprecation.

'Please don't talk in English for my sake,' Melanie said. '*Qué hermoso vestido tenés, Zou-Zou,*' she added, to prove her proficiency in Spanish.

'Oh, this,' Zou-Zou replied, not even glancing at her Paris dress. 'Thank you, it's just an old frock.' She swept back her blonde hair, her emerald bangles sliding down her elegantly thin arm. 'Your Spanish sounds marvellous, Melanie,' she added, 'but it's better not to use the word "*hermoso*" for "beautiful" here. Use "*lindo*" or "*bonito*" instead.'

'Diego already corrected me about "*esposo*" a while ago,' Melanie said. 'Apparently he is my "*marido*". He told me only vulgar people say "*mi esposo*" for "my husband", and he gave me a long list of what I can and can't say. I'll never remember all of them.'

'It's all very silly,' agreed Teresa. They had been chatting for a while on the difficulties of learning the subtle points of languages when Melanie noticed Diego pointing at his watch.

'I think Diego wants to go home. He's flying to Miami tomorrow morning,' she said. They exchanged goodbyes and kisses before Melanie left. She was only a couple of steps away from them when she heard Teresa's aristocratic voice.

'She seems very nice,' Mme de Tannerie commented to Zou-Zou, in a tone as angelic as her beautiful face. 'But she worries too much about learning to talk properly. All she has to do is listen to her ghastly father-in-law, and then she'll know how not to speak.'

'Was your father born in Buenos Aires?' Melanie asked Diego as they drove home.

'No, he wasn't. He comes from Salta, a province in the North. Why do you ask?'

'Because . . .' Melanie couldn't say it was because someone had planted doubts in her mind about her father-in-law's pedigree, any more than she liked finding herself curious enough about it to ask. It was the kind of enquiry María would make.

'Because I've noticed he speaks differently from your mother,' she said in the end.

'Your ear for Spanish is getting sharper,' Diego said approvingly. '*Mamá* also comes from Salta, but she speaks with a Buenos Aires accent because she came to school here, to the *Sagrado Corazón*. Her mother was Tita de la Force, and they are a very old Salta family. I showed you Simón de la Force's house near ours. He was Tita's half-brother, and he was the richest man in Argentina. He died on his wedding night. His wife Arianne inherited everything, and for years *Grandmère* Tita and her sisters wanted to sue her, because they were sure she had killed him for the money, but they had no firm evidence. Arianne lives abroad now. She is incredibly beautiful, and apparently she lives with some gigolo. Simón married her after his first wife died of a snake bite, when she was at their estate in Salta . . .' Diego went on, and Melanie wondered how he had ended up talking in detail about his half-great-uncle's wives, when the starting point of the conversation had been his own father.

'Tell me about your father's family,' she interjected at last.

'My father was an only child, and my grandparents died before I was born, so I can't tell you much about them. Going back to Arianne . . .'

For a family that thrived on dynastic legends, Amilcar seemed surprisingly short of them himself.

Diego came out of the bathroom, a towel wrapped around his waist, rubbing his hair dry with another. Melanie was already in bed, reading *La Nación* with a pen in her hand, a dictionary by her side, making the occasional mark on the page.

'You don't need to look up the words in the dictionary, just ask me,' he said, standing next to her. She smiled, and put the newspaper aside.

'I'm marking apartments, not words. Now that I can speak a little Spanish, I thought it was time we started looking for our own place. Your mother hasn't said anything, but I'm sure she doesn't want us here for ever.' Melanie noticed Diego's face. 'Has she said anything to you already?' she asked.

'No, and I'm sure she wouldn't.' Diego stopped rubbing

his hair and sat by her side. 'This *is* our home, Melanie. It's been in the family for seventy years, and I'll inherit it one day. It will be our children's home. There's no reason for us to move. It's not as if we are short of space,' he added.

They most certainly weren't. Their dressing room alone was the size of Melanie's old apartment, and they had their own sitting room, as well as a study for Diego. There was enough wood panelling in their rooms to build a ship, enough antique furniture to set up a couple of shops, and enough pelmeted, tasselled and fringed curtains for Scarlett O'Hara to cope with a lifetime of impromptu engagements, but Melanie felt exactly as she had when staying with Diego at the St Regis: every luxury was either there or available on request, and yet nothing belonged to them.

'You can redecorate our rooms if you want,' Diego said, reading her thoughts. 'I'm sure my mother won't mind.'

'*That* is the point,' Melanie snapped. 'I can't see why whether your mother minds or not should matter to us. Home is where you don't have to bother about anybody else.'

'I didn't mean it like that,' he said instantly. 'Of course she'd have no say, one way or the other. Throw the whole damn lot out tomorrow, and start again.'

Even if he meant it, even if it were true that María wouldn't mind, even if she changed absolutely everything, Melanie knew that it would make no difference. Diego saw it as his home, but she would never be able to see it as hers – as theirs. It was Amilcar and María's house, and she could feel their presence all the time, even if they weren't there.

'We may buy our own place eventually, but now is the wrong time to do it,' Diego said. 'The economy will crash soon, and that'll be the time to pick up bargains. Two people told me at the party that they're going to Miami this week. Everybody is sending their money abroad.'

'But you always say that everything is fine,' Melanie protested.

'Only fools are pessimistic in public. And we have better things to do in private than talk economics,' he murmured, pulling aside the bedclothes.

. . . and Diego is away. He goes to New York or Miami once a month, because everybody here is taking their money out of the country. He loves flying, but he refuses to take me along. Diego says he and the co-pilot need to concentrate very hard, and he would be so afraid of making a mistake and putting my life at risk if I'm on board that it would make handling the plane twice as difficult for him. He's never there for more than a couple of days anyway. Sometimes I miss New York, and I'd love to see you. But I'm trying to get used to a new language, new people, and new friends. You should see the house! It looks like one of those big piles on Fifth, the rooms are fit for the Queen of England, and I don't have to do anything: there are seven live-in staff, plus the driver, and three security guards. Everybody is crazy about security, because they all seem to have a friend or relative who was kidnapped, or almost kidnapped. They say things got much better since the Army took over, but they keep the guards just the same. They are so used to them that they talk about their sex life in their cars, with the bodyguard and the driver in the front seat, listening to every word. I expected people to be much more snooty, but they tell you everything, because they all go to the psychoanalyst all the time (not my in-laws or Diego though).

The country is beautiful, but we haven't been there

much because it's been winter here (we're upside down!). You wouldn't believe it, because it feels like spring if you're used to our winters. We'll start going there at weekends once Diego is back. He's had a new polo field built, and he's dying to try it out . . .

Melanie stopped and stared at the page. She was writing to Donna for the first time since her wedding, the sheets piling up by her side, and suddenly she saw the letter as her friend would. She and Donna had worked together, split lunch bills to the last dime, and travelled on the subway at rush hour. Now she was going on about a lifestyle that would either make Donna feel like a cockroach, or show Melanie for the dumb airhead she feared she might have become.

Melanie crumpled the letter and flung it into the wastepaper basket, pulled a blank sheet from the desk drawer and started again, in much more circumspect style. It was no good, she thought after a while. She couldn't write a polite note to Donna, any more than she could tell her about her lifestyle, or ask her to come and stay with them. Their lives were too different now. Melanie could imagine María's muted horror at Donna's brashness while her friend was here, and her scathing comments once she had gone.

The thought of her mother-in-law made her reconsider the wisdom of leaving the unfinished letter in the wastepaper basket. Melanie suspected that the maids might report everything about her to their mistress. At least she disliked her mother-in-law enough to suspect her capable of encouraging spies under her roof. She dropped the crumpled sheets into the grate, and lit a match. Once the flames took hold, she prodded at the pieces with a poker until they sifted to ashes through the grate, on to the small dune of grey dust in the marble hearth.

*　　*　　*

Melanie settled into her new life. A pattern was developing in her everyday routine, and she felt bored, or perhaps it was a feeling more complex than boredom. She didn't feel bored when Diego was around, and she spent the rest of the time in the company of friends who had vast experience in the art of keeping tedium at bay, or with people who were prepared to relieve Melanie and her friends of significant sums of money in exchange for giving purpose to their days. There was always a new art gallery, a new antique dealer or clothes designer, some Hungarian countess who was fabulous at aromatherapy, some *bruja* who was a genius at reading the future. If all else failed, there was lunch. Or dinner. Or a party. There was always something. When it came to the art of killing time, Melanie had joined a world of serial killers, so she felt wasted rather than bored. She needed a job, a feeling of purpose, and she said so to Diego.

'I don't have much to do during the day. Could I come and work with you in the office?' Melanie asked him one evening.

'You should count yourself lucky that you don't need to work,' he replied.

'I want to. Then I wouldn't have to ask you for money all the time.'

'You don't have to ask,' he reminded her. It was true. Melanie never paid for anything. All the bills were sent to the office, and Diego left an envelope with far too much cash in it on her dressing table at the beginning of each month.

'I'd like to earn some money. It would make me feel better,' she insisted. 'I could be your secretary, and we'd see each other during the day.'

Diego smiled.

'You wouldn't want to be my secretary for the money,' he said. 'Mirna earns two hundred dollars a month, and she is very well paid. You'd have to be pretty desperate to work in Buenos Aires for a salary.'

Melanie couldn't quite believe him. She realized that she had no idea about what anybody earned, not even her own maid.

'How much is Felisa's salary, then?' she asked.

'You ought to ask my mother. Much less than my secretary, for sure, but don't forget the maids get bed and board. It's a pretty good deal for the girls.'

It sounded to Melanie like an even better deal for their employers, but she didn't want to change the subject.

'*Why* can't I be your secretary?' she insisted.

'Because Mirna needs the job, and you don't. Her husband doesn't earn very much, and they have two kids. Do you want me to fire her?' Diego asked.

'Don't be stupid.' Melanie couldn't reconcile his flippant remarks about the maids a moment ago with his concern for his secretary. Unless there was another explanation. Not the obvious one, though; even if Melanie had entertained the possibility of Diego being unfaithful to her for a second, Mirna was short, fat, and nobody's idea of a sexual fantasy.

'You sound as if you don't want me near your work,' she joked.

'That's a lie!' Diego replied, far more vehemently than necessary, and he noticed Melanie's surprise.

'You're right,' he admitted. 'You need something to do, but it wouldn't be a good idea to work with me. It's a small office, my father is very difficult, and you don't like him. It would be an impossible situation.'

She could understand Diego's point, but his outburst still baffled her − unless *he* didn't want her near him all day, but to press the point could lead to an argument, and Melanie didn't want that. Screaming matches between her

84

parents had been the bugbear of her childhood, and she was determined to have a good marriage.

'You could work somewhere else,' Diego suggested. 'I could ask Sergio, or Peti . . .' He ran through a long list of friends, and Melanie had second thoughts. Her Spanish wasn't fluent enough yet for her to handle a real job, and she didn't want to become somebody's office pet, the glamorous Mrs Santos being offered a job just to look decorative behind a desk, for the sake of ensuring Diego's friendship. Nor would it be that easy for her to fit into *any* job: she was trained in banking, and Melanie wanted a real job, not a pastime.

'Maybe I should wait until the summer is over,' she said. That would be in March, and it was early November now.

'The fucker nailed me for three hundred thousand dollars, Diego, can you believe it? My own cousin, and we grew up together . . .' Paco Larregui's voice carried from the other end of the colonnaded gallery at the front of the house. Diego and Melanie had come to Las Acacias for the weekend. The men were discussing business after lunch, while Melanie and Dolores, Paco's wife, sat in wicker armchairs, having coffee. Dolores was telling Melanie about some adultery going on among country neighbours, a story Melanie found as unoriginal as Paco's. Suddenly everybody had a tale of financial horror. Investment houses vanished as suddenly as they had appeared, embezzlement was rife and, as was bound to happen in a tightly knit society, it often entailed family tragedy: widows bankrupted by their sons-in-law, uncles ripped off by their favourite nephews, blood relationships and fortunes crashing simultaneously. At least Paco's tale had the ring of genuine feeling about it, so Melanie focused a frozen smile on his wife and kept listening to the men's conversation.

'. . . I had borrowed the money in the first place, and now I have to pay it back.'

'What are you going to do? Just let me know if you need help,' Diego volunteered. Paco smiled, and slapped his friend's shoulder affectionately.

'You're great, Diego, but I think I'll manage. I'll sell some land I own near Azul; Uncle Quico left it to me in his will last year. Easy come, easy go. It's just over a thousand hectares, so it should be enough.'

'Sell quickly,' Diego advised. 'The way things are going, soon you might not be able to find a buyer at all.'

'I know. Otherwise, I'll have to sell you my ponies. We'd better get going,' Paco said. 'Darling, I need my siesta,' he added loudly, to catch his wife's attention. Dolores stood up.

'Do you have any sleeping pills, Melanie? Paco likes me to take a siesta with him, but I can't sleep during the day, so I take a pill. I've run out,' she explained apologetically.

'I'm sorry, I don't,' Melanie replied, trying to keep a straight face. She and Diego saw their friends to their Range Rover, parked in the cool shade of a group of jacarandas near the house. The trees were in full blossom, a splash of dense, velvety lilac under the sun.

Melanie stared at Diego asleep, his chest rising and falling with his breathing, a golden-brown pointer of hair leading her eye from his flat, taut stomach to his groin. She smiled and stretched her arms out behind her head, luxuriating in the deep contentment of after-lunch sex on a hot, sunny day, the dust in the air glinting golden in the sunlight filtering through the jalousies. Sex was the best aspect of siestas in the country, at least for Melanie, who also found it hard to sleep during the day, although she was not prepared to take sleeping pills for the sake of marital accord.

She got out of bed quietly, put on her clothes and left the room, enjoying the peace shrouding the house at this time of the day. It was the stillness of night without the menace of darkness, the silence broken only by the low of cattle in distant fields. Melanie loved the feeling of having Las Acacias to herself. It had been love at first sight for her, confirmed at every visit, and she wished they would live here all the time, instead of their hollow, frenetic life in Buenos Aires. She thought it would make sense for Diego to live close to the heart of the family business, for their children to grow up in the freedom of the countryside, and had said so to him. Not mentioned, but much more important from her point of view, was the possibility of living apart from Amilcar and María.

'It wouldn't be practical for us to live here all the time,' Diego had replied. 'My father needs me in Buenos Aires, I'd still have to go to America on business, and the country is a very lonely place in winter. You wouldn't like it.'

His answer had disappointed Melanie, but as the weather improved they had been here virtually every weekend; they would leave town early on Friday and go back on Mondays, sometimes Tuesdays if Diego was practising polo, and Amilcar and María never came with them. From passing comments, Melanie gathered they usually went to visit distant friends or relatives. She never asked María about her activities, to avoid giving grounds for questioning about her own – social or otherwise. However briefly or imperfectly, at Las Acacias Melanie could have the illusion of her own home.

Her steps echoed on the terracotta tiles of the gallery, polished by the years to the colour of old bloodstains. The house enclosed a large courtyard on three sides. Built in the early 1800s, its original Hispanic simplicity had been embellished a few decades later with Italianate columns and a balustrade crowning the flat roof, but the original layout remained unchanged, owing little to the notion of comfortable privacy. Every room led to the inner gallery, the only means of independent circulation around the house, regardless of the season, until some ancestor or other of María's had had the openings glazed earlier in the century. The French doors were open now, letting in the rich scent of lemon blossom and jasmine from the courtyard. Melanie reached the front of the house. The broad floorboards creaked as she crossed the drawing room, followed by the eyes of the men and women in the Colonial ancestral portraits on the whitewashed walls.

She opened the heavy, panelled door at the end and went into the study. It was the room Melanie liked best in the house, with windows on two sides, overlooking the lagoon and the wood. Diego and Paco had been here before lunch, playing billiards, and their drinks had not been cleared away yet. Melanie could imagine María's politely glacial wrath at the maid responsible for a similar oversight in Buenos Aires, and decided to have a word with Evelina later.

Spread on a huge partner's desk was a bound collection of cadastral maps of the area. Melanie guessed that Diego and Paco must have had one of their recurrent discussions about who had owned what, and when. She began to fold one of the maps, taking great care at the creases because it was quite old, and she glanced at the title block in search of a date. '1904' was printed boldly, in vaguely Art Nouveau characters, and Melanie's curiosity was aroused. She looked at the map in detail; blocks of different colours showed the various estates in the region, detailing the name of the properties, their owners and the area for each plot. Most of the map was taken up by a pink, slightly irregular rectangle: '*Las Acacias – Doña Luisa de la Force de Gonzalez Golbin – 24,472 Hectareas*' read the caption. The owner must have been María's much-mentioned Aunt

Lulu, Melanie deduced, and she couldn't help being awed by the size of the place. She had assumed that Las Acacias extended as far as the eye could see, but that notion seemed less impressive than the blunt fact of sixty thousand acres of good farming land. María had plenty of reason to be grateful to Aunt Lulu.

Melanie unfolded another map. This one showed the estate in 1945. The pink rectangle was divided into a number of much smaller quadrangles, their colours all different, their owners all named 'Gonzalez Golbin'. The plot holding the lagoon and the house was now listed as '*Las Acacias – Carlota Gonzalez Golbin de Lier – 3,783 Hectareas*'. The name meant nothing to Melanie, and there was no reference to María or her own family name anywhere on the map.

Melanie checked the rest of the maps in the binder. It was only in 1970 that ownership of the estate changed to '*Las Acacias SA*', the Santos' family company. By then, the area of the property had shrunk to 2,667 hectares. It was still sizeable, but very small compared to the original holding.

Melanie had a good head for numbers, and business interested her. She remembered the much-heard complaint from farming friends of Diego's during her first months in Buenos Aires about the absurdity of holding on to their land, at best yielding three or four per cent a year in hard cash, when it was possible to earn five per cent *a month* by investing their money in the right *financiera*.

Paco had said that he was counting on covering three hundred thousand dollars of debt by selling one thousand hectares of land. At that rate, Las Acacias was worth less than a million dollars, and would produce an annual income of less than fifty thousand dollars. Her left hand was holding the corner of the map, the stone on her ring glowing a deeper green against the blue background. She was wearing two hundred thousand dollars on her finger; the more colourful magazines had described their wedding reception as 'the million-dollar party'. Their Lear Jet had to be worth more than that. There were millions invested in America.

It didn't add up.

That evening, as they lay in bed, Melanie brought up the subject that had puzzled her since the afternoon.

'Why are we so rich?' she asked.

Diego laughed softly.

'Because we have more money than most people,' he replied. 'If you mean it as a philosophical question, you should ask Padre Angelotti. I'm not very good at serious explanations.'

'I don't mean it like that,' she said. 'I want to know where the money comes from.'

Diego raised himself and rested on his elbows.

'Hey, you sound as if you're planning to see a lawyer,' he said, his eyebrow raised in mock suspicion, but Melanie detected a hint of guardedness behind his flippancy.

'I'm not. It's just . . .' Deciding it was better to be open about it, she told Diego about the maps, and her assumptions drawn from what Paco had said that afternoon. Diego rested back on the pillows again and drew her close to him.

'You're not just a pretty face, are you? You're right about the *estancia*, but we have other sources of income . . .'

'Like what?' Melanie asked.

'My mother had lots of relations. They left her things . . .'

The multiple spectres of rich aunts rose in Melanie's mind.

'. . . And my father is very good at investing money. He makes a little go a long way.'

'But how rich are we?'

'I really don't know. If you can be precise, then you're not truly rich,' Diego laughed. He kissed Melanie good-night, and pulled the sheet over his shoulder. A few moments later he was sound asleep.

'Chiquita Balmaceda is leaving my Hospital Committee before Christmas. I thought you might like to take her place, Melanie. I can put your name up for election at the next meeting, if you want.' María rang the small silver bell by her side; the butler came in and cleared away the plates.

'That's really nice of you. I ought to know my way around a bit more before taking on such a responsibility, though,' Melanie replied, trying to sound grateful and regretful at once. She did not want to join María's charity committees, and wondered if María had heard about her intention to find a job. Charity was probably the only kind of work María would consider suitable, but what really irked Melanie was the possibility of Diego discussing her with his mother.

'Of course,' María agreed. 'Everybody is going away after Christmas for the summer holiday, so I won't need to do anything until March. You might feel differently about it then.'

At times Melanie thought she had reached a modus vivendi with her mother-in-law, or at least that she understood the rules of coexistence. Not long ago, the fact that María's request for Melanie to have lunch with her at the house had been relayed through Pilar, the housekeeper, would have seemed like another indication of María's hauteur, a reminder of Melanie's lesser standing, but now she knew it was a long-established habit. María used Pilar whenever she wanted to ask Diego to do something she feared he might decline, thus avoiding the unpleasantness of a face-to-face rejection. There was nothing tentative about María's manner when it suited her, so Melanie reluctantly admired her mother-in-law's skill at sidestepping small frictions for the sake of everyday harmony.

Reluctant admiration was also Melanie's reaction to María's disregard for the increasing gloom among their friends. Only the imminent summer break and the blanket of heat over the city softened the mood of accelerating crisis. From trade deficit to external debt, from silent mothers in the Plaza de Mayo to vocal supporters screaming for the release of Isabel Perón, everything contributed to a sense of drift. General Videla would step down in March, and General Viola would become President. The Army's new Commander-in-Chief would be General Galtieri. Other faces, perhaps other policies, but the air was thick with decay and fear.

Pessimism was the norm, even for the many friends of the Santos to whom the situation would not make much difference: their money was already abroad, and would stay there. Nothing would change for them, but nevertheless they joined in the widespread lamentation. Not María. She would politely upbraid her dinner guests if they expressed any doubts about the future of the country. 'It is our duty to behave in a way that sets an example to those less lucky than we are,' she would say, followed by an exhortation to make the most of the country's opportunities. Amilcar usually said nothing on those occasions. When he did, he would express similar views to María's, but the rasping, menacing sound of his voice would deprive them of their upbeat message, and conversation would stop.

'Have you thought about redecorating your rooms?' María asked as she helped herself from the silver tray proffered by the butler. Melanie was slightly thrown by the non sequitur, until she realized it wasn't one. Diego *had* been talking to his mother about Melanie's grievances. It was as if she remained an outsider, even in the process of being acknowledged as a member of the family.

'If so, you might want to use a good decorator to help you,' María went on. 'It is important to have someone you can trust.'

Suddenly Melanie liked the idea. A change in look might make their rooms feel more personal to her, even if this would never be their home.

'I love the look of the rooms at Las Acacias. Who did them for you?' she asked.

'Oh, somebody called Eduardo de Charcas. But there are much better decorators than him,' María replied coolly.

The combination of good work with the opportunity to contradict María was irresistible.

'Finita told me about him,' Melanie replied. 'I'll ask him to come and see me.'

His chin cupped in his hand, one huge cameo ring on his forefinger, Eduardo de Charcas stood in the middle of Melanie's sitting room after a tour of her quarters, and sighed.

'My dear, we'll simply have to start all over again. You want something *really* stylish. This furniture is not antique, it's just *passé*,' he moaned. 'These must be discarded pieces from María's former house.'

They probably were, Melanie decided.

'I love what you did at Las Acacias,' she said.

'I always thought it was one of my best jobs. I wish I could see how it has mellowed.'

Melanie decided to ignore his obvious angling for an invitation to the *estancia*.

'How long ago was that?' she asked.

'Oh, quite some years ago. 1970 or 71? I can't remember. Whenever they bought the *estancia*. That *was* hard work. There wasn't a picture or a piece of furniture in the house. *Nothing*. Luckily María likes auctions, so we had a lot of fun. She couldn't stop. I remember when she bought the *Regence* console in the hall downstairs. It was at the Marquez Lagos sale. "You can't have that at the *estancia*!" I told her. It's a good piece, although I have my doubts about one of the legs. It is a bit more Louis XVI than the rest. I suppose that María wasn't very happy in the end about the fact that I knew better than her.'

Melanie wondered if he was talking about Aunt Quiqui's table.

'You seem to know so much about furniture, Eduardo,' she said. 'I wish you could teach me about it. I always feel so ignorant listening to my mother-in-law.'

It was one of María's charity afternoons, so they had the reception rooms downstairs to themselves. After a couple of hours of information, gossip, and French expressions, Melanie had heard enough about the makers, styles and origin of all the main pieces on display. Eduardo de Charcas's knowledge about the fate of great collections in Buenos Aires was encyclopedic, but the subject wasn't of real interest to Melanie.

What did interest her very much was to find out that every single one of María's so-called ancestral possessions, Aunt Meme's portrait, Aunt Celia's commode, Aunt Quiqui's console, as well as the house itself, had been bought at auction within the last ten years.

Eduardo de Charcas rearranged the fabric samples on the table and stepped back.

'I think that's *it*,' he said emphatically. 'In the drawing room, we should have the Colefax and Fowler *bleu de Nanking* chintz on the walls, then, with the Brunschwig cotton satin for the curtains, and the bedroom will be all in the Kirk-Brummel silk, in that lovely shade of *bois-de-rose*. It will be like ... ooooh!' He shuddered in delight.

'It will be gorgeous,' Melanie agreed. She wasn't interested, but she had a reason for having dithered so much over possible choices. During their first meeting at Eduardo's office, he had bombarded her with a mountain of gossip about Buenos Aires society, but he had become reticent as soon as she tried to steer the conversation towards the Santos family. He didn't know Melanie, and his apparent rift with María, however petty the reason, obviously rankled. His social standing mattered a great deal to Eduardo, Melanie noticed, and he might be reluctant to worsen his problem with her prominent mother-in-law by indiscretions that Melanie could repeat at home.

She had to gain his confidence, which could only be achieved by giving him information in turn, so earlier today, as he pulled out more swatches and samples from the shelves, Melanie steered the conversation towards her wedding. The innocuous start led naturally to the much more interesting revelations about María and Amilcar's opposition to her at first. Eduardo's eyes glittered as he heard the story of the poor little American girl, which Melanie guessed would make the rounds that evening, but she didn't care. She hadn't told him anything that many people didn't know or hadn't guessed already.

'So it's settled, then,' Eduardo said, gathering the samples. 'It's time for a drink, and we deserve one.' He pulled out a bottle of champagne from a small refrigerator concealed in a cabinet, opened it, and poured two glasses.

'I'm so sorry to hear that things were so difficult between María and you,' he said as he gave one glass to Melanie, eager for more details.

'Oh, that's all behind us,' Melanie said blithely. 'We get

on very well now. The one I find difficult is Amilcar. He is so dour . . .'

'You're being kind, darling. It took me at least a year not to be terrified of him on sight. It's that voice and those eyes. I can't understand why someone like María married him in the first place. I don't think he was rich then, Cary Grant he certainly was not, and nobody had ever heard of the Santos before.'

'But María had money,' Melanie said.

'*Had* is the right word. There might have been money once, but the only rich person in that family in recent times was Simón de la Force, and he made all the money himself.'

'I thought María had been left things by all those aunts,' Melanie insisted.

'Which aunts?'

'Celia, Meme, and the others. She always talks about them.'

'Well . . .' Eduardo said with a scathing smile, 'María always mentions them, but they were all dead when she was born, and I doubt they would have seen much of her when they were alive anyway. The link comes through María's mother, and her branch of the family always lived in Salta. There was a de la Force in the nineteenth century who married a very rich girl from Potosí, moved to Buenos Aires, and bought a lot of land with his wife's dowry. Celia, Meme, Quiqui and Lulu were his daughters. They were very big in Buenos Aires society in their time, but by then the two branches of the family were quite separate. I don't think they would have left anything to María's mother, let alone to her. Did she ever say that to you?'

'No, she didn't.' María had never said anything other than 'this used to belong to Aunt so and so', but in such a way that the implication of linear descent was inevitable.

As she had made much of a blood link which, now that Melanie knew the facts, seemed only marginally stronger than a connection to Adam and Eve.

'How did Amilcar make his money then?' she asked.

'You should be the one telling me,' Eduardo laughed. '"Business" is what everybody says, because no one knows for sure. There are only two ways of making lots of money quickly. Either you're very clever, and very lucky, or you have friends in Government. Take your choice.'

Melanie remembered the sprinkling of guests in uniform at her wedding, and the regular appearance of Generals or Admirals for dinner at the house. She thought she knew the answer.

Worried about being late, Melanie raced across the hall, and up the stairs. By the time she and Eduardo had finished the champagne, she had heard enough scurrilous gossip to see her through a year of cocktail parties, laughed so heartily that her mascara had run, and an unexpected friendship was established, even if it meant staying far longer than she had intended. They were going out to dinner that evening, and Diego would be at home by now. Unlike most people in Buenos Aires, he fussed about punctuality.

She walked into their bedroom expecting a mild sermon, but Diego wasn't there yet. Relieved, Melanie chose her evening clothes and took them to the bathroom. Only when she was ready did she notice Diego's briefcase on a chair. Perhaps he had gone to see his mother.

The double doors from the gallery into her in-laws' hallway were open, and the lights in the corridor leading to María's bedroom were on, but she wasn't there. Melanie went back to the hall. The door to the sitting room was closed, and she could hear voices inside. María's came first, then Amilcar's distinctive drone, but Melanie was unable to understand their words. Perhaps it was better not to interrupt them. As she turned away, she heard the door open behind her.

'What *are* you doing here?' It was Diego, sounding almost as menacing as Amilcar.

'I was looking for you. We are going to be late,' Melanie explained. She felt as if she was coming up with an alibi, because Diego seemed to expect one from her.

'Did you hear . . . ?' He took in her perplexed face and stopped. '. . . The good news?' he completed in a much more relaxed voice. 'I've just agreed with *Papá* that we can stay in Punta del Este for as long as we want this summer.'

Melanie wondered why such a conversation justified a family meeting behind closed doors. Then she saw María and Amilcar behind Diego, staring at her. Judging from their expressions, it seemed very unlikely to her that they had been discussing holidays.

SEVEN

'Do you see the big red roof? That's the San Rafael Casino, and the swimming pool ahead is La Terraza's. The white house behind belongs to the Tanneries . . .' As soon as they had approached Punta del Este and started their descent, Diego had begun to point out landmarks or buildings. Some Melanie couldn't miss, others were lost in the vast panorama from the cockpit: prairie and forests on one side, the ocean on the other, the pale yellow line of the beach pointing to the horizon, and the cloudless sky encompassing it all like a bell jar.

Melanie had assumed that they would travel on Diego's plane. It was Diego's admitted extravagance, his passion, and he owned to it with a slight feeling of embarrassment, as the evidence of rich parents' indulgence. Because Diego enjoyed flying the plane so much, Melanie minded the fact that she never accompanied him. She didn't care about planes, private or otherwise, but she was vulnerable to the sense of being left out, and the knowledge that there was something in Diego's life that gave him such pleasure from which she had so far been excluded. Melanie was no expert on aircraft, but as they walked across the tarmac, even she could see that the sleek, twin-engine turbo-propeller plane couldn't be Diego's jet.

'Whose plane is this?' she asked.

'Ours. My father's, in fact. Did you think I was stealing someone else's?'

'No, but I thought we would fly in yours.'

'It would be a bit extravagant to use the Lear and the

co-pilot for a hundred-mile flight, even for me,' Diego smiled.

No more extravagant than being a two-plane family, Melanie thought, but then perhaps there was still a lot to get used to in her new life.

'I thought your father didn't like flying,' she said.

'He shouldn't, because of his sinuses. That's why they need a plane that can fly at lower altitudes. He hardly ever uses it, but my mother does.'

Melanie was surprised.

'I can't imagine when,' Melanie said.

'Whenever. At weekends, I suppose.'

Since they were seldom in Buenos Aires at weekends, Melanie had never thought much about what María and Amilcar did. Diego's comment triggered her curiosity.

'Where does she go on her own?' she asked.

'To see friends in the country, I suppose. I don't ask her.'

Diego seemed both impatient at and embarrassed by the turn in the conversation. Melanie felt sorry for him.

'You can tell me,' she murmured.

'I can tell you what?' he snapped.

'Whatever it is. I know you, Diego. You're hiding something from me, something that concerns her. Nobody buys a plane just to see friends at weekends.'

'I'd better check if they're loading the luggage properly,' Diego muttered, and he started to move away, but Melanie grabbed his arm.

'No, you'd better tell me, otherwise I'll ask her myself. I don't like secrets between you and me,' she insisted.

'You're right,' Diego sighed, then he looked away, as if distressed. 'It's difficult to be open about something you've been hiding for years, something your parents told you not to talk about ever since you were a little boy,' he said. 'My mother is supposed to be an only child, but it's not true. She has a brother who is one or two years younger than her. Nobody knew about him. My grandparents lied, and said that he had been born dead.'

'Why?' The story was already so unlike anything Melanie could have imagined that it sounded like a tale to her.

'Pride. Stupid old pride,' Diego said with a tight-lipped smile. 'The baby was severely malformed, you see, and my grandfather must have found it unacceptable to be seen as the father of a monster, so they kept him in an attic, out of sight. Don't look so astonished, it wasn't so unusual for their circle in a small provincial society. There was a lot of intermarriage, and they all had a story about the family idiot, the *opa* in the attic. My grandfather died when my mother was in her teens, and her mother couldn't cope with anything, so she took charge of the family. She has looked after her brother ever since. He lives at their estate in the mountains, in Salta, and that's why my mother goes there every weekend, to see him. It would be impossible if she didn't have the plane ...' Diego's voice had been nearly a whisper at first, but now it was almost normal, as if he was relieved, pleased in a way, to have disclosed the family secret to Melanie. She couldn't understand the need for secrecy in the first place, but she could imagine the burden on María, the need to uphold a fiction imposed on her since childhood.

'I feel very sorry for your mother,' she said. 'It must be terrible for her.'

'It must be, but she's quite remarkable, you know. She told me about it many years ago, then she said, "We'll never talk about this again," and we never did. You must promise me that you'll never, ever, ever, mention *anything* about this conversation to her. You don't know about Salta, you don't know about her brother, you know nothing, OK? She made me swear then that I would never tell anyone, and I have always respected her wish.'

'Of course,' Melanie said. 'I'll never mention it. We'd better go.'

His arm around her waist, Diego led her to the plane. A moment later Melanie sat behind him in the cockpit. Diego was busy at the controls, in preparation for take-off.

The plane veered left now, away from the sea. They were flying quite low, over empty country, and Melanie saw the runway ahead. The ground got nearer and nearer, as if she was on a gigantic fairground wheel, and she closed her eyes. A moment later, they had landed.

'Isn't it beautiful?' Diego asked exuberantly as soon as they left the plane, indicating the rolling countryside around them. It reminded Melanie of the first lines of 'Morning Has Broken'; there was a fresh, unsullied quality to the landscape, perhaps because it was so empty. There were a few horses grazing in a distant field, but she could see no houses, no sign of human presence other than the airstrip. The solitude around them was even more remarkable after the sight of beaches, buildings and yachts from the air moments ago.

'Where are we?' she asked.

'At the San Diego Polo Club,' he answered proudly. Melanie looked again. There was no clubhouse, no grounds, nothing.

'It's just beginning to happen,' Diego explained. 'Polo is becoming very big business. I had the idea some years ago, but it was hard work to convince my father to put money into it. Punta del Este is a great place and we have reversed seasons, so the club could be a big hit with American players. That's why we need the runway, because you have to make it accessible for private planes.'

'Shouldn't you have built the facilities first?' Melanie asked.

'That's the sensible way to go about it, but I'm dealing

with my father,' Diego laughed. 'It's easier to convince him to do the cheaper things first, and get him to commit himself step by step. I made him buy the land, then we built the airstrip, and now I'm working on him to do the rest.'

They heard the sound of an engine, and Diego turned.

'There's Remigio,' he said. 'He's late.'

'Who is Remigio?'

'Our caretaker,' Diego explained as a small, dark blue van approached along a dirt track, trailing clouds of dust. The van stopped a few yards away from Diego and Melanie, and she saw the words 'San Diego Polo Club' in elegant white lettering, and a logo of crossed polo mallets, also in white, emblazoned on its side. A short, stocky man with thick black hair and a bushy moustache got out of the van.

'Good morning, Don Diego. Good morning, Doña *Melaní*,' he said courteously. He stressed the last syllable rather than the first, but otherwise the man got her name as right as could be expected without an introduction, as had happened before when Melanie had met other members of the Santos staff for the first time. Diego seemed to judge introductions unnecessary as far as Melanie and his employees were concerned, since they should obviously know who his wife was.

'Good morning, Remigio,' she said, her mention of the man's name completing the elliptical introduction ritual. A young man, in his early twenties at most, got out of the van and opened the tail gates.

'*Vamos! Apurate!*' Remigio snarled, more as an assertion of authority than as a need to spur the young man into action, since he seemed both agile and very familiar with his task. He had already climbed on to the plane and brought out the hand luggage, then removed the big suitcases. Diego opened the van door for Melanie, and sat at the wheel. Once the luggage was inside, Remigio tapped on Diego's window.

'Everything is ready, Don Diego,' he said, then he and his young assistant climbed on to the rear.

'We don't have to drive very far in this,' Diego told Melanie. 'Remigio always leaves my car by the gate on the main road. He spends a lot of time polishing it, and he doesn't want to ruin his work by driving it on the dirt road.'

A few moments later, they saw Diego's two-seater Mercedes gleaming by a white-painted gate. Steel tubes formed a double arch over the entrance, framing the club's name in cut-out letters. They stopped by the car, and Melanie got out before Diego had time to come round and open her door. The silver tips of her Maud Frizon slip-ons glinted in the sun; she breathed the fresh, sharp air from the sea, looked at Diego, tanned, sleek and beautiful in his Calvin Klein casual clothes, and felt as if they were living in some *Vogue* feature, two graceful gods moving from their plane to their car, on the way to their villa by the sea. Only it was all real, not illusions on a page.

Melanie started to close the van door, when she noticed that the safety belt was caught at the side. She moved the back of the seat forward, and released the strap. As she pushed the seat back into place, her gaze fell on the gap behind. She was familiar with the sight of guns in the country, either rifles for sport, or revolvers or pistols, but until now she had only seen one like this in movies or on TV. Melanie didn't know that the matt black, box-shaped automatic pistol could fire seventeen rounds per second, .45-calibre bullets that sliced their way through steel. What she did know was that it didn't belong in the van of a genteel polo club.

Nor in the world of *Vogue*.

*   *   *

'Victoria! How lovely to see you! We weren't expecting you back so soon, darling.' Teresa de Tannerie stood up and kissed the newcomer. 'You're just in time for coffee.' Victoria's linen shift fluttered in the breeze, and the light from the torches shone on her tawny blonde hair as she slid gracefully on to one of the oversize white cushions on the terrace with the others.

'I only wanted to see Clarita and the baby,' she explained. 'I wasn't going to stay in that awful heat in Buenos Aires for a moment longer than necessary.'

'How's your sister?' somebody asked.

'She's fine, and the baby is gorgeous. It's quite funny, in fact,' she said, 'because the baby is supposed to be three months premature. You know what my mother is like, Diego, yours is a liberal by comparison, so she'd rather not admit that Clarita was pregnant when she got married. The doctor and the nurses were fabulous about it. They put the baby in an unplugged incubator for my mother's sake, and they looked concerned but reassuring whenever she asked them about his progress. She stands in front of the incubator and prays for the poor little thing's health. Can you imagine? The boy weighs at least nine pounds!' Victoria laughed.

'She can't be blind,' Melanie said. 'Surely your mother must see that the baby is very healthy.'

'Of course she does, but what option has she got? She's been telling us about the evils of sin for years. It is much easier for her to accept a lie than to have to face facts, don't you think?'

'No, I don't,' Melanie replied. 'Lies are lies, and I don't like them.'

Victoria's eyes flashed angrily.

'Oh, dear, this is about to become a serious conversation,' moaned Teresa, turning to her husband. 'Please be an angel and pour some more wine, Jacques. Now *I* have a problem,' she announced. 'We love to have lunch in the park when we are in the Dordogne, but the maid can't see us from the kitchen window because of the trees, so she can't tell when we need her to clear the table. Jacques's sister was going to bring me some kind of cordless bleeper you can get in New York which would have solved everything, but now she's cancelled her trip, and I really don't know what I'm going to do . . .'

Melanie looked away, at the breakers foaming white in the moonlight, the soothing sound of the sea muffled by the din of conversation so vacuous that it made her feel like screaming. Then she heard Diego's voice.

'I'm going to New York in a couple of days. I can get the bleeper for you, Teresa . . .'

'Diego, you're such a darling!' Teresa gushed, and Melanie's irritation became sudden, hot anger. She stood up.

'We're leaving, Diego. Goodnight, everybody,' she said curtly to the group at large before walking away. As her steps echoed on the tiles, she could hear Diego making excuses for their sudden departure. Melanie knew that they were leaving too early, that she was supposed to thank Teresa and Jacques for a lovely dinner, to confirm to everyone that they would see them the next day, as if there was any chance of missing them. She couldn't care less. She got into their car a second before Diego, who rushed up behind her.

'What the hell is all this about?' he fumed, turning on the ignition. 'You're behaving like a lunatic. I can imagine what they must be saying about us now.'

'And what would that be?' Melanie snapped back. 'Something like "Poor Diego, stuck with that American nobody?" Or "He should know that you don't have to marry a secretary, you just fuck her?" You're the one who knows what classy people talk about, so you tell me . . .'

'You're crazy. I don't understand what's come over you, Melanie. They all adore you.'

'What's come over me is that I don't want to spend my time listening to a hypocrite like Victoria, then being told off by your Teresa, as if she smelt bad drains, and then have to listen to an unbelievably silly story about a bleeper. I don't like to live with stupid people who put up with me only because I'm your wife, that's all.'

'Now hang on a minute,' Diego said. 'Victoria is an idiot, and everybody knows that. She would have been at your throat in a second because she doesn't like being contradicted, that's why Teresa made a joke about the conversation being too serious. The story about the bleeper was her way of changing the subject, and she chose the most trivial thing she could think of because it would defuse the situation. She knew what she was doing.'

'And I don't.'

'I didn't say that.'

'Maybe that's our problem, what you don't tell me,' Melanie retorted. 'I don't like to find out that you're going to New York only because you tell your friends at a party, and I don't like not knowing why you need to go there so often. I don't like it when you tell me that Remigio has a machine gun because he moonlights as a security guard at the bank in Maldonado, but then he looks at me as if I'm crazy when I ask him about his other job. You told me what a wonderful time we would have here, in our own house, but you didn't tell me that your parents would be in the house next to ours. I don't like . . .'

'Melanie, stop this right now!' Diego interrupted her. 'I'm sorry I didn't tell you about the trip, but it only came up this afternoon. I knew you'd hate my having to go away as much as I do, so I was trying to find the right moment to tell you. As to what I do there, you do know about it more than anyone. I have to look after our money.'

'That's bullshit,' she said. 'You don't need to go in person. That's what telephones are for, you know.'

'And there is something called the *Dirección Impositiva*, darling. Nobody likes paying taxes and the Government knows it, so they probably tap the phones of every rich person's office. You'd have to be very stupid to call an American bank from Buenos Aires. In any case, *Papá* is obsessed about the possibility of anyone tricking us out of our money. When we make an investment, it is a condition that the money can only be moved or withdrawn after the manager receives instructions from me *in person*. As for Remigio, OK, I lied to you, and I admit it. He has a machine gun because he was our bodyguard during the guerrilla years. Things are better now, but you never know, and Remigio is very fond of his gun. I thought you'd be worried if I told you that there is a danger of being kidnapped, no matter how unlikely.'

'Not everybody keeps guys with machine guns around,' Melanie said.

'Because most people are not supposed to be as rich as we are.' Diego reached for her hand. 'Let's not poison our lives for the wrong reasons, Melanie. What you and I have is magic, I love you more than anything, and the rest doesn't count.' He looked at her, and saw her biting her lip, staring hard ahead as if fighting her tears.

'You don't believe me?' he asked. 'I love you too much to lie about something like that.'

She shook her head.

'I believe you,' she said. 'But I don't want to live like this for ever, with you coming and going at your father's whim, having everything in the world except a place of our own, surrounded by people we don't care about. I'm not like your mother. I can't live just for show.'

They were near the turning towards their house. Diego pulled in, took Melanie in his arms and kissed her, a long, slow kiss as his hands moved restlessly over her back. Suddenly Diego started the car and made a sharp U-turn, the tyres spewing sand to the side as they climbed on to the tarmac again.

'I don't want to live like this either,' he said. 'I promise you that we *will* live as you want one day, and much sooner than you think. We've talked enough now. Just close your eyes, and let's go for a little mystery tour.' Diego slipped a tape into the deck, then pressed a switch. The soft top of the car folded away as the voice of María Creuza, as luminously dark as the starry night itself, came out of the speakers. They raced along the coast, and Melanie felt the wind on her cheeks, her skin still slightly taut from the afternoon sun. The song went on; the words were in Portuguese, so she couldn't understand them, but the voice alone was so pure, so moving, that Melanie didn't need to.

'Do you know what she is saying?' Diego asked, and Melanie smiled. He always seemed to guess her thoughts.

'She must be talking about love, and I'd guess that what she says must be very sad,' she said.

'And very beautiful. She tells her love that they both know that nothing in the world can tear them apart, as they know that distance doesn't matter, but that love only becomes great through suffering. That's why, my love, she says, don't be afraid of pain, because every road will take me to you in the end.'

By then they were driving in complete darkness, other than the lights of the car and the lustre of the sea reflecting the moonlight. The paved road had come to an end. There were no houses, only the beach, the land, the music and the stars.

'Where are we going?' Melanie asked.

The track turned sharply to the right, and Diego stopped the car.

'Only this far,' he said. He picked up a travel rug from the back seat and gave it to Melanie, then went round the car and opened her door. He leaned down, one arm around her shoulders, the other behind her knees, and he effortlessly swept her off her feet. The ground dipped away suddenly, and Melanie could see the lagoon now, its water as still as mercury, cut off from the open sea by the dunes and the beach.

'We are going for a swim,' Diego whispered in her ear as he walked down the slope. 'You think that it will be very cold, but it won't be. It will be perfect. Cool enough to make your heart beat faster at first, but then you'll feel warm water all around you. We'll float on our backs, and you'll stare at the stars and I'll stare at you, because there can't be anything more beautiful than your skin in the moonlight. I'll reach for you and then you'll feel me against you and you'll feel the water around us, and you'll rest your body against mine because you want to let yourself go, to feel light in my arms, and then you'll feel my hands over you, and we'll wait because we know that the longer we wait the better it will be, so we'll cling to each other and we'll wade towards the shore, until the water is shallow enough for us to be able to run, and then there'll be warm dry sand under our feet, and the cool wind on our bare skin, so we'll hold tight and fall on the blanket and we'll kiss and we'll taste the salt on our lips, and I'll lick every bit of you . . .'

Their clothes scattered on the ground, they rushed towards the edge hand in hand, cleaving their way through swarms of brilliant fireflies. There was a splash, the murmur of rippling water growing fainter as they left the shore behind them and moved deeper into the warm, dark lagoon, just as he had foretold.

'Come with us to Fernando and Marisa's this evening, Melanie. We'll pick you up around ten,' Dolores Larregui said as Melanie got out of her car.

'Thank you, but I want to stay home tonight. I think that the sun has given me a headache,' Melanie replied, hoping that the excuse would sound less tired than she felt. Not that she had over-exerted herself. They had all spent a languid, perfect day cruising along the bay on the Lobos's yacht, followed by drinks at the club bar, but the company of twenty people made Diego's absence even harder to bear. He had said that he would be away for only two days, but it had turned into a week already. The only reason to consider an evening out was that otherwise she was expected to have dinner next door at Amilcar and María's house, with a few other couples of their age, the numbers adding up to a perfect complement for bridge afterwards. As she walked across the lawn towards her house, Melanie could see Remigio in the distance, lighting the fire for the barbecue at the far end of Amilcar and María's garden. They were staying in that evening, and she should turn up. The prospect was boring, but almost preferable to being on her own, or the frenetic, mandatory *joie de vivre* of Diego's friends.

She went into the house and headed for the kitchen.

'Any messages, Casilda?' she asked her maid.

'Señor Diego called, about an hour ago. He said he's fine, and that he'll be back tomorrow morning, Señora.'

Diego called her at least twice a day from New York. Often they missed each other in the evenings, especially if he was going out to dinner, too early to find her at home here. Melanie wondered if his outings at night were really business: Diego could have practically any woman he wanted, and she had witnessed the inviting looks he got whenever they walked into a crowded room, but the fact that he didn't call her again on those evenings reassured her. It was much easier to phone from a hotel bed-room, and pretend he was calling during dinner, than to phone long distance from a restaurant. Her jealousy was self-indulgent in the end, because she didn't really believe Diego was unfaithful, and the thought of seeing him again tomorrow morning made her feel elated, so much so that Melanie almost cheered up at the prospect of dinner with Amilcar and María.

'Thank you, Casilda. I'm having dinner next door tonight, so you can have the evening off.'

'Thank you, Señora, but I think I'll stay in my room. There might be something I want to watch on TV later.'

Melanie wondered if the late-night show wasn't Remigio. She had seen them whispering together in the garden.

Once in her bedroom, she chose her clothes for the evening as if it mattered, and toyed with the idea of putting up her hair, before deciding that she could do better things with her time. She had a quick shower, slapped on some make-up and got dressed. By twenty past nine she was sitting with a novel that Dolores had lent her. Melanie had little trouble with spoken Spanish by now, but reading was still a struggle, and after a few pages she put the book down. It was a clear evening; it would be nice to go for a walk before dinner, she decided, leaving the house and heading for the woods. She meandered among the trees, enjoying the scent of pine, until she found herself on Amilcar and María's grounds, at the back of the house. Rather than go in via the kitchen, she decided to skirt the sprawling building to reach the main entrance. She smiled and nodded at the maids through the pantry windows, as they busied themselves over the food, then turned the corner. The sprinklers had been on recently, soaking the grass; Melanie was wearing sandals, and she could feel her feet getting wet, so she moved on to the narrow brick path around the house. The picture windows on this side were dark, except for one. As Melanie approached it, she heard a familiar twangy voice coming from inside, through the half-open sliding doors. It was Amilcar.

'... Diego said it wasn't easy, but they've taught the bastards a lesson.'

'I don't like Diego dealing with this. He's too young,' María said. Melanie's first instinct was to move away, not to pry into Amilcar and María's private conversation. But it concerned Diego, and she felt entitled to know. She was tired of being treated like a visitor – or behaving like one, because part of her had been only too keen to ignore the insidious hints of a dark aspect to her perfect life. She came up to the edge of the doorway and listened.

'Nonsense. I was dealing with trouble like this or worse when I was his age.'

'The rules have changed, Amilcar. They have wiped out the Chileans and the Cubans already.'

'Diego can deal with them ...' Amilcar must have moved in the room, because now Melanie could hardly hear him. She moved closer, feeling the light from the window on her cheek.

'Can I help you, Señora *Melani*?'

Melanie gasped. It was Remigio, a few steps behind her.

'Who's there? Who's there?' María stepped outside, coolly elegant in a beige raw silk trouser suit and her customary pearls, but there was nothing cool about her voice – or her face when she saw Melanie.

'I found the Señora here, standing against the wall, *patrona*,' explained Remigio.

'I ... I came from the wood, and I was making my way to the front. The grass is very slippery,' Melanie explained. She knew that her face was red and her excuse was preposterous, so she avoided María's eyes.

'It is indeed. It's very slippery at times.' María's voice had regained her refined languor. 'Take Señora Melanie to the front terrace, Remigio, and hold her arm just in case. We don't want any more accidents, do we?' She looked at her watch. 'I'd better come with you, Melanie darling. My guests should be here any time now. Did you hear what I was saying to Amilcar, my dear?'

'No. I heard your voices through the window, but I wasn't listening,' Melanie replied.

'They've just announced on the news that Queen Fredrica of Greece has died. She was absolutely charming. I saw her at a ball in Madrid a few years ago, wearing the most wonderful dress. Dior, I'm sure. They say that the Greek shipowners are paying the Royal Family's bills while they are in exile . . .'

Melanie was tempted to confront María with her blatant lie, but she held back. It would only lead to animosity, because her mother-in-law would deny whatever Melanie said. Better to wait for Diego, and ask him.

Escorted by Remigio, the two women headed for the terrace, María babbling away. Much later, as the guests made their way home, they all commented on how lovely Melanie looked that night. The more observant among them also picked up on the fact that she was very clever too. After an unfavourable start, *la Americana* had managed to gain the affection of her mother-in-law in a few months. Now María seemed unable to stay away from her side for a single second.

As soon as she woke up, Melanie jumped out of bed, impatient for Diego to arrive. She had read in bed till the early hours, to wake up as late as possible this morning and cut short her wait. It was nearly eleven o'clock, so Diego should be here any minute now. She showered, dried her hair, and got dressed. María and most of the women she knew had their breakfast brought to them in bed, but Melanie couldn't get used to it, particularly if she was on her own. Like siesta, breakfast in bed was not a solo occupation for her.

She headed for the door and pulled at the handle, but

the door didn't open. Only then did she see the sheet of elegant pale blue stationery, edged in darker blue, lying on the floor by the door. It was María's writing paper.

Melanie darling:
  Casilda came to see me this morning in floods of tears. The silly girl decided to make sure that the duplicate keys were working, so she tried them. She locked your bedroom door, but when she tried to unlock it, the key snapped, and it is jamming the lock now. Remigio has gone to Maldonado to get some tools he needs to fix it, and he shouldn't be long. If you wake up in the meantime, please ring the bell, and Casilda will bring you whatever you need via the window.
  María

Melanie glanced at her window. It would be impossible to get out between the bars. She rang the bell. A moment later she heard Casilda's voice on the other side of the door.

'Please bring me my breakfast, Casilda. How long ago did Remigio leave?' Melanie asked.

'I don't know, Señora ... Some time ago ...' Casilda sounded very contrite.

Melanie did not like the idea of being trapped in the room.

'Any news of Señor Diego?'

'Doña María asked Remigio to collect him on his way back from Maldonado, Señora.'

Typical of María to make her son the priority, Melanie thought. Diego must have spoken to his mother in the meantime if she knew at what time he would land.

'Please ask Señora María to come and see me, Casilda.'

'She's gone with Remigio, Señora.'

After a while, Casilda appeared at the window. Melanie

collected her breakfast things and the newspaper through the bars, laid them on a small round table in a corner, and sat down. She had barely had time for her first cup of coffee when she heard footsteps and voices in the corridor outside.

'Darling, it's me,' Diego said. 'Remigio will fix the lock now. It won't take him long.'

Melanie could hear the gentle scraping of metal against metal, and then the key turning at last. The door burst open and Diego came rushing in.

'I was worried sick about you all the way here,' he said after a long, breathless kiss. 'You must have felt trapped, as if you were in jail. That girl will hear from me . . .' Diego was beginning to work himself up into a rage, as if he needed it to release his pent-up anxiety, and Melanie interrupted him.

'Hey, don't make it sound so terrible,' she said lightly. 'I've only been up for half an hour or so, and I wasn't exactly incommunicado. I've even had breakfast.'

'Good.' Diego went to the door and locked it again.

'There's something I want to ask you,' she said.

'I'm sure it can wait,' he replied, his eyes twinkling. He came back to Melanie and took her in his arms.

Melanie snuggled up to Diego in bed.

'I heard your mother talking to your father last night. It was about you, and it worried me,' she said.

'Remigio told me that you twisted your ankle outside *Mamá*'s bedroom last night. Are you all right now?'

'I just slipped on the wet grass, it was nothing. But . . .'

'But what?' His hand tightened almost imperceptibly on her shoulder. 'Come on, tell me, you know I don't like mysteries,' he said impatiently.

'I heard your mother say that you were in danger.' Melanie gave him a word-for-word account of what she had heard. Diego listened intently.

'So you have no idea what she was talking about then,' he said.

'No, but I don't like the way it all sounds,' Melanie replied.

'Because you think that I'm involved in some sinister mission. I wish my life was so interesting,' Diego said almost wistfully. 'Guess what it's all about.'

'What?'

'Broccoli,' he laughed. 'Not very exciting, is it? There are all sorts of trading agreements between Latin American countries and the United States, and sometimes it pays to grow something to take advantage of an incentive or a loophole. Mexico, understandably, wants to keep as much of the American market to itself as possible and has a lot of pull on the South American side of the State Department. Many years ago, Chile started to export cucumbers to America, but the Mexicans killed the trade. Then the Cubans started to export artichokes very successfully, before Fidel, of course, and again the Mexicans managed to stop it. We started exporting broccoli a couple of years ago, and now there are a few Mexican guys trying to edge us out of the market, that's all.'

'Your father said you taught them a lesson.' After so much anxiety, Diego's explanation was so banal as to be almost credible, and Amilcar could make even the most innocent line sound sinister.

Almost credible. The words remained on Melanie's mind, because, much as she wanted to believe his explanation, it didn't justify Maria's blatant lie about her discussion with Amilcar.

'Your mother could have told me last night.' Melanie didn't want to elaborate, because Diego might tell his mother, and then she would have to put up with María's polite fury at being pictured as a liar.

'You know what my parents are like. They have a thing about being secretive about anything concerning our business. It wasn't such a big deal, I just made the other side see reason after hours of boring talks.' Diego pulled Melanie tight against him. 'I'm sorry that I can't live up to your fantasies,' he said, and Melanie decided to ignore her misgivings. Perhaps he was right in calling them fantasies, and life was easier without them.

'You do,' she said, resting her head on his shoulder, and catching sight of their reflection in the bedroom mirror as Diego embraced her. The feeling of closeness was so strong that it dispelled her fear that he was lying. Not entirely though; her doubts lingered like still dark clouds on a clear day's horizon, either threatening rain or waiting to be blown away by a good wind. She wondered if she ought to tell him her period was late, but perhaps it was better not to say anything until she was absolutely sure. She knew Diego would be as excited as she was about what that might mean.

It seemed a hot, sunny February morning like any other. By midday, traffic thickened on the coastal road and cars started to converge on the focal points along the uninterrupted beach, where young girls in bikinis conversed with fit young men just back from windsurfing and made arrangements for the evening. The more sedate female crowd were to be found further back on the beach, gathered under sun umbrellas and surrounded by bags, books and board games, their deep tans showing off the lines on their faces and the gold jewellery on their wrists and fingers. Their men weren't there; they were either still at home, frantically trying to get through to Buenos Aires on the dilapidated telephone system, or grouped at tables on the bar terrace, nursing stiff gin and tonics and punching figures into calculators, or on their way to the airport.

That morning, they had learned that the Argentine Government had announced an unprogrammed, substantial devaluation of the peso, as unexpected as frost in midsummer, as brutal as the facts: the foreign debt had trebled in a year, the summer holiday lull had failed to slow down bankruptcies, and capital was haemorrhaging out of the country. Not even the brightest summer sunshine or bluest sky could dent their fear. Or their disconcertment. Some of them had second thoughts about military rule as rumours of brutal repression spread, or friends of friends disappeared, but this was balanced by the stupendous boom in which riches gushed out of the ground for so many of them. Now they found themselves without democracy, without freedom and, worst of all, without money.

On a small green hill by the sea, a dune ennobled by tonnes of soil, acres of turf, and automatic sprinklers, stood the pristine white buildings of La Terraza, Punta del Este's most exclusive club. Among the tacit requirements for membership were money, connections and upper-class manners, the latter accounting for the fact that the conversations around the pool were less panicky than on the beach. But there was fear here too. Amilcar Santos had organized a game of *truco* that morning, only to see the other players leave the table one by one, to take or make phone calls, in the end forcing Amilcar to play patience. María, the patron saint of composure, protected her face from the sun under her black straw hat and wraparound glasses, and flicked through a copy of *Paris-Match* on her lap whenever the tone of the conversation around her became too despondent. Diego was at his reassuring best, buying drinks and talking up the future, and Melanie was perplexed, glad that the crisis didn't seem to affect them while unable to ignore the feeling of foreboding that surrounded her.

It was a feeling she remembered that night, when she woke up suddenly and noticed that Diego wasn't by her side. He was standing by the window, his face in the moonlight. It was the face of a cornered man, so frightened that Melanie hardly recognized him, so frightening that she closed her eyes and pretended to sleep.

EIGHT

'Isn't this the most beautiful room in Buenos Aires? Gorgeous, just gorgeous!' Eduardo de Charcas exclaimed, his hands dancing in the air as they encompassed Melanie's sitting room, completely redecorated during her stay in Punta del Este.

'The fact that you designed it has little do with it, I'd guess,' Melanie said. She poured the tea, her legs elegantly crossed, her fingers resting on the lid of the silver teapot, her waist-length strings of baroque pearls and chunks of turquoise dangling from her neck as she leaned forward.

'You're so chic it's awesome, darling,' Eduardo complimented her. 'You look like . . .'

'. . . María,' Melanie cut in. 'At least that's how I feel now, pouring tea in my new drawing room and pretending to be *so* gracious.'

'Balls,' Eduardo said dismissively, 'you have natural chic, while María is all airs. I have an eye for things like that, you know. You have the quality of Dulce or Malena when they were young. You're a real star . . .'

For a second, Melanie saw the scene in her mind, a rich society woman making idle talk with her name-dropping gay decorator friend, and she hated it.

'Oh, fuck off, Eduardo!' she exploded. 'You don't need to make an ass of yourself.'

'Well, well, well. Snappy, aren't we? You used to be more fun, Melanie. You've only been back for three weeks, but maybe you need another holiday,' sniffed Eduardo, clearly offended. Melanie moved to the sofa and sat next to him.

'I'm sorry. I really am,' she apologized. 'It's just that I feel awful, but I shouldn't take it out on you. You're the only real friend I've got.'

Her words mollified him.

'We'll always be friends. You know why? Because we're both outsiders,' Eduardo said, patting her hand before adopting his languid social persona again.

'Everybody is very tense everywhere these days, darling,' he moaned. 'The Army is split, Galtieri will make himself President any day, and the economy is catastrophic. It really is Valium time, so don't worry about it, just go on and have a nervous breakdown like everybody else. It's the chic of the month, believe me.'

'You have an odd way of cheering people up,' Melanie smiled. 'I suppose it could be that, but nobody seems to worry about the situation very much around this house, as far as I can see. The problem is Diego. Suddenly he's not the same man, as if there's something on his mind. He seems so distant . . .'

'Don't be so coy, darling. Do you mean he doesn't fuck you any more?'

'Don't be so coy, darling. Do you mean he doesn't fuck you any more?'

'You're more imaginative about rooms than about people's problems, Eduardo. Diego and I are fucking very well, thank you, but . . .'

María stopped the tape, her face scowling in disapproval.

'That girl really is trash. How can she discuss her private life with that pervert? Eduardo Charcas will tell everybody,' she complained to Amilcar, who was standing behind her. He leaned down and started the tape recorder again.

'. . . there is something odd about his behaviour. I can't explain it, because he acts exactly the same as usual, and he hasn't said anything, but he's worried. I only wish I knew what's on his mind,' the tape went on.

'So do I,' muttered Amilcar.

They listened to the rest of the conversation, then Amilcar switched off the tape deck.

'I don't think she knows anything, because there's nothing to know. You always suspect Diego for no reason,' María said.

'And you're only too ready to defend him.' Amilcar cracked his knuckles. 'It was a mistake to let him handle so much. I've told him that the next time he goes to New York I'm going with him.'

Melanie jostled her way along the narrow pavement of Reconquista Street, thick with the midday crowd. She was in that hybrid area of downtown Buenos Aires where solemn turn-of-the-century bank or office buildings, carved out of granite more solid than most of the businesses they housed, give way to apartment blocks, now also turned into office space by the growth of the financial district. The offices of Las Acacias SA were in one of these, but Diego had asked her to meet him at El Pulpo instead, a couple of blocks away. She saw the sign over the corner entrance, a lovelorn octopus eyeing a mermaid, opened the old-fashioned glass door and walked in. Men in shirt sleeves, their jackets on the back of their chairs, discussed business with varying degrees of fervour, frantically busy waiters shouted back their orders to the kitchen, and wine bottles and preserve tins lined the shelves along the walls. It was a typical, no-frills, traditional Buenos Aires restaurant, and very different from the kind of establishment Diego usually took Melanie to.

He was sitting at a corner table, in a quieter area of the

room. His half-hearted attempt at standing up and kissing her would have been judged more than adequate by most casual observers, specially since it involved a married couple, but it struck her as disturbing. There had never been anything perfunctory about Diego's way of greeting her. Melanie was used to his full attention, but she wasn't getting it now. She sat down; his eyes remained fixed on the door.

'Are we expecting somebody else?' she asked at last.

'No, it's only us, of course,' he said. A waiter appeared and placed menus in front of them. Melanie glanced at the long list of food.

'I want the grilled *langostinos* with a salad, please,' she said.

'The same for me. No wine, just a bottle of Villavicencio,' Diego told the waiter, without opening his menu. Usually he examined it with care, or asked the waiter for suggestions. Once they were alone again, he kept his eyes down.

'You might wonder why I've asked you to have lunch with me at short notice. I have a problem, and I need your help. Will you help me?' Diego asked. It wasn't a rhetorical question, and Melanie wondered how bad his problem could be, if he doubted her willingness to become involved.

'Of course I'll help you,' she replied, feeling as close to him again as when it had been just the two of them in New York. He took her hand and smiled a tight-lipped smile, as if trying to keep his face under control.

'Thank you, *Ojos de Jade*.' Diego used the nickname rarely, and usually only at very special moments. 'You know I love you more than anything in the world. I won't be able to explain everything now, so you have to trust me.'

Something stirred in Melanie's memory. She recalled one of Donna's pearls of wisdom over a lunchtime sandwich:

'Only men who are liars ask you to trust them. The others don't need to.'

'You haven't told me what I have to do,' she said.

'I'm about to, but you must promise that you won't interrupt me until I've finished, OK?'

'OK.'

'I have to go away for a week,' Diego said, 'but my parents must believe I'm with you. I'll tell them that we're going to Rio on the Lear to celebrate the anniversary of the day we met, and that we'll be staying at the Copacabana Palace . . .'

They had met in January, not March. It was a detail, a small fact except that it meant something special to her.

'But that's not . . .' she started to say. Diego raised his hand.

'Please don't interrupt me, darling. I find all this very difficult, and I've asked you to wait until I've finished. Here's your ticket.' Diego pulled a small Varig folder from his pocket and put it on the table, by her plate. 'We'll leave the house together this evening, and I'll drive you to the airport. In Rio, you'll check into the hotel, and you'll ask the desk to put through any calls for me to our suite. If my parents call, tell them that I'm playing tennis or that I'm having my hair cut, or a massage, or whatever suits the time of day, and then call me at the number in New York I'll give you, so I can phone them back. It might be easier if you stay out of the room as much as possible, then you'll only have to relay the message that they called. I'll join you there in four or five days, we'll have a couple of days together, and then we'll come back. It won't be too hard for you, I hope.'

Her amazement was beginning to give way to anger.

'Sure it won't be too hard,' Melanie scoffed. 'I'll polish my tan in Rio while you'll be somewhere I don't know, doing I don't know what.' She pushed the ticket across the tablecloth. 'But since I'm not *that* cool, or that stupid, you'd better have this back.'

'Do you think I'd be such a shit, to involve you in all this for the sake of cheating on you? Why would I make such a fuss about keeping my parents out of the picture, while making it so obvious to you?'

'Precisely for that reason,' Melanie snapped. 'Because it would be such a clumsy way to go about it that it becomes incredible.'

'Come on, Melanie, this is crazy,' Diego said. 'If I needed to go away because I wanted to cheat on you, I could tell you that it is one of my usual business trips, and you wouldn't suspect anything. Don't imagine things that aren't there.'

It was true. Sometimes she worried that she had become too suspicious about everyone: the servants, her in-laws, and now Diego; she was always reacting like an unwanted intruder.

'Why do you need to go away, then?' she asked.

'I can't tell you. I'm sorry, but I really can't,' he said quietly.

Her mood of confidence, born a second ago, died equally quickly.

'I don't know what you are up to, and there might be very good reasons why I shouldn't know. But then you should leave me out of it.' Melanie opened her handbag, took out her sunglasses and put them on. Diego took her hand.

'I hate to see you cry,' he said. 'I didn't want to tell you because it would hurt you, but I was stupid. I should have realized it would be much worse to ask you to help me without telling you why. It's . . .'

The waiter arrived with their order, and Diego stopped.

'It's about my sister,' he continued once they were alone again. 'I have to take her out of the country.'

'But she's out of the country already!'

'Sshhh ... Keep your voice down,' Diego whispered, glancing at the tables nearby. 'You never know who might be listening. That's what my mother says, but I've found out it's not true. Marina is kept under watch in our *estancia* in Salta. That was the deal . . .'

'What deal? With whom?'

'With people my parents know in the security services. Marina was a guerrilla, but there was an informer in her group, and they were all taken away one night, four years ago. My parents managed to get her out of the detention centre, but only on condition that she be kept out of sight, effectively under house arrest. She couldn't be free; there was no guarantee that she wouldn't talk to journalists about what she saw in jail, or she could go underground and rejoin the terrorists. She was sent to Salta, and she's been kept there ever since. She's not allowed to see anyone from the outside world. Apparently she's in a terrible state, and that's why I want to take her away. Casildo, Remigio's brother, is in charge of her.'

As with all of Diego's family stories, Melanie felt a mixture of astonishment and disbelief at the possibility of ever being able to *understand* them.

'I can't see why it's become so urgent for you to take your sister away now,' she said.

Diego toyed with his fork.

'My sister is hooked on heroin. I don't know if she was addicted before, or if they injected her at the detention centre, to make her crave for it and talk. I know that Casildo is her supplier now, and he gives her as much as she asks for, because it makes his job easier. The more hooked she is, the less likely she'll run away, but she managed to get hold of a telephone and she called me a few weeks ago, at the office. She told me everything, and I was horrified. Marina said that she was afraid of killing herself because of her addiction. She begged me to get her out of there. I stopped in Salta on my way to New York, and it broke my heart. She looks so ill, so wasted . . . She was a lovely girl, Melanie. I made enquiries when I was in New York, and I found a clinic that specializes in the treatment of addicts. It's supposed to be one of the best, and I was lucky. They can take her now, so I'm going to go to Salta tonight, to take her away. It has to be tonight, because Casildo is away until tomorrow morning.'

Melanie remembered her brother Dan, found dead in the basement of a condemned building. He had been fifteen at the time.

'You must do all you can to help Marina. I'll come with you,' she said impulsively.

'I'd love you to come with me, but I need you in Rio for my plan to work, Melanie. My parents can't know that I helped her escape, otherwise they'll force me to bring her back.'

'Why? Surely they must want her cured as much as you do.'

Melanie found it hard to read Diego's face at that moment; she settled for a mixture of melancholy and disgust.

'It's not that simple. My father would be very worried about breaking his deal with the security services, and his way to cope with the problem of Marina is to blame my mother and distance himself from the mess. My mother deals with the problem by hiding or denying it. I'm pretty sure that she's been paying for the drugs, because Marina has no money herself, but I'm also sure she pretends not to know what the money is for. If Marina is out, in a clinic, they would have to face a lot of unpleasant truths, and they don't want to. I can't have a confrontation with them. That's why I need you in Rio, to put them on the wrong track . . .'

'I can't believe that your mother would let her own daughter die. You must talk to her,' Melanie said.

Diego smiled bitterly.

'My mother believes whatever suits her own version of events,' he replied. It was a fact that Melanie had learned long ago.

'It won't work,' she said suddenly. 'As soon as your parents hear tomorrow morning that Marina has disappeared, they'll call us in Rio and ask us to come back immediately. Your mother will be in hysterics. She's bound to want you here, with her.'

'No, she won't be able to acknowledge what's happened, you see. After years of saying they had no idea where Marina was, they can't tell me that she was living at our place all along. Once you start lying, it's not so easy to stop . . .'

The banality of the restaurant scene around them made Diego's revelations seem even more bizarre. It was hard to imagine María being able to sit at the head of her Georgian dining table, her hair, dress and pearls all perfect, making small talk to her guests, week after week, never letting her mask slip, when every weekend she travelled hundreds of miles to face the decline of her drug-addicted, terrorist daughter, whom she claimed not to have seen for years. It was far-fetched enough for Melanie to wonder if Diego could be inventing it all.

'There's something else, Melanie,' Diego said. 'I know about your brother, because my mother told me in New York last year. I know how it must have hurt you, since you've never mentioned it, and that's why I didn't want to tell you about Marina at first. I didn't want to make you relive all that in any way . . .'

Melanie felt ashamed of doubting him, although in some corner of her mind a shadow of suspicion refused to melt away.

'I'll help you,' she said. 'What time do you want to leave for the airport?'

'At six o'clock this evening. I'll be back at home around four thirty,' replied Diego.

Her appointment with the doctor was at three o'clock. Melanie had missed her second period; by now she was certain she was pregnant, but the need for certainty was as much for her own sake as for Diego's. She had time to keep the appointment, and she would phone from Rio to ask for the result.

She would tell Diego then.

María pressed the bell. A second later, a concealed door opened in the damask wall, next to the huge Aubusson tapestry that dominated the dining room, and the butler came in. He laid a silver coffee service by her side, bowed discreetly, and left. Amilcar lowered his paper.

'Where the fuck is Diego? He's late for breakfast. Pablo is ill, and I need him to drive me to the office,' he growled from the opposite end of the table.

'*Watch your language!*' María snapped in English, nodding towards the kitchen door. 'In his room, of course. He might have overslept. They were out yesterday night, and they must have come back very late, because I didn't hear them.'

'Benito!' roared Amilcar, and María grimaced in disgust. The butler rushed into the room.

'Go upstairs to Diego's room, and tell him I want him here in five minutes,' Amilcar instructed.

'You must call him *Niño* Diego, or *Señor* Diego, in front of the servants, please,' María reminded him once they were alone. 'If *we* don't uphold the rules in the house, Amilcar, nobody will.'

'I have no time for that crap now,' he said.

'Every detail matters,' María retorted crisply. For a

moment, the silence was broken only by the rustle of Amilcar's newspaper and María's butter knife scraping against her toast, then Benito came back, looking rather flustered.

'Señor Diego and Señora Melanie have gone, Don Amilcar,' he announced.

Amilcar jumped to his feet and stormed out of the dining room, followed by María.

'Oh, my God, he's had an accident! He might be in hospital, Amilcar!' she cried as they stared at the empty, untouched bed.

'Or cleaning us out, more likely.' Amilcar looked at his watch. 'It's another hour until the banks open in New York. I'd better go to the office now. I'll call them and freeze the accounts immediately.'

'Don't be ridiculous. Diego would never do anything like that, and there's nothing you can do from here anyway. You'd have to be there. That's the way you wanted it,' María said dismissively.

'Now don't blame me, María. *You* started the whole shit about being watchful, because *you* thought that the gringa would turn him against us.'

'But she didn't, did she? You've heard what they talk about, day after day, and there's not a shred of evidence against Diego. You must calm down.'

'What I have to do is to go to New York. Now. I told him yesterday morning that I was going to go with him next week. That's why the little shit left yesterday.' Amilcar paced up and down the room, opening drawers and cupboards at random. Benito came in, holding a small silver salver.

'Telegram for you, Don Amilcar,' he said. Amilcar tore it open, then flung it at María.

Dear Mamá and Papá. Completely forgot about anniversary meeting Melanie. She was furious. Decided to take her to Rio to make up. Not much time before

going to New York with you, Papá, so left in a hurry.
Love is crazy. Sorry. See you on Monday. We are at
the Copacabana if you want us. Love, Diego.

'You see? There's nothing to worry about. He's young,
and in love, Amilcar. Just let him be reckless, enjoy himself,' María said.

Amilcar was on the phone already.

'I want the Copacabana Palace, in Rio de Janeiro. Yes,
now. Immediately,' he told the operator, then he covered
the mouthpiece with his hand. 'You didn't used to be so
understanding about his love life,' he said acidly.

'Because now I'm sure she loves him, and it's only a
matter of time until they have children. She wouldn't want
Diego in jail.'

Amilcar held his hand up, asking María to stop talking.
'Mr Santos. Mr Diego Santos,' he said. 'Melanie? It's Amilcar here. I have to speak to Diego . . . What? . . . Then tell
him to call me right now.' He put the phone down and
looked at María.

'He's playing tennis,' he said.

'I told you there's nothing to worry about,' she replied,
obviously pleased to be right.

'Pushing off to Brazil to play tennis and fuck your wife
is no way to run a business,' Amilcar countered. 'He can't
handle anything. He's had it all too easy . . .'

'A moment ago he was going to fleece you, now he is
good for nothing. You must be fair to him, Amilcar. Diego
is not perfect, but he is our son, and you should be proud
of him. You've always expected too much, always made
him feel that he lets you down . . .'

'Because he does.'

'You'd rather have Marina here, I suppose. *Your*
baby . . .' María sneered. Amilcar stared at her in rage.
The phone rang, and he answered it.

'What the hell are you doing in Brazil?' he growled, but María wasn't fooled by Amilcar's tone. She heard the relief in his voice, which matched her own.

'I miss you. I'm dying to see you.'

'That's what you said yesterday, but you're still there,' Melanie replied. 'I hate the answering service, and that girl with the gushing voice.'

'It's the only way I can keep in close touch with your messages, darling. The clinic is outside New York,' Diego said. 'I've had to spend a lot of time with Marina, but she's settling down at last.'

'I've been thinking about her. I wish we'd met. Does she know that you're coming back here?' Melanie asked.

'Yes, of course, it would be very cruel to her otherwise. I've told her I'm leaving today, although we have to change our plans. Listen, darling, the trouble with the plane's fuel injection system has turned out to be a real nuisance. They got the spares today at last, and they've assured me it will be ready in a couple of hours. If not, I'll be stuck. You'll have to fly here tonight instead. I'll tell my father he has to make his own way here, because the plane broke down in Rio, and that we flew to New York together from there. Oh, God! Once you start lying, it never stops. I hate this,' Diego moaned.

'They lied to you first. It's not your fault,' Melanie replied, trying to encourage him. 'It would be great to be together in New York again,' she continued, genuinely excited by the prospect, even if it included Amilcar.

'You *are* wonderful. Thank you,' he said, sounding more upbeat. 'Book your ticket now. I'll call you back in half an hour.'

'There are no seats on any flight to New York until tomorrow morning. I'm booked on the ten A.M. Pan

Am flight,' Melanie said. 'I'll be there in the evening.'

'That's impossible!' Diego cried. 'There has to be a seat tonight. Fly economy, if necessary. Or go to the airport now and wait for a cancellation.'

'There are no seats, Diego. I was there when the concierge tried every airline. I'm not going to sit in the airport on my own for hours, just on spec. What's the hurry? A few hours make no difference,' Melanie said.

'I suppose you're right. It's just that I'm desperate to see you. I feel like flying there now, but I can't, damn it.' He sounded forlorn, and Melanie felt sorry for him.

'Cheer up, I have great news,' she said, breaking her self-imposed vow of silence. She wanted to tell him in person, but suddenly it seemed the right moment. 'I spoke to Dr Arriola yesterday afternoon. We're going to have a baby . . .'

'What? When? Are you all right? When will it be born? You must call him back and ask him if you should be flying. You must take it easy, look after yourself. I'll make sure of that.' Diego sounded frantic.

'Don't be silly,' Melanie laughed. 'I'm not crippled, and I'm only ten weeks pregnant, according to him. I feel exactly the same as usual. I should have kept it as a surprise until I saw you.'

'I'm glad you didn't. You must rest a lot, though.'

'I've done nothing but rest here. I'm bored! In fact, I was planning to go for a walk in a minute.'

'That's the craziest idea I've heard in a long time. Everybody knows that Rio is a dangerous city. You must promise me that you won't leave the hotel.'

'OK, if it worries you. I'll stay here.' Melanie had no intention of doing so, but there was no point in arguing over the phone.

'I can't wait to see you,' he said.

'Neither can I.'

Melanie waited for an endearment.

'Listen, darling, if my parents call, don't say anything about you coming here, OK? I'll tell them myself,' Diego said instead. 'I'll be waiting for you at the airport. I love you.'

'I love you too. See you tomorrow, my love,' she said quickly, because for some reason she was about to cry and she didn't want Diego to hear it. Melanie hoped that being pregnant would not leave her at the mercy of sudden mood swings like this. She put the phone down, picked up her shoulder bag, and left the room. Instead of waiting for the lift, she swept down the broad stairs. The airy grace of the foyer reminded her of Fred and Ginger in 'Flying Down to Rio'; the view of the palm-fringed, sweeping bay through the monumental windows was almost as unreal as a painted backdrop. People lounged by the pool, beckoning white-jacketed waiters, and the romantic perfection of the scene made her miss Diego even more. She wondered if she should go back to her suite and change into her swimming costume, but she knew from experience that she would be bored after five minutes on her own by the pool. She'd go for her usual walk instead, up along the landward side of the avenue, enjoying the sight of the bustling open-air cafés and back by the beach, on the wide, swirling-patterned black and white mosaic sidewalk, feeling the breeze from the sea on her face.

Melanie went down the front steps and turned left, when she heard a sweet, small voice: *'Missis! Missis!'* It was a child, calling her. The boy was very beautiful, with skin the colour of pale milk chocolate, thick black hair and smiling eyes. He was ten years old at most. He was squatting on the pavement, a tray of flowers in front of him. Another boy sat by his side.

'Flowers, *sim*?' the boy said, pointing at the tropical blossoms. Every morning a huge floral arrangement from

Diego was delivered to her suite; flowers were the last thing Melanie needed, but she felt sorry for the children, so decided to buy some. The boys stood up respectfully as she approached them, their dazzlingly white teeth flashing as their smiles widened. Melanie was about to lean over when she felt an arm encircling her waist from behind, pulling her away, and she realized she was about to be robbed. She screamed, expecting the children to leap at the thief, or to cry for help, but they didn't. They ran away instead. The man released his grip on her. Melanie turned to face him.

'I'm terribly sorry to barge in on you like that, but you'd have lost your bag otherwise,' he said, his accent as English as his apology. He was pleasant-enough looking, in a rather bland way, and Melanie guessed he was in his late thirties, maybe younger. Everything about him suggested he couldn't wait to embrace middle age.

'I'm so sorry,' he repeated. 'But I saw them do it a couple of days ago. They rush across the road as soon as the doorman goes inside the hotel. If you had leaned far enough over the tray, the other boy would have cut your shoulder strap with a blade and grabbed the bag from you. They would have run in opposite directions before you could react.'

'They left their flowers behind,' Melanie noticed.

'They probably cut them from some park nearby, and the tray is a piece of cardboard. They'll be sitting outside another hotel at the opposite end of the beach in no time at all, with new stock,' he smiled.

'You seem to know the local customs ... I'm sorry, I should thank you before anything else. I guess I'm still shaken,' Melanie said.

'I often come to Rio on business. I was robbed myself a couple of years ago, so I know how you must feel. A drink might help,' he suggested. His manner was vague enough for his words to be either an invitation or a piece of friendly advice. Melanie decided to treat it as the latter.

'I'm on my way to meet friends. I shouldn't keep them waiting,' she replied. 'But I really appreciate your help.' She felt guilty at leaving it at that, but if he was here on business he was likely to be on his own. Melanie didn't feel like spending the rest of the evening making small talk, or fending off a pass.

'I'd better get going too. Good luck, and do be careful,' he said, and started walking towards the Leme end of the avenue. Melanie stood there for a moment. The sun was beginning to set, and night fell very quickly in Rio. Suddenly she didn't feel like walking on her own. She turned round and went back inside, into the safety of the hotel.

Melanie threw the bedclothes aside. There was no point in trying to fool herself that she would get back to sleep. It was just after six o'clock, and she had been awake since four, tossing and turning in the dark at first, then reading, then turning off the light and hoping that she would fall asleep, but she was too impatient for morning to arrive, to be on her way.

She phoned room service and ordered breakfast, then went to the bathroom and turned the shower on at full force, clouds of steam swirling in the air and veiling the marble walls under a mist of microscopic dew. Melanie felt the water running through her hair and over her shoulders, sliding down her breasts, trickling down her navel; the familiar image of Diego holding her tight against him, his hands gliding over her soapy skin, became so intense that she could almost see him.

She stepped out of the shower. As she rubbed herself vigorously with the white bath sheet, she saw herself in the mirrored wall. The velvety cloth showed off the golden-brown glow of her tan, and she enjoyed the sight of her body. She dropped the towel and reached for her bottle of body milk, squirting the thick cream on her palm until it oozed between her fingers, then she daubed it all over, blending the long, glistening smears on her skin into a smooth sheen. The memory of Diego filled her mind.

A knock at the door shattered her thoughts. She wrapped her damp hair in a towel, slipped into her terrycloth robe, and let the maid in. The girl laid breakfast on the table by the window, and left.

Melanie picked up the silver coffee pot and poured the strong, black brew, as densely fragrant as chocolate, her fingers clenched around the warm hardness of the handle. She took a sip, then reached for the halved papaya in a crystal bowl; the core of darkly viscous, lustrous seeds glistened inside the cleft of the peachy-pink flesh, ripe with juice. Melanie picked up the spoon and dug into the fruit, its firm texture yielding cleanly; the delicious, acid sweet taste filling her mouth, piece after piece, was a perfect balance to the rich bitterness of the coffee. There were other tropical fruits in an ice-filled bowl. Mangoes, guavas, and pineapples she could recognize, but many she didn't know, all of them probably as rich and exotic in flavour and scent. Their skins glowed purple and red and orange and yellow in the sunlight, the same bright light that burnished the slightly choppy sea into a metal sheen and painted gold on to the mountains beyond, their smooth, rounded bare rocky tops emerging from the coat of dense greenery covering their almost vertical slopes.

The sun reached deep inside the room now, and fell on the bed, on the soft, crumpled warmth of slept-on sheets. It would have been a perfect start to the day if Diego had been there, having breakfast with her, a towel around his waist, his hair slicked back after his shower. They would look at each other across the table; he would take her up in his arms and carry her away from the table. Laughing, their lips sweetly sticky from the fruits, they would fall on to the bed, her hand swiftly pulling his towel off him, and they would make long, languorous early morning love. She wanted Diego here.

It was nearly seven o'clock. Melanie called the front desk, and asked for a porter and a taxi. She had just finished getting dressed when the phone rang.

'It's the concierge, *Senhora*. I've got Mr Santos here, asking for you.'

Melanie smiled. Diego hadn't been able to wait either, and he had come to fetch her instead. 'Send him up immediately.' Melanie dropped the phone in its cradle and rushed to the door. Footsteps echoed along the corridor, getting closer. Melanie threw the door open and flung out her arms.

She found herself staring at Amilcar. His eyes were bloodshot, two black discs in a ring of red. He was dead pale, even paler than usual. Sombre, silent, Remigio hovered in the background, behind his boss. Melanie's arms dropped slowly to her sides.

'Diego's plane crashed in Mexico at midnight. He's dead.' Amilcar shoved her aside and moved into the room, followed by Remigio.

'You'd better tell me everything,' he said.

NINE

Wearing black, their heads and shoulders shrouded in lace mantillas, Melanie and María stood by the bronze gates of the Santos family tomb, its walls invisible under the oversize wreaths piled high against them. Amilcar was next to María, his eyes masked by dark glasses. Everbody else stood behind them, packed shoulder to shoulder in the narrow lane, among the marble vaults. Friends and servants, nuns and social climbers, country people and drawing-room habitués, people too young to care and old people for whom the ceremony was a painful reminder of things to come, they all stood under the morning sun as Diego's coffin was lowered into the crypt. Their sad, grieving countenances were, by and large, genuine. The funerals of the rich are always crowded, but Diego's zest for life, his cheerfulness, had made him many friends. Even for those who were not really close, the fact that he had died so young, so blessed by fortune in every other respect, and so happily married, was more than enough reason to feel sorrow for him. And for his family. Not even tragedy could obliterate his widow's good looks entirely, but it was hard to recognize her in the sad figure in the front row. Her shoulders slightly hunched, her eyes swollen and red, her lips blistered from days of biting them in anguish, the sight of Melanie Santos broke everybody's heart.

Only those who knew her well were able to detect similar signs of grief in María Santos. Standing straight, her hair immaculately dressed, her pearls discreetly visible through the veil of lace, she seemed her usual self, a woman in total control of her emotions and her surroundings. Only the occasional movement at the corner of her mouth, and her unblinking stare, suggested otherwise. She led the way into the vault, and her family followed. As soon as they were out of sight, paying their last respects inside the crypt, the crowd broke into small groups. Some people chose to comment on how sad it all was, others made a deliberate effort to talk about something else, anything that would lift the gloom of the occasion, until the re-emergence of the Santos family from the crypt silenced them.

Flanked by his wife and his daughter-in-law, Amilcar led the cortège towards the cemetery gates, and it was now, as she stared at the perspective of cypresses and ornate mausoleums ahead of her, that Melanie felt brutally alone for the first time. The previous days had been a blur of grieving, waiting for confirmation of contradictory reports on the accident, and never-ending offers of condolences, either over the telephone or in person. Drawers and closets had to be emptied, and private papers sorted out – something Melanie refused to do; she kept the few letters she had sent to Diego, and the album of their photographs together. The other papers she emptied into a huge crate, and asked the driver to take it to the office, for Diego's secretary to see to.

Domestic and social routine had helped a great deal, and for the rest of the time there were pills: blue ones to sleep, white ones to relax, orange ones to perk up. Then Diego's coffin had arrived from Mexico. Melanie had intended to be by its side from the moment it entered the house, but when she glimpsed through her bedroom window the huge crate being unloaded outside, and heard the angry instructions from the foreman to his crew about how to handle the heavy load, she decided to wait in her room until they were gone. Eventually, Melanie heard the men climb on to the lorry again and drive away. As she walked along the first floor gallery, she saw María climbing up the stairs in a hurry, looking angry. Melanie jumped back from the balustrade, and stood by the side of a long bookcase, waiting for María to go into her rooms.

Melanie was surprised that her mother-in-law had not stayed by the side of Diego's coffin, in the library which had been turned into a funerary chapel for the wake. Although nothing was said, Melanie sensed that her mother-in-law saw Diego's death as the full restoration of her rights over him. María had explained the arrangements for the wake that morning, before the coffin was brought to the house. People would start arriving in the early evening, and there would be a continuous stream of visitors until midnight, when only relations and very close friends would stay for the final vigil, keeping the family company and comforting them. At nine o'clock in the morning friends would start arriving in the house again, and they would all set out for the Pilar church shortly afterwards, for the Requiem Mass before the burial. Since they would not sleep during the night, María advised Melanie to have a rest after lunch. It all sounded strangely barbaric, particularly having to spend the only time Melanie would have to mourn by Diego's side making polite conversation instead. She wanted to be alone with the coffin.

She opened the door to the library; the air smelt of hot metal. People had been working in the room in the morning, under María's supervision, but Melanie thought they had finished just before midday. Black velvet hangings covered the walls and the windows, and a large silver crucifix presided over the room. At its feet, flanked by six tall silver candlesticks, was Diego's coffin. Amilcar and a man in overalls stood by the bier; the man was holding an electric saw.

Only then did Melanie notice the coffin's lid, its wood as polished as black mirror, lying on the floor, the man's bag of tools next to it. Her first thought was that the man was sealing the coffin, and she was angry at Amilcar and María for not having given her the chance to see Diego for one last time. But then she remembered that one of the many officials had said, after identification of Diego's remains through his dental records – here the man lowered both his voice and his eyes – 'The coffin will be sealed, of course. I'm sure you understand . . . in the circumstances . . . it's more . . . it's easier for the family . . . terrible accident . . . the ladies, you know . . .' Amilcar had nodded and remained silent. Now, in the same room, he stared at his daughter-in-law.

'I thought you were resting, Melanie.' He shouted to be heard over the grind of the saw, but the workman stopped as soon as Amilcar spoke.

'What the hell are you doing?' Melanie approached the coffin and pushed the man aside. The sheet of zinc sealing the box had been cut along the edges of the upper section, and across the middle. 'You must be crazy!' she screamed at Amilcar.

'I want to see my son for one last time,' he murmured. Amilcar nodded at the man, who picked up a small crowbar from his bag. He lifted one edge, then removed the metal plate and stepped aside.

Melanie glimpsed the white satin buttoned padding, and the white cotton shroud, covering Diego's shoulders and his head. A square opening revealed what had once been his handsome face, scraps of torn skin and mashed flesh put together into some semblance of human form. As her father-in-law leaned over the coffin and stared at Diego's remains, Melanie rushed out. Amilcar crossed himself, and turned to the man.

'Seal it,' he said before leaving the library. The workman put on his goggles, and picked up a blowtorch.

Melanie saw Amilcar come into the hall, but he ignored

her and headed for the stairs. She waited until the man left the library, and then went in again. Much later, when María came in, escorted by two maids bearing vases of calla lilies, she found Melanie sitting beside the coffin in the candlelit penumbra.

The wake turned out to be less daunting than Melanie had feared. During the early part of the evening, the constant stream of people offered a distraction from her thoughts. By midnight, numbed by hours of listening to small talk and endless cups of black coffee, she went into the kitchen for a glass of water, rather than ask one of the servants to bring it to her. As she went through the pantry, she was respectfully greeted by three women, sitting at the table and talking quietly. One of them was very old, and they all had the dry, craggy skin of people who have spent their life in the sun and the wind. The women were dressed in cheap, old black clothes, and Melanie assumed that they must have worked for the Santos family at some point. The women nodded in humble recognition of Melanie's polite smile, but they looked down when she came back from the kitchen, as if to be acknowledged twice was beyond their expectations.

Most people had left by one o'clock. Only the inner core of María's circle remained, sitting around her in the gilt and cream drawing room. Melanie went back to the library; she had been there only for ten minutes or so when the door opened, and she heard Amilcar's voice outside.

'*Venga, Mamá,*' he said. The oldest woman Melanie had seen in the kitchen came in, followed by her companions, and Amilcar quickly closed the door behind them. He noticed Melanie only then, but he ignored her. Standing by the coffin, the women brought their hands together and bowed their heads in prayer. Melanie guessed that the younger women must be Amilcar's sisters. After a few

144

moments, Amilcar coughed discreetly, then took his mother's arm and led his family out.

Neither Diego's grandmother nor his aunts were at the funeral now, or perhaps they were lost among the crowd, where Melanie – or anybody else – wouldn't see them. The episode had brought back memories of the early days with Diego, when Melanie herself had been assigned the role of Untouchable; she had been tolerated by Amilcar and María only because they had no alternative. Melanie wondered what would happen now, with Diego gone, when they had no further reason to accept her.

The family reached the cemetery's portico and stood by the gates to receive the last round of condolences from the departing mourners. Melanie saw Eduardo de Charcas, who came over and hugged her.

'I don't know what to say, other than that I love you, and I'm desperately sorry,' he murmured. 'I wish I had been here with you this week. I was in Chile, and I only saw the papers yesterday morning.'

His words, and the simple comfort of his embrace, shattered Melanie's hard-won control. She didn't care about all these people, and she had no time for their hollow politeness.

'Take me away, please,' she sobbed quietly. 'I have to go, or I'll start screaming.'

María heard her, and gave her a disapproving glance. Melanie took Eduardo's arm and he led her towards the exit, nodding at people without stopping to speak to anyone. They crossed the wide road and reached the far side, where a long stretch of fashionable restaurants and cafés faced the cemetery.

'Where do you want to go?' Eduardo asked.

'Anywhere but home. And I don't want to bump into anyone we know,' Melanie said.

'Then we'd better get out of here quick, before they all come this way. My car is round the corner. Let's have lunch in the Costanera,' he suggested. 'We're unlikely to see anyone there.' A moment later, they drove past the cemetery, and saw María and Amilcar still standing near the gates.

'I don't know how they do it,' Melanie said. 'She hasn't cried once, not even when they brought the coffin home yesterday.'

'María is a tough old boot. Now what are *you* going to do?'

'I don't know,' Melanie replied. 'Go back to New York and find a job, I guess. I have nothing to do here any more.'

'Don't rush into anything. Take your time, and let things happen for a while.'

Melanie looked out of the window.

'That's what I've been doing ever since I came here, for Diego's sake. I want to feel that I'm in control of my life again, for a change,' she said.

The butler closed the tall wrought-iron gates behind the black Mercedes. Helped by the driver, Amilcar and María got out of the car, and went into the house. Slowed down by their vigil, no longer forced to keep up appearances in front of witnesses, they seemed aged by their grief. Inside the main hall, Amilcar led his wife through a side door, into a small vestibule, and called the lift. Creaking announced the arrival of the old, birdcage-like cabin, slowly coming down the open shaft. They remained silent until they reached their rooms. There, María unfastened her pearls and bundled them in her hand, then kissed Amilcar on the cheek.

'I'm *so* tired. I'm going to have a rest,' she told him.

'We must talk,' Amilcar replied.

'I don't want to talk now. Later.' She turned but Amilcar grabbed her wrist.

'You've been saying that for the last two days. We must talk, María.' He pulled out a sheet of paper from his pocket.

'Twenty-six million, three hundred and twenty-seven thousand, five hundred and forty-eight dollars,' Amilcar read. 'And that's not counting interest earned. Gone. And there's no evidence of any money found on the plane either.'

'Do you expect anyone to travel with twenty-six million dollars *in cash*?' María sneered. 'He'd need a jumbo jet. You're so desperate to accuse Diego you can't even think straight any more.'

'Unlike you, I don't want to fool myself. I'm talking about the money he was supposed to bring back. It was nearly one and a half million dollars. Burnt notes are no use, so the Mexican police would have told us if they had found anything like that.'

'Maybe the money was on board, and they kept it. Or told the Americans about it. They might be after us now, for all we know,' María countered.

'We *would* know, and I haven't heard anything. There's no question that the rest of the money is missing. Only Diego could have taken it.'

'Diego might have decided that it was better invested elsewhere, and moved the money before coming back.'

Amilcar stared at her in disbelief.

'You forget that he shouldn't have been there in the first place. He went to New York to clean us out,' he said.

'There's plenty more in Panama, and in all the other accounts too. I don't care about the money,' María said dismissively.

'*I* care. I didn't work my ass off for the sake of that parasite. Don't be ridiculous.'

María raised her head. Suddenly her tired air vanished.

'What on earth do you want me to say, Amilcar? I don't know what you're getting at.'

'He was planning to run away with our money. You just don't want to face it.'

'That is ludicrous. He'd never leave Melanie behind.'

'Maybe he didn't mean to. Maybe they had arranged for her to go to Rio, to fool us, and then he was coming back to pick her up and go somewhere else. With our money,' Amilcar added bitterly. 'She's in it too. I know she lied to me in Rio. She said Diego went to New York because there was a fault with the plane, and he wanted it serviced in America. I've checked, and there was nothing wrong with the plane before it left. She told me that Diego had asked her to cover up for him when we called because he didn't want us to worry. It's bullshit. She was covering his tracks. She's in it up to her neck.'

'That's ridiculous. That girl can't lie convincingly to a five-year-old. She knows nothing, I'm sure of it.'

'They were in it together, I tell you. I bet you she knows where the money is, and soon she's going to tell us that she wants to go back to America. We'll have to keep her under surveillance,' Amilcar hissed.

'I've had enough, Amilcar!' María started to cry. 'I can't stand here, listening to your horrible speculations. First Marina, now this . . . For years I lived with the uncertainty of not knowing where she was, if she was dead or alive, and now you want to poison my memory of Diego. He was our son . . .' She stormed out of the sitting room and went to her bedroom, slamming the door behind her. María put her pearls inside a velvet-lined box, and removed the matching studs from her ears. The mirror offered her an escape from her thoughts, and she stared at her own reflection. Her grey roots were beginning to show. A quick glance at her diary confirmed that she had booked a hair appointment for the next morning.

Other symptoms of ageing in her looks hadn't bothered her. Unlike many of her friends, María had not had her face lifted, or the skin on her hands subjected to treatments as expensive as they were useless, in an attempt to get rid of liver spots. Now she wished she had. She pulled at the skin on her cheekbones with her thumbs, her fingers pushing up her hairline at the same time, but it was still *her* face in the mirror, the face of a woman in her mid-fifties, with sad eyes. As she looked down, she saw the silver-framed photograph of her children on her table, Diego and Marina on a see-saw, in Playa Grande, smiling at the camera, when they were six and four.

Standing by the door, Amilcar could see her from the back, her shoulders shaking gently as she cried. María hadn't heard him knock, and she didn't hear him come in. She only noticed his presence in the room when he stood behind her, his hands on her shoulders.

'I didn't want to hurt you,' he murmured. 'Please forgive me; sometimes I'm an ass. You know you're the only one who matters to me, María.'

'And you are the only one who matters to me,' she said. It was true, now that Diego was dead, but Amilcar never bothered beyond the immediate facts. María relaxed in the reassurance of her husband's arms, in feeling the warmth of his cheek against hers, then she felt his lips on her neck, an unusual gesture from him. Very slowly, his hands moved up over her ribs until they held her breasts.

'Amilcar!' she exclaimed in surprise. There hadn't been anything sexual about his demonstrations of affection for many years, by mutual – and silent – consent. Once they had had children, María saw little point in sex. Never too fond of it in the first place, it became like a holiday resort visited year after year, its attractions paling through familiarity, until the journey became more tiresome than the visit was rewarding. Once, long ago, she had seen Amilcar on the street with a young, expensive-looking girl, of the type she had seen at some hotel bars. María was momentarily hurt, but then she reasoned that she wouldn't have minded seeing Amilcar coming out of his dentist's surgery or his lawyer's office: they were all practical solutions to practical needs. As for herself, María remained faithful. Amilcar made her happy in those aspects of marital life that mattered to her, and she respected the demands of religious belief and social convention, particularly if they bolstered her own inclination.

Now Amilcar was unzipping her dress. At any other time, María would have found it objectionable, absurd. They were too old, and they hadn't seen each other naked for at least ten years. She would have worried about the light streaming through the windows, revealing the puckered skin around her nipples, their sagging bellies, shuddering at the thought of having to put up again with the stickiness, the discomfort of it all. But today was different, and she found herself willing to relive an easier, simpler time.

'Oh, Amilcar . . .' she sighed. He turned her around gently, and kissed her. María noticed that he must have brushed his teeth before coming to her room.

'I told you I don't think you should leave immediately. Don't rush into anything,' Eduardo de Charcas reiterated, carving his huge steak with enthusiasm.

'I don't want to stay. The sooner I start again, the better,' Melanie said. 'I can't live like this, Eduardo. I cry when I wake up every morning; I expect to see Diego there, next to me, and he isn't. It happens all the time, because everything here reminds me of him. Memories are awful, if you have nothing else.'

'Has Diego left you any money?' Eduardo asked. Melanie gave him an angry look.

'I didn't mean it in that way,' she retorted. 'I don't give a damn about money, and you are thinking like María now. I didn't marry Diego for his money.'

'I'm sorry. I didn't mean that, but sooner or later you'll have to think about practicalities. You can't depend on Amilcar and María's charity. It would be much better for you if you had your own money.'

'As far as I know, Diego had nothing to his name. Everything belongs to his parents.'

'It doesn't surprise me, knowing Amilcar and María,' Eduardo said acidly. 'All rich parents are the same, they give their children just enough to keep them on the hook, so they keep coming back for more. You shouldn't leave with nothing, though. You should stay, and find out a bit more about what you might be entitled to.'

'I don't care,' Melanie said impatiently. She understood his concern, but she found it gross of Eduardo to bring up the subject of money only an hour after Diego's funeral.

They were sitting on the terrace of one of the many open-air restaurants in the Costanera, a tree-lined avenue along the shore of the River Plate. Miles of parkland to one side and the sea-like infinity of the river to the other almost created the illusion of open country, but it was ruined by the traffic on the road, and the noise of aeroplanes taking off or landing at the airport nearby. In spite of the open air and the breeze from the river, the aroma of roasting beef from the giant barbecues in the restaurants was overpowering.

The smell made Melanie feel nauseous, which reminded her that going back home wouldn't be easy. Her baby would be born in less than seven months. Nobody would employ her while she was pregnant, and it would be very difficult to work once she had a newborn child. Amilcar and María might give her an allowance, but as soon as they knew about the baby, they would make it a condition that Melanie brought up the child in Buenos Aires. Perhaps she had a legal right to live wherever she wanted *and* receive some support from Diego's parents, but she would have to fight her case in an Argentine court. Melanie had seen enough Generals and Admirals dining at their table to have a fair idea of her chances of winning.

Her engagement ring shone in the sun. I'm being stupid, Melanie thought. She knew Diego had paid two hundred thousand dollars for it. Even if she got only half that, it would pay for a few years in New York – not in her present style, of course, but comfortably enough. She should be able to organize herself long before then, finding a job and someone reliable to look after the child during the day, but it would be much easier if she was free from money worries in the meantime.

'I'm not going to start arguing with Amilcar and María about what I may or may not be entitled to,' Melanie went on, more calmly now that she realized she needn't face financial difficulties.

'Only people without a cent bother to be as grand as that,' Eduardo sighed, rolling his eyes. 'Come on, honey, don't tell me you look forward to cooking your own meals.'

'I don't mind that, you know. I even like the idea,' Melanie said.

'You're crazy.'

She thought about life in the house without Diego: the suffocating silences, the perennial smell of floor wax, flowers, and old silk, the stilted conversations at table with María, Amilcar's chilling dourness.

'No, I'm not,' she replied. 'At least I'll be able to live as I want. I'll be free.'

'We all have the freedom to sleep under bridges,' Eduardo retorted.

'That's not in my plans, don't worry.'

'Still, you married a rich man, and you are entitled to what should be yours,' he insisted.

'I never saw Diego's money as *mine*. It wasn't even his, so it doesn't matter.'

'Of course it does, and you benefited from it. I hope you're not turning this into some version of Indian widowhood, using poverty as your own pyre. I know you loved Diego madly, but his money must have mattered to you. You're not a saint, and thank God for that.'

Melanie sat back.

'It mattered, but not in the way you think. Of course I enjoy being rich, but I know I could go back to my old life. What I didn't want was for my children ever to go through what I went through, growing up with the uncertainty that you might be thrown out of your house because the rent money was gone before it was collected, to see my parents argue about nickels and dimes all the time. It ruined their marriage, and it got even worse after my father left us. My brother became a small-time crook and a junkie, and I felt that my life only began when I got away. That's the only reason why Diego's money was important, because I knew that my child would be safe. It's funny, isn't it?' she said with a bitter smile. 'You think that you've got it all worked out, and then it blows up in your face, when it matters . . .'

'Are you pregnant, then?'

Eduardo's question shook her. She wasn't sure she could trust him to keep quiet about her pregnancy. For Melanie to have her child in Buenos Aires, as a member of the Santos family, was no hardship from his point of view. He would be unable to resist the temptation to pass on the information to Patricia, or Teresita, or any of his glamorous girlfriends, to whom he fed gossip like a circus tamer giving tit-bits of raw meat to his lions to keep them at bay. Cocktail party chat would do the rest. It would take a day or two at most for the news to get back to María, and Melanie could imagine the Santos' obsessive concern once they knew she was carrying Diego's child. It would be much more difficult for her to leave, or to cut them off from decisions concerning the child's future. Melanie didn't want to keep them in ignorance about the child, but it would be very different if she told them only after she had settled in New York again. She wanted her baby to be born in America, where she would be on her own territory, living on her own money. It wouldn't be so easy for Amilcar and María to lay down the rules.

'Don't be ridiculous. Of course I'm not.' She could hear the hesitation in her voice, and Eduardo leaned forward, his antennae tuned to the possibility of revelations.

'I don't believe you,' he said. 'You look different, and that's why you're in such a hurry to leave. You don't want Amilcar and María to know about it!'

'Don't be silly, I'm not.'

'What is it, then? What's the secret? I know that you don't want to tell me something.' It was the kind of challenge Eduardo found irresistible, and Melanie knew he wouldn't stop now until he had found out the truth – or believed that he had. Otherwise his accurate guess about her condition would keep him on the phone for hours that evening, without any obligation of discretion. She had to reveal something far more significant than a pregnancy, if he was going to believe her.

'I'm not pregnant,' she insisted. 'But you're right, there's a reason why I want to go as soon as possible. You must promise me you won't say anything to anyone. Ever. OK?'

'OK,' he nodded.

'You promise?' she insisted, for effect.

'Yes, yes, come on,' Eduardo agreed impatiently.

'Shortly before he died, Diego heard that Marina was alive, but kept prisoner on the *estancia* in Salta. Apparently it was a secret deal between Amilcar and María and the Government. Diego was planning to get her out on his plane . . .' As soon as she started talking, Melanie realized that if she admitted her knowledge of Marina's current whereabouts, and María heard about it, it would be as powerful a reason as any for her mother-in-law to follow her to New York.

'. . . But I don't know if he did it. Diego didn't want me to know too much, for my own sake,' she finished.

'Are you saying that Diego died because of Marina? Is that why you can't stay with Amilcar and María?' Eduardo gasped.

'No, that's crazy. I don't even know if it was true that she was in Salta. But *if* Diego helped her escape, Amilcar and María will find out sooner or later. They won't believe I don't know where Marina is, and it would be an impossible situation if we are living together. That's why I want to go now, before it's too late.'

'It's incredible, but I suppose it's no more astonishing than many things one hears these days,' Eduardo murmured, shaking his head. 'I can understand now why you're so keen to go.' Melanie felt guilty about lying, as she felt guilty about betraying Diego's confidence. But lying to Eduardo was necessary, and Diego was dead.

'I'm going to miss you, Edu,' she smiled.

He opened his eyes wide in amazement.

'Miss me? With you there, I'm going to be in New York even more often than I am now, darling. I like my walks on the wild side, you know,' he smiled back.

'Is Señora María at home, Benito?' Melanie asked the butler as she came into the house.

'Yes, Señora, she is with Don Amilcar in the Round Room.'

The grand name of the room was at odds with its mundane use. It was one of the smaller reception rooms, next to the library, where María and Amilcar watched TV. Melanie walked across the hall and knocked at the carved double doors before going in. They were sitting side by side on a small sofa in the dark, holding hands, their faces glowing in the dim light from the screen. María reached out and turned on a lamp on a side table.

'We missed you this afternoon, Melanie,' she said.

'I had lunch with Eduardo Charcas at the Costanera, and then we went to the cinema. We went to see "Kramer vs Kramer",' Melanie explained. As was often the case when giving an account of her activities to María, she found herself volunteering more information than necessary, a habit from the days when her mother-in-law's approval mattered to her. To her surprise, Amilcar reached for the remote control and switched off the TV. Melanie couldn't believe that he was interested in conversation with her, but at least he was trying to make an effort. Sometimes things improve only when it is too late, she thought.

'I hear it's very good,' María commented. 'I'm so glad you've joined us. Please sit down, Melanie, we ought to have a little talk *en famille*.' She paused until her daughter-in-law had made herself comfortable in an armchair.

'Would you like a drink?' Amilcar asked them.

'I'll break my rules for once,' María said, an announcement as unexpected as Amilcar's attempts at being affable. 'I'll have a sherry, darling.'

'The same for me, please,' Melanie said, for the sake of diplomacy. A moment later, glasses in hand, they all relaxed in their seats, or at least tried to, in their unusual attempt at closeness.

'These have been very difficult times for us all, Melanie,' María said. 'Diego's death is as horrible a loss for you as it is for Amilcar and I, and we only have each other now. I fear there have been times when you may not have felt as close a member of this family as you are entitled to. It might have been my fault, and I'm sorry. I just want you to know that you are like a daughter to us. Never forget that.'

In spite of herself, Melanie was moved. She had never liked Amilcar and María, and she never would, but it was also true that Diego's death forged a link between them, which made it harder to announce her wish to leave. Her resolve weakened for a moment, but then she imagined how much more difficult it would be once they knew she was pregnant. Her condition would begin to show soon.

'It's really nice of you to say that, María,' she murmured. 'And I appreciate everything Amilcar and you have done for me.' Melanie had mentally rehearsed her speech on her way home, and she had settled for an expression of gratitude as the best opening. 'I also think of you both as my family,' she finished.

'That's very touching, my dear,' María replied. 'A family must stay together, finding comfort in each other. Amilcar and I were wondering about your plans.'

Melanie was pleasantly surprised by the turn in the conversation. It would have been much more difficult to bring up the subject herself.

'I have none, other than to return to America, to stay with my mother for a while. I would like to go soon, if you don't mind. Maybe in a week or two,' Melanie replied. There was something in the look exchanged between Amilcar and María that made her feel cut off from them again.

María smiled.

'Of course,' she said. 'Such a sensible idea. You could ask your secretary to make all the arrangements, darling,'

María suggested to her husband, then she turned towards Melanie. 'You just give Amilcar your passport tomorrow morning at breakfast, and you won't need to worry. Everything will be arranged.'

Melanie stood by her bedroom window, staring at the back of the monument in the square, at the bronze statues streaked by the rain. There were lights in the Jockey Club and a few other windows around the square, and the occasional car passed by, but it was just after midnight, and the scene was very quiet. A Ford Falcon drove slowly around, the Federal Police crest painted on its door. It reminded Melanie of the similar, unmarked car she had seen near the airport on her first visit. As usual, the memory involved Diego, and she moved away from the window. The thick silk curtain fell smoothly into place again.

She had felt restless ever since María's suggestion earlier that evening that she should give her passport to Amilcar. Melanie had remarked that she didn't need a visa for the US, but María had launched into some complicated explanation about exchange controls, airport taxes and ticket reservations, making it essential for Amilcar's secretary to have Melanie's passport. The explanation sounded bizarre – but no more than other bureaucratic procedures Melanie had come across in Argentina, and she had no excuse to turn down their offer, other than instinctive suspicion, out of habit. There was nothing to worry about, she thought, and there was no reason not to hand over her passport to Amilcar tomorrow morning. She could always go to the American Embassy and ask for a duplicate, if necessary. Amilcar and María would not be able to keep her here against her will, nor was there any reason that they might want to. In spite of María's surprising warmth towards her that evening, Melanie found it hard to believe that they would ever really see her as part of their family.

The phone rang. It was her private line, to which very few people had the number. Even fewer would call her after midnight. For a second, she thought she would hear Diego's voice when she picked up the handset, but it was Eduardo.

'I hope you weren't asleep,' he said. 'I'm not alone, but my gorgeous new friend is in the bathroom. I was worried about you. How are things there?'

Melanie stretched herself on the bed and smiled.

'Everything is OK,' she said.

'Did you tell your in-laws about leaving?'

'Yes, I did. I told them I was going to see my mother for a short stay, and I think they believed me.'

'You shouldn't count on that. María is nobody's fool . . .' Eduardo paused. 'The hunk is back,' he went on in English. 'He doesn't look as if he speaks foreign languages, but I'd better be careful just in case. I've been thinking about what you told me about that Salta business. If it turns out to be true, they must suspect something. The sooner you leave, the better . . . Oh, dear, my rough diamond looks unhappy . . . Don't be so impatient, Raúl!' Melanie heard him whisper in Spanish.

'I think you'd better go back to your guest,' she said, 'and I should go to sleep now. I want to get up early to go to the American Embassy tomorrow. But you're a sweetheart to worry about me. Thank you.'

Amilcar got out of bed at six thirty A.M., as he did every day, without the need for an alarm clock. By seven he had showered, dressed in one of the many virtually identical permutations of pale blue shirt, grey pinstripe suit and black brogues available from his wardrobe, all custom-made in England, paused momentarily over the choice of tie among the selection prepared for him by María before they went to bed, then went downstairs for breakfast. He had barely managed to reach the third page of *La Nación* when María swept in. To Amilcar's astonishment, she was still in her dressing gown.

'You must come with me immediately,' she said.

Amilcar followed María into her dressing room, and listened to the recording of Melanie's conversation with Eduardo de Charcas. He turned off the tape recorder, went to the phone and dialled Remigio's number.

Melanie was surprised to see the butler busying himself in the hall below. It was just after eight, and usually he was around the kitchen area by this time in the morning, verbally whipping the staff into activity. 'Benito,' she called from the half-landing. The servant raised his head and moved to the bottom of the stairs, waiting for her.

'Good morning, Señora Melanie,' he said respectfully.

'Good morning. Señor Amilcar asked me to give you this,' she replied, handing him her passport in a brown envelope.

'I know, Señora, Don Amilcar told me before he left. Oscar is waiting to take it to the office.'

Melanie started towards the door.

'Señora María wants to see you before you go out, Señora. She's in the drawing room.'

Melanie was surprised by the announcement. She knew that María had breakfast early with Amilcar, but then she went back to her room upstairs, while the maids cleaned the ground floor. They didn't seem to be around this morning. María was alone in the drawing room, among her forest of *signé* French furniture, plucking out baby's breath from a floral arrangement in a Chinese vase.

'I've told them that I don't want this in my flower arrangements. It's so vulgar. Please sit down, Melanie. I won't be a moment.

'Do you have any plans this morning?' María asked once the flowers were organized to her satisfaction.

'I . . . I was planning to go downtown to do a few things,' Melanie replied vaguely.

'Nothing you can't postpone, I hope, because I'd like you to come with me, if you don't mind. Amilcar and I have been thinking about what you said last night, and it would be selfish of us to expect you to live in Buenos Aires, much as we would like you to. It would be much easier for you and for us if you were to go back to America sooner rather than later . . .'

Melanie was delighted by the unexpected announcement. None the less, she felt obliged to demur.

'I wouldn't want to cause you . . .' she started, but María raised her hand.

'Sometimes it's better to face the facts squarely,' she said. 'It doesn't make sense for you to stay here for our sake. No, you must leave as soon as possible. Amilcar's secretary will make arrangements for you to leave on Monday; I thought we could have a quiet farewell party for you tonight, before everybody goes away for the weekend. I used to mind about rules, but hardly anyone observes mourning these days, and I'm sure Diego would approve of you saying goodbye to your friends. It would be a waste of your time to stay here to pack all your belongings; just take your personal things, and I'll have the rest sent to you.'

Melanie was taken aback by María's candour. Eduardo had been right. Her mother-in-law had seen through her lie, but she was gracious enough not to make any reproaches.

'But I'm not planning to leave for ever. I'll be away only for a short time,' she mumbled, for politeness's sake.

'Why, Melanie? You have no obligation towards us, and we might as well be open with each other. Diego was the only reason for you living here. Amilcar and I will be delighted to take care of you, wherever you might be, but we don't expect you to live with us for a day longer than necessary. We are too old for that.' María smiled wanly.

For the first time in nearly two years, Melanie felt a surge of affection for her mother-in-law. She was absurd in many respects: prejudiced, obsessed with 'the right thing' from cutlery to flowers to people, imbued with esoteric notions of class duty as if she was a member of a Royal Family. The positive side was her graciousness. María had lost both her children, Diego had been buried only the day before yesterday, and yet she was able to be generous, even in the knowledge that her daughter-in-law didn't like her.

Melanie kept her eyes down.

'I misjudged you,' she said. 'I wish I could stay. Maybe in the future . . .'

'Now, now,' María replied briskly, 'the future is uncertain for all of us. Let's not make promises we can't keep, shall we?'

Melanie smiled, and nodded.

'There is something I want to ask you before you go, though,' María went on. 'I would like to build a memorial to Diego in Las Acacias, and I have arranged to see Lier Tonconogy, my architects, this morning. I'd be so happy if you could postpone whatever you were planning to do, and come with me to their office instead. We could go to the country tomorrow, to choose the site. There isn't much time left before you go. We'll come back here afterwards, and I'll help you with the invitations for tonight. We'd better phone people as early as we can.'

Melanie's visit to the American Embassy had become unnecessary, and she very much wanted to be party to any decisions concerning Diego's memorial. She could ask Felisa to pack for her while she was in the country.

'I'd love to come with you,' she said.

'I'm so pleased,' María replied, standing up. 'Oscar

should be back with the car any minute now. I'll go and make myself ready.'

Melanie followed her out of the room, and watched María ascend the stairs before going into the library. She closed the door, and picked up the phone. She dialled Eduardo's home number, and waited. Melanie was about to give up when he answered at last, his voice heavy with sleep.

'I'm leaving on Monday morning. I've just had a chat with María, and it's all arranged. We are going to the country tomorrow, for the weekend, so I hope you can come here tonight.'

'The Lobos are giving a dinner party. I'll cancel,' he said.

'You don't need to. I'll ask them anyway. You can all come after dinner,' Melanie replied.

Eduardo stayed silent for a moment.

'So you *are* going,' he said. 'I'm sad to hear it, but it's great news for you, Melanie.'

'*You* don't sound great,' she replied.

'I had a really rough night,' he chuckled, 'but it was worth it.'

'I hope so.' Melanie heard a noise behind her, and saw María at the door.

'I have to go now,' she said. 'I'll see you this evening.'

Eduardo de Charcas dropped the phone, and slumped on the pillows. He had a vague recollection of Raúl leaving some time during the night, but it was as fuzzy as his perception of things now. Hoping he had asked the enthusiastic young man for his phone number, he glanced at the bedside table, but the only thing there was the mirror they had used for doing several lines of coke. Perhaps what he needed now was a cup of black coffee and another hit.

He went to the kitchen and turned the kettle on. The water had just begun to boil when the entry phone buzzed.

'Mr Charcas?' asked a man's voice.

'Yes.'

'I've got a parcel for you from Mrs Melanie Santos,' a man said, and Eduardo smiled as he pressed the button; it was typical of Melanie to send him a farewell present, as it was typical of her to keep it a surprise. A moment later he heard the lift doors, and the bell rang. It was only after he moved to answer it that Eduardo realized he was stark naked.

What the hell, he thought, and opened the door. Since Eduardo had never met Remigio, he had no reason to pay any attention to the messenger, other than the unusual fact that the man was wearing tight-fitting, supple black leather gloves.

Late that evening, the illuminated windows in the Santos house offered glimpses of the crowd gathered under the curlicued ceiling of María's drawing room. To passers-by, the sight would have suggested yet another one of those sparkling social events that were an intrinsic part of the family's legend. But it was different for those inside, who were here to say goodbye to Melanie. A hint of melancholy hovers in the background of any farewell scene, and all of them had been in the house only a few days ago, mourning Diego. Everybody noticed the slight discrepancy between Melanie's description of her trip as a visit to her mother for an indefinite period of time, followed by her eventual return to Buenos Aires, while her mother-in-law made it quite plain that Melanie had decided to go back to America for good, much to María and Amilcar's regret – the latter nodding his agreement, in his usual, taciturn silence. For once, María seemed unwilling to pay even lip service to the appearance of family harmony, and was ready to admit implicitly that their relationship might be fraught enough for Melanie to wish to leave so soon.

As for Melanie, her air of melancholy was genuine. The

discussion with the architects that morning, and her imminent visit to Las Acacias tomorrow, had focused her mind once again on the reality that Diego was no longer here, as the party tonight was another reminder in a subtle, insidious way. People were very polite to her, too much so, in a way that real friends are not. The plain fact was that they had accepted her because she was Diego's wife; now he was dead, they accepted with equal ease that she would disappear. They were here because of María, really, and as she joined the group around her daughter-in-law, Melanie could feel their attention shifting away from her.

'It's so kind of you to have come at such short notice,' María said. 'It's really at sad times that one needs friends around. I only hope that Melanie won't lose touch with us, and that she will remember her Argentine family and friends.'

'I don't forget the people I love, María,' Melanie said, noticing that Eduardo hadn't arrived yet. He was always late, she thought, but then she noticed that the Lobos hadn't arrived either. Their dinner party was still going on, she guessed. As if on cue, Zou-Zou Lobos and her husband came through the door, followed by their guests.

'Melanie darling, Juanjo and I wanted so much to say goodbye to you that we rushed dinner. The poor darlings had to gulp down their food,' Zou-Zou said.

As they rubbed cheeks and kissed air, Melanie glanced at the newcomers over Zou-Zou's sable-wrapped shoulder.

'Didn't Eduardo come to your house tonight?' she asked.

'Don't mention that beast,' Zou-Zou sighed. 'He stood us up, but it doesn't surprise me. He always finds something more interesting to do at the last moment.'

As soon as the newcomers blended in, and conversation started again, Melanie drifted away quietly and left the room. The noise from the party hummed in the vast hall, but there was nobody there. She walked into the library, and dialled Eduardo's number.

There was no reply.

The driver was silent, as usual – and so was María, which was unusual, so Melanie kept staring out of the window as the black Mercedes sped towards the outskirts of Buenos Aires. Once they were outside the central area of the city and the northwards corridor of Avenida Libertador, Melanie felt lost, in alien territory, particularly as the city frayed at the edges into a no-man's-land of motorways, gritty industrial suburbs, and shanty towns. It had felt very different the first – and only – time she had made this journey four months ago, to fly to Punta del Este with Diego, when what now struck her as menacingly shabby had seemed almost picturesque.

Melanie had been surprised to hear that morning that they would be flying to the country from the small aerodrome where the Santos plane was kept, but María explained that it was a much better option than driving, given the short time available. After half an hour of gloomy silence in the confines of the car, Melanie was glad of the change. It took four or five hours to drive to Las Acacias, while it would be an hour at most on the plane.

The suburban patchwork gave way to an illusion of open country as they skirted Campo de Mayo, a twenty-five-thousand-acre Army training camp northwest of the city. Then they turned, and soon Melanie saw the perimeter fence of the aeroclub. A moment later they parked outside one of the hangars, where the white aircraft waited for them. She noticed that Remigio was already there, talking to the pilot.

They boarded the plane. Remigio dealt swiftly with their hand luggage, then they sat down and fastened their seat belts. The plane taxied away from the hangar, heading for the runway. Melanie could feel the vibration of the engines increase, and María turned to Remigio.

'Do you have a newspaper, by any chance?' she asked. Remigio gave her his copy of *Clarín*. As the plane raced down the runway, María started to read; they would take off any second now, and Melanie closed her eyes. By the time she opened them again, they were a hundred feet or so off the ground, slowly climbing towards the low cloud.

'Oh, my God!' María exclaimed. 'This is awful, really awful . . .'

'What is it?' enquired Melanie.

'Nothing, nothing . . . I shouldn't have said anything . . . Oh, Melanie . . .' She put the paper aside, and Melanie picked it up. It was opened on the page devoted to local crime, from where the headline glared at her: 'Society decorator murdered.' As soon as she saw it, she knew it was Eduardo, and the letters danced in front of her eyes. '. . . de Charcas's naked body found by his part-time cleaner . . . brutally strangled . . . dead for several hours . . . evidence of drug use . . . homosexual connection suspected . . .'

Melanie's scream ricocheted around the cabin. She did not even try to control herself. 'We have to go back!' she sobbed, fumbling at her belt buckle and trying to stand up, but Remigio grabbed her arms, pinning her to her seat.

María reached for her bag. She pulled out a small box, opened a bottle of mineral water in the compartment by her seat, and poured a glass.

'Take this, it will relax you,' she said soothingly, slipping a pill between Melanie's lips, then holding the glass for her. María sat on the arm of the chair, stroking Melanie's brow.

'Steady, steady . . .' María murmured over and over, as if she was calming a small child, until she noticed Melanie's eyes closing.

'That was quick,' Melanie heard Remigio saying, far, far away.

'It should knock her out until tomorrow morning...' Melanie could hear the sound of María's words, but that was all they were for her, unintelligible sounds. A moment later she was deeply asleep.

TEN

At first, all Melanie saw was white, pure white, and she thought she was looking at the clouds out of the plane window. She awoke slowly; her headache made her close her eyes again, but she felt safe in her own bed, in her own room. As she reopened them, she realized her mistake; she was staring at a plain plaster ceiling, not the ornate mouldings in her bedroom. Only then did she remember her last moments of consciousness, the news of Eduardo's death, and that they had been on their way to Las Acacias. Somebody must have put her to bed once they had arrived.

Gingerly, she got up, and looked around her. This wasn't her usual bedroom in the *estancia* either, nor one of the guest rooms. It wasn't that different; another big, white colonial room with a blood-red tiled floor and a barred window deeply set in the thick wall, the furniture equally sparse. But the rooms she knew were elegant in their expensive austerity, while this one was cheaply furnished, almost spartan in character. A small hatch and a shelf next to a door added to the utilitarian air. Melanie tried the door, then the hatch, but they were both locked. Another door led into what must have been a bedroom originally, turned into a bathroom in the 1920s or 1930s, as she guessed from the cracked, yellowing fittings. There was a clean white towel on the rail, Melanie's wash bag was on a small, painted table by the basin, next to which she found toothpaste and soap, still in their boxes. The hairbrush did not look new but, to Melanie's astonishment, her initials were engraved on the ivory handle. The table rested against another door, and she tried this handle too. It was also locked.

Back in the bedroom, she put her ear to the door, but she couldn't hear a sound. 'Hello,' Melanie called, then shouted. After a while, she started banging at the door until her fists hurt. There was no reply, and by now she was sure that she couldn't be in the main house. The window was rather high in the wall, so Melanie pulled up a chair to stand on.

The first thing that struck her was the unusual, extraordinary vividness of the sky; it was as if the blue had been artificially enhanced, as on a postcard, and then she saw the landscape. It wasn't the infinite green prairie she knew; craggy, rocky mountains rose beyond the narrow strip of a valley, their peaks dappled by snow in the far distance. The barren grey of the slopes was abruptly replaced here and there by a blanket of shrubs, or by bold sweeps of red or ochre earth. Wherever she was, it wasn't Las Acacias.

Neither did the ground around the house look like any country garden she knew. It was too small to be called a park, and purists would hesitate to call it a garden either, since there weren't any flowers. Trees and spindly shrubs grew in rectangles of stone-edged grass, in an attempt at symmetry defeated by the exuberant intromission of tall, huge cactuses sprouting everywhere, as if reclaiming their territory. Suddenly Melanie was distracted by loud, wild barks, and then she saw a pack of dogs racing along the garden, a sinister sight as unusual as everything else. The dogs were white, as large as ponies, but there was nothing tame about them. Thick saliva streamed from their square snouts. Even from the distance, she could see their formidable teeth as they snarled at each other.

Her attention shifted to another noise, much closer: the bolts were being drawn. Melanie stepped down from the chair. She could see the head and shoulders of a dark-skinned, Indian-looking girl on the other side of the now open hatch, wearing a pale blue dustcoat.

'Did *la señora* want anything?' she asked politely in a lilting, provincial accent Melanie had not heard before.

'*La señora* wants you to open that door right now. Where in hell am I?' Melanie bristled, annoyed by the girl's languid indifference, so unlike the deference she had come to expect.

'I'll bring you breakfast, Señora,' the girl replied, shutting the hatch in Melanie's face.

At least she had her watch, so she knew it was just after nine in the morning. The clothes she had been wearing yesterday – or whenever it was that she had arrived here – were neatly folded on a chair, and she found the change of clothes she had brought along hanging in a varnished wardrobe, her expensive white cotton shirt looking absurdly out of place on the shelf lined with a sheet of coarse green paper, held at the corners by drawing pins.

Not knowing where or why she was kept under lock and key was maddening, but then Melanie began to feel fear. She remembered Diego's stories about friends of theirs being kidnapped for ransom; some returned but many didn't, and the Santos were foremost among the list of possible targets during the 1970s. There had been one or two cases since Melanie's arrival, but they were said to be organized by ex-bodyguards – or by paramilitary groups within the security forces themselves. Melanie wondered if they could have been betrayed by Remigio, but kidnappers wouldn't have bothered to provide toiletries or unpack her clothes.

The hatch opened again, and the girl pushed a tray on to the shelf before closing it once more. Melanie took the tray, on which she found a small pot of coffee, a glass of orange juice, and half a grapefruit, carefully sliced into segments: whoever had prepared it knew exactly what she liked in the mornings.

After breakfast, Melanie went into the bathroom. The door had no lock, so she left it open, and she didn't pull the shower curtain behind her either. Being able to see or hear beyond her immediate surroundings made her feel less vulnerable, but she didn't linger under the hot water as usual. Back in the bedroom, she got dressed and then heard bolts being drawn once more. The door opened, and Melanie caught sight of Remigio before he stepped aside.

María came in.

She strode confidently into the room, the deep folds of her dark red, black-fringed poncho swaying to her brisk step. Surprisingly, María was wearing trousers, riding breeches tucked into well-polished black boots with silver spurs, and her black hair was pulled back into a roll, not her usual style at all. She looked younger, trimmer in her rather masculine get-up, as if she found it easier to move in it. The gleam of pearls around her neck, half-seen through the black-edged slit in the poncho, was the only reminder of her habitual image.

'I hope you slept well. This used to be my room years ago,' she said. The banal courtesy made Melanie even more indignant.

'I did, but where on earth are we? That girl is crazy, María, she keeps my door locked!' she said.

'I asked her to,' María replied. 'We are in Salta, in my *finca*.'

'But you said that we were going to Las Acacias!'

'I don't think I did, but it doesn't matter now. You said the other day that you had misjudged me, as I must confess that I misjudged you. Please sit down,' María said, indicating one of the straw-seated chairs flanking the breakfast table. The barking of the dogs outside filled the room for a second, then it was quiet again.

'The poor darlings want their food,' María smiled. 'It's a pity you haven't seen my dogs, because they are rather unusual. It's a breed called *Dogo Argentino*. They were bred in colonial days, to hunt runaway slaves, but they are almost extinct now. I started rearing them some years ago, and I'm very pleased with the result, I must say. Not the kind of dog you can keep in town, though.' Momentarily, María's demeanour was as if she and Melanie were making small talk before a shopping morning, but then she regained her stern countenance.

'I always thought myself a better judge of people than Amilcar, but he was right about you, Melanie. He was right about me too. Amilcar always said that my weakness for Diego would get us into trouble one day . . .' María's voice was wistful, making Melanie perplexed. She had never believed totally in María's acceptance of her, but it made no sense to reopen old grievances now that she was leaving. Perhaps her mother-in-law was cracking up after the death of her son.

'It doesn't matter any more, María. You know I'm leaving. You won't see me again, if that's what you want,' Melanie said, and María gave her a sardonic look.

'I wouldn't have expected you to agree on that particular point, Melanie, but I'd rather we didn't waste time pretending. The game is up. What I would like to know is how you found out about us. Did Diego tell you?'

'I don't know what you're talking about.'

María sighed.

'It's stupid to carry on bluffing once the other person has stopped believing you. You were clever enough to work out that we were far too rich for what you could see, but now you disappoint me. Don't look so surprised. Diego told me of your questions about where our money came from. He always came to me when something bothered him. We had no secrets, Diego and I . . .'

It was the kind of remark – and the tone – that Melanie couldn't stand, that had made her detest María on sight, a feeling she didn't have to suppress any more.

'. . . and now I no longer have any secrets from you. They say that truth is better. I always thought that truth is like going around in your underwear. It might be more comfortable, but very few people look their best that way. Were you disappointed when you found out?'

'I don't know what you're talking about,' Melanie said brusquely.

María went to the window. 'It's preferable to be able to see only the sky,' she murmured. 'The landscape here always made me feel entrapped. Well, not always, only when it became inevitable, when there was nowhere else to go . . . Did I ever tell you about Simón de la Force? I don't think I did. He died about fifteen years ago. He was my mother's half-brother; I used to hate him but now I find him interesting, because I suppose we had things in common. Being a survivor is like being a spy, or a Jew: you recognize your own kind even at a distance . . .' She shook her head, as if dismissing her thoughts. 'Sorry, I'm digressing, and we don't have much time. Simón was my grandfather's son by an Indian maid, long after he became a widower. The silly old man only had daughters from his marriage, so he went crazy over his baby boy, and married the mother. He died soon after the wedding, and his new wife was ignored by the family. Simón hated us for that, but I don't know how he could expect my mother and my aunts to fraternize with an Indian bastard. He grew up hating everybody, and then he claimed that the family had tricked him out of his rightful inheritance. It was nonsense, he got his share like everybody else. I admit that his land was not so good as the other *fincas*, but it was much, much bigger. Then he became a Peronist, and that's when the real trouble for us began . . .' There was something feverish about María's monologue, as if she could only bring herself to tell her story by speaking very fast. 'My parents and their relations were Conservative, of course. A year or two after the election, the only credit available to farmers was from state banks, and they were all controlled by Peronists. Simón not only had any further loans cancelled, he had all the previous loans called back. We were wiped out. My parents, my aunts and uncles, they all lost everything.'

María paused to catch her breath. She kept her back to Melanie, as if her presence there had no significance.

'It wasn't so terrible at first,' María went on. 'My father was a lawyer. He hadn't practised much until then, because he hadn't needed to. Now he thought it would make up for the loss of their land, and he reopened his office. If he had been cleverer, he would have realized that nobody was going to employ a lawyer on bad terms with the party in power. We had to live by selling things: our house in town first, then pieces of jewellery or silver. There wasn't much to start with, and soon there was nothing. We ended up living here, in San Matías, because nobody wanted to buy the estate. The land was useless.

'Do you know what the worst thing about it was? That it wasn't total destitution. Hunger either kills you, or it makes you fight back. You have to. This was like an invisible poison, cutting down your options, weakening you a little more every day, without you noticing it, like a gas leak from a water heater. Which is how my father died, a few years later. They said it was an accident. Simón de la Force sent a wreath of orchids the size of a stable door; I'm sure that the bastard did it to spite us, to make our flowers look shabby next to his. By then he was the richest man in Argentina . . .'

The hatred in María's voice was as vibrant as if the events she described had happened yesterday, not decades ago. Melanie couldn't see what it all had to do with her.

'I was engaged at the time,' María continued. 'Fernando was said to be the handsomest young man in Salta; I certainly thought so. My father suggested that we postpone the wedding: we were very young, and there was no need to rush things, he said. With hindsight, I realize that he was terrified about having to pay for a big wedding, and he might have hoped for better times eventually. Then we moved out of town, and I saw Fernando less frequently, until he sent me a letter, soon after my father's funeral. He had met another girl, and this was true love, he said. I'm sure it was,' María smiled bitterly, 'the girl had inherited a thousand hectares of sugar cane and five hundred hectares of tobacco plantation from her mother, and her father had a big car dealership in Tucumán and excellent contacts with the Peronists. People talked about the wedding reception for months . . .'

She shook her head slightly, as if amazed by her own words. 'So I found myself in this God-forsaken place, the house crumbling around us, without my father, with my mother going quietly mad, planning an imaginary social life, telling me about parties given by our relations in Buenos Aires as if she had been to them. It was then that I met Amilcar. He was quite well known locally, because he had a Pontiac when the other young men around here went about on horseback. There is such a thing as luck, you know, but there is also the ability to see opportunities, as you must have realized when you met Diego. Two years before I wouldn't have given Amilcar the chance to speak to me. Nobody knew very much about him, other than he had been born in Bolivia, somewhere near the border. I suppose that Salta must have seemed a land of opportunity to him, and he moved here when he was very young. He seemed to be doing well, but I didn't take that into account at first, I was merely intrigued by the idea of talking to someone so inappropriate, and flattered by his attention. Then I found, to my surprise, that I was looking forward to seeing him. You know why? Because he worshipped me. For Amilcar I was like a goddess. I needed a man who would take me out of that ghastly life, and there weren't any around San Matías. Even if there had been a more suitable man, he would have thought that he owned me, that I was in his debt, and that's no way to start a marriage.'

María came back to her seat. Her back straight, her legs elegantly crossed, her hands resting on her lap, the red folds of her poncho trailing on the floor, she looked like a portrait of a Creole lady by an Art Deco artist.

'I'm sorry it is taking me so long to reach the part of the story that really concerns you,' she said. 'So, I married Amilcar, but he only told me that he was in the cocaine business some months later. I think I was expecting Diego by then. Amilcar had started as a runner when he was in his teens, and then he built his own distribution network. In those days cocaine wasn't such big business, so he also did a bit of smuggling: cigarettes, radios, nothing too big, but it all added up to something that, from his point of view, was quite a successful operation. That's where I made a difference in his life, because the world I knew was much broader than his, but one has to be careful about making a man feel small. The first step was to move to Buenos Aires. From there we branched out into Uruguay first, then Southern Brazil . . . Don't think that because you're keeping quiet I can't sense your disapproval, Melanie; you have a very expressive face. I think Diego found it one of the loveliest things about you, and I saw what he meant the first time we met.'

Disapproval played only a minor part in Melanie's rage at the hypocrisy that had made her life so miserable. Her mother-in-law's grandeur, her house, her damned furniture, everything had been bought with drug money. Her inclination would have been to lash out at María, if it weren't for the fact that to show surprise, to acknowledge her shock, would add to the old viper's evident pleasure in her complete command of the situation – and Melanie's fate. As to the latter, Melanie realized that her previous ignorance made no difference. She knew now.

'Don't you have anything to say?' María asked. 'I was expecting you to shriek that you despise me, at least. You never struck me as someone who could be shocked into silence.'

'You're right that I despise you, but I was rather bored at the end of your story, María,' Melanie replied. 'I've known about your revolting business for quite a while.' Her lie gave her the small satisfaction of seeing María perplexed, for a change. 'That's why I wanted to leave, and never see you again. If you weren't Diego's parents I would have gone straight to the police.'

'That wouldn't have done you much good,' María countered with a sarcastic smile. 'The outcome would have been the same, and at least now you are in a more comfortable place. Did Diego tell you?'

Melanie heard the almost suppressed anxiety in María's voice. The temptation to mortify her, to make her believe that her adored son had loved Melanie enough to breach the family secret was quite irresistible, if it weren't that it would force her to accept that Diego knew. To lie to María now was a pleasure, but the idea of Diego lying to her was poison.

'I found out myself,' she said instead. 'That evening in Punta del Este wasn't the first time that I eavesdropped on you and Amilcar. Family habits are catching, you see.'

'Curiosity has its drawbacks, Melanie,' María replied drily. 'As your friend Eduardo found out. I heard you on the phone.'

'What did I say to Eduardo?'

'It's what Eduardo said to you. "I've been thinking about what you said, about the business in Salta. You must leave now . . ." Those were his words, more or less. You must have told him.'

Fear came over Melanie like icy water. She realized what had happened to Eduardo, as she realized why Remigio was waiting outside.

'Since we understand each other at last, I might as well finish my story,' María went on. 'I also worked very hard at establishing us socially in Buenos Aires. I had lots of relations there, but there was no question that I felt closer to them than they did to me, and Amilcar didn't help; he is a remarkable man, but nobody can expect him to be a social success. I persevered however, and it got easier as we became richer. Also Diego was at school by that time. He always was very popular. Then we had our real break, in the late 1960s. People had started to emigrate to America from all the Latin American countries, and soon there was a fairly large community in Long Island, in places like Queens. Amilcar had a number of contacts, and he started supplying them. It was all very basic in those days, air hostesses taking a kilo or two at a time, nothing spectacular, but then it started to grow, and that's when I told Amilcar that we ought to make the most of the opportunity. Until then we had been wholesalers, buying the finished powder from laboratories in Chile, but it was much more profitable to buy the paste in Bolivia and process it here. It costs us a thousand dollars to produce a kilo of pure coke; when they cut it in New York, it becomes two kilos, selling for sixty thousand dollars. By the time it reaches the customer, it's worth anything between one and two hundred thousand dollars, but it's stupid to operate at street level. They are the ones who get killed, who run into trouble. The 1970s were marvellous for us. Suddenly everybody in New York was a potential customer. Our own pilots fly the product to Venezuela or the Caribbean, and we hook up with a number of freelance transport networks. It is a very solid business,' María said with proprietorial pride, 'but there are always risks. Like you, for instance.'

'I'm not a risk, María. I just want to go back home and leave all this behind me. I won't say anything,' Melanie said.

'It's so easy to want the impossible,' María said in mock wistfulness. 'Even if I were prepared to consider it, you can't expect me to trust your discretion. You couldn't keep your mouth shut to Eduardo Charcas, of all people.'

'It wasn't what you thought at all . . .' Melanie explained about Diego and Marina.

María stared at her.

'That is the most preposterous story I've ever heard,' she hissed. 'I wish it was true. Marina was killed after interrogation by the security services, and she was buried in an unmarked grave. That's what we were told, and it took a lot of influence for us to find out, believe me.'

'But Diego told me that Marina was here, with the *opa*, that she was looked after by Remigio's brother,' Melanie insisted.

'What *opa*? Who do you mean?'

'Your brother, the one that . . .'

María stood up.

'There's no point in carrying on this conversation, Melanie. You do have the most fantastic inventiveness – or Diego did. It makes no difference to me.' María went to the door, and opened it. Melanie could see Remigio, wearing black leather gloves. María turned to her.

'Goodbye, Melanie,' she said. 'I'm so sorry.'

'You're crazy,' Melanie said. 'You can't get away with this. People will start asking where I am.'

María paused by the door.

'I suppose you mean our friends, since I can't imagine anyone on your side worrying very much,' she replied. 'They all came to say goodbye to you on Friday, remember. You've gone, as far as they are concerned. I'll tell them that you were so eager to leave you brought your trip forward, and we took you straight to the airport from Las Acacias. In a couple of hours, Amilcar's secretary is boarding a flight to New York. I believe it's virtually impossible to detect that the photograph in your passport has been changed. Officially, you will have left Argentina, and I'll be delighted to give your old address in New York to anyone who asks me, as I'll share their sadness when you fail to reply to letters, or your phone isn't answered. Everybody's heard how often people in America move from one place to another, without leaving any trace . . .'

For the last few weeks, Melanie had imagined her life, real life, starting again in the future, weeks or months ahead. Now she found she could only think of the next minute.

'But I'm pregnant, María. If you kill me, you'll be killing Diego's child,' she said.

Much later, long after María had left the room, once Melanie had stopped shaking, she calmed down enough to think about what she'd heard. María's disclosures about their drug-dealing shocked her far less than she would have expected; they revolted her, but only as a rational fact, not because of trust betrayed or love misplaced. Melanie had never loved or trusted Amilcar and María; on the contrary. The revelation suited her, because it gave her a genuine reason to detest them, a feeling that she had been forced to temper into mere dislike until now because of her love for their son.

What she had heard about Diego was another matter. It

was inconceivable that María would have lied about her own daughter, particularly when she had every reason to believe Melanie would be killed a few minutes later, and she had admitted that Marina had been murdered. Diego had lied, about his sister, about his invented uncle, and his possible reasons for lying were as painful to her as the actual fact of it. He had probably lied about everything.

Melanie went to the bathroom and washed her face. The hairbrush was still on the table; María would not have bothered to provide her with a personalized brush if she was going to have her killed. There were long, auburn hairs caught in the bristles, and Melanie remembered the photograph in Diego's wallet: Marina had had long, auburn hair. The monogram could be hers. The window bars and the bolts made it quite likely that the room had been used to keep someone prisoner before. Perhaps Diego hadn't lied after all, but María had no reason to keep on lying now, when it made no difference. She said this used to be her room: the brush could have been hers.

Someone knocked at the door.

'May we come in, Señora *Melaní*?' It was Remigio, and his whole demeanour had changed. Once again she was Señora *Melaní*, of whom he asked permission.

'Come in,' Melanie said, and heard the bolts and locks being undone. Some things hadn't changed; she was still a prisoner.

Remigio entered the room, followed by two men. 'My brother Casildo, Señora,' he said, introducing the swarthy man by his side. Melanie remembered Diego saying he was Marina's keeper. Remigio turned towards another man.

'And this is Dr Gomez, from the village. Señora María asked him to come and see you . . .' he added.

María was standing by the fireplace, staring at the flames, when the phone rang.

'At last,' she said as soon she heard Amilcar's voice. 'Why didn't you call me back earlier? I have a problem.'

'Whatever it is, it's small compared with the problems here,' Amilcar said crustily. 'I'm on my way. I'll be there in the morning, but you must start our alternative arrangement now. Tito called me an hour ago. The Americans are very keen to see us, and they have asked their local friends for help. *Real* help. It's over, María. Tito said he can delay it for a day, but that's all he can do. They're coming to my office tomorrow.'

María understood the urgency in Amilcar's voice. The DEA must have blown their operation in America. They had to have strong evidence if they had been able to overcome the Santos' protective network in Buenos Aires.

'I see,' she murmured, suddenly conscious of the danger of the telephone now. She could wait until Amilcar was here to ask for more details.

'Can you tell me about your problem?' he asked.

'Melanie's expecting Diego's baby,' María replied. 'She told me this morning, and I asked Dr Gomez to check if it's true. He'll have the result of the blood test soon, but after examining her he's pretty sure that she is expecting a child.'

'Does that mean you didn't buy her a one-way ticket?'

'That's not possible any more, Amilcar. It's our grandchild. She's one of us now,' María said.

Melanie switched off the TV, and took one of the books from the pile brought by the young maid when she came to collect the lunch tray hours ago. She had been accompanied by Casildo, who carried a TV set and a radio.

'Señora María sends you these,' the girl said. There could only be one reason for these sudden comforts, and Melanie silently congratulated herself on her wisdom in allowing Dr Gomez to check her without resistance. It hadn't been calculation at the time, merely her repugnance at the thought of being overpowered by Remigio and Casildo if she refused.

'There's also a bell here, if you need me,' the girl added, showing the bellpush concealed behind the headboard.

'Thank you. What's your name?' Melanie asked.

'Violeta, Señora.' The girl bowed her head slightly, and left the room. Melanie heard the now familiar noise of the the door being bolted behind her. If possible, her options had narrowed. Before she knew about Diego's baby, María's only interest in Melanie was her silence. If she could have been assured of it, it was remotely possible that María might have allowed her to go away eventually. Now the child would create a permanent bond between them.

Melanie spent the afternoon alternating between moments of despair, stabs of self-pity, bouts of useless planning, and sessions of mindless television-watching. María and Amilcar would never lose touch with Diego's child. Even if Melanie reported them to the police, and they were sent to jail, they would come after her one day.

Soon after sunset, there was a deep, ominous rumble in the near distance, followed by an orange glow in the sky. Melanie climbed on a chair and looked out of the window. There was a big fire, some two or three hundred yards away.

She rang the bell several times.

'What's going on?' she asked as soon as Violeta came in.

'I don't know. Señora María wants you to join her for dinner in half an hour,' the maid said, her expression as immutable as usual, and she left. Melanie heard the bolts close again.

'I'm so glad you decided to join me. Please sit down,' María said when Melanie walked into the dining room. 'Thank you, Remigio, you can wait outside now,' she added, ringing a small bell set before her on the table. A maid came in, another young Indian girl like Violeta, bearing a huge orange pumpkin on a silver tray, which she placed by María's side.

'You may have noticed that the food here is rather simple, I'm afraid,' María said apologetically, in the tone she used at her table in Buenos Aires. She lifted the top of the pumpkin by the stem, revealing the hollowed-out inside. She stirred the beef, rice, and vegetable stew with a hammered silver ladle, and began to serve the food. 'This is *carbonada*, a very typical local dish. It's rather nice, and it's better to stick to what the girls can prepare, I find.'

'You don't have to make dinner party conversation, María. I'd rather you answered my questions instead,' Melanie said. 'First of all, I want to know if Diego was involved in your . . . business.'

'Of course he was,' María replied as she handed a plate to Melanie. 'Amilcar brought him in a few years ago, and he didn't disappoint us. Diego had a very good head for detail, and he was particularly useful to me. Once he joined us, I did not need to go to New York so often, to deal with the banks. As you know, Amilcar's English is not very good.' María tasted her food, then reached for the silver saltcellar on the table. 'They always forget,' she murmured in disapproval.

'But did Diego know how the money was made?' Melanie insisted.

María gave her an amused glance. 'It would have been rather absent-minded of him if he didn't. Look, Diego's role was much more important than just dealing with our investments. He was to be Amilcar's successor. He had to know every aspect of the business, and his role was crucial. He was bringing the money out of America in the Lear. Amilcar couldn't fly himself, and you can't trust anyone outside your family with so much money, month after month.'

'I don't know what you mean. I thought that the money never left America.'

'It would have been very unwise to do that,' María said, rather didactically. 'It's the weakest link in the chain. You can't deposit one or two million dollars in cash, month after month, without someone eventually wondering where it comes from. The simplest way was to take it out of the country in our plane, bring it to Uruguay, where the banks are not controlled, and they don't ask questions about cash. The idea of the polo club in Punta del Este was Diego's. It was the perfect excuse to build a big private landing strip without raising suspicions. From there the money went to Switzerland, through perfectly legitimate bank transfers, and only *then* it was sent back to America. It's silly to leave your money in Switzerland, their interest rates are ludicrous. As far as the American banks were concerned, Diego was a very wealthy foreign customer, and his money came from abroad through impeccable channels. Like so many very rich investors, he travelled in his own plane. He was never stopped, but if he had been, the plane was always clean going *into* America, and nobody cares about planes that are leaving. It was working so well, but the trouble started two or three years ago, first in Miami, and then in New York. The Colombians wanted everything to themselves, and they killed a lot of people, including some of ours. They are expanding the market so much that they'll force Reagan to do something. You can make millions without upsetting anybody, but not billions. It's crazy. You always have to have a sense of proportion.'

'In drugs?' Melanie asked, astonished.

'In everything. There was no need for trouble, really.'

'Are you saying that the Colombians killed Diego?' Melanie asked.

María joined her hands in a prayerful gesture.

'I don't know. There was some fault with the plane, but it could have been sabotage,' she replied. 'I'm not sure that I want to know.'

'Why? Because you think that Diego wouldn't have died if it weren't for your business?'

'Because it wouldn't make any difference to the fact that he is dead,' María snapped. 'And the fact that he took all the money from our accounts in New York before he died. There were millions. I made a great mistake about him ... but one shouldn't dwell on such sadness,' she said soothingly, 'when there's so much to look forward to. Your baby is the most precious gift you could have made us, Melanie. I'm so happy. Amilcar is thrilled at the news. After so much grief, the family will survive.'

Only that morning María had been ready to have her killed. Melanie wondered if María's new plan was to keep her incarcerated here until her baby was born, and then get rid of her anyway.

'I want to have my child in America, María,' she announced, as if it was in her power to lay down the rules. María gave her an ironic look.

'I can understand that, but it might not be very sensible in the circumstances. You'll have the best possible care, but the baby will have to be born here. The Santos are always born under the Southern Cross,' María said rather grandiloquently, as if she was referring to an ancient dynasty. There was another explosion, near enough this time to rattle the cutlery on the table. 'We're pulling down a few redundant barns,' she explained. The dogs howled outside, a haunting, primaeval sound, and the smell of burning kerosene wafted into the room.

'We aren't going back to Buenos Aires, in any case,' María went on. 'Not for quite a long while at least. Amilcar and I have decided to take a rest on our estate in Paraguay;

he'll be here tomorrow morning. It's a lovely place, very secluded, very quiet indeed, and we have marvellous security there. I'm sure you and the baby will love it.'

'You're assuming I'm coming with you,' Melanie said.

'Aren't you?' María's tone left no doubt that she considered her question rhetorical. By now the stench of kerosene fumes in the air was overpowering.

'You can't keep me against my will for ever, María. It's too absurd.'

'I don't intend to, because it won't be necessary after a while. You see, Melanie, in a few months you'll have your child. You'll need an extremely convincing lawyer for anyone to believe that you married Diego and lived with us for nearly three years, without having a clue about what we were doing. Everybody heard you announce that you were leaving, and Amilcar and I will be leaving Argentina at the same time. It is too much of a coincidence, there are lots of witnesses to the fact that you lived with us willingly, and it wouldn't make much difference if you were to strike a deal with the police, become a witness against us, and walk away free. We aren't alone in this, we have powerful friends who were our partners, and they will worry about what you might know about them. I'm sure that you don't want to live the rest of your life looking over your shoulder. After a while, really intelligent people decide that they like what they can't change. It makes everything so much easier.'

'That might be how you justify your life to yourself in order to sleep at night, but I don't need to. You're mad. Worse than mad, you are a total shit, María,' Melanie shouted.

'Sometimes you are so . . .' María's voice trailed off into a sigh.

'Vulgar? Common? Say it. You don't need to leave sentences unfinished any longer, you know.'

'On the contrary. I was going to say "prissy", in fact, but perhaps you're right. It's all the same problem.'

'This is too much,' Melanie exploded. 'You are scum, a drug-dealer, but you think you have the right to patronize me!'

María closed her eyes for a second, in a gesture of resigned impatience.

'It's difficult for someone like you to understand,' she said. 'We are very different, Melanie. I was born to what I have, and all I did was regain the life that should have been mine, if there had been any justice. You had no right to marry Diego.'

'Sometimes it seems as if you thought that right was yours and yours alone,' Melanie replied, and María's glare shot across the table.

'Don't be impertinent,' she hissed.

'You asked for it. You still believe that you have the right to judge, to feel superior to me. You made such a big deal of who I was, of the fact that I wasn't refined enough for your son, when the problem, the *real* problem, was that you were criminals and I wasn't.'

'I never said anything other than that I would have preferred someone who wasn't an outsider, someone who understood our values better. What I do is incidental to who I *am*. The trouble with somebody like you is that you believe people are their occupation: a secretary one month, a princess the next. I suppose you must be the kind of person who finds Grace Kelly admirable.'

'I don't give a shit about Grace Kelly, what are you talking about? She doesn't go around killing people. My brother died because of people like you.' After two years of dissembling, Melanie was relieved that at least she didn't have to hold her tongue any more. 'You murder people, and then you dare to pontificate about the right way to behave. You make me sick.'

'Your views are as simplistic as your language, Melanie. I thought you were more intelligent than that. People buy what we sell because they want to. Some might ruin their lives as a result, but it's their own choice. You can't blame me for that any more than you can blame General Motors for car crashes. I don't force anyone to do anything.'

'Don't you? I'd rather be having dinner on a flight to New York than here, you know.'

'I'm not holding you. You're perfectly free to go,' María smiled, nodding towards the glazed doors to the gallery. 'But the dogs are loose outside, and some of the fields around the house are mined. You may or may not be able to find the way out on your own. I have no way of reaching Casildo and his men, who are patrolling the area, to tell them I've changed my mind and I'm prepared to let you go this evening. They would shoot first, and ask questions later.'

'Great. Then I can go tomorrow morning, in broad daylight. I'll find my way without any trouble,' Melanie replied.

'These are the circumstances tonight. You have to decide what is the best option for you, as we do all the time. Tomorrow morning is another day. We'll be on the plane, on our way to Paraguay. You'll love it there,' María smiled, and rang the bell. The maid came in to clear up the dishes. In spite of the argument, Melanie had endeavoured to eat everything on her plate. She couldn't take anything for granted, let alone her next meal.

'*Buenas noches*, Señora Melaní,' Remigio said courteously as he let Melanie into her room, before locking the door again. On their way back from dinner, she had glimpses of frantic activity around the place, men removing boxes and crates and burning papers in the courtyard, the glow of the flames matching the red in the sky from some much larger fire nearby. Something had happened, something that had triggered Amilcar and María's flight. Probably the police were after them, a fact that gave little comfort to Melanie. They would arrive too late, after the Santos had left, taking her along. If the police found them, Melanie might prove her innocence in the end, but it wouldn't spare her months of jail. Her child would be born in prison, one way or the other.

As from tomorrow, they would be in Paraguay. Melanie would be kept under permanent watch, and she had heard enough to know that the country was a haven for anyone with enough money and contacts to buy protection. 'After a while, really intelligent people decide that they like what they can't change. It makes everything so much easier,' María had said, and Melanie could see it happening. After one or two years together, with her child becoming used to the life there, it would be far easier for her to accept the situation than to escape.

She had to run away tonight, before she was truly trapped. She looked at the hatch, the barred window, the door. Maybe Remigio was sitting in the corridor, but maybe he wasn't. She knocked at the door.

'What do you want, Señora Melaní?' he asked, his voice muffled by thick planks of wood between them. He *was* there.

'I . . . I've been ringing the bell for Violeta, but she hasn't come, and I would like a cup of coffee,' Melanie said.

'I'll go and tell her,' Remigio replied, then Melanie heard his steps fading into the distance.

Five minutes later, the maid came in with a tray, and left it on a table by the window.

'Thank you, Violeta,' Melanie said. 'Oh! There's something in the bathroom I want to show you.'

'Fuck off,' the girl replied. 'I'm not your slave any more.' She headed for the door, but Melanie was encouraged by her outburst. Discipline was breaking down, a sign that the maids knew that their bosses were on the run, and that they were being left to their own devices.

'There's a lot of money in it for you,' Melanie whispered. Violeta stopped, gave Melanie a sly look, and followed her. In the bathroom, Melanie closed the door, to make sure Remigio couldn't hear them.

'How much?' Violeta asked.

Melanie showed the girl her Rolex watch. She wished she had put on her gold one before leaving Buenos Aires.

'Not enough,' the girl shrugged.

'You can have my earrings, too,' Melanie said, showing Violeta her discreet pearl studs. The girl remained unimpressed.

'This is the most valuable jewel I have,' she said at last, holding out her hand. 'I'll give you my engagement ring, if you get me out of here.'

'How much can I get for it?' the girl asked.

'It's worth . . .' Melanie paused. The true value of the ring was beyond the girl's comprehension. '. . . a lot of money. You should be able to buy a house, and you won't have to work for the rest of your life.'

Greed and disbelief fought a short battle in the girl's eyes. Greed won.

'I can't stay here for long,' she said. 'Give me the ring, and I'll bring you the key in a moment.'

Melanie wondered if the girl was so dumb as to expect her to fall for such an obvious trick. She went back to the room, poured the coffee and spilled it on her bed.

'Oh, look at the mess I've made! You'll have to change my bed now, Violeta,' she said loudly. 'Bring the key when you come back with the sheets, and then we can talk,' she whispered. The girl stomped out, and Melanie couldn't be sure whether they had a deal or not.

After a while, she heard voices in the corridor. Violeta came in with a bundle of fresh linen.

'Is there someone outside the door all night?' Melanie asked as Violeta started to strip the bed.

'Not tonight. Casildo and Remigio are leaving with Don Amilcar and Doña María in the morning, and they have lots of things to do. Remigio is going now. He just asked me to make sure that you were in bed, and lock the door. Here's what you want. I stole the duplicate for you,' Violeta said, pulling an old-fashioned steel key from her pocket. Melanie took it.

'How do I get out of this place? I want to get to Salta, and I don't have any money,' she said.

'There's a door to the garden at the other end of the corridor. Turn left, go behind the old kitchen, and you'll find a small gate in the garden wall. There used to be a man there during the nights, but not any more . . .'

'Was that when Marina was living here?' Melanie interrupted her. Violeta looked nonplussed by the question, but then ignored it. 'Once you're outside, keep going straight ahead,' she went on. 'You'll come to some *chañar* trees, and then you'll find a creek. It's very shallow, so you can walk in the water, and that should keep the dogs off your scent. After two miles, you'll come to the railway. Around five o'clock in the morning, there's a freight train going to Salta. It has to slow down over the bridge, so you should be able to climb on board. We all do it, but it might be more difficult for you. You are not used to it; you're a *señora*,' she added scathingly. 'The train reaches Salta around midday. Wait on the train until half past one, because by then the railwaymen will be having lunch, and you'll be able to get out without being seen.' Violeta tucked in the blankets, then held out her hand, palm up.

'You have the key, and I've told you what you wanted to know. Give me the ring now,' she said.

Melanie wasn't sure what to do. She had no way of knowing if the girl had told her the truth or not.

'If you don't give me the ring, I'll scream, and I'll say that you took the key from me. Give me the ring now,' Violeta insisted.

Melanie went to the door, tried the key in the lock, and turned it. She pulled the ring off her finger, and gave it to Violeta, who stuck it in her apron pocket and left. A second later, Melanie heard her lock the door behind her, as she had said she would.

Then she heard the bolts slotting into place.

The moonlight streaming through the window cast a square of light on the floor. After the girl's betrayal, Melanie had lain on the blankets, fully dressed, desperately trying to figure out a way to escape. The key was useless, and there were bars on the window. She stared at every piece of furniture, every object in the room, but there was nothing that could be turned into a tool or a jemmy.

She glanced at her watch. It was nearly two o'clock. In a few hours, they would be leaving for Paraguay. She'd never be free again. There was no point in sleeping, even if she had been able to, so she reached for her bedside light. As her finger was about to turn the switch on, she stopped. If there was someone outside the house, the light would attract attention. Keeping up the pretence that she was still able to get away gave her a faint illusion of hope, at least, and they must not know that she was awake.

Groping her way in the dark, Melanie reached the bathroom. She felt the weight of the key in her trouser pocket, the metal pressing against her thigh, and slipped it into the lock of the other door. The key turned sufficiently for her to try again, this time applying gentle pressure, and the lock yielded. Her heart beating fast, she moved the table aside as quietly as she could, then opened the door, inch by inch. There was only silence at first, then she heard a low, rasping sound, like an animal snoring. Melanie paused. María had mentioned the guard dogs, and she was terrified at the prospect of one of them pouncing on her in the dark. She waited, until she decided to take the risk. She had no other option.

Melanie walked into the room on tiptoe, trying to discern what was there in the faint gleam of moonlight through the curtains. The room was fairly similar to hers, and there was a door that had to lead to the corridor. There was also a bed, where she could see the contour of a head on the pillow. An armchair stood to one side of the bed.

She started to cross the room, when the rasping sounds from the bed became slightly louder, faint snores turning into guttural words. There was a man in the bed, only a yard away from her. She stared at him. The sight of his features in the vaporous light of the moon made her freeze. It was as if his face had been hit with a sledgehammer, a grotesque misalignment of bones and flesh. What she supposed to be his eyes and his mouth tried to convey some meaning. They looked at each other, then Melanie realized that what she took to be a seat by the bed was a wheelchair. The man was María's brother, the *opa*. Maybe Marina had been here too. Maybe Diego hadn't lied to her.

She could see the mist of cold on the window panes, so she took a blanket from the man's bed, wrapped it around her shoulders, and left the room. The corridor outside seemed as dark and quiet as the rest of the house, the only light coming through the glazed door to the garden at the end.

The door wasn't locked. Once outside, Melanie turned left, as Violeta had said, towards the dark side of the house. Across a few yards of open ground, she saw an abandoned building. The old kitchen, she supposed, and fought the temptation to race towards it. She could hear voices in the distance, probably Remigio and his men in the front yard. She bent down and crawled over the hard soil, which scratched her hands, until she reached the other side. She skirted the kitchen, and faced the perimeter wall of the compound. There was the gate.

The creaking of the rusty hinges sounded as loud as a pistol shot to her. She paused, but she heard nothing: no lights came on, nobody shouted, dogs didn't bark. Melanie felt as if her heart was pressing against her ribs, ballooning in fear, and this time she abandoned caution. She ran towards the trees in the distance, dark outlines against the black sky, then she felt the ground slope down under her feet. She heard the quiet murmur of the stream long before she reached it.

The chilly mountain water bit at the skin on her bare feet, until she stopped feeling the round pebbles at the bottom. Melanie guessed she had waded for about a hundred yards, but she had no idea how long she should stay in the water to put the dogs off her scent. The searing pain in her feet and her calves had nearly convinced her that she had been there for long enough, when she heard the barks in the distance, amplified into roars by the darkness. She ignored the pain and kept going, until she was sure that the sounds were receding into the distance. A minute later, she climbed out of the water and sat down, huddled in the blanket, rubbing her feet and calves until her shaking became mere shivers. She pulled her shoes back on, and started to follow the edge of the stream. At times the water cut through rock, and she was forced to move to higher ground, along thorny bushes, feeling her way in the dark. It was as she was cutting across some boulders that she heard another sound, coming from the sky this time, getting louder by the second. It was a helicopter, and she could see the powerful beam of light aimed at the ground, approaching her. She raced forward, desperately searching for some cover, the thorns of the cactuses scratching her skin, until she saw a thick bush. She dived into it and sat on the ground, her arms wrapped around her legs; a second later, light showered on her, splinters of clarity filtering through the leaves. She closed her eyes, as if it would make her invisible. The light came and went as the helicopter circled the area, and Melanie waited, hearing the thumping of her heart. Then she heard the rustle of dry leaves very near to her. It could be a foot or a yard away, she couldn't tell, because the noise stopped immediately. *Simón de la Force's wife died in Salta, of a snake bite,* she remembered Diego saying, and she struggled to choke her scream and her urge to run away, into the open ground, because the helicopter was still around. She kept waiting, shivering in panic, a panic that only lessened when it started to turn into fury. Now it didn't matter whether Diego had lied to her or not. It was because of him that she was here, gasping in terror.

Eventually, the noise of the helicopter faded away, and she jumped out of her shelter, into the safety of the open darkness. She felt tears of exhaustion in her eyes, but she forced herself to go on, focusing her thoughts on revenge. She would get back to Buenos Aires, and she would report María and Amilcar to the police. It worked for a while, then Melanie merely started to count her steps, thinking about nothing else but the next one. Hundreds became thousands, until she saw the railway bridge ahead, spanning the water.

Standing on the side of the tracks, she looked at her watch for the first time since leaving the house. It was twenty past five, and she froze at the thought that she might have missed the train, but then she heard a rumbling noise in the distance. A minute later, she saw the light of the engine, slowing down as it approached the bridge. Melanie ducked behind a rock until the engine had gone past. The first carriages were inaccessible, but those at the rear were low-flanked. She trotted alongside the train until she matched its speed, then grabbed a handrail and heaved herself on to the steps.

Fuck you, Violeta: *señoras* can jump, she thought with glee as she rolled on top of a load of granite chippings, on her way to whatever came next.

ELEVEN

The man barely glanced at the watch and the earrings on the glass counter, as if it was a waste of his time.

'Seventy thousand pesos is the best I can offer you, Señora,' he said. Melanie made a quick calculation. It amounted to approximately two hundred dollars, a steal.

'You can always try somebody else, but I don't ask any questions,' he said mellifluously, pointedly looking at Melanie's dirty clothes and hair. The man was quite good at judging degrees of despair. Melanie took off her gold wedding ring, and dropped it on the counter.

'Make it ninety thousand with the ring,' she said. 'Otherwise I'm going,' she added, gathering up her jewellery. The man decided it wasn't worth risking the best deal he had had that week, and reached into his pocket.

Outside the small jewellery shop, Melanie joined the late afternoon crowd in central Salta. She had no idea where she was, other than that the station was at the other end of the street. Her body ached after hours on the train, lying in an open freight carriage full of granite chippings, but she had more urgent worries on her mind. Like her appearance, for instance. People stared at her, at the unusual sight of a tall, green-eyed blonde covered in granite dust. She noticed a clothes shop across the street, and headed straight for it. Ten minutes later, she left the store wearing a cheap blue wool coat and a grey dress, the kind of clothes she wouldn't have dreamed of buying three days ago. The bag with her old clothes went into the nearest dustbin.

As she walked past a news stand, she saw the headline

'Police in Buenos Aires raid the Santos family home' emblazoned across a newspaper. Amilcar and María's pictures featured prominently on the front page; Melanie wondered if her picture was published too, but she didn't dare to pick up a copy. She kept on walking instead, until she found a drug store, where she made a few purchases, including a pair of sunglasses. Melanie put them on immediately, before heading for the station again. The night train to Buenos Aires would be leaving in three hours.

There were a number of cheap hotels in the vicinity, and she chose one at random.

'I need a room for the night, but I don't have any luggage. I'll pay you now,' she told the man at the desk, under a fly-encrusted light, as he looked at her suspiciously .

The man pushed the register towards her.

'Ten thousand pesos,' he said. Melanie saw the sign advertising single rooms for seven thousand, but she handed him the money without comment. Key in hand, she went upstairs.

The room was miserable. A torn net curtain covered the window, and the metal bed dipped in the middle, the bedspread sagging into a stained hollow, but Melanie had no intention of sleeping on it. She tried the taps on the basin. The cold water ran freely, the hot spurted rusty water at first, then a tepid stream trickled out. It was enough.

Stripped to her underwear, she draped a towel over her shoulders and stood in front of the basin, then pulled out a comb, a pair of scissors and a bottle from the drug store bag. Melanie leaned down, dipped her head into the water, ran her fingers through her wet hair, and started to snip away at her shoulder-length locks. After a while, she had achieved a more or less passable urchin haircut. She put on plastic gloves, and rubbed the dark chestnut rinse on her hair, working at the thick lather. She waited for twenty minutes, rinsed it off, then stood patiently under the electric fire over the door, running her fingers through her damp hair. When it felt nearly dry, she went back to the mirror. It didn't look too bad, she decided, and she certainly didn't look like herself any more.

She got dressed, picked up her sunglasses, and left the room, staring straight ahead as she walked past the desk. A minute later she was at the station, standing in front of a ticket window.

'Buenos Aires, please. One way,' she said.

Nearly thirty-six hours later, the train pulled into Retiro station in Buenos Aires. Melanie stretched and stood up, pulling herself away from the battered green leather upholstery that felt like her second skin by now. She pushed her way through the other passengers trying to disentangle cases and luggage from the overhead metal racks, and stepped out on to the platform, desperate to get away from the smell and the stifling air of the carriage.

The sight of the Torre de los Ingleses, the clock tower facing the station, of the long grassy slope of Plaza San Martín across the avenue, filled her with the confidence of recognition. They were familiar sights, and she knew her way around here. For a second, she felt as if she only had to call a taxi to be home in five minutes, where Benito would respectfully open the great gates for her, and she would race up the stairs to her bedroom, where her bath would be filled and her clothes laid out by Felisa, but then the fantasy shattered. She was on the run, nearly weeping with exhaustion after two nights of almost no sleep, and she had little money left in her purse. There was a public telephone nearby, but the only phone numbers she knew by heart were the Santos' home, their office, and Eduardo's. Everybody else's was in her address book, in the house.

Even if she had her book, who would she call? She had

met dozens, hundreds of people here, some of them often enough to be considered friends, but not to the extent of hoping that their friendship would survive the scandal. Amilcar and María's flight was public knowledge. If she were to call anyone and arrange to meet them, Melanie had no way of telling that she wouldn't find the police waiting for her at their house, and she dare not even try to leave the country. Even if she could afford to buy a ticket, she had no papers.

Melanie raised her glasses just enough to rub her eyes, then leaned against a wall and thought for a moment. Her best option was to go to the American Embassy, and give herself up there.

She raised her hand, and called a passing taxi.

'The American Embassy, Señora.'

Once out of the taxi, Melanie stared at the elegant façade behind the railings, at the American flag waving in the breeze among the stone urns on the balustrade, and she remembered when Diego had showed her the building, on their way to his house from the airport the first time she visited Buenos Aires.

Melanie headed for the huge gate at the corner.

'Good morning, ma'am,' said the young marine standing guard, and she almost wept with relief at the familiar sight of his close-cropped blond hair under the white cap, and the sound of his accent.

'Who are you coming to see?' the marine asked.

It would be pointless to explain her situation to the guard.

'I need to speak to someone about ... my passport,' Melanie said.

'You've come to the wrong building. This is the Ambassador's residence, and you want the office. It's only a short walk from here,' the marine said, pointing to the right, to the street flanking the park. 'It's the big white building beyond those trees, on Colombia Street. You can't miss it.'

Melanie started walking along beside the stone wall, which screened the garden from view. She could hear the sound of a tennis game on the far side, the noise of the rackets hitting the ball, the voice of the players engaged in a good-humoured dispute over a particular shot. Another world.

As Melanie caught sight of the bunker-like building a couple of hundred yards away, she decided that her situation wasn't as hopeless as she thought. She hadn't married Diego in America, so she was still Melanie Clark on the records there, and she hadn't taken Argentine nationality. The only record of her maiden name here was her wedding certificate, and she doubted that anybody bothered to transcribe the huge ledgers into computers. If the police were after her too, they would be looking for Melanie Santos, and Melanie Clark had a clean file in her own country. She could report her passport as lost today, and get a new one. Then she could say that her money and ticket had been stolen with her passport, that she needed to be repatriated . . . Melanie was getting more and more excited as her plans fell into place, when she noticed two men standing at the corner of the Embassy building, some hundred yards away. They seemed to be involved in conversation, but they also seemed to be keeping an eye on everything around them.

A few feet closer, Melanie was able to see the men more clearly, although not clearly enough to make a definite identification. The younger man looked like the one who had helped Remigio unload their luggage from the plane in Punta del Este. He had been wearing summer country clothes then, and this man was wearing a winter suit, but there was something about the way he stood that made his figure recognizable. The other man walked to a car parked nearby, and said something to the driver. The car was a blue Falcon, just like Remigio used to drive. Or the police.

Melanie stopped. If she got close enough to be able to recognize them, they would be able to recognize her. It made sense for Amilcar and María to send their men to keep watch on the Embassy, to catch Melanie at the one place she was bound to turn up. As it made sense for the police to do the same; only wishful thinking could have made her believe a moment ago that they wouldn't know her real name and nationality. They had raided the house and the office. They had the Santos' files and papers. They must have notified the Embassy staff, who would be expecting her. Everybody was an enemy. There was no way out.

Turning on her heel, Melanie retraced her steps. A minute later, she heard the tennis players again, and she almost banged her fists against the wall in despair, as if hoping that it would crumble and she would be readmitted into a world of sunny mornings and easy living. She ran across the road instead, and collapsed on one of the stone benches by the edge of the park, near a circular, temple-like pavilion, sheltering the marble statue of a young god. The park was virtually empty, adding to her feeling of loneliness. Melanie started to cry.

'Pehrdohn, Senhiohra . . .' The man gave up on his Spanish after two words, with good reason. 'Are you all right?' he asked.

Melanie raised her head and nodded, barely able to see his face in the sunlight through her streaming tears.

'Yes, yes, don't worry,' she said, then started sobbing helplessly again. The man sat down.

'I know you, don't I?' he said suddenly. 'We met in Rio, a few weeks ago, outside the Copacabana, remember?'

Melanie recalled the scene: the Englishman who rescued her from the street thieves.

'You were blonde then,' he added.

'You have the most amazing memory,' Melanie said.

'There aren't many eyes like yours.' He looked down, as if embarrassed, and Melanie found his awkwardness endearing. The unexpected contact, the feeling of friendly company, no matter how tenuous, allowed her to regain her composure.

'I can't remember your name,' she said.

'I'm Norman Fellowes. You didn't ever tell me yours.'

'I'm Melanie . . . Clark. What are you doing here?'

'I've been in BA on business for a few days,' he replied. 'I was on my way back from your Embassy, enjoying the sunshine. It's a lovely morning.'

Melanie said nothing.

'I'm flying to New York this evening,' he said. 'I have a few meetings this afternoon, but I'm free for lunch. Would you like to join me?'

His invitation was another poignant reminder of normality, of what life could be for everybody but her, and Melanie burst into tears again.

'I'm sorry. I have no right to intrude into your life like this,' he apologized. 'Please excuse me. I'm sorry . . .'

She guessed he was about to move away, and grabbed his arm.

'Please don't leave me,' she begged. Suddenly she didn't care any more. She needed to talk, and talk she did; Melanie told him everything, about her marriage, about Amilcar and María, about her flight from Salta, until she ran out of both words and breath.

'There's no reason why you should believe me,' she added eventually. He smiled.

'Why shouldn't I? It's all in here,' he said, giving her his copy of the *Buenos Aires Herald*.

The first thing to catch Melanie's eye as she scanned the front page was a blurred picture of María, a close-up of her face lying on the ground, blood streaming from one side of her face and neck, matting her hair and smearing her pearls. The report said that San Matías, the family property in a remote valley in Salta near the Bolivian border, had been raided by the police in the early hours. Mrs Santos and some of her gunmen had died in the ensuing siege. Her husband was still at large. There were rumours that Mrs Santos's daughter-in-law had been in the house, but immigration records confirmed that the young Mrs Santos had left Buenos Aires last Sunday for New York.

'Nobody will believe me now,' Melanie said. 'They'll think I faked my own departure with their help, and then joined them in Salta, to run away with them. Nobody will believe I didn't know what they were doing.'

'You worry too much,' Norman replied. 'It's obvious that you are innocent, and you must have faith in justice.'

Melanie marvelled at his Englishness.

'You don't understand,' she sighed. 'It takes a long time for cases to reach the courts here. I would be kept in jail in the meantime, and the Santos had very powerful friends.'

'Perhaps they could help you, then,' he suggested.

'Help me? They'd want me dead!' Melanie cried. 'They don't know that I really know nothing about their dealings, so they'll make sure I never get a chance to give evidence. They've killed thousands of people here, for less reason than that. I have to get back to America, even if it means going to jail. I can't stay . . .' She stared into the void, and Norman sat by her side, his arms crossed, his chin cupped in his hand. He seemed to be thinking too.

'I might be able to do something for you,' he announced after a while.

* * *

'. . . So you are Frances Fellowes, my wife, and . . .'

'I was with you in Brazil, but then you flew to Chile, and I joined you here yesterday. My bag was stolen this morning, and we *must* leave for New York tonight. We can't wait here for a new passport for me,' Melanie cut in. 'We live in London, at 78 Woodfall Street, in Chelsea, and we have a dog called Bonzo, a Dalmatian . . .'

'I never mentioned a dog,' Norman said.

'Stories are always better if you embellish them. I thought all English people had dogs,' Melanie said, looking out of the car window, at a plane climbing towards the clouds in the distance. They would be at the airport soon.

'It's better to stick as close to the facts as possible,' he countered, and Melanie thought that Diego's baroque style of deceit had rubbed off on her.

'You're right,' she said.

She had found during the day that Norman Fellowes was meticulous in the extreme, as he had insisted on rehearsing their story far too many times, but on the other hand his intervention had been nothing short of miraculous. Now she could be minutes away from freedom.

That morning, after their meeting in the park, Melanie had gone back with him to the Plaza Hotel. From there he had called 'a friend'. Melanie stood outside the phone booth, so she couldn't hear a word of the long conversation, but he was smiling when he finished.

'No problem,' Norman said. 'Someone will be waiting for us at the Aerolineas Argentinas counter, and he will take you through immigration. Once we are near New York, you'll have to tell the air hostess that you must have dropped your passport outside the terminal here, and you'll have to deal with immigration at Kennedy yourself. I can't help you there, I'm afraid.'

He took Melanie's arm and led her towards the exit. They turned right and walked for a hundred yards or so.

'How could you arrange it so quickly?' Melanie asked.

'I know a few useful people here, and they owe me a few favours,' he replied enigmatically. By now they were walking along the Kavanagh building. Norman stopped in front of one of the the shops and opened the glass door.

'Your ticket is ready, Mr Fellowes,' said the smiling travel agent behind the counter as soon as they went in.

'This is my wife,' Norman said. 'Frances was planning to go back to London from Brazil, but she changed her mind, and she's coming to New York with me. I need a ticket for her on the same flight.'

'Of course, Mr Fellowes.' The man busied himself at his computer terminal.

'Economy, if you don't mind,' Norman said, putting his American Express card on the counter. The travel agent raised his eyes.

'I'm sorry, but economy is full, Mr Fellowes. There are only business or first class seats available.'

Melanie noticed the slight tightening of the muscles around Norman's jaw, and prayed that he wouldn't back down now because of the cost.

'I shouldn't miss Danny's bar mitzvah, darling,' she said. 'His father is a very important client of my husband's,' she explained to the agent, 'but unfortunately we can't charge my ticket to his company. I'll pay you back. Every cent, I promise you,' she said, smiling mischievously in order to turn the remark into a joke between husband and wife for the sake of the travel agent, but there was anguish in her green eyes as she looked at Norman.

'Business will be fine,' he muttered to the agent.

As soon as they were outside, the small blue and white folder tucked into her coat pocket, Melanie took his hand.

'I meant it about paying you. You must give me your address in London, and I'll send you a cheque as soon as I have a job,' she said.

'We can sort that out on the plane,' he said. 'Let's have lunch now, shall we? You can tell me what on earth you do at a bar mitzvah,' he continued with an unexpectedly impish smile.

'I've never been to one either. There's always a first time,' she replied, feeling light-hearted at last. They were about to go into the hotel when Melanie stopped.

'Is your real wife called Frances?' she asked.

'No. I'm divorced,' he replied. 'But you remind me of someone I used to know many years ago.'

It was as good a name as any, she supposed. Inside the foyer, Melanie raised her hand to her glasses, as if to reassure herself that they were in place. In the grill, the maître d' greeted Norman with a smile.

'Good morning, Mr Fellowes.' The man scrutinized Melanie, and she wondered if he had recognized her. She had been here with Diego a few times, but she had been blonde then, and much better dressed.

'This way, please,' he said, heading towards the huge windows overlooking Plaza San Martín, and Melanie saw Teresa de Tannerie and Zou-Zou Lobos with their husbands, sitting at one of the window tables. She took Norman's arm.

'I know those people,' she whispered. 'I don't want to stay here.'

'Excuse me,' Norman said to the maître d'. 'We've changed our minds. We'll call room service instead.' He put his hand in his pocket and slipped a folded note into the man's hand.

'Of course, Mr Fellowes, of course.' The maître d's voice was full of worldly understanding, and Melanie hated him for that. She and Norman walked to the lift, avoiding each other's eyes.

'It's more sensible to have lunch up here,' he murmured as they walked down the corridor. He opened a door, and

Melanie went in. A small, dark hallway led into a light, airy room; Norman took Melanie's coat and hung it in a cupboard. The first thing she noticed as they went into the room was the huge double bed, taking up much of the space.

'It's a lovely view,' she said, walking up to the window and surveying the tops of the trees in the square, and the city around it. Norman pulled out one of the chairs by the table for her, and offered Melanie a green-bound menu after she sat down.

'Please choose whatever you want,' he said. It was only as she scanned the list that Melanie realized she was ravenously hungry.

'I'd like the prawn cocktail ... and the *lomito* with champignons ...' – she struggled with her sense of discretion for a moment – '... and the chocolate mousse,' she added. Norman picked up the phone, dialled a number and repeated the order. '... And a steak with a mixed salad, mineral water, and a bottle of Norton red,' he added. He put the phone down, left the room and came back a few moments later.

'If you'd like ... the bathroom is there ...' he mumbled, nodding almost imperceptibly towards the hallway. Melanie realized that she hadn't had a bath for the last two days.

'Could I use your shower, please?' she asked.

'Of course.'

The first thing Melanie noticed in the bathroom was the raised lavatory seat, reminding her of her days with Diego, then she saw Norman's jockey shorts and socks, left to dry on the radiator. He was rich enough to buy her a business class ticket and to stay at the Plaza, but sensible enough not to pay room service prices to have his underwear washed. After two years of Diego's non-stop extravagance, the sight made her feel unexpectedly fond of this stiff Englishman, who had appeared from nowhere and rescued her.

Melanie took off her clothes, and washed her tights, panties and bra in the basin. As she rubbed them between her hands, her eyes fell on Norman's open washbag, catching sight of a half-full bottle of aftershave, and the box of condoms. Melanie concentrated on her task, then carefully put her underwear to dry next to Norman's. She turned the shower on, full force, and clouds of steam swirled in the air, misting up the wall mirror. She soaped herself thoroughly, enjoying the feel of hot water and scented lather on her skin. There was a sachet of shampoo next to the soap dish. Melanie reached for it, the water running under her breasts as she leaned down, and washed her hair, closing her eyes as the foam slid over her forehead. She had begun to rinse it off when she felt a draught. She opened her eyes; through the gap between the edge of the shower curtain and the wall she could see the mirror, and a hazy reflection of the half-open door.

Melanie stepped out of the bath immediately, reached for the towel, and wondered what she would do if Norman came in, but the door didn't move. She peeped through the opening: he was sitting at the table, his briefcase on his lap, reading some papers. Melanie pushed the door shut, only to see it open again. She pushed really hard this time, and she heard the latch engage at last.

She rubbed her hair until it was nearly dry, and reached for the terrycloth dressing gown on the hook, but thought better of it. Nothing in Norman's behaviour so far showed that he expected her to go to bed with him, but if Melanie went back to the room dressed only in his dressing gown, he could see it as an invitation. She would have little choice if he wanted her to go to bed with him, but he hadn't suggested it, and Melanie didn't want to encourage him.

There was a wall-mounted hair dryer next to the mirror. It didn't take her long to dry her bra and her panties until they were only slightly damp. She dressed quickly, combed back her hair, and came out. Lunch was waiting.

Norman made most of the conversation, and Melanie learned that he had his own business in electronics, which was apparently very successful, and the reason for his frequent trips to Brazil, Chile and Argentina. He lived on his own in London, in a small house in Chelsea, 'a mews house, almost'. If there were children from his marriage, he didn't mention them.

After lunch, Norman said that they ought to coordinate their stories, in case they were questioned at the airport. After three or four rehearsals, Melanie stopped him.

'Why are you taking so much trouble over me?' she asked.

'I've been wondering myself,' he smiled. 'I suppose that no gentleman can resist helping a lady in distress. I don't know.'

It could be the truth, or a most diplomatic excuse. She remembered his mention of Frances.

Norman glanced at his watch.

'I ought to go now,' he said. 'I'll be back around six o'clock, and I've arranged for a car to collect us at seven. You should have a rest. You need it.'

After he left, Melanie walked around the room. His case was packed, but still open. There were shirts on top, neatly folded, even the ones that were worn – all bearing London labels. Socks were fitted carefully into the gaps around the edges; the clean ones were rolled into balls, dirty ones tied in knots. Norman Fellowes was tidy. She felt tempted to dig deeper into the case, but then felt ashamed of her curiosity. She stretched herself out on the bed, her head on his pillow, and fell asleep instantly.

Now, as the car slowed down as they approached the airport terminal, Melanie felt refreshed, excited and fearful at the same time. With a little more luck, soon she would leave all of this behind her. Norman paid the driver, and he opened Melanie's door. As she stepped out, she saw two men in uniform coming towards them. They were Army uniforms, and Melanie could tell from the stars on their epaulettes that they were officers.

'Señor Fellowes?' one of them asked. 'We are here to help you.'

'Thank you very much,' Norman replied. 'It's my wife who needs help actually. She lost her passport this morning. You know what women are like . . .'

The plane slowed down to a gentle halt, the engines became quiet, and the passengers started to retrieve their hand luggage. Norman and Melanie stood at the top of the queue, near the door, waiting to disembark.

'An immigration officer is waiting for you, Mrs Fellowes,' the stewardess said. Norman looked at Melanie, a tight smile on his lips.

'It's going to be all right,' he said. 'I'll be at the Inter-Continental this week, otherwise call me in London. Are you sure there isn't a number where I can contact you?' he asked.

'Not at the moment,' Melanie replied. 'If you haven't heard from me soon, try all the women's jails.'

The stewardess cleared the exit, and the queue moved on. Three steps later, Melanie was on American soil. She was safe at last.

The man from the IRS Criminal Investigation Division turned to the man from the FBI who looked at the man from the Drug Enforcement Agency. None of them said anything. It was the man at the end of the table, someone from the federal prosecutor's office, who broke the silence. After two days of constant questioning and fruitless sessions over the photographs of men with countenances as Latin as their names, Melanie wasn't even sure who was who among the officials facing her.

'Let's go over it once again, Mrs Santos,' he said. 'You knew about the Unity Investment Bank account, but you knew nothing about the other accounts. You didn't know that the money came from drugs, you never met anyone involved in your husband's activities here, and you only found out about them a week ago, when your mother-in-law told you her whole story. You could have been a witness against her, but she is dead, so she can't be charged, and you have no direct evidence against Amilcar Santos, other than what his wife told you. We'll find him eventually, but uncorroborated evidence is no use to us. You could press charges against him for kidnapping, but the evidence only incriminates your mother-in-law. Amilcar Santos wasn't there.'

'Am *I* going to be charged?'

The man made a few scribbles on his pad.

'This morning we got a copy of Remigio Arteaga's confession in Buenos Aires, confirming your version of events. Nothing has been found, here or there, linking you to the Santos organization.'

'So . . .'

'You're free to go. We don't need you.' The man stood up. 'We'll arrange a car to take you wherever you want.'

Melanie watched the revolving doors as people flowed out of the building, into the plaza. In the distance, the windows of the World Trade Center grew brighter against the fading daylight. Then she saw a familiar figure.

'Donna!' she called, breaking into a run. Her friend took a moment to recognize her, and then she smiled.

'Hey, it's good to see you! What are you doing here? Shit, you should sue your hairdresser, honey!' Donna laughed.

'I need help, Donna,' Melanie interrupted. 'Can you put me up for a few days?'

'Sure, no problem, but I thought you only stayed at the Pierre these days. Where's your prince of the Pampas?'

'I'm on my own again. It's a long story . . .'

'They always turn into frogs in the end,' Donna said, a knowing look in her eyes.

'He's dead, Donna.'

'I always put my foot in it, don't I? I'm so sorry.'

'You didn't know. I should have kept in touch . . .' Melanie said contritely. Arm in arm, they headed for the subway, among the crowd of office workers.

TWELVE

In the distance the Super-Mart car park, empty for the night, was eerie under the sodium lights. Melanie dropped the net curtain and turned her back on the window. She was wearing Donna's dressing gown, her hair still damp from the shower.

'Coffee is ready,' announced Donna from the closet-size kitchenette. Melanie collected her mug and they sat at the table.

'I'll start looking for a job tomorrow,' Melanie said. 'Are there any at the bank now?'

'I'll find out,' Donna replied, 'but nobody is going to love you if you start feeling sick a couple of weeks later.'

'I haven't felt sick so far. It won't happen,' Melanie countered, sounding far surer than she felt. She glanced at her bare finger on her left hand. It had all seemed so simple when she had planned her future over lunch with Eduardo in Buenos Aires, a few weeks ago.

'It's not going to be easy, honey. You're three months pregnant,' Donna said gloomily.

'Two and three quarters,' Melanie corrected her, as if it made any difference. As for Donna's first point, Melanie needed no reminder that life wouldn't be easy, and not only because of her pregnancy. She had imagined that she could adapt to her former existence with no trouble, that her year in Buenos Aires had had little effect, but it had taken only a couple of days here to realize how wrong she was. Donna's poky apartment depressed her, in itself and as a token of the best she could now hope for, as depressing as the need to count every cent. Life with Diego, in his world, had changed her, and not only with regard to money. Even Donna's company, which she had found so invigorating in the past, grated on her. Their conversation used to be like a tennis rally; now it limped along, punctuated by gloomy silences.

'Have you thought about . . . ?'

'Yes,' Melanie said tersely, closing the subject. She wasn't going to have an abortion. It was the only thing she knew for sure.

'I'm really glad you called. You're looking wonderful tonight,' Norman said, as he had already when they met in the lobby, and again during drinks at the bar, and earlier during dinner. The look in his eyes confirmed to Melanie that he meant it, as it confirmed that repetition was not something that bothered him. Although she had done the best she could with Donna's most sedate evening outfit, she still felt like a puffball, drowning in clouds of cheap nylon organza, but Norman didn't seem to notice.

'Thank you. I've applied for a couple of jobs today. Soon I'll be able to pay you back . . .'

'You don't need to tell me that.' Norman stopped her. 'Don't worry. I'm in no hurry.'

She wondered if he was being too kind, too concerned about putting her at ease, or if it was a reminder that she was in his debt.

'I *want* to pay you back. As soon as possible,' she said. He raised his hand, his cheeks slightly flushed.

'Don't mention it again. Some things are better left unsaid,' he murmured, and Melanie remembered María using the very same words. 'I'm leaving tomorrow morning,' Norman went on, stirring his coffee although she had noticed he didn't take sugar. He had already mentioned that too. 'I wonder if you would like to come to London for a long weekend. When and if you have the time, of course.'

'That's really nice of you,' she replied, 'but I want to get myself organized here first.'

'I understand,' Norman said, looking away, and Melanie felt a complete heel. He was perfectly pleasant, and she owed him a great deal.

'No, you don't,' she said impulsively. 'I want to come and see you.'

He smiled, as if he had been reprieved.

'Shall we have a brandy at the bar?' he suggested. They left the restaurant. As they walked past the elevators, he paused.

'I have a very good brandy in my room, in fact,' he said awkwardly. 'Would you like to try it?'

It was his discomfiture that made up for the transparent excuse, for the clumsiness of his invitation. His nervousness touched her, making her sorry for him. She owed him her new life.

'I'd love to,' she said.

John Ravazzi glanced at the single sheet of paper in front of him, then looked at Melanie, sitting on the other side of his desk.

'I've checked your references with Unity Investment. I liked what I heard,' he said. 'You don't have much experience as an Account Sales Assistant, but they told me that you were among the top five during your training course . . .' He paused, and Melanie tried to hide her rising excitement. She sensed that Ravazzi was about to offer her the job.

'You don't say anything about your marital status in your resumé,' he went on. 'Are you married?'

'My husband died a few months ago. That's why I need a job,' Melanie replied.

'I'm sorry, but I had to ask, you see. My best Sales Assistant is leaving because she's having a baby, and she wants to give up work. I'd rather not employ someone who's planning to have children soon, and leave. But that doesn't apply in your case, so the job is yours, if you want it.'

Melanie stood up.

'Let me think about it. I'll call you tomorrow,' she replied. She shook his hand, pretended not to notice his puzzled expression at her sudden reluctance, and headed for the door.

The queue in front of the 'Other Passports' desk moved slowly, but eventually Melanie made it through immigration control, and followed the signs to 'Baggage Hall'. Carrying the small case she had borrowed from Donna, she walked swiftly past the luggage carousels and through the Green customs area, until she found herself at Heathrow's meeting point. After a moment, she saw Norman smiling at her, and went over to him.

His lips brushed against her cheek. Although Melanie had expected a full kiss on her lips, she wasn't surprised. By now she had learned that demonstrativeness in public places made him uncomfortable.

'It's good to see you. Did you have a pleasant trip?' he asked, taking her bag.

Melanie felt the muscles in Norman's back hardening under her hands, and then he groaned. She tightened her arms around him, holding him as he relaxed after his orgasm. It was the fourth time they had made love since her arrival two days ago, and she was beginning to get used to him, or at least not to think of Diego every time Norman touched her. He was kind, considerate, and eager to please her; if gratitude had been her motivation the first time in New York, by now Melanie wasn't sure it was the only reason.

'I love you,' he murmured. She had expected him to say it, sooner or later, and in a way she wanted to hear it. She snuggled up against him, and kissed him.

'Tomorrow I'll be back home. Don't make it harder for both of us,' she said, for his sake.

'You don't have to go,' he replied. 'You said that you haven't found a job. You could help me with my work here.'

'I know nothing about electronics.' Melanie came out with the first excuse to cross her mind.

'It's nothing to do with that,' he smiled. 'I'm selling my business, in fact. I've always wanted to go into politics, and I've been selected as a Parliamentary candidate for West Swanton. The by-election is in a couple of months. I have an enormous number of letters to write.'

'I thought your business was doing very well.'

'That's always the time to sell up. I won't need to work any more.'

Melanie thought about his Jaguar, and the affluent if impersonal ambience created by the mahogany furniture and chintz curtains around his house. He had money, as she had suspected in Buenos Aires, but now she disliked herself for the thought.

'You can stay here for as long as you wish. Nothing like a good night's sleep to make us see things more clearly. Think about it. Goodnight, darling.' Norman kissed Melanie, and reached for the light switch.

'You cook as well as you . . . do everything else,' Norman said, smacking his lips in exaggerated appreciation.

'I hope you mean my typing,' Melanie teased him. She stood up and began to clear the table. 'And you can give me a hand. Dirty plates won't bite you,' she added. Norman followed her into the kitchen, and put the dishes on the counter. Once Melanie finished rinsing them and loading them into the dishwasher, he drew her to him and nuzzled her neck.

'These have been the best ten days of my life, Frances.' Occasionally, as a joke, Norman used the name he had invented for her in Buenos Aires. Melanie thought these had been the best ten days for her since Diego had died, but perhaps there was no real difference between his qualification and hers. Those intervening weeks felt like a lifetime to her.

'I don't want you to go back to New York,' he said, and Melanie realized she didn't want to go back either. She didn't want to return to a mattress on the floor of Donna's two-room apartment, to living on social security, to the increasingly less likely prospect of a job that would soon turn into a crisis once her pregnancy became visible. It would be like going back to the misery of her childhood, as if all her efforts over so many years counted for nothing. To stay for a bit longer, feeling safe and protected, suddenly appealed to her.

'I'm very happy here, but I can't stay indefinitely,' she said.

'You can. You can marry me. Please.'

Unable to help it, Melanie burst into tears. She hated herself for finding Norman dull and stodgy at times, for thinking about Diego every time they made love. She was deceiving him.

'I'm pregnant,' she sobbed. 'I can't marry you. It's . . .' Norman put his hand over her mouth.

'I love you more than I've ever loved anyone in my life, Frances. And I'll love *our* baby too.'

Three weeks later, Mr and Mrs Norman Fellowes left Chelsea Register Office. By now everyone knew her as

Frances. She liked the idea of a new name, a new start for a new life, confirming her break with everything she had left behind. The change became official by deed poll, but nobody other than Norman and the clerk who performed the ceremony had a chance to use her new name that day, because Frances insisted on a completely private ceremony. The wedding was on a Friday, allowing them a honeymoon in the Cotswolds over the weekend. On their return, they held a small reception at the Churchill Hotel for Norman's friends, a mixture of businessmen and lesser Tory politicians. The following weeks were taken up by Norman's frantic election campaign. After his victory, everybody agreed that Norman's performance had been tremendous, and he was particularly touched by Mrs Thatcher's letter of congratulation, welcoming him to the House. His young American wife had been marvellous; so helpful, so charming, everybody said.

Five months later, Mrs Norman Fellowes gave birth to a healthy boy in the Lindo Wing of St Mary's Hospital. If her husband had been an MP for longer, some acid paragraph might have made the gossip columns about the birth of a severely premature nine-pound child, but Norman wasn't yet newsworthy. The only comment was from those who visited the Fellowes in hospital: they all agreed that Peter was a truly beautiful baby boy.

PART TWO

THIRTEEN

'Guess what? You have more flowers, Mrs Fellowes!' the nurse announced cheerfully as she came into Frances's room; she managed to clear a corner of a table, already overcrowded with bouquets, laid down a pretty basket of lilies of the valley, and she unpinned the card from the white satin ribbon.

'From your husband, who will always love you,' the nurse read aloud. 'Isn't that nice?' she chirped before moving to Frances's bedside and taking her pulse.

'Mr Malone will see you shortly, but you had a good night. I'm sure he'll send you home before midday,' she said.

'That would be nice,' Frances replied. 'I really look forward to a night of proper sleep.' Concussion had been diagnosed as soon as she had been brought into the London Hospital yesterday, and she had been awakened every two hours during the night, to make sure she hadn't lost consciousness. Other than an ugly bruise on the side of her head, she felt fine, and eager to see Peter. Norman had taken him home yesterday, once the boy had been checked over at Casualty and found to be unharmed.

Frances glanced at the riot of flowers. In the overheated air of the room, their scent was suffocating.

'Please leave the azaleas and the lilies, and take all the other flowers to the wards, Dorothy,' she said. 'It's a shame to waste them.'

'I'll send someone to do it, Mrs Fellowes. I'm afraid I don't have time to do it myself now,' the nurse replied. As soon as she was gone, Frances got out of bed and collected the cards from the arrangements before taking them out of the room herself, and lining them against the corridor wall. Back in the room, she had just finished arranging the lilies and the azaleas on the table when there was a knock at the door. She got back into bed quickly, in case it was the consultant.

'Come in,' she said. The door opened, and Norman walked in. He kissed his wife, then gave her a huge bunch of roses.

'I'm glad to see you looking your usual self, darling. You gave me a fright yesterday,' he said.

'And you make me feel like a movie star, giving me flowers and more flowers,' she smiled.

'I saw the garden in the corridor. Everybody is very worried about you,' he said. Frances gave back the roses to him.

'Please put them next to the others, darling. The azaleas are from the Majors, so I thought you'd like to see them.'

'With love from John and Norma,' he read aloud, leaning over the exuberant display, clearly pleased by the size of the offering. 'Not everybody gets flowers from Downing Street,' he added. Frances had got used long ago to Norman's weakness for stating the obvious, when it reflected well on him.

'How's Peter?' she asked.

'Very well. Eugenia is spoiling him rotten, and he should go back to school tomorrow. If it weren't that you wanted him to stay at home, I could have taken him back this morning, on my way to Swanton.'

Frances heard the tacit criticism between the lines. As was often the case, Norman was suggesting that she overprotected their son, an accusation he found easier to articulate when it came to Eugenia, their housekeeper.

'It won't make any difference if he misses one day at

school,' she said. 'Both of us can do with a quiet day.'

'I phoned Miranda before coming here, to tell her you wouldn't be in the office today. I didn't say why, though.'

As usual, Norman had done the right thing, Frances thought. Her secretary would drive her crazy with concerned phone calls otherwise.

'I saw Mr Malone on my way in,' he went on. 'He says he'll come and see you as a matter of routine, but since you had a good night, there's no reason to keep you here any longer, so I arranged for a car to take you home. It must be waiting by now.'

'Then I might as well get dressed,' Frances said, pushing the bedclothes aside.

Norman glanced at his watch.

'There's a policeman outside waiting to talk to you, and I have to be in Swanton before lunchtime. Why don't you see him now, so I can be with you during the interview? You might feel more comfortable that way.' As with most of Norman's suggestions concerning their life, it was difficult to extricate genuine worry from expedience. Frances said nothing, and Norman opened the door.

'My wife will see you now, Inspector,' he said, then stood aside as a man walked into the room.

'Good morning, Mrs Fellowes. I'm Inspector Lucas,' he said courteously. 'I'm glad to see that you have recovered so well. I would like to ask you a few questions, if you don't mind.'

'Not at all,' Frances replied. 'Please sit down.'

Inspector Lucas opened a small notebook and rested it on his lap.

'I have your son's statement, but it would be helpful if you could give me your recollection of events,' he said.

'We stopped at Spitalfields Market on our way to meet my husband in the country. My son was desperate to try out his new skates, and he discovered that there is a special track open on Sundays. We stayed in the market for half an hour or so, then we left. As we were approaching our car, a white van appeared. Two men got out, and they simply attacked us.'

'Do you remember any details of the van, other than the colour?'

'No.'

'Describe the men, please. Did you see their faces?'

'I didn't look at them too closely, Inspector. One of them was taller than the other, and both of them were of medium build. One of them was wearing a blue jogging suit, the other was in jeans and a black leather jacket. I'd say they were in their late twenties or early thirties and they had brown hair, but I can't remember anything much about their faces, though I might recognize them if I actually saw them again.'

'Did they talk to you?'

'No. I offered them money before I was hit, but they never said anything.'

The Inspector raised his eyes to Frances.

'Did you see the other man, the one who chased them off?'

Frances shook her head.

'I heard a voice, but very faintly, as if it came from far, far away, and then I blacked out.'

The Inspector looked at his notes.

'We are interested in this man, because he knew you. He gave your name and your son's when he called 999, but Peter says he didn't tell him who you were. The operator took down the caller's name and address. They were false.'

'I'm afraid I can't help you. I have no idea who he was.'

'Frances and Peter's picture was in *Hello!* two weeks ago, Inspector,' Norman suggested. 'He might have seen it.'

'I hope that not every *Hello!* reader walks around with a gun, Mr Fellowes. Peter said he thought the man was armed, although he never saw the weapon.' Inspector Lucas put his notebook in his pocket and stood up.

'I won't keep you any longer for the time being, Mrs Fellowes, but we'll contact you again in a couple of days. It would be very useful if you and your son could help us put together an Identikit picture of these men.'

'I don't want my son involved,' Frances said. 'The experience was enough for him as it is.'

'It would be helpful though,' Inspector Lucas insisted.

'It was just another mugging, and they happen every day,' Frances replied. 'I know you are doing all you can, but the police can't be expected to find every mugger in London. It was very nice to meet you,' she added, politely dismissing him with a charming smile.

Norman saw the policeman out.

'I would appreciate it if this matter is kept confidential, Inspector,' he said once they were in the corridor.

'I had a call from Mr Nesbitt at Central Office this morning, Mr Fellowes. Don't worry, it won't be reported to the press.'

By the time Norman went back into the room, Frances was putting on her clothes.

'Was it really necessary to say that there are muggings in London every day?' he asked.

'For God's sake, Norman. It wasn't a press conference about law and order, and the man is likely to vote Tory anyway. The Identikit would be a waste of time; they want to make a fuss of me because I'm your wife, that's all,' she replied.

Frances got up well before seven the next morning. As usual, she left her bedroom only after she had showered, dressed, and attended to her face and hair. She went up the stairs, into Peter's room. He was sound asleep; Frances stared at his sweet, peaceful face, then stroked his hair gently and decided to let him rest for another half-hour. His school uniform was neatly laid out on a chair, as she herself had arranged it last night, but she checked it again, just in case, before leaving the room.

On her way downstairs, she stopped at the first floor, walked into the drawing room and drew the curtains; she disliked darkened rooms if it was light outside. She stood by a window, looking out at Hans Place and the garden square still shrouded in the calm of early morning. Everything looked as usual, and yet it didn't. It had been only after she had been back in the safety of her home, of every-day life, that the incident at Spitalfields had started haunting her, a feeling that struck her first when she went to bed alone last night, because Norman had been delayed at Swanton. On impulse, she went to the telephone and dialled their country number.

'I was waiting to call you,' he said. 'I thought you'd sleep late this morning. Did you have a good night, darling?'

'Yes, thank you,' she lied. 'I'm taking Peter to school this morning, so I had to get up early anyway. I spoke to Mr Thompson yesterday, and I told him that Peter would be there around ten o'clock.'

'You could come here afterwards,' Norman suggested. 'I'll be canvassing this morning. It would be nice to have you with me.'

'I'd love to, but I really must go to my office. It will be easier for me to come in a few days.' She decided to tackle the real subject on her mind. 'I'm not very happy at the thought of Peter being on his own at school after what's happened. Do you think it would be possible to arrange some kind of police protection for him?'

'I think you might be overreacting, darling. You yourself told Inspector Lucas that it was a mugging like any other.

They can't provide protection for every person that has gone through an unpleasant experience.'

'Peter is a child, and he is your son. It might have been the IRA, for all we know.' She could hear Norman sigh.

'You *are* overreacting,' he said. 'Be reasonable, Frances. Even Cabinet Ministers don't have police protection all the time, let alone their children.'

'We could hire someone, then,' she insisted.

'That's not on, darling. People will find out, and some Labour trouble-maker will make a mountain of the whole thing. They'll say that street crime has become so bad that rich Tory Ministers hire protection for their children, while the rest have to brave the streets as best they can. I'm sorry, but I don't think it's a good idea.'

'That's easy for you to say, because you aren't a ten-year-old,' she snapped. 'Peter is scared.'

'All the more reason for his life to return to normal as soon as possible,' Norman said firmly. 'I can understand your concern, but we must keep our sense of proportion. I must go now. I'll be home this evening, my love. See you then.'

Tight-lipped, Frances put the phone down and headed for the kitchen downstairs, to the comfort of her house-keeper's company. Not that she was going to mention it, but Eugenia would understand her concern.

'Good morning, Eugenia,' she said. No matter how early Frances got up, she always found Eugenia in *her* kitchen, as the housekeeper described it with pride, always dressed in black, her greying hair tidily arranged into a bun. 'Peter's still asleep. I thought he could do with some extra rest this morning.'

'*¡Por supuesto! El pobrecito necesita descansar.*' Eugenia approved. The boy had been her darling ever since she had started working for the family, when Peter was a newborn baby. Eugenia had spoken English fluently enough then, but once she had realized that her boss understood everything she said in Spanish, in spite of Frances's denials, she would only use her native tongue.

'*Le prepararé huevos revueltos para el desayuno, como a él le gustan,*' Eugenia announced.

'His doctor doesn't think it's a good idea for Peter to have eggs too often. He had scrambled eggs yesterday,' Frances said. She always replied to Eugenia in English; slowly, as if answering a tourist's halting request for directions to Buckingham Palace. Each woman pretended not to speak the other's language, a logic more powerful than reason because it responded to their own private motives.

'*Doctores . . .*' Eugenia shrugged. Her theory, as Frances knew, was that doctors were only good for killing their patients at great expense, another idiosyncratic aspect of Eugenia's philosophy of life. Frances also knew that there was little point in contradicting her, so she headed for the table instead, where her coffee and her grapefruit were waiting for her. She paused in front of the wall-mounted pinboard, to check if Peter had a birthday party next weekend. The invitations, an assortment of cards ranging from Ninja Turtle stationery to blue-edged Sloane paper, had been moved to one side by Eugenia, to make room for the picture of Frances and Peter which the housekeeper had clipped from *Hola!* The Spanish edition of the magazine had also carried the wretched article; as with the spoken language, Eugenia considered her thirty years in England a mere interlude until she could return to her native Santander, so she only read Spanish publications.

Satisfied that no special arrangements were necessary to accommodate Peter's busy social life, Frances poured her coffee.

'Has your niece had her baby yet?' she asked. There were more pressing subjects on her mind, but she welcomed the opportunity of soothing small talk.

*   *   *

'. . . There's a new Super Mario game out, Mum. Could you get it for me this week, please?'

'I bought you two new games a few days ago. I'll think about it,' Frances replied. Her qualification was more a matter of form than anything else, and they both knew it. The school's entrance was only a few hundred yards away, so she slowed down.

'I'll buy it for you if you promise me something,' she added. 'Please don't talk to strangers if you go on an outing.'

'You've told me that a million times already,' Peter moaned. 'Are you worried about what happened on Sunday?'

'Are *you*?' she asked, glad for the opening. She had tried to talk to him about the incident once they were back at home, but he had dismissed her attempt as 'boring'.

'It wasn't so special, Mum. They showed something like that on "Crimewatch" last month,' Peter replied with worldly wisdom. He must have seen the programme during half term, Frances guessed, deciding to have a word with Eugenia about enforcing the ban on watching TV after eight in the evenings when Peter was at home.

'The police told me you saw the man who saved us,' she said, to keep the subject going.

'He was very nice. He looked like a movie star,' Peter said, and Frances smiled at an obvious case of hero-worship.

'Who did he look like then?' she asked.

'Like Bruce Willis,' Peter said enthusiastically. Ever since *Die Hard II*, there was no higher god in Peter's pantheon of heroes. 'But he was very tall, and had long dark hair and black eyes.'

'He didn't look like Bruce Willis at all then!' Frances laughed, making light of the conversation.

'Well, it was the way he walked, you know what I mean . . .'

They drove through the gates of Doddington Hall, and Peter's face clouded over.

'Mum . . .'

'What, darling?'

'Remember the party for your wedding anniversary last year?' he asked.

'What about it?' She and Norman had never bothered about wedding anniversaries until then, when he had insisted they should have a big celebration for their tenth. She wondered why Peter would bring it up so unexpectedly, nearly six months after the event.

'Was that the month you got married?'

'No, we got married in June, but everybody is out of London in the summer, so we decided to have the party in September instead.'

'I see . . .' Peter looked down.

'You see what?'

'My birthday is in October. I'm ten . . .' he mumbled.

At last she knew why he had seemed embarrassed when he'd started the conversation.

'What do you mean?' she asked, just in case. Peter was good at maths, but even so he was too young to be worrying about such a specific concern.

'Alexander told me last week that his mum joked about it when she got the invitation.' Alexander was a school friend of his. Frances's inclination was to slap his inanely grinning mother next time she saw her. She guessed this was the real reason for Peter's reluctance to come back to school. Not the silly magazine article.

'You were a bit premature, sweetheart, that's all,' she said blithely, knowing he wouldn't quite believe her. Peter wasn't stupid. He gave her a knowing look.

'Alexander says that you were pregnant before you and

Daddy got married,' he said. Frances kept staring ahead. Their life was public property now; it would be too easy for this nonsense to become an item in a gossip column.

'You were premature, darling. And I wasn't pregnant when I married your father. I promise you. Alexander is talking rubbish,' she replied.

Peter believed her. He could always tell when his mother was lying, and Frances saw the relief on his face. A moment later, the school buildings were visible through the windscreen.

'You don't need to come in, Mummy,' Peter said as he got out of the car. He put his cap on, tossed his bag over his shoulder, and started to walk towards the main block, the gravel crunching under his feet.

'Hang on a minute,' Frances said, running after him. She still couldn't believe how easily he seemed to have recovered from his ordeal.

'Don't go wild with the kisses,' Peter muttered as they neared the school door. 'Somebody might see us, and they'll tease me later.'

Norman would be pleased, Frances thought. Life *had* gone back to normal.

'Is one kiss all right?' she smiled, her lips brushing his forehead, and restraining herself from hugging him. Peter moved away and went inside, without looking back. Frances stood there for a minute, tempted to go in and talk to his teacher, or the headmaster, anyone who would reassure her that they would take special care of him. But she had already spoken to them over the phone, and Norman had warned her not to make too much of a fuss. She stared at the grounds around the building, at the bucolic scene that had always struck her as a picture of safety and rural serenity – like the park at Las Acacias, a memory she had pushed to the back of her mind for years, but which now came back with startling vividness. For an instant,

Frances considered taking Peter back home with her, but she could imagine Norman's reaction, and he would be right. This was England, not Argentina. Her own fear was the only link between Peter and what had happened there.

She went back to her car and drove away.

'The latest Harris poll gives us a five per cent lead. It was three per cent last month, and the campaign has been going for only a week,' Norman beamed as Frances sat down. He was scanning the front page of the *Daily Express*, before moving on to the other newspapers piled beside him on the breakfast table.

'I spoke to the housemaster,' Frances said. 'Peter is fine.'

'I told you he'd have no trouble. Peter is a very sensible boy.'

'He is, but it would be quite normal for him still to feel shaken,' Frances countered.

'He's coming home next Friday anyway,' Norman reminded her.

'What time do you want to leave that evening?' Frances asked. Soon after Norman became an MP, they had bought an old rectory in his constituency, where they spent most weekends.

'We're having a meeting at Central Office on Saturday. I have to stay here, but you can go down with Peter, if you want. I'll manage,' Norman replied.

'We'll stay here, then. He'll feel safer if we are all together. We could do something with him on Saturday evening, to cheer him up.'

'I've already asked David to dinner that night,' Norman said. 'We have to discuss a few things. I'll ask him to bring Judith, since you are here.'

An evening discussing election tactics wouldn't be Peter's idea of fun, Frances thought. Nor hers, but she said nothing.

*　　*　　*

Norman folded his trousers and laid them carefully on the clothes stand by his side of the bed. His extreme tidiness had once seemed endearing, but now Frances saw it as slightly absurd, and tried her best to ignore it.

'How's your work?' he asked.

Already in bed, Frances raised her eyes from her book.

'I'm having trouble with that crazy marchesa,' she said. 'I got a fax from her this morning. She wants a lot more money to let the group stay in her villa, and it would be difficult to change the arrangements now.'

'What are you going to do?'

'I faxed her back, reminding her it was all agreed in writing, and I haven't paid her anything yet.'

'Good. You're cautious in business; I like that,' Norman approved, taking off his shirt and folding it.

Frances looked at him.

'You used to like me better when I was less cautious.' Their eyes met, and she regretted her remark. Sexual innuendo to a man in his underpants could only be an invitation or a snub. From the sudden – and by now most unusual – spark in his eyes, she assumed that Norman took it as the former. Norman was very good at finding the least troublesome solution to any problem. Making love to her now might be an impulse – but it could as easily be the best way to obscure the fact that he hadn't touched her for weeks.

He moved towards the bed. Frances closed her eyes for a second and imagined what would follow, his mouth on her breasts, her legs entwined around his hips. She would feel breathless, crushed, giddy, biting her lip until the taste of her own blood and his skin would mix in her mouth.

But then she opened her eyes again and saw Norman by the bedside, stretching out his hand towards her, his waist overflowing the elastic of his boxer shorts, faint traces of that morning's dusting of Floris talcum powder still on his chest – or perhaps his body hair had begun to turn white. The taste in her mouth was not blood, but the pleasant, half-medicinal, oily scent of her very expensive night cream. Frances looked around: mellow wood, mellow lights, mellow colours, mellow good taste in every detail. Middle age hung heavily in the air, like an emanation from the roses on the chintz lining the walls and the furniture. Perhaps their sex life was dying of over-decoration, she thought as she closed her book and put it on her bedside table.

'I can't keep my eyes open. Goodnight, darling, sleep well,' she said, snuggling up under the bedclothes. Norman's hand fell on his pillow and he reached for his pyjamas, as if it had always been the intended destination; he put them on, turning his back to her, opened his briefcase and took out a thick file, then got into bed. He picked up his glasses from the bedside table, adjusted his reading light, turned to Frances and kissed her. A moment later he was completely engrossed in the Conservative Political Centre's assessment of the Opposition's challenge in marginal constituencies.

As she walked along the King's Road, Frances wondered if she should fire Miranda that morning, a recurrent dilemma over the last two months. A secretary had become a luxury in a small business like hers, and she was aware of Norman's private views on the economy, at odds with the brave promises in his speeches. The recession was going to get much worse after the election, and perhaps she would be doing Miranda a favour by letting her go now, when she still had a chance of finding another job. The decision would have been easier if Miranda, who was just about competent by the skin of her teeth, didn't get on Frances's nerves with her constant, enthusiastic prattle, confusing the issue between a sensible decision and mere exasperation. The fact that Miranda's father was one of Norman's senior colleagues didn't help.

When Peter had been one year old, Frances had forced herself to go back to work again. She guessed that Norman wasn't as happy about her decision as he pretended to be, but it had been through one of his business contacts that Frances had got a junior position in a merchant bank in the City. Frances had some experience, she was bright, and she had access to useful people through her husband. The exhilarating atmosphere of the mid-Eighties in the City also helped her, and she started to climb fast within the Corporate Finance department. Her chances of a directorship grew more and more likely, just as the possibility of a Cabinet post for Norman became more certain. But the financial scandals following the Stock Market crash and the onset of the recession revealed the danger of her position. If Frances were involved in a scandal, no matter how unwittingly, it could damage Norman's career. As she didn't need the money, Frances resigned from the bank in 1989 and set up in business on her own, organizing expensive tours to France or Italy, accompanied by a suitable expert to lecture on buildings, paintings or sculptures. It was an anodyne – and therefore riskless – occupation, and it left Frances enough time to help Norman while giving her an excuse to keep some distance from his life. Until the recession began to bite, she had even been able to make a little money, just enough not to feel a complete fool.

She crossed the road at Wellington Square, reached her office and pressed the bell. After a while, she searched for her keys. Miranda was late, and Frances let herself in. She raised the venetian blinds and looked out at the square for a moment, a sight she always enjoyed because it reminded her of her afternoons there when Peter was a toddler. They had moved out of the area when he was nearly two, because Norman insisted they needed a bigger place, and they had bought the house in Hans Place. For a while, Frances regretted the move. They had been happy here, although it would have been impossible for them to have had a housekeeper in the old house, enabling her to work full time, or to entertain on the scale demanded by Norman's rising status.

The fax machine came to life. Frances expected it to be the marchesa's reply, but it wasn't. It was from the Palace Hotel in Madrid, confirming reservations for the Ribera exhibition tour. Frances made herself a note to phone Dr Fonseca in Seville later, and stuck it on her desk.

Only then did she notice the blinking red light on the answering machine. Frances rewound the message tape, and pressed 'Play'. The first message was from Miranda, saying she had had a terrible night (at the clubs, Frances assumed), and that she would be a bit late this morning. The second one was from Frances herself, asking Miranda to call the printers about some catalogues as soon as she came in. Since she had phoned the office last night, Miranda must have called earlier, before leaving for her night out, and Frances decided she should certainly fire her, not so much for being unreliable as for being so stupidly careless, even about her own alibi.

She dialled the printers' number.

'Could I speak to Mr Bingham, please?'

'He's on the other line. Would you like to hold?'

'Please tell him that Frances Fellowes called. I'd like to speak to him as soon as possible.'

She went downstairs and collected the post, the usual assortment of bills, a couple of elegant-looking envelopes from clients, and lots of direct mail. Frances was sitting at her desk, reaching for her letter opener, when the phone rang.

'Hello,' she said briskly, ready for the printers' excuses.

'You still sound the same, *Ojos de Jade*.' It was a man's voice, and Frances thought that she was imagining that accent, that voice, as she used to do for so many years. Nobody else had ever called her 'Eyes of Jade'.

'Who's that?' It was an unnecessary question, but it was all she could say.

'You know who it is. My voice can't have changed that much, my love.'

'Where . . . how . . . why do you . . . ?' There were too many questions, so she settled for reassurance first. 'Diego, is that you?'

'Meet me at the Ritz, in the Palm Court, at four o'clock. Be alone,' he said, and the line went dead.

Frances put the phone down. She tried to think, to coax her shock into understanding, but she couldn't, just as she couldn't stay here, alone. She thought of going back home, but it would be worse, and she would have to invent some excuse for Eugenia's sake. She could claim to be ill, but then Eugenia would make an enormous fuss if Frances attempted to leave the house later. At first, she was over-whelmed by a feeling way beyond curiosity, a desperate need to know *now*, this minute, without delay. But then she needed time to get used to the idea that he was alive. She had always mourned him in some corner of her mind, a memory so painful that she had protected herself by tossing and turning it over to blunt the edges, like an oyster secreting nacre over a piece of grit digging into its flesh until it becomes something harmless, both precious and unrecognizable from the original irritant. It was eleven years, more or less to the day, since she had seen Diego for the last time. Now she had another husband, another country, another name. Another life.

And she had Peter.

The thought of her son made her angry. Diego had known about her pregnancy, and yet he had left her. For another woman, probably, as she had feared when he announced his plan to go to New York on his own. He had discarded her without any thought at all. His parents might have killed her. Frances was about to embrace her anger like a long-lost friend, when she remembered that, in Salta, she had decided to believe his story. Diego had asked her to join him in New York. It was only because of Amilcar's appearance in Rio that she hadn't been able to go. Maybe she hadn't told him about her pregnancy. She was sure she had phoned for the result of the test in Rio, but after so long she couldn't remember now if she had mentioned it to Diego or not.

The thought made her feel better, but then her anger returned in a new version, far more hurtful because it was addressed to *what if*, to what could have been. If Diego had been open with her, if he had asked her to go to New York with him, they would have been together now.

Or perhaps not. She'd never know. The only thing she was certain of was that she wanted to see him again.

'Mrs Santos?'

Startled at the mention of the name she hadn't used for so long, Frances turned towards the bellboy who had materialized from nowhere. Or so it seemed to her; for the last fifteen minutes she had kept her eyes on the door, her back to the gilded figures of the fountain. The thought of Diego not turning up was almost as disquieting as the possibility of seeing him again.

'Yes,' she said.

'Your husband apologizes for his delay. He'll be here soon.'

'Where is he?'

'I don't know, madam. The concierge asked me to find you and give you the message.'

'Thank you.' After a moment, exasperated and impatient

in equal measure, Frances got up to leave. She stopped before the glass doors at the bottom of the steps, glancing outside in case Diego was approaching, until she noticed that the doorman was looking at her. She wondered if the man had recognized her, and she turned around to leave by the main entrance. As she faced the Palm Court again, she saw Diego sitting at her table, looking at her.

He stood up, smiling as he had smiled when they met in New York for the first time, and Frances wondered how he could have impressed her so much then, when he had been merely the sketch, the outline of the man he was now. There were a few lines around his eyes, a few grey strands in his thick black hair, and his figure seemed sturdier, not in weight but in presence. The passage of time had not detracted at all from his looks, investing them with a patina, an elegant finish that added to his attractiveness. Only the admiring look in his eyes retained the spontaneous exuberance of the younger Diego.

'You haven't changed, Melanie. You are still the most beautiful woman in the world,' he said, pulling out a chair and solicitously helping her into her seat. There was no unease in his manner, as if they had never parted.

'Thank you, but I have changed a lot. Maybe your memory is slipping after being dead for so long,' she said acidly.

He smiled.

'You didn't used to be sarcastic,' he said.

'One of the many changes, probably.'

He caught the waiter's eye, and ordered tea.

'It's the best tea in London,' Diego said. He noticed her look.

'I know. I still say that whatever I like is the best. But it's always true,' he smiled.

'That's a funny word for you to use,' she snapped.

'Truth, you mean? Why? I never lied to you. I might not

243

have told you everything at times, but it was only for your own sake.'

'You lied to me all the time. You lied about your trip to New York. You went there to empty your parents' accounts. You faked your own death . . .'

'How do you know about the money?' he interrupted her.

'Your mother told me, when she told me about the drugs.'

The waiter came and started laying plates and cups on the table, so they waited until he moved away. The fact that Diego seemed so unperturbed only added to Frances's rising anger.

'You'd better pour it now, you don't like strong tea,' Diego reminded her. She poured a cup and handed it to him.

'How odd of my mother to tell you. She must have been fonder of you than I thought,' he commented. 'It *is* true that I took the money, but it was my money as well as theirs. I invested it. I made it grow.'

'You never told me about the drugs. You knew I wouldn't have married you if I had known.'

'I didn't know either,' he countered. 'I only found out after we were married. You must believe me.'

'Don't be absurd. Why should I believe anything you say?'

Diego sighed, then leaned towards her.

'Because it is true,' he said, lowering his voice. 'My father always told me that our business was agricultural exports, and that he ran a double-account system. He declared a nominal export value in Argentina, and the bulk of the money was paid abroad, mainly in America, but then it had to come out, to avoid American taxes. I thought I was helping him to hide black money, not profits from drugs, but then I found out. I was shocked.'

'Not as shocked as I was when your mother told me you ran the whole drug operation in America,' Frances said. 'I don't know why you even bother to lie any more.'

Diego sat back.

'That's an invention of my mother's. She was always jealous of you, and she must have been trying to hurt you. I promise you that I didn't know about the drugs until that summer, but it makes no difference now. I wanted to get out, Melanie. That's why I went to New York, to report them to the police and the DEA.'

'I see. You saw the light, then betrayed your parents, took millions of dollars as moral reparation, and decided to start a new life. Pity you forgot to tell me,' she replied, struggling to stay calm.

'I've told you that the money was mine as well as theirs. If I hadn't taken it, it would have been confiscated by the Government. I couldn't see why it was acceptable for them to reap the benefit, so I thought that I might as well keep it myself.'

'You're wasting my time. I don't want to hear any more of this,' Frances said, pushing back her chair and reaching for her bag. Diego grabbed her hand.

'Please don't go,' he pleaded. 'I only did it because of us. I really wanted to break away from them, for you and I to have a new life elsewhere, like you wanted. I might have been wrong about the money, but I couldn't live without it. It's not a sin, and my parents always said that one day I would be very rich. I couldn't face starting from nothing, and I wasn't sure that you would have loved me if I didn't have money.'

'I would have loved you exactly the same,' Frances retorted. She had tried to – wanted to – believe his explanation, because it exonerated him, but his last words hurt her. He had doubted her. Or her love for him, if there was a difference.

'That's what you think, but you don't know. I wouldn't have been the same man. I still remember your face when you saw Las Acacias for the first time.'

'I loved the place,' Frances accepted. 'But I loved you more. Money wasn't everything, at least for me.'

'Poor people don't have parks and lakes,' Diego replied, brushing his hair back with his left hand, a habitual gesture she remembered well. He noticed Frances's glance.

'It's your ring. I'm still married to you,' he said. 'But those aren't my rings, and you're not a diamond-solitaire type. Your new husband can't be very imaginative.'

Frances dropped her hand to her lap, under the table, out of sight.

'I had to be able to get to New York without my father suspecting anything,' Diego went on. 'I couldn't take you along, because I needed you in Rio, as my alibi.'

'The story about your sister wasn't true then.'

'Yes, it was.'

'Where is she now?'

'She killed herself in the clinic, a few months after I took her there. It was a terrible blow, and it took me a long time to get over it.'

Frances remembered the hairbrush in her room in Salta, and the maid's comment about the watchman. María had denied Marina's presence there, but she also had denied her brother's, and Frances had the evidence of her own eyes about that. Diego could be telling the truth again, but now she didn't want to absolve him. Hating him had been the only consolation available to her at first, the palliative for the pain of not having him. Now it was the best antidote to the possibility of having him back.

'Once I was in New York, I made contact with the DEA and gave them the names of my father's people there. I had taken the list from our office. Then I realized that the DEA would arrest me as soon as they had hard evidence, and I decided to leave immediately, as soon as we were together again. It took me a few days to get fake papers made for you and me, that's why I invented the story of the fault on the plane. Since I didn't want it, I hired another co-pilot to take my place, and sent the plane back to Buenos Aires after I called you. If they hadn't crashed in Mexico, you would have left Rio by the time my father arrived. I was waiting for you in New York, but you didn't come.'

Frances sat back. Diego's betrayal of his parents to the DEA explained what had happened in Salta, but the rest was a pack of lies. This time she was certain, because María had mentioned sabotage. Diego had sent someone to die in his place, as a cover-up, and disappeared with the money afterwards.

'I don't believe you,' she said. 'You left me. You could have contacted me in Buenos Aires, if you had been the least bit concerned about me.'

'How? I knew that my parents had bugged the phones in the house. We only got our post after they had checked it. My "death" was a fluke, but it was the best possible new start for us. I was trying to find a way to contact you, but then you disappeared. Do you think I would be here now, if I had wanted to get away from you?'

Frances didn't know what to think.

'How did you find me?' she asked.

'I saw you in *Hola!* You may have changed your name, but I knew it was you at once.'

'Are you living in Spain then?' she asked.

'I live here and there these days,' Diego replied guardedly.

'Must you keep looking around while you talk? It's as if you were expecting somebody else to join us,' Frances said.

'I'm sorry. I always worry about being followed. It's

difficult to shake old habits,' he apologized, then looked at her.

'You don't believe me,' he said.

'It doesn't make any difference, Diego. You have your life, and I have mine. Let's keep it that way. Goodbye.' Frances stood up.

'It's too early to leave. We haven't discussed Peter yet,' he said.

'There's nothing to discuss,' she replied.

Diego gave her a hard look.

'It's not only *my* memory that fails at times,' he said. 'You told me that you were pregnant, remember? Even if I didn't know, he looks exactly like me in the photograph. I want to see him, talk to him. You should sit down, you're drawing attention to yourself. I'm sure you don't want to be noticed.'

Frances slipped back into her seat. At least now she knew *why* he had bothered to find her again. Peter.

'You must be crazy,' she said in an angry whisper. 'Do you imagine that I would ruin Peter's life by telling him about you? Leave us alone.'

'You wouldn't have said that last Sunday morning,' he smiled. It took her a few seconds to understand what he meant. She was so startled that she could hardly speak.

'Was it you who . . . ?'

'I wouldn't have known about it otherwise, would I?' he interrupted her.

'You were following us.'

'Of course I was. Do you think I didn't want to see you, once I knew where you two were?' He sounded impatient, as if her surprise annoyed him. 'I thought you'd guess as much from my flowers in hospital. I wrote the card myself. You used to be very observant, Melanie. I sent you lilies of the valley before. You know my writing.'

Frances remembered the basket.

'I didn't see the message. The nurse read the cards to me. I had lots of flowers; you can't expect me to remember every single one of them . . .' There was no need to explain, but it gave her a breathing space in which to overcome her confusion at Diego's revelation. Her first reaction was gratitude, and she welcomed it as a reason to approve of him in some way, but then she didn't want to. It was easier to face him behind the shield of contempt.

'Why did you come back? Did you expect to come here and pick up where you left off?' she asked, uncomfortable at the fact that the question could apply to her presence here as well.

He smiled.

'In a way, and I wasn't wrong. Your eyes don't lie. I want you to bring Peter to me, as if you were meeting an old friend, so that I can see him. He's my son, Melanie. I have the right to know him.'

'I told you not to use that name.'

'You used to like it when I whispered it in your ear. As I'll whisper it again, when I hold you. Let's go upstairs. I'm staying here . . .'

'You *are* crazy.' Frances grabbed her bag and rushed to the door without looking back. She hoped she'd never see Diego again.

'*Su marido llamó para decir que va a venir tarde,*' Eugenia called loudly from the kitchen, as she heard the front door.

'Thank you, Eugenia. Any other messages?' Frances asked from the foot of the stairs. Norman being late was a fact of life.

'*No, ninguno.*'

Frances went upstairs. She knew that Diego couldn't call her here, but she had to ask. He had been on her mind ever since she had left the hotel, and now she felt as if, somehow, he had followed her into her house. She went into her bedroom, threw her coat on the bed, and sat in an armchair by the window, staring idly at the square below.

It had been stupid to lose control, she thought. Now she had to wait for Diego to make the next move. Much as she wanted him to, he wouldn't go away. She knew him. The question was how far he was prepared to go to get what he wanted.

The bell rang. She went to the landing, and heard Eugenia opening the door.

'Who is it?' Frances shrieked, shocked by her own shrillness, her hands clenched on the polished handrail.

'The milkman,' Eugenia replied, clearly startled. Frances almost smiled in relief, but only for a second. It would be just like Diego to ring her bell, although he might wait for a time when Norman and Peter were here. Perhaps he would go to Peter's school . . . She went back to her bedroom and rummaged through the magazines neatly piled on a glass table. She found that particular copy of *Hello!*, and flicked through it until she came to the article: there was no mention of the school's name in it. Frances threw the magazine aside.

I can't live like this, she thought. Then she realized that she was stupid to fear Diego so much. He hadn't told her where he lived, nor what he did. Probably he had even better reasons than she did to avoid a scandal, or anything that might blow his cover. It was a question of staying calm, of being reasonable, and making him see sense. Frances reached for the phone, and dialled Directory Enquiries.

'The Ritz Hotel, please.' She scribbled the number on her notepad, then dialled it.

'Mr Diego Santos, please. S-a-n-t-o-s.' She would have to meet him again. It would be impossible to discuss Peter over the phone, she thought, while she waited to be connected.

'I'm afraid there's no one registered under that name, madam,' the operator said.

FOURTEEN

'Goodbye. So wonderful to see you – such fun.' Norman waved at their departing guests. Frances waited for her husband to turn off the entrance hall lights and set the burglar alarm, then they went upstairs together.

'David and Judith are very nice, don't you think?' Norman asked.

'Yes, they are,' Frances agreed.

'You seemed . . . not your usual self tonight.'

'What do you mean?'

'I don't know. It was as if you weren't paying much attention to the conversation.'

'It wasn't that riveting,' Frances replied. She wished she sounded less offhand.

'Is something troubling you?'

Two days ago, Frances made the decision not to say anything to Norman about Diego, or at least to wait until she heard from him again. Now she reconsidered, tempted by the possibility of confession, of unburdening her concern, but there would be no absolution, or at least not for long. Ever since his political career took off, Norman had become terrified of putting a foot wrong, about anything that might affect his image. The election campaign was on, and his sensitivity was at a peak.

If she told Norman about Diego's reappearance, he would most likely do nothing about it. To be fair, there was very little Norman *could* do. 'My wife had tea with a man she used to be married to,' was not something the police would be inclined to act on. If they knew that Diego was the man at Spitalfields, it could turn the matter into a criminal investigation. Norman wouldn't want that, and neither did she. Diego alive meant that her marriage to Norman could be bigamous. Officially, Diego had been dead at the time of her second marriage, and she and Norman had acted in good faith, but the possibility was hardly an election bonus.

'No, not at all. I'm just tired, I guess. I'm going to check on Peter,' Frances said as they reached their bedroom landing, and she climbed the next flight of steps. She opened her son's door and peered inside, reassuring herself at the sight of the sleeping boy in his bed, surrounded by the usual chaos of clothes, video games, and half-put-together aeroplane models, most of them strewn on the floor. Frances tidied up the room as best she could, then she stood next to Peter's bed for a while, looking at him. She loved the sight of the curve of his cheek against the pillow, the way his dark hair formed into clumps when he slept, as she loved the sweet, innocent smell of his skin when she leaned down and kissed him, forcing herself to leave his room. She lingered outside, by the open door, listening to his steady breathing. By the time she went back to her own bedroom, Norman was already in bed, his glasses perched low on his nose. There were papers next to him, and a sheaf of them on his lap.

'It would be nice if you could come to Swanton with me on Monday morning,' he said. 'There's a walkabout scheduled around the new shopping mall, and then I'll stand outside Sainsbury's, talking to people.'

'What am I supposed to do?' asked Frances.

'Just be there, or talk to people yourself. They all love you, you know.'

'I can't see how I can help you,' she replied, although she knew perfectly well what he meant. Encouraged by Norman, Frances had spent years taming down her

American openness, but at election time she was expected to bring it back on cue. 'I really don't know enough about the issues, and I have my own work to do.'

Norman took off his glasses and rubbed his nose, a clear sign to Frances that he was upset.

'The Liberal Democrats are doing quite well in the constituency,' he said. 'But their guy is unmarried. There are rumours about him . . .'

'And your agent has nothing to do with the stories, I suppose,' Frances said.

'Of course not. Sometimes you have the most extraordinary ideas. But people like family values, and it would help me if they see you by my side. Every vote counts, Frances.'

'You know what the trouble with you lot is? That you're all the same, you and all the rest. You make promises, and then you don't keep them. Mrs Thatcher was the best of the lot of you, and you threw her out. Disgusting, I say, that's what it is . . . You must be one of those who want to send murderers to some school, and throw money at them instead of hanging the bastards.' The man ranted at Norman, who grinned back at him, as crisply unperturbed as the blue rosette in his lapel. Frances thought that she would make a very bad politician. When Norman approached the man, she had been deceived by his appearance; jogging sweats, trainers, and a gold sovereign ring made her assume an allegiance to Labour, but he had turned out to be a Tory fundamentalist.

'I couldn't agree with you more,' Norman said soothingly. 'But there's no firmer pair of hands than John Major's, and we need your support. We've put the "Great" back in Great Britain. We can walk proud again, but it can all be ruined so quickly, if the socialists get a chance. Can we count on you?'

'Yes,' the man grumbled. 'But I tell you that my mortgage is killing me.'

'I know, I know. What's your name?'

'Charlie Falconer,' the man said.

'Sometimes sacrifices are inevitable, Charlie, but I assure you that, once we win the election and confidence returns, the economy will take off again. You must meet my wife, Frances. This is Mr Falconer,' Norman introduced him, before turning to his next prey, a mother with a small child in a pram, already softened up by Norman's entourage.

'My wife saw you in *Hello!*' Mr Falconer said. The whole world read that magazine, Frances thought.

'Thank you,' she replied. There was nothing to thank him for, but it did no harm. 'Do you have any children?' Frances asked, glancing at the clock in the middle of the square, and hoping she could stop soon. It was nearly half past twelve; Miranda would disappear for lunch any minute now.

'. . . And the boy is on the dole. My daughter Cherry is training as a beautician. She wants to find a job in Ipswich when she finishes . . .'

'I'm sure she will,' Frances reassured him, trying to stem the biography of the Falconer family. 'Could you tell me where I can find a phone, please?' By the time they parted company outside Boots, Frances had gathered additional information about Cherry and Rick, the unemployed son, which she forgot as soon as she had crammed all her change into the coin box.

'Miranda, it's me . . . Don't worry, I'll be back around two o'clock, and I'll deal with that . . . Anything in the post? . . . Right . . .' Frances had left her reason for phoning until last, as if it was an afterthought. 'Any calls? . . .' She nodded at the familiar – and irrelevant – names, then her face tightened.

'What did he say? . . . I see . . . Let's hope he's a new client,' Frances said. 'I'll see you later.'

As she put the phone down, she thought that the man with a foreign accent who had asked for her but didn't want to leave his name was unlikely to be interested in Italian tours.

'. . . Wait a minute, please.' Frances put the phone down on her desk and searched among the papers there, until she came to a thick, glossy brochure. She took it, and walked to Miranda's desk.

'I need you to go to the photocopying place now, if you don't mind,' she said. 'I want two colour copies.' That should keep Miranda away for half an hour at least, by the time she'd made a couple of stops on the way. Frances picked up the phone again as soon as she heard the door close.

'Did you get rid of whoever it was?' Diego asked. 'Since I phoned this morning, I thought you would have made sure that you were alone.'

'I don't sit here waiting for you to call,' Frances lied, 'and I can't close my office for your sake.'

'Would you rather I phoned you at home then? I'm sure your husband wouldn't like it.'

Frances knew he was bluffing. Her home number was ex-directory.

'Don't try blackmailing me, Diego, although I suppose it's part of your repertoire.'

'I could call you there, if this is the right number' – he read it out correctly – 'but I won't, unless I have to,' he added. 'I just wanted to say goodbye, in fact. I have to leave this evening.'

'Good. And don't come back.'

'That's not what I had in mind. I'd like to be back on Thursday, but I have some engagements I might not be able to change, so next Monday is more likely. I thought that we could meet for lunch, or a drink if you prefer,' he said. 'And you could bring Peter along.'

'I've told you to leave him out of this!'

'You don't have to explain anything to him. Just say that you're meeting an old friend. It's true, as it happens.'

'Peter doesn't give a damn about my friends. He'll say he doesn't want to come. He couldn't, even if he wanted to. He's at school . . . at lunchtime.' To say that Peter was a weekly boarder would be a clue to his whereabouts, and she had enough proof of Diego's ability to find things out already.

'You can bring him here for the day,' he suggested. 'You could say that he needs a medical check-up. I could collect him from school, if you want.'

'You are a shit!' she screamed. 'I'll kill you if you start bothering him!'

'I just want to see him once, Melanie, that's all. You can tell him that your friend has a nice present for him. He would like that. Let's say Tuesday, shall we? I'll contact you on Monday, to tell you where we should meet. See you then.'

The line went dead. Frances sat there, the phone still in her hand.

'I'm glad you're up. I have to talk to you,' Norman said as soon as he came into their bedroom. Frances's immediate thought was that Diego must have contacted him. She had felt more at ease over the last two days, hoping that he had left London, as he said he would, but there was no certainty.

'What's happened?' she asked, trying to sound calm.

'Inspector Lucas phoned me this evening. The police raided a house in Tottenham and they arrested two men there. One of them had the magazine picture of Peter and you in his wallet.'

Frances was relieved, both by the news in itself, and by the fact that her fears about Diego had been unfounded.

'Who are they?' she asked.

'Inspector Lucas told me that they are drug dealers. Customs and Excise had been watching a warehouse near Tilbury that handles containers from South America. It was supposed to be a coffee business, but they knew it had been set up as a front for drug smuggling. The police broke into the warehouse last night, and arrested other people in the ring. They confessed, and that's how the police found these two.'

'I'm glad they got them,' Frances said, but she knew that there was something else he wanted to discuss.

'It might help if you went to identify them,' Norman said after a pause. 'Lucas said that they have enough evidence to nail the men for drug-dealing, but attempted kidnapping is a serious crime too. He'd like you to help him, but he realized at the hospital that you seemed reluctant.'

'I don't think you'd like the publicity either,' she retorted, irritated by Norman's attitude. Passing on responsibility for an unpalatable but necessary decision had become so instinctive for him that he no longer noticed himself doing it. 'I'd be in every newspaper, and so would Peter. I'm sure you don't want *him* turned into tabloid news.'

Frances knew it was all she needed to make her point. Ever since their marriage, they had never spoken again about her past. It had been a silent pact. They both understood the rules, without any need for explanation. From the start, Norman had seen himself as Peter's father, because it suited him, as it suited Frances. Peter *was* Norman's son, a fiction that had become so successful that Norman seemed to believe it.

'You're right,' he said quietly. 'I'll call Lucas and tell him that we'd rather drop the matter.'

She noticed his use of 'we', and smiled at him.

'Thank you,' she said. Her smile froze at an unexpected thought. If her attackers were drug dealers, a connection with Diego was very likely. He could have arranged to have her and Peter abducted. He might have seen something that forced him to change his plans on the spot, and then he had reversed his role to save his own skin. The possibility seemed as likely to Frances as his claim to have been their saviour.

'. . . My dear, they have *so* much money you wouldn't believe it. Apparently she brings her own hairdresser from Athens because he knows her hair, she says . . .' Melissa, Lady Harvey, cooed with longing admiration, and Frances nodded politely, half-listening to the stream of gossip about her hosts for the evening, Vlasos Kalomeropoulos and his wife, Arianna. The Greek shipowner was said to be the largest single contributor to Tory Party funds; looking around her, at the lush, padded opulence of his house in Eaton Square, Frances could believe it. Every wing of the Party was there, but only the really serious players, a large factor in Norman's joy at receiving an invitation. There were just two Junior Ministers among the guests, both rumoured to be about to join the Cabinet after the election, and Norman was one of them.

'Vlasos is a sweetie, I used to know him well before his marriage,' Melissa Harvey said meaningfully, then she paused for breath and looked around, over Frances's shoulder. She stretched her neck and grinned at someone, tossing her voluminous blonde hair in the process. A moment later, the target of her smile, another good-looking woman in her late thirties or early forties, joined them.

'Frances Fellowes, Lady Bromfield,' Melissa introduced

them, to Frances's irritation. Class pretentiousness infuriated her; no matter how many years she lived here, it was an aspect of English life she still found hard to swallow.

'My friends call me Frances. Please do,' she told the newcomer, who smiled.

'I'm Victoria,' she said in a curious foreign accent with American inflexions, and Frances suddenly remembered her from the *Daily Mail* gossip column: 'Beautiful New York divorcee bags Mrs Thatcher's favourite tycoon', had been the headline at the time of her marriage to Jack Bromfield.

'I'm sure we've met before, but I can't place you,' Victoria Bromfield said, and Frances felt a cramp of fear in the pit of her stomach, a familiar feeling over the last two weeks. 'Did you ever live in New York?'

'Eleven or twelve years ago, but only for a few months, then I met my husband and came to England. Otherwise, I lived all my life in Los Angeles,' Frances replied. It was the condensed version of her past invented at the time of her marriage, which she had always used for parties. If necessary.

'I've never been to LA. But I'd swear I've met you though . . .'

'Victoria is from Argentina, but she lived in New York for a few years,' explained Melissa.

'Too many. My second husband was a mistake,' Victoria laughed.

'No marriage is a mistake if you have the right lawyer, darling,' the multiply-divorced Lady Harvey countered with the voice of experience, and Frances remembered at last. She had met Victoria in Punta del Este, at the house of Teresa de Tannerie, before Diego drove her to the lagoon. A feeling of vulnerability chilled her skin as effectively as if every window in the room had been thrown open, letting in the night air. Over the last few days, she had had to face Peter's questions about his birth, then Diego's reappearance, and now the intrusion of this woman here, where she least expected it.

'Excuse me, I must find Norman,' she said abruptly. Frances cut across the crowd, until she found him in a convivial circle of Government chiefs, starry enough to make Norman the only Indian among them. She took his arm and drew him reluctantly aside.

'I want to go,' she whispered.

'Why? We can't leave so early,' he whispered back.

'I'm not feeling very well.'

'You could ask Arianna if you can lie down in one of the bedrooms upstairs. I'm sure you'll feel better in no time at all.'

'Don't be ridiculous. I'd rather go home. I'll take the car,' Frances snapped, moving away before Norman could object. She looked for her hostess to say goodbye, and saw her at the other end of the drawing room. As Frances got closer, she realized that Mrs Kalomeropoulos was talking to Victoria Bromfield. She turned back, hurrying towards the stairs and the marble hall. Waiting for the uniformed maid to find her coat, she decided she would write a letter of apology tomorrow. A sudden, crippling migraine would be a good enough excuse.

She left the house, walking along a line of double-parked, chauffeur-driven cars, the ministerial Rovers and occasional Jaguar humbled by the Mercedes and Rolls. Frances got into her own car. As she drove away, she noticed another pulling out across the road. It made a U-turn and followed her, twenty or thirty yards behind, enough for her not to be able to see the driver clearly.

The traffic lights were red. The other car stopped a few yards behind her, enough to prevent Frances from seeing the driver clearly. She turned into Belgrave Place, the Friday night traffic thinning away as she left the King's Road.

She accelerated, but the gap between the cars remained unchanged, almost as if she was towing the other car. At Belgrave Square, she swerved into Chesham Place without indicating; a second later, she saw the lights of the other car in her mirror. The traffic lights at the Pont Street junction were green, then turned to amber. Frances raced across them; the other car did so too, just as they changed to red. As she was about to reach Cadogan Place, she thought of phoning Norman, but she was in the middle of Belgravia, in her car, there were people and policemen about, and the other driver had done nothing so far other than drive in the same direction, at the same speed. It wasn't reason enough to be so frightened, unless she explained her suspicions to Norman. Frances kept going, but the lights at Sloane Street changed to red. She locked the doors, picked up the car phone, and dialled her home number.

'Eugenia? I'm sorry to get you out of bed, but I left my keys. I'm very near home. Could you wait for me downstairs? And leave the door open, so I don't have to knock, but be there, please.' She rang off, before Eugenia could grumble.

Frances drove across the junction slowly, with deliberation. As she raised her eyes to the mirror, she saw the other car turn into Sloane Street. She caught a flash of red from its tail lights, and then there was an empty road behind her.

'Piers is great, really great. His eyes are incredible . . . He looks like Michael Bolton, you know . . .'
Frances was used to Miranda's gushing inanity about her weekend activities on Monday mornings, but today it was particularly unbearable. Miranda had met her latest interest at some friend's party on Saturday night, and she had told Frances in detail about what they did together on Sunday – or at least those aspects that she guessed would

not excessively shock someone who was nearly twice her age.

Pretending to make herself busy over forms and letters, Frances had listened with half an ear, waiting for Diego's call. She supposed she should be grateful for anything that took her mind off things. If she had been on her own, by now she would be sitting at her desk, staring at the phone. Over the last few days, she had gone over her conversations with Diego many times, in search of clues. He could be living anywhere in the world, but her guess was that it had to be somewhere in Europe, since he was able to come and go so easily. He wouldn't have stayed in America, and it would have been impossible for him to fly back to South America on Monday, and consider the possibility of being back in London by Thursday. He had to live in Spain, as she had guessed, and she tried to find comfort in a scrap of certainty that made little difference in any case.

It was almost half past ten. He could be in London already, if he had taken an early flight. Her hand reached for the bookshelf by her desk, ready to pull out the IATA manual to check on Madrid–London flights, but she changed her mind. It would be hard to explain why she was looking at those particular flights in such detail to Miranda. She must be careful.

Miranda picked up the phone. Diego could be at the airport now, dialling this number, and Frances had to restrain herself from asking her to leave the line clear. Miranda noticed her anxious look.

'Piers said he would call me before ten this morning, to arrange something for this evening. I'd better give him a ring,' she explained.

'You should let him call you. Don't seem too keen,' was Frances's suggestion.

Miranda had started to dial, but now she rang off, and Frances was glad that she seemed to heed her advice. After a second, though, she tried again, and this time she looked at Frances. There was panic in her eyes.

'The phone isn't working,' she said.

'You *must* fix my phone. Not this afternoon, not "as soon you can". You must fix it *now!*' Frances shrieked into the mouthpiece. It was after midday now, and it was her third trip to the public telephone, to call the engineers. She listened for a second, before starting to rant again.

'I don't care how many faults you have to repair today. I want to talk to the area supervisor, then . . . That's my problem, not yours. Give me the number, please.' She rummaged through her bag until she found a pen, and scribbled down the number. Ignoring the ostentatiously irate looks from the woman waiting by the side of the booth, she fed a coin into the slot and dialled again.

It was only when she finished her call, marginally pacified by the assurances received, that Frances realized the extent of her impatience. She had pulled rank shamelessly, mentioning Norman and half the Government in the process, something she had never done before. At any other time, she would have been angry with herself for doing it, but not now. Nothing mattered to her, other than to have the damned telephone fixed without delay.

'It's working now,' Miranda announced at two o'clock. She had been checking every few minutes, as Frances herself would have done if she hadn't been worried about triggering Miranda's suspicions.

'Good,' Frances said without raising her head from her papers, as if the matter was of little importance to her. She carried on working, and waiting. After half an hour, she realized that knowing the phone was in order again only doubled her anxiety. Perhaps Diego had called before, and given up. Perhaps he wouldn't call at all. She persevered at her work, letters, forms, and schedules blurring into a single, half-seen irrelevance.

The phone rang just after three.

'I'll take it,' Frances blasted across her desk. A second later, she put the receiver down.

'It's for you,' she told Miranda, who picked up her extension with alacrity.

'Who? . . . Oh, Piers . . . I'm sorry, I wasn't expecting your call at all . . .'

Frances ground her teeth in irritation.

'Don't be too long, please,' she said, although she knew better.

'Goodnight, Frances,' Miranda chirped, almost dancing her way out of the office. She was meeting Piers at a wine bar near Sloane Square.

As soon as she had gone, Frances was pacing the room; at least while Miranda was there she had been forced to pretend to be calm. Now she was alone, and night was falling. The silent phone dominated everything else in the room.

She hated being forced to stay here and wait for Diego's call, as she hated the knowledge that she wouldn't leave until he phoned. Perhaps it would be better if Diego didn't call, if – for whatever reason – he disappeared from her life as swiftly as he had come back, but she knew that it wouldn't be that easy. Frances would spend the rest of her life in fear of his reappearance, and it would be impossible to keep him away from Peter indefinitely. She couldn't make Diego forget Peter's existence, even if he had been able to forget her for so long.

To turn him in to the police was also out of the question. Diego might go to jail, but there would be no way of keeping Norman out of the picture. The scandal would destroy her marriage, but far worse than that was the prospect of what it would mean for Peter. Whatever happened from now on, her life had changed irreversibly. It would never be the same again.

Unless Diego died.

The shrill ring of the phone jolted her. Frances stretched out her hand to pick it up, when she realized it was actually the fax machine, beside Miranda's desk.

The machine clicked as the connection was made. The paper roll retracted, then the sheet began to emerge from the felt-edged slot. There was no letterhead. A hand-written line appeared. Frances recognized Diego's writing immediately. The machine slowed down, and she became frantically impatient to read his message.

'I tried to phone you earlier, but couldn't get through. Wait for me tomorrow at five o'clock, on the corner of Grosvenor Crescent and Belgrave Square, north side,' she read line by line as the sheet emerged. Unsigned.

FIFTEEN

The pavements around Belgrave Square were empty, but for a policeman standing outside the Turkish Embassy, a few dozen yards away from Frances. She wondered if he had noticed her, idly waiting at the corner for the last ten minutes. Diego was late.

That morning, she had managed to trace the source of his fax message through the number printed on the paper. It belonged to a photocopying shop off Oxford Street. 'We can't remember every customer, love. We only make sure we're not sending anything obscene. Is that what you've got, then?' the man asked, and Frances hung up.

It was just after ten past five. A wave of traffic came round the far corner of the square. A dark blue car veered to the left, near the kerb, and slowed down as it approached Wilton Crescent, until it stopped next to her. Frances could see the driver through the windscreen, a nondescript man in a grey suit, but all the other windows were of dark glass, making any passengers in the back invisible. The rear door opened.

'Come in quickly. We're blocking the traffic,' Diego urged her from inside the car. It was only as she closed the door and sat next to him that Frances became worried about the wisdom of what she was doing.

'Just drive around the park,' Diego said, leaning towards the mirrored screen between them and the driver, then he pressed a switch.

'He can't hear us now,' he told Frances. 'I thought this

would be better than meeting in a public place. I knew you wouldn't bring Peter in any case.'

'He can't miss school at your whim,' she replied brusquely. Perhaps it was time to mislead him. 'Peter is at school in Yorkshire. He can't come to London during the week, without missing at least two days. It's out of the question.'

Diego smiled with his eyes only.

'You look even more beautiful when you lie,' he said. 'I went to Doddington Hall yesterday, and I saw him there, playing cricket. I don't understand the game at all, but he seemed good at it.'

'You couldn't have seen him! They wouldn't have let you in.'

'Why not? I made an appointment to visit the school. I told them I was considering it for my son, and they're very keen on foreign parents who can afford the fees. Times are hard, I gather. They showed me everything. I liked his house, his dormitory in particular. Does he get on with the other five boys? It must be fun to share your room with friends at his age. I wish my school had been like that. It's a good place for him. Once we are together again, he could stay there, if he wants.'

Frances glared at him.

'Your drug-dealing friends would look after him then, I suppose,' she snapped.

Diego looked at her in astonishment.

'What the hell are you talking about?' He sounded quite genuine, as always he did when he was lying. Or when he wasn't; Frances couldn't tell any more. Perhaps her suspicions of Diego's plot to kidnap them were mad; nothing in Peter's recollection of the scene suggested that Diego had been with the men. It would be dangerous to explain her outburst, and put ideas into his mind. If they weren't there already.

'Someone was trying to sell drugs outside the school a few weeks ago,' she said.

'That *is* cheap,' he replied, sounding genuinely appalled. 'You know I wouldn't do anything like that.'

'I don't know what you might or might not do, but leave him out of this. I'll kill you if you don't. I mean it,' she said.

'I don't think you would. It's not your style – and besides you love me. I didn't talk to Peter at the school anyway, but I liked seeing him again. He's a very good-looking boy. I'm sure he's very clever too.'

Frances sat stiffly in the corner. She decided not to pick him up on his cocky remark about love, but it was maddening to feel so impotent.

'You can't have him. Please go away.'

'I'm his father. You can't change that. The problem is yours, Melanie, not mine. You lied to him.'

Suddenly she was enraged.

'How dare you?' she cried. 'How can *you* talk about lies?'

'I never lied to you about us. Since I'm sure you haven't told your husband or Peter about our meetings, I wonder if you can say the same. We are all liars, when it suits us. The first time you met my mother, you were quite inventive about your own past, as you may remember . . .'

Frances didn't want to remember.

'How did you find out about the school and my home number?' she asked instead.

Diego gave her an amused look.

'There's very little that money can't buy. You just need a diligent detective, and there are lots of them around. Very discreet too. Almost impossible to see them. But we were talking about Peter,' he reminded her.

'I heard you. You want me to tell him about you.'

'I haven't said that. It's up to you to decide.'

'Are you expecting me to tell Peter that his father is not the man he thinks, but a supposedly dead Argentine drug dealer I happened to have been married to years ago, who has reappeared out of the blue? You must be able to imagine what it would do to him. Do you want to ruin his life?'

'It doesn't need to be like that,' Diego replied. 'You can tell your husband you've found someone else, and that you want to leave him. He won't want a scandal, and I'll stay out of the picture until it's all settled. After your divorce, you and I will live abroad. Peter can come with you, if he wants, or he can stay at school here, and live with us during the holidays. Peter must have plenty of friends with divorced parents. Divorce among civilized people doesn't need to be a drama, and your husband will understand. He's used to dealing with facts, and making the best of them. He wouldn't lose touch with Peter, and there would be no drama that way.'

He had it all figured out. Frances was speechless, as enraged by Diego's easy assumptions about her as she was uneasy about his assessment of Norman's possible behaviour; it was more credible than she would have liked.

'You're mad,' she said eventually. 'You must believe that I've spent all these years thinking about you.'

'I thought about you. I could never forget what we had, and neither could you. I know that.'

'I don't care about you now. Not one bit,' Frances said.

'Then you wouldn't be trying so hard to hate me.' Diego moved close to her and took her hand.

'Words are easy,' he said, 'but your skin feels the same to me. Your eyes are the same. I still love you more than anything; nothing has changed.'

Frances broke away from him.

'Stop the car. I want to get out,' she said.

'I won't go away. Don't force me to do something you

might regret later. I don't want to hurt you. Or Peter.'

Frances felt tears gathering in the corners of her eyes.

'If you *really* don't want to hurt him, please go. Let him grow up happily, away from you. That's all I ask you.'

'Why should I?' he asked.

'Because I beg you. And because it would be best for Peter.'

'You always talk about Peter, never about yourself,' Diego said. 'You're using him as a shield to avoid facing what *you* want.'

'That's not true!'

'Why are you so angry then?' he asked. Frances didn't say anything.

'I'll take you at your word,' Diego said after a while. 'I'll leave you both in peace, on one condition. I have to go back this evening, but I'll return on Wednesday. Keep that afternoon free for me. If, as you say, I don't matter to you any more, it would only mean an hour's sacrifice, at worst. Then I'll be gone for ever, I assure you, and you'll have what you want. I'll let you know where to find me.' Diego lowered his window. They were driving along South Carriage Drive, near the gate to Knightsbridge. He switched on the microphone.

'The lady is getting out at the Scotch House,' he told the driver.

'I didn't say I agreed,' Frances said.

'Then I'll keep coming back,' Diego replied. The car stopped, and he opened the door for her. 'But you want to agree. We know that. See you on Wednesday,' he said.

'. . . John was fantastic today. People cheered like crazy when he spoke about nightmare on Kinnock Street. I bet you it will be the headline in the *Sun* tomorrow. Things are definitely shaping up.'

Norman's voice came to Frances through the half-open

bathroom door, as he shouted to make himself heard over the running water. She heard the hum of his electric toothbrush, and welcomed the absence of conversation, leaving her momentarily alone with her thoughts, followed by a stark realization: she didn't care. She didn't care about his obsession with the election, about his wish to win, about what the papers would say tomorrow. It all seemed so petty, so meaningless.

'The headlines were all about taxes today, and that's good. Even when the *Guardian* says that we'll have to put them up, it reminds people that we cut them in the first place.' Norman had come into the bedroom, changed into his striped pyjamas, and continued talking. Her face slightly turned away from him, Frances watched his reflection in the cheval glass. Suddenly she felt choked by everything that had happened over the last ten days, and by ten years of accumulated guilt, slowly piling up in her heart like sand running into the bottom of an hourglass. She had never loved Norman, or at least not as she should, although this knowledge had nothing to do with Diego's visit. She had known it ever since their life together had settled into a pattern, but a combination of gratitude, comfort, his love for her, and their mutual love for Peter, had seemed to fill the void.

'Scotland is looking a bit ropy . . . What's wrong? Why are you crying?' Norman asked, astonished.

'It's this new eye cream,' Frances replied lamely. 'It's supposed to do wonders for your skin, but it stings like hell.'

'You don't need it, darling. You're absolutely lovely without that rubbish.'

'Do you mean that?'

Norman gave her a surprised look.

'Why would I say it otherwise?' he asked. Frances got out of bed, walked over to her husband and hugged him.

'Hold me. Just hold me,' she said, then to his surprise she kissed him as if there were no memories, no guilt. Her hand undid his pyjama buttons, one by one, and her fingers brushed his chest until they reached his waist, then they gripped the cord and pulled.

'Good God, Peter will think he's walked into somebody else's house when he comes back,' Norman exclaimed as he entered his son's bedroom. For the last two hours Frances had been tidying up the boy's cupboards and shelves: clothes, books and electronic games were immaculately arranged. It had been dark outside when she started; now the morning light came through the window.

'I thought you were downstairs, but Eugenia told me she hadn't seen you. Why did you get up so early?' Norman asked.

'I just woke up, and I couldn't go back to sleep,' Frances explained. 'Have you had breakfast yet?'

'Yes. I have to rush. There are a couple of meetings at the Ministry this morning, and then I'm going to Swanton in the afternoon. I'll be there for the rest of the week. Why don't you come with me?'

'I'd love to, but I can't leave the office. Miranda is useless on her own. I'll drive down on Saturday morning,' she said, walking downstairs beside him and cherishing the feeling of early morning companionship, like an augury for the rest of the day.

'Can't you be there tomorrow evening? I'm having dinner with Geoff and some people from the association, and I was counting on you. Why do you want to wait until Saturday? I hate being apart.'

'Because I'm collecting Peter from school on Friday after-noon, remember, and I'll bring him here first. He needs new trainers, and his school trousers are much too short.

Saturday morning is the only time we'll have to buy new things.' At least this excuse was true.

Norman opened the front door.

'I'm sorry you can't come,' he said. He kissed Frances goodbye, perhaps more ardently than usual, or so she thought. Guilt stung her like a scorpion, invisible in the grass, but present none the less: she would have gone with him if it weren't for Diego. Frances watched him get into his car. For a second, she made the perfect picture of a wife in her dressing gown saying goodbye to her husband as he left for work; it almost made her believe that life could be normal again.

An hour later, as Frances was putting on her coat in the hall, the front bell rang.

'Mrs Frances Fellowes?' asked a delivery boy, holding a lavishly wrapped box. 'Sign here, please.'

Frances closed the door after him, and tore at the wrappings. Inside there was a small bunch of lilies of the valley, and an envelope. The card bore a short message: 'Flat 5 – Remington House – Curzon Street. Wednesday. Four o'clock.'

Life could be normal again, but only if she met Diego. There was no other option, and Frances didn't stop to consider why she was neither outraged nor humiliated by the fact.

'That's a new dress. *Very* sexy,' Miranda said as she hung up her coat. 'Sexy' was a word Miranda used for everything she liked, but it sounded like an accusation to Frances.

'Oh, this,' she said dismissively, trying to sound casual. 'I got it at Joseph's sale. I thought it would be useful for the office.'

'It certainly clings to all the right places,' was Miranda's comment, and Frances looked down, at her loose, charcoal-grey knitted shift. When choosing her clothes that morning

274

she had made a point of discarding anything she thought would flatter her, or anything reminiscent of the kind of clothes Diego used to like on her.

'Please get your pad, Miranda. We have some correspondence to do,' Frances said briskly. She took the first letter from the pile on her desk, and began to dictate a reply.

'. . . And I would be very grateful if you could confirm in writing that the terms are acceptable . . .' Suddenly Frances saw Diego's face, his naked chest, his brown skin fading to white below the waist, his hand reaching for her. 'In the event of cancellation, we would require three weeks notice . . .' she went on, unsuccessfully trying to stop the scene unfolding in her mind.

'Hold on. You're going too fast for me,' Miranda complained, her pencil scratching desperately on her pad.

At half past three, Frances left her desk and put her coat on.

'I won't be back this afternoon,' she told Miranda. 'I have a dentist's appointment.'

'Oh, poor you. I hope it won't hurt too much,' Miranda clucked, glancing at the diary on her desk. 'You didn't write it in. That's unusual.'

Frances wondered if she suspected something. 'I forgot. I made the appointment from home last week,' she said. Without thinking, she opened her bag to search for her mirror and lipstick. When she realized what she was doing, she closed it again.

'See you tomorrow.' Frances rushed out as fast as she could, to prevent Miranda asking anything else. As soon as she was outside, she scanned the King's Road for a taxi, and soon saw one approaching. She was about to raise her arm, when she thought about the prospect of being incarcerated with a talkative cabbie for the journey, forcing her to make conversation. Worse still, the man might recognize her. 'I drove Norman Fellowes's wife this afternoon, you know, that guy who's a Minister or something,' he would say to his mates later. 'I took her to one of those blocks of flats on Curzon Street, you know where I mean . . .' It was unlikely, but better to be careful.

Frances put on her sunglasses, and kept walking towards the Underground station at Sloane Square.

The building blended with the other grey stone and brick façades around it, as discreet as the rectangular, polished brass plate on the broad, dark wood door announcing 'Remington House' in cursive black lettering. Frances climbed the short flight of steps leading to the entrance. She could still go back. She *should* go back, she thought as she pressed the button marked '5'. The door buzzed open too quickly for her indecision, and she went in, relieved to find herself inside. She was in no position to bargain with Diego, let alone contradict him. The sooner this was all over with, the better, a thought she found more comforting than the shivers of guilty anticipation running over her skin like busy ants.

After the noise of traffic in the street, the first thing that struck her was the sudden silence. The hall was only remarkable for its anonymity: thick carpet, marbled wallpaper, and a side table near the stairs, on which stood a vase of silk flowers. There was a small perspex stand next to the flowers, holding leaflets. 'Remington House: an enclave of luxuriously elegant apartments nestled in the heart of Mayfair . . .' she read, glad for an excuse to stay in the foyer. The words 'privacy' and 'seclusion' featured a number of times, and daily or weekly rates 'on application' were mentioned in the small print at the bottom.

Frances heard the lift gates open a few yards from her. There was nowhere to hide down here, so she rushed up the stairs, catching sight of a couple leaving the building as she turned at the landing. Arrows and numbers were painted on the wall. Diego's flat was to the left. The door was ajar.

The entrance hall was a miniature version of the foyer downstairs, silk flowers included. An archway faced the door, leading to the sitting room. There was no sign of Diego. Overpadded leather armchairs and a sofa, the kind of furniture that filled Harrods windows during the sale, surrounded an empty fireplace.

'I'm in here.' Diego's voice came through a half-open door to one side. It had to be the bedroom, and Frances wondered if he was waiting for her there. 'I won't be long,' he added before she could decide.

'I was putting some things away,' he explained as he came in. 'You know I'm a pain about tidiness,' he smiled apologetically. She thought he would kiss her, but he didn't.

'Please sit down. What would you like to drink?' he asked, heading for the drinks cabinet at one end of the room. 'I hope you didn't have any trouble finding the place. I don't understand this business of addresses without numbers . . .'

It would have been easier if Diego had been wearing only his dressing gown, if soft music was playing, the curtains were drawn and a fire burned, if he had prepared a scene of staged romance as luxuriously tacky as the setting itself. But light streamed through the windows, and he was wearing grey flannel trousers, shirt and tie, and a blue cashmere cardigan. Anyone watching them, a woman sitting bolt upright, her arms crossed, while a man stood away from her, making small talk, would have been more likely to read it as two not very close friends meeting for a drink than as a seduction, or the improbable reunion of a dead man and his ex-wife.

'I don't want anything,' she replied. Diego opened a

small fridge concealed within a cabinet, and pulled out a bottle of white wine. He opened it, poured two glasses and handed one to Frances.

'I hope you'll change your mind,' he said, sitting on the sofa. 'I took some trouble to find this particular vintage.' He raised his glass.

'To us,' he toasted, his eyes on her. 'You didn't used to wear dark grey,' he said. 'It suits you, although I prefer your hair blonde. It's a shame that you've changed it.'

'Maybe it's not only gentlemen who prefer blondes, then,' Frances snapped. Diego smiled.

'You wouldn't want a gentleman this afternoon,' he said. 'They're fine for marrying, but shits are much more exciting in bed. You should know that.'

Frances stood up.

'Is that my cue for taking my clothes off? We are wasting time, you know.'

Diego sipped his wine.

'You're letting your wine get warm. What I said doesn't apply to you and me, so you don't need to be so puritanical about it. We're married, if you remember, although it might be more fun to pretend we're not. Imagination always makes everything more exciting.'

Frances sat down, and reached for her glass.

'Do you remember the wine?' Diego asked once Frances had tasted the rich, mellow flavour. 'It's Corton-Charlemagne 71, the same wine we drank our first evening together, at La Côte Basque. Very few white wines improve with the years. Only the really good ones. At first you think that nothing could improve that taste, but just let it stay in your mouth for long enough. Give it a chance.'

Frances left her glass on the coffee table.

'Drink some more. Enjoy it,' Diego insisted, coming up to her. He sat on the arm of her seat, took the glass and offered it to her again, but Frances didn't respond. He put the glass to her lips; a few drops of wine trickled down her chin. Diego wiped them away with his fingers, running them slowly over Frances' moist lips, then he held her head between his hands and pushed her gently against the chair back, his face close to her.

'Is this how you want it?' he asked. 'Do you think that by pretending you're here against your will, that by going through it as if it was a sacrifice, it will be easier for you once I'm gone? I'll give you what you want then.' Diego grabbed her wrists and pulled Frances to her feet, then he pulled off her dress and led her across the room, until her back was against the wall, his forearm hard against her chin, pushing it up. He looked her in the eyes, and smiled.

'Bras that fasten at the front make things so much easier,' he said, his fingers brushing her breasts as he undid the clasp. 'Now you will undress me. First you undo my tie . . .' He waited until she did it. 'Now my shirt . . . Yes, take it off. The belt next. And the zipper, that's good. Very good. I didn't say I wanted your hand on me. Not yet.' Diego kicked his clothes aside, and stepped back until they stood at arm's length.

'Take those off,' he nodded, and Frances removed her tights and her pants. It was painlessly easy. Somebody else was moving her hands, not her. Her mind was blank.

He took her hands and held them up against the wall, forcing her body forwards against his own, skin to skin. She felt his breath on her neck, and then his lips at her ear.

'I'm going to lick every bit of you. When you ask me,' Diego whispered, and Frances closed her eyes.

'When you ask me, I said. And look at me, don't pretend it isn't happening.' Diego pressed himself against Frances, his face an inch away from hers, then he let her hands free. Frances could feel his lips just brushing hers, as she could feel his prick pressed hard against her. Her mouth parted, waiting for his kiss, but there was only air. Diego didn't move.

'You haven't asked yet,' he said. His hands slid along her arms, then her sides, like summer rain on parched ground. When Diego raised Frances off her feet her legs moved in spite of herself to grip him around the waist. His mouth skimmed one nipple, then the other; touch became kiss, and kiss gave way to gentle bite.

'I remember that shiver,' Diego murmured. One arm hooked under her legs, the other supporting her back, he carried Frances next door. The huge bed stood in a pool of light, under the ring of ceiling spots. It was unmade, sheets and pillows still crushed, rumpled by the weight of his body, more welcoming than crisp, starched linen because his skin had already touched them, as her fingers touched him now, his skin smelling of good soap and hot afternoons, the sun still glinting in the flecks of gold in his eyes. She dug her fingers into his hair and pressed her mouth to his.

They rolled on to the bed. Everything became as it had been years ago, because neither of them had forgotten anything. There was no shame, their lips and their hands making up for lost time. Diego spoke only when Frances sobbed out loud.

'I love you,' he said, then he kissed her, a kiss as eager as a question. He knelt on the bed. Frances closed her eyes and waited.

'Say it, damn you. Just say it,' Diego hissed.

Frances looked at him, towering above her.

'Say it,' he insisted.

'I . . . love you,' she whispered.

'Louder. I can't hear you.'

'I . . . love you.'

'Say it again.'

'I love you ... love you love you love you,' Frances sobbed, and Diego kissed her again. Gently this time.

'Now it's going to be really good,' he said. His hands slipped under her buttocks, lifting her slightly, and Frances closed her eyes. She felt no guilt, only the blissful touch of his cock sliding into her, his body on hers, flesh upon flesh, a pleasure that killed both doubt and guilt.

Suddenly, out of nowhere, the image of Norman kissing her goodbye filled Frances's mind with terrifying vividness. She had justified coming here as inevitable, as something she had to do in spite of herself, an unavoidable sacrifice. Now she realized that if she stayed with Diego a second longer, she might never leave. She shoved Diego away from her and jumped from the bed.

'I hate you!' she screamed, rushing out of the room. She started getting dressed, half-fearing, half-expecting Diego to come after her. Frances glanced at the bedroom door one last time, but he didn't appear, and she left.

Fifteen minutes later, Frances was at home, shutting off the outside world. She resisted her impulse to draw the bolts and lock herself in; she ran upstairs instead, to the drawing room. She poured herself a large brandy, her fingers shaking as she tried to fit the stopper back into the decanter. Holding the balloon glass with both hands, she sat on a sofa and gulped down her drink as if it were medicine, as if she expected it to give her instant peace. It didn't. It merely burned her throat, and gave her an excuse for the fact that her eyes kept filling with tears.

The phone rang. Her hand lifted the receiver, then she let it drop again. She walked to the window and stood close to the curtain, to avoid being seen from the road. There was nothing unusual in the scene outside: a blonde woman walking a dachshund, an old couple loading Harrods bags into their car, a traffic warden issuing tickets on the other side of the square, but for Frances the familiar had ceased to be reassuring.

She forced herself to move away from the window, and started to straighten the pictures on the walls, although they didn't need it. She started to rearrange the objects and books on the coffee table, until she realized that what she was really doing was waiting for the phone to ring again. She left the room immediately and went to her bedroom, avoiding the sight of her bed. In her dressing room, she took a bag out of a closet, and threw in a few clothes chosen at speed, then rushed downstairs, to the kitchen. She found Eugenia in the laundry room, busy with the ironing.

'I'm going to be with Norman until Friday. I'll be back with Peter that evening, Eugenia,' she said. By the time she got into her car and drove away, it had started to rain.

'. . . But can the Government win? It is in marginal constituencies like Cheltenham, Darlington and West Swanton that the fate of John Major and his team will be decided.' The image of Norman Fellowes canvassing in the railway station filled the screen for a brief moment, then it faded. 'That report was by Mark Conroy,' said the presenter. 'And now to America, where George Bush is . . .' Norman reached for the remote control and turned off the TV.

'They gave me the closing shot. That's really good,' he beamed at Frances, full of hope and Frascati after their dinner with his agent and other members of his team in an upstairs room at a local restaurant in Swanton. The owner, who kept pictures of Mrs Thatcher and the Pope over the bar, among straw-wrapped Chianti bottles, gave special rates to the local Conservative Association. The evening had finished early, so they could all go home to watch the special report on marginal constituencies on 'Newsnight'.

Norman put the remote control on his bedside table,

turned off his light, and moved across the bed, until his leg touched Frances's, who was snuggled under the duvet, lulled by the sound of the wind in the trees outside. London seemed a world away from here, and she had forced herself to participate in the conviviality during dinner, pushing the memories of the afternoon out of her mind. Not for long.

'I'm so glad you came tonight. It was the nicest possible surprise,' Norman said, taking her hand, and she relaxed in the safety of his presence, until he began to stroke her forearm. He never approached sex directly, leaving himself a way out if Frances didn't respond with an encouraging signal.

'I wouldn't have thought so, since you chose to dance with Gail after dinner,' she scolded him lightheartedly.

'That's not fair. It was Luigi who turned on that ghastly music, and pushed me on to the floor. You were near the door by then, and I couldn't reach you.'

'You could have called me over.' The conversation seemed to have the desired effect, since Norman's hand now rested on her arm, motionless.

'You know I couldn't. Luigi pushed Gail on to the floor too, and she works like a dog for me. It would have been very unkind to leave her standing there.'

'You *are* nice,' Frances replied, glad for the meaningless banter, keeping her mind off her own obsessions.

'Don't tell me you're jealous of Gail, of all people. She's leaving after the election anyway. She's getting married.'

'Oh, I'm so glad for her. She's a very nice person,' Frances commented.

'I wanted to talk to you about that. If we win, and I move to the Cabinet, I'll have even less time for constituency matters than I have now. I'll need someone really efficient, whom I can trust, to be my secretary in the House.'

'I can't think of anyone right now,' Frances said.

'I thought *you* might want to help me. You're wasting yourself on that business,' he said, and Frances was touched by his embarrassment. Not at the suggestion, but at the likely possibility of being turned down. As she would have done, without second thoughts, if she felt less guilty towards him.

'Can you do that? It might seem like nepotism, and I wouldn't want you to get into trouble because of me,' she said, trying to find a gracious way out.

'That's not a problem. Lots of MPs employ their wives, and it makes sense. What do you think?'

'I don't know. I . . .' Frances was searching for an excuse other than her own work – she couldn't bring herself to use it. She didn't *really* care about it, and Norman knew that.

'Don't turn me away, Frances,' he pleaded. 'I know what's going on.'

'What do you mean?' She could feel her face turn white.

'You're drifting away from me. I could feel it the other night. You . . . pretended . . .' It was so unlike him to mention sex, no matter how obliquely, that Frances realized the depth of his concern. She was relieved by the fact that he was talking about them, not Diego. He didn't know anything.

'I don't blame you,' he went on. 'It's my fault, because we don't spend enough time together, and it will get worse after the election. I thought that it would help if you worked for me. We'd see each other during the day that way . . .'

Words can be filtered, emotions can be denied or controlled, but thoughts run free. Frances's first reaction was that Norman's offer would make it harder for her to see Diego in secret if he ever came back, and then she felt shame, as if lice were crawling over her head, unnoticeable to anyone else but intolerable to her, making it impossible to air her otherwise acceptable misgivings. Her work didn't mean *that* much to her; she saw it as marginally more exciting than being an interior decorator, an antique dealer, or any of the ersatz careers popular among women in her position. But having something that was hers, a part of her life that was independent from Norman, was important. In other circumstances, she would have been able to put her case convincingly, to him as well as to herself.

'Let me think about it,' she bargained. 'I'd have to close the office, and I can't do that from one day to the next.'

'I don't expect you to. I know you need time to sort things out,' Norman replied. Frances could sense his relief at not being turned down outright. She couldn't share his feeling, because she knew that her reason for being amenable was the very problem he was trying to stave off.

'We only have to try a bit harder, and everything will be fine,' he said, edging towards her under the blankets. Every problem has a straightforward solution for him, she thought enviously, then she felt his hand on her shoulder. She squeezed it gently before moving it away from her. No more was needed, in the unwritten code of gestures between any couple who have shared a bed for years.

'I'm terribly tired, darling. Do you mind if I go to sleep?' she said, aware that she was hurting him, and feeling helpless about it. She couldn't pretend again. Not after meeting Diego.

'Of course not. Goodnight, darling.'

Norman's tone was as loving as usual, but he didn't try to kiss her again. He made himself comfortable in bed instead, his back to her. Soon afterwards he was snoring, and Frances wished for his peace of mind. Norman loved her. He didn't need to lie. He had nothing to feel guilty about. He could sleep.

She couldn't.

Outside, the trees creaked and groaned in the wind.

SIXTEEN

'Peter, are you ready? We ought to go,' Frances shouted up the stairwell. There was no reply, so she went to his bedroom. Peter was sitting on his bed, his Sega on his lap, his fingers furiously punching at the controls.

'We *have* to go and buy your shoes now. I told your father we'll be in Swanton before lunchtime. He'll start worrying if we're late.'

'Oh, Mum!' Peter groaned, his eyes fixed on the screen. 'I was about to kill the dragon, and you made me die! Now I'll have to start all over again.'

'No, you won't. Turn that damned thing off.' Frances moved forward, ready to snatch the game away from him, but Peter rushed to the bathroom and locked the door.

'Come out now. This is ridiculous,' she bellowed.

'When I finish this game. It'll only take me a minute,' he pleaded.

Frances stood by the door. She would have to make a deal with Peter, the usual way to get him to do something he didn't really want to. At any other time she wouldn't even think about it, but today she couldn't bring herself to bribe him even in the smallest way.

'You've got five minutes, otherwise I'll throw that game away. I'll be downstairs, OK?' She left without waiting for an answer, and the inevitable further bargaining.

In the kitchen, Eugenia was giving a last-minute wipe to the immaculate worktops, her coat already on, her bag by the door. She was spending the weekend at her sister's home in Finsbury Park.

'I'll be helping Norman on Monday, so I won't come back after I take Peter to school, Eugenia. You can take the day off and stay with your sister, if you want,' Frances offered. Eugenia's expressions of gratitude were curtailed by the ringing phone. Frances was about to pick up the kitchen extension, but thought the better of it and went to the study to take the call there, preparing herself to hear Diego's voice. As she had done every time the phone rang during the last two days, even in the country.

'Is that Frances?' It was a woman's voice, and Frances relaxed immediately.

'Speaking. Who is this?'

'It's Victoria Bromfield. I met you at the Kalomeropoulos party. I tried to find you there, but you had left, so I asked Arianna for your number.'

Frances remembered Eugenia saying that a lady had called a couple of times while Frances was away, but she hadn't left any message.

'Oh, hello,' she said, endeavouring to sound politely distant. She had a pretty good idea why Victoria Bromfield was so keen to talk to her again.

'I placed you at last. I think we met in Punta del Este, years ago, at the house of Teresita de Tannerie . . .'

'I'm sorry. You must be making a mistake,' Frances replied, fighting her impulse to slam the phone down. It was a situation she had rehearsed in her mind for years, and at any other time she would have found it easier to handle, but now she felt like a besieged army trapped in a valley, with the enemy in control of the commanding heights, coming at her from all directions.

'Mum! I'm fed up with waiting! Let's go!' Peter bellowed through the door.

'I'm sure it's you. You were married to Diego Santos. Your name was Melanie then,' Victoria persevered, and

287

Frances held on to the phone in numb confusion. She heard the front door slam shut.

'Melanie, you said? You must have met my sister there. I know she married an Argentine, but we weren't very close. I lived in Los Angeles, and she moved to New York when we were in our teens.'

'How extraordinary. Eyes like yours are so unusual that I thought . . .'

'They run in the family. We both look very much like our mother,' Frances interrupted her.

'I see . . . Do you know what became of her? She was so charming . . . She had quite a hard time in Argentina in the end, and then she disappeared . . .'

Frances guessed that Victoria didn't believe her, but she didn't care.

'I have no idea. We lost touch before she married, as I told you. I'm very sorry, but you caught me when I was about to leave for the country with my son. We ought to have lunch though. It's difficult for me now, because of the election campaign, but . . .' *I'll call you* wouldn't be enough, so Frances reached for her diary. 'I'm free on April 17th . . . Oh, I'm so glad. Shall we meet at San Lorenzo at one? I hope you and Jack are free on the evening of the 20th. I'm planning a small party for Norman then, if everything goes well . . . Lovely . . . See you on the 17th, in any case.'

Frances put the phone down. She hadn't thought of a party until now, but Norman would like the idea, and cultivating the Bromfields was the only, remote chance of Victoria accepting her story; she was likely to rate a useful social friendship higher than making an enemy of Frances for the sake of gossip. She wished she'd never have to lie again: to Peter, to Norman, to Diego, even to meaningless people like Victoria. Not least, she wished she didn't have to lie to herself, a dream easily achieved if she were prepared to give up everything she had.

Frances waited for a moment, until she had stopped shaking, then opened the door. There was no sign of Peter. She called him, then she heard noises from the kitchen.

'Come on, darling, let's go. We're late,' she said. Eugenia came through the door, carrying her bag.

'Peter said he was fed up with waiting for you. He'll meet you at Harrods, in the sports department,' the housekeeper announced. In her mind, Frances saw Peter walking alone down the street, among the Saturday crowd at the store, and she remembered the scene at Spitalfields. She had refused Diego, and she couldn't tell what he would do next. No matter how hard she tried, in spite of all the evidence to the contrary, a side of her still wondered if he hadn't sent the men after them in the first place.

'You should have stopped him!' she cried.

'But Señor Norman said that Peter should come and go as usual!' Eugenia protested. She was right, but Frances had no time to apologize. She ran out of the house, hoping to find Peter walking up the road. There was no trace of him.

She raced into Harrods through the Hans Road entrance, looking left and right as she swept through the men's department, ignoring indignant looks as she pushed past shoppers blocking her way. The lifts were too far away, and they would take too long. She headed for the escalators instead, rushing the steps, floor after floor, until she found herself in the white glare of the sports section. There were dozens of children and teenagers around, some on their own, some with their parents, but none of them was Peter. Frances stood by the shoe display, then she grabbed a passing assistant fiercely by the arm.

'I'm looking for my son. He's ten, about this tall, with dark hair, and he's wearing a red track suit . . .'

'I haven't seen him, madam. You're sure he's in this department?'

'He asked me to meet him here. He's looking for trainers . . .'

'He's ten, you said? He might have been told to go the children's shoes department, on the fourth floor.'

Frances ran downstairs. It only took her a couple of minutes to realize Peter wasn't here either, as it took all of her sense of control not to give in to a combination of panic, anger at Peter for being so careless, and despair. She couldn't believe that he had been snatched from the street, because it was Saturday morning in Knightsbridge, and there were hundreds of people about. Frances tried to guess where he could have gone, but the options were endless: he might be looking at toys, or records, or electronic games, and she had been in the store for twenty minutes already. Defeated, she approached one of the women behind the till.

'I can't find my son,' she said, hearing the rising panic in her own voice. The assistant beckoned a security guard nearby, who asked Frances for a description of Peter.

'I'll take a look around for him, and I'll tell my colleagues on the fifth floor. Don't worry, madam. Please wait here.'

A few minutes later, the man came back.

'My colleagues are looking for your son. We'll page him if they can't find him. Please come with me, madam.'

The guard accompanied Frances to the lower ground floor, where he explained her predicament to one of the women at the Customer Services desk.

'Don't worry, Mrs Fellowes, it happens all the time. Your son will be here soon. Please sit down,' the woman said with a sympathetic smile. A moment later, the message was given over every loudspeaker on each floor: 'Peter Fellowes, your mother is waiting for you at Customer Services. Please contact a member of staff immediately.'

'They'll find him,' the woman at the desk reassured Frances, who was looking in every direction, and hardly heard her. She didn't want to face the possibility that she would never see him again. There were so many stories in the papers about children being snatched by their fathers and taken abroad, and now it could happen to her. Almost as horrifying as that possibility was that it would be her fault, for taking Diego at his word, for hiding the facts from Norman.

'Peter!' she screamed, when she saw him walking towards her at last, next to an uniformed guard, a glowing smile on his face. A second later she hugged him, tears pouring down her face.

'Don't do this ever again, do you hear me?' Frances sobbed, then she turned to the woman at the desk.

'Thank you very much,' she said, still crying. 'Excuse me for making such a fool of myself.'

'Don't worry, Mrs Fellowes,' the woman replied cheerfully. 'It's always the mothers who cry in these cases, never the children. What were you doing, young man?' she asked Peter. 'That's a big box you've got there.'

It was only then that Frances noticed the large cardboard box under Peter's arm, half-wrapped in a green and gold Harrods plastic bag. At first she thought that Peter must have bought the trainers on his own, but the box was too big, and he had no money.

'It's a present. A video camera,' he beamed.

'Must be your lucky day,' replied the lady, smiling at them as they walked away.

'A present from whom?' asked Frances as soon as they were out of earshot.

'That nice man at Spitalfields. He came up to me. He said he was glad to see me again, and he asked me if you were all right . . .'

'What else did he say?' Frances interrupted him.

'Nothing much. He said I deserved a present for being so brave, and he asked me if I would like a video camera.

Can you imagine! He must be filthy rich. I heard the announcement while he was paying. "Your mother is looking for you. You shouldn't keep her waiting. Tell her to be careful. I'll call her next week," he said, and he left. What did he mean?'

'I've no idea, darling. I wish you'd remember what Daddy and I told you about not talking to strangers, particularly after what happened.'

'But he wasn't a stranger, Mum. I'd met him before, and he saved us. He's jolly nice.'

'Just do what I ask you, OK? Now come on, let's go,' Frances replied. Her panic was turning into fury, and she struggled to keep it under control. She pushed the door open.

'We haven't bought the shoes,' Peter protested.

'Forget the shoes. We'll get them another time.' She couldn't wait to get out of London.

As usual, Norman woke up earlier than necessary. Time to himself in the morning was his daily self-indulgence. Or used to be; like everything else in his life, it had been largely encroached on by his duties. By the time he had showered, dressed, shaved, and was ready to face the world, it was still too early for the newspaper boy to have made his round; he went to the kitchen and turned the kettle on. He found the silent house oppressive; he didn't like being on his own, particularly at the times meant to be family occasions, so he prepared his solitary breakfast and ate it at speed. Cup of coffee in hand, he picked up the bundle of late correspondence he had left in the hall the night before, and went to his study.

It didn't take him long to scan the few letters in the pile, delivered to the local Conservative Association by constituents either too thrifty or too hard-pressed to post them to the House of Commons, then he picked up a video cassette.

Although it was unlabelled, Norman guessed that it came from Nick Ball's public relations agency. He had engaged their services a few months ago, and coaching him on television was part of their brief. This would be the recording of his recent appearance on 'Newsnight', and Norman wished it wouldn't be so easy to identify the programme, because he hadn't been on any others yet. He was surprised not to find the usual report with their comments; it was annoying to pay dearly for less than perfect service.

He turned on the video and slipped the tape into the slot. The screen became a flurry of lines and dots in black, grey and white, then turned into a recognizable scene in colour, showing a naked couple in bed, under a flood of light. The grainy image and the unprofessional lighting only contributed to the grossness of the picture, and Norman sighed in mild annoyance. Obscene mail was an inevitable fact of life for politicians; years ago, at the beginning of his career, Norman had found a turd with a blue rosette on his doorstep. As the torrid action unfolded on the screen, his initial disgust gave way to mild curiosity, but good sense prevailed, and he reached for the 'Eject' button.

As he was about to press it, Norman froze. Sharply in focus, unmistakable, Frances's face came into view. He stood still, shocked by what he saw. It wasn't the evidence of her infidelity that hurt him at first: that would follow. It was Frances's hunger, her passion towards the unknown man that wounded Norman; it was a side of her he had never seen before. At last he managed to turn off the TV, before slumping into an armchair.

Norman disliked emotion, because he didn't trust it. He knew it could spread over his perception like bacteria in the bloodstream, an invisible enemy that had to be checked before it inflicted permanent damage. Reason was the best medicine, so he applied his mind to his problem. 'Crisis' was a word he never used for himself; he had learned that words too often became facts.

He loved Frances. In his own imperfect way, but he loved her. He couldn't imagine loving her more, even as a possibility. Falling in love with her had been the second and last time in his life when Norman had allowed recklessness to take over, and he had never regretted it. Unlike the first time, when he had left his first wife – or lost her – because of hurt pride. After a few years of marriage, they had found that Norman couldn't have children. Some time later, his wife told him she was having an affair, and Norman reacted as he thought he should, a moment of anger that led to three years of sorrow. With hindsight, he was grateful for his impulsiveness then, because otherwise he wouldn't have been free when he met Frances, nor would he have fallen so strongly for her.

Like all politicians, Norman knew the importance of luck and timing, both pivotal to the appearance of Frances in his life. She had really needed him then, and being able to play her saviour, feeling that he was indispensable to her, was irresistible. He would have loved her in any case, but circumstances are as crucial as essentials, all of them cards in a constantly reshuffled deck that only rarely produces a winning hand.

Therefore Norman had reasons to be both grateful for and mistrustful of impulsiveness. Cautious by nature and from experience, he was not going to allow emotion to influence a fundamental decision, particularly if it could mean great personal loss. He wouldn't make the same mistake again.

After the initial shock, the evidence of infidelity didn't surprise him. He had sensed for a long time that something was wrong in their marriage, but the tape couldn't have come from Frances. It was unlike her to bring up the issue in such a shabby manner. If she had decided to mention it, she would have taken the opportunity when Norman himself had raised the subject of their marriage a few nights ago. The tape could be an attempt at blackmail, but then it would have come with a demand for money, or a threat. The likelier explanation was that it was a desperate act by her lover, whoever he was, to force the issue, to make it impossible for Norman and Frances to stay together. The man wanted Norman to take the step Frances couldn't bring herself – or didn't want – to take. If so, it was his battle to fight, not Norman's, and desperate people made mistakes.

Norman stood up, and went back to the TV set. He pressed the 'Eject' button, took the tape, and walked to the fireplace. Calmly, he lit a match, which he dropped on to the bed of crumpled newspaper, kindling and logs. At first, only wisps of smoke emerged, then the budding flames licked the wood. He waited patiently until the fire was established, then he dropped the tape among the flames, watching as the black box began to melt.

He stood by the fire, staring at the bubbling mass of burning plastic belching foul-smelling smoke, then he wiped his eyes and left the room, shutting the door behind him.

It was only while they were cruising along the M11, when she had given up on any further attempts at conversation with Peter, who was examining the camera on his lap and the instruction manual in his hand with the concentration of a heart surgeon, that Frances wondered how Diego could have known she and Peter would be going to Harrods that morning. Frances tightened her grip to regain control of the wheel and stop the slight swerve as the next possibility hit her. Eugenia knew. She knew their plans for the weekend, as she knew everything about the family. 'There's very little that money can't buy,' she remembered

Diego saying. He could have offered Eugenia money beyond her dreams, all the money she needed to buy a house in Santander. She had been saving for it ever since arriving in England.

Frances was ashamed of her suspicions as soon as she considered them seriously. Eugenia was scrupulous to the point of silliness, producing laborious accounts of every penny spent on household bills. She had sat by Peter's bedside when he had been ill as a small child, forcing Frances to go to bed to rest. She didn't like Norman, but no more than she mistrusted men in general. 'The source of all evil,' she called them, with the same intensity of feeling she deployed in taking care of Frances and Peter. If Diego had approached her, Eugenia would have been more likely to smash a bottle over his head than to take his bribe.

Diego was making her distrust others, when it was a virtual certainty that he was having them watched – or watching them himself. He could have been waiting for his opportunity to find Peter alone, until it came along. Frances glanced in the rearview mirror, as if she expected to see him tailing her car. Perhaps he was, but she couldn't tell. He could be in any of the cars behind, unidentifiable in the usual Saturday morning traffic on the motorway. But Diego wasn't stupid. He had said many times that he wanted Frances back with him, the only statement he had made so far that she believed without qualification. To snatch Peter away from her would make Frances hate him irrevocably, as she should hate him now – but couldn't. Diego wouldn't kidnap Peter alone. He would abduct both of them, as he might have tried to do that Sunday, and Frances found herself cherishing the possibility. It would free her of any responsibility or any guilt for the consequences. She wouldn't betray Norman, or at least not willingly. Like most self-absolutions, the fact that it would be based on an excuse wouldn't make it less effective.

Like a greyhound released from a cage, her memory raced over the years, and she saw herself and Diego naked on the boat, drifting away in the Caribbean without a care in the world, a scene as concrete in her mind as the flat, banal landscape of Essex in front of her eyes. It was possible to leave everything behind, and start again; she had done it twice before. Frances allowed herself the luxury of her fantasy, like a sleeper who wakes up before the alarm clock rings, snuggling up under the bedclothes and refusing to go back to sleep to prolong the illusion of freedom, an illusion that shattered as soon as she thought about it seriously.

Excuses weren't enough. Diego had given her a excuse to meet him at his flat. Frances had convinced herself that she despised him then, that she was only agreeing in order to see him off, although she knew he couldn't be trusted to settle for less than what he wanted. She had gone to bed with Diego regardless because she wanted to, a knowledge that she found intolerable, not only as evidence of her own disloyalty to Norman, but as proof of the shallowness of her current life.

She glanced at Peter, who was still absorbed in his manual, and regretted her thoughts. Not everything was shallow in her life, and she couldn't leave everything behind again. Life without Peter was unthinkable, and to bring him along would mean wrenching him away from all he knew and loved. His life would be wrecked, and Peter was *her* life now.

'Give me a hand with this bag, Peter,' Frances said, leaning over the open boot. As they approached Swanton, she had phoned Norman's office from the car. He wasn't there, and Frances was told that his schedule for the day included canvassing the residential estates around the industrial park, at the edge of the constituency, and that he wouldn't be back until the evening.

Peter took the bag with one hand, holding his treasured video camera carefully with the other, and Frances wondered how she would explain Peter's new toy to Norman.

'Listen, it would be better if you hid that camera for the time being. Daddy will never believe what happened, and he will think that I bought it for you, and that we made up the whole story. He always says I spoil you,' she told him as they walked towards the house. The green shoots on the clematis beside the door had spread exuberantly since she left two days ago, Frances noticed. She also noticed from Peter's face that the idea of not using his new treasure during the weekend did not appeal to him at all.

'You can tell him that you bought it to film him when he talks to people. He'd love that. He wouldn't mind if you lent it to me,' Peter suggested.

'That would be a lie,' she said sternly, and Peter gave her a slightly puzzled look.

'I thought you didn't want any trouble,' he said.

Frances sighed, and opened the door. The first thing that struck her was the acrid smell of burnt plastic. Alarmed, she checked through the house, but everything seemed as impeccably normal as usual.

'Can I go and play with Nicky?' Peter asked while Frances was clearing the table after lunch. Nicky Howard was Peter's best friend in the village. Frances was still shaken after her experience that morning; the prospect of letting Peter out of her sight terrified her.

'Ask him to come here instead, so you can show him the camera,' she said. Five minutes later, as she finished putting the dishes away, she could see Peter through the window, rushing up the path to meet his friend.

The phone rang.

'Hello, Mrs Fellowes.' Frances recognized the twangy voice of Gladys, her cleaning lady. 'Mr Fellowes asked me to come in this morning, because he said that you were coming back today, and he wanted your bedroom and your bathroom to look really nice. It took me a couple of hours to tidy up everything.'

Frances was touched by Norman taking the trouble to have the house prepared for her arrival, in spite of his busy schedule, and she was amused by Gladys's tactful way of ensuring she would be paid promptly for the extra work.

'I noticed everything looked impeccable,' she said. 'I was going to call you anyway. I'd be grateful if you could come up for a couple of hours in the morning next week, because we'll all be here then.' She had promised Norman to stay with him until the election, next Thursday, and Peter's Easter break at school started on Wednesday. There was no point in sending him back on Monday, only to live in terror for the next two days.

As she hung up, Frances realized she had forgotten to tell Miranda about being away from the office next week. She started to look up Miranda's home number, only to put her diary aside. It would make no difference if she called now or later. Her work seemed almost irrelevant.

The thought of Diego kept haunting her, the image of his face closing down on hers, his breath on her cheek, and Frances immersed herself in domestic chores to exorcise it. She checked the larder and wrote out a long shopping list, then took a leg of lamb out of the freezer for Sunday lunch. There was no point in making plans for dinner until she heard from Norman. He might want to go out, or ask some of his colleagues to join them here. Frances took one look at the boys playing ball in the garden, then moved to the other side of the house.

She unpacked Peter's small bag in his bedroom, checking that he had enough clothes in his cupboard for the week ahead. Gladys had cleaned his bathroom; there were unused bars of soap in the dishes, a new roll of lavatory paper in the basket, and clean towels on the rail. Their bedroom was equally tidy. Now she regretted Gladys's early endeavours, because they deprived her of the most expedient way of ignoring the thoughts buzzing in her head. She considered joining Peter and his friend in the garden, but she knew that her appearance would put an instant end to their fun. Frances felt as trapped in the house as she felt in her life, suffocating in lies that multiplied by the day, like weeds. She was both accomplice and perpetrator, victim and guilty party, and there was only one way out.

'Hello, darling! Did you have a good journey?' Norman shouted cheerfully as he closed the front door. The drawing room lights were on, but there was nobody there. Or in the kitchen. He went back to the hall. He could see that Peter's room was dark, and so was their bedroom.

'I'm here,' he heard Frances voice call as he walked past one of the spare bedrooms.

'I wish you had seen how wonderfully it all went this afternoon,' he said, coming into the room. Frances was sitting in an armchair by the window, away from the circle of light thrown by a bedside lamp. 'I'm sure I'll win. People were being incredibly supportive.' There was something too glib, too strained about his enthusiasm, as if Norman was putting it on for her benefit, she thought.

'What are you doing sitting here on your own? Where is Peter?' Norman asked.

'He's with the Howards.' Frances stood up. 'He's having supper with them. I want to talk to you.' She expected him to ask, 'Something wrong?' in the concerned tone she knew well, but he didn't.

'Is it something to do with our conversation the other night?' Norman asked instead.

'In a way.' Frances had been rehearsing this moment for

hours, waiting for it, but now she confronted Norman's trusting face, and she hesitated. Telling him was necessary, if she was to save what they had, but nothing would be the same afterwards. She could pull back still.

'Diego has come back. He faked his death all those years ago, and now he's found me again,' she said bluntly, denying herself the chance to prevaricate. At the time, Frances had been surprised by the relative ease of her acceptance of Diego's unimaginable reappearance, only to realize that it was because somewhere in her mind, unseen but unrelenting, she had always nursed the hope that one day he would. Now she expected Norman to be shocked, astonished or angry, but he seemed unmoved by her revelation. The man who lined up his socks in the drawer according to colour and sorted out his change into tidy piles when he emptied his pockets appeared to be perfectly at ease with a fact that disrupted every aspect of their lives. Perhaps she knew him as imperfectly as she had known Diego during their marriage. Perhaps marriage was as much an understanding between strangers as anything else.

'What does he want?' he asked as calmly as if Frances had announced that a travelling salesman was at the door.

'He wants me to go back with him. And he wants Peter.'

'That's absurd,' he said, and Frances wondered if his statement applied without qualification, or only as far as Peter was concerned. Or maybe *she* was filtering his words through her own uncertainties.

'I've . . . gone to bed with him.' Frances remembered her botched attempt at Catholicism in Buenos Aires, the awkwardness of confession only relieved by the certainty of absolution. 'Diego forced me to do it. He said that otherwise he'd make a scandal, and ruin our lives. That's why I agreed, but I couldn't go through with it.

'You must believe me,' she added after a pause, guessing

from his silence that he didn't, and she couldn't blame him. Frances didn't know if she believed herself.

'I believe you,' Norman said finally. 'I only wish you had told me as soon as he contacted you. It must have been hell for you, but panic is a bad counsellor. He's in no position to threaten us. It would mean jail for him, and he knows it.'

Norman was offering supportive understanding, the best Frances could have hoped for, but now she realized that it didn't solve anything. It left her with a choice she didn't want to face.

'Is he still in London?' Norman asked.

'I don't know. He told me he was leaving on Wednesday,' she replied.

'He might not come back. He must be travelling with false papers, and I could arrange for him to be stopped at the airport.'

'I don't know his new name,' Frances said.

Norman thought for a moment.

'The election is on Thursday. Try to stall things if he contacts you before then,' he said. 'If he insists on making trouble, you will arrange a meeting, and we'll have him arrested. He will be deported immediately for travelling on false papers, and then it will be someone else's problem.'

She could be free of Diego if she betrayed him. It hadn't been an option until now, before Norman knew.

'I don't want Peter or you dragged into a scandal,' she replied.

'He doesn't want a scandal either. It can only be a scandal if he owns up to who he really is, and then he would lose everything. He's bluffing, Frances.'

She hoped it was true.

'Did he have anything to do with the attack on you?' Norman asked.

'I don't know. I don't think he had, but I can't be sure.'

Frances looked down, avoiding Norman's eyes. She hadn't mentioned the incident at Harrods that morning.

'I thought Peter should stay here this week,' she said. 'It doesn't make any difference if he loses a few days at school, and I'd rather have him with us.'

'He loves school. It would be a shame for him to miss it unnecessarily,' Norman said. 'But you must do whatever you think is right,' he added quickly, as if eager to dispel the slightest chance of disagreement. Now Frances wondered if his words went beyond what he seemed to be saying.

'Perhaps you're right,' she agreed, partly in conciliation, but also because she realized that Peter would be bored alone with her in the house for days. He was getting too old for that. As soon as she made her decision, she wondered if she was being honest with herself. Not having to look after Peter made it easier for her to come and go. Every option was double-edged.

'Is there anything else you want to tell me?' Norman asked quietly. If there was any doubt in Frances's mind as to his ability to read the situation, it vanished now.

'No, not at all,' she heard herself say. There was relief on Norman's face.

'They're showing that Schwarzenegger film Peter was so keen on, and we'd be just in time for the last show. We could take the boys,' he suggested, now in his usual brisk voice.

'I'm sure they'd love that, but I can't stand that kind of film. I don't mind staying here; I have quite a few things to do, in fact,' she replied.

'I'll go and fetch them. We'll be back around eleven,' Norman said, kissing her. A moment later, she heard his car driving away.

Frances remained where she was, long after he had gone. Norman hadn't rejected her. He hadn't even suggested that she stopped seeing Diego, *unless he made trouble*. Norman wasn't putting pressure on her in any way. As usual, he had come up with the most sensible solution. Or a compromise. If there was a difference.

It was just after eleven that night when the lights of Norman's car shone through the windows. By the time he and Peter came in, Frances was waiting in the hall.

'Go to bed now, darling, it's terribly late,' she said.

'You should have seen it, Mum. He could turn into *any-thing*!' Peter bubbled, giving Frances an excited account of the film on their way to his room.

'That's great, sweetheart. Now brush . . .'

'. . . your teeth, wash your face, do a wee, and go to bed. I know,' Peter said, and Frances smiled.

'I'm glad you've learned it at last. Goodnight, darling.' She kissed him, closed the bedroom door, and went back to the front of the house. Norman was in his study.

'The boys really enjoyed the film,' he said as she came in. 'It's getting late. Shall we go to bed?'

While she was on her own, Frances had considered sleeping in the spare bedroom that night. The idea of lying next to Norman, as if nothing had changed, had seemed ludicrous to her then, as ludicrous as rejecting his offer of peace and normality seemed now. She followed him, hoping that his reconciliation strategy would not include making love. Tomorrow perhaps, but not tonight.

Her misgivings were unnecessary. While she made herself ready for bed, Norman gave her a detailed account of his campaigning that day. He moved into the bathroom as soon as she got into bed. Unusually for him, he ran a bath, and seemed to linger in it for an inordinately long time. When he came out at last, the sleeping pill Frances had swallowed was about to take effect; she fell asleep almost immediately after he kissed her goodnight.

She woke up around four o'clock in the morning.

Norman asleep by her side, Frances stared at the ceiling. It would never be the same for them; Norman knew about her infidelity. His generosity embarrassed her, although his silence could be as expedient as it was admirable. It all depended on his reasons, but then she could say the same about herself.

Frances was trying to fall asleep again, when a scream broke the silence.

'Mummy!'

There was terror in Peter's voice; Frances jumped out of bed, rushed to his room and turned on the light. Her son was sitting bolt upright in bed, his eyes wide open. She sat next to him and embraced him.

'I'm here, darling. What is it?'

'I saw them! I saw them here. The two men were standing by my bed . . .' Peter began to cry, and Frances held him tight.

'They were here . . .' he sobbed. She looked at the window. The shutters were closed, and the burglar alarm was on.

'It was a nightmare, sweetheart. There's nobody here, except us. Nobody can get in,' she said soothingly.

'Don't go, please! Don't leave me alone.'

'I'm not going anywhere, silly. I'll stay with you all the time, I promise.' Frances cradled him in her arms, and stroked his head until Peter fell asleep. She didn't break her promise. She was still there holding him in her arms when morning broke.

The vicar blessed the congregation, and people started to leave the village church. Standing in the second pew on the right, Norman, Frances and Peter waited until old Lady Walsham, piloted by her family, left the front pew, then followed down the aisle. As soon as they reached the font near the entrance, Norman rushed ahead.

'I want to make sure that the photographer from the *Swanton Chronicle* is here,' he whispered to Frances. He was, and the family posed for a few shots in the spring sunshine. Norman immediately moved on to greet members of the congregation, followed by the photographer, while Frances and Peter stood amidst the tombstones, waiting for him. Mrs Jameson, a sweet old lady who lived down the lane, came over to them.

'My, you have grown up, Peter,' she said in her crackling voice once they had exchanged pleasantries, then turned to Frances again. 'I've got something for you. There was a very good-looking young man standing next to me. I've never seen him before. He left halfway through the service, but he asked me to give you this.'

Frances took the folded service sheet. Inside, she found a scribbled note.

'Two guys are following you. I'll call you at your office tomorrow. Be there.'

The message was in Spanish, and it was in Diego's handwriting.

SEVENTEEN

'Why don't you come back after taking Peter to school? You were going to stay here this week,' Norman said. They were in the kitchen, clearing up after an early supper. Peter had gone to his room, to change into his uniform.

'I wanted to, but I really ought to talk to Miranda, otherwise she'll mess up the bookings for the opera tour to Bordeaux. I'll try to be back as soon as possible, probably by tomorrow night. I'll be here in good time for election night,' she added. Her guilty conscience turned conversation into dialogue through an interpreter. She hadn't told Norman about Diego's message. It will work if we *both* make it work, Norman had said; she took it as an invitation to frankness, but it could mean complicity in silence too.

'Peter showed me the video camera you bought,' he said.

'I thought you'd like to have a record of the last days of the campaign. They told me it's very easy to use,' she said glibly.

'That would be nice,' Norman agreed. 'Although I'm not sure it's a good thing to have a video camera around all the time.'

Frances dried her hands. There was the merest shade of an edge to his tone, as if there was more to the remark than a mere comment, although his face remained entirely guileless. She wondered if she had reached such a degree of hypersensitivity that she assigned a double meaning to even the most banal words.

*　　*　　*

307

'Goodnight, darling. See you on Wednesday.'

Frances kissed Peter. Pyjamas on, teeth brushed, he and the other boys in his dormitory were ready for bed. In the corridor, the headmaster's wife was busily moving from door to door, supervising bedtime, and Frances wondered if she should ask her to keep Peter in the school grounds at all times until the holiday.

'Goodnight, Mrs Stewart. Please keep an eye on him, he's still a bit nervous after the mugging,' she said instead, before she joined the other mothers on the stairs.

'You must be very busy with the election. It's so exciting,' one of them said to Frances. 'I saw you in *Hello!* You looked marvellous, as always.'

Frances wondered if *everybody* read that damned magazine.

'It is very exciting. Only a few more days to go now,' Frances replied, trying to get away.

'I'm sure your husband will win. It would be a disaster if the socialists got in now,' the woman went on.

'You're absolutely right,' Frances agreed mechanically. Until this moment, she had never considered the possibility of Norman's defeat, and how much easier everything would be if he weren't a public figure.

'You know, people are talking about the curse of *Hello!*, because every couple they interview ends up in trouble afterwards, like the Yorks and the Spencers,' the woman added with a sweet smile. 'It's nonsense of course, but it's rather funny, don't you think?'

'Hilarious,' Frances snapped, walking towards the stairs without saying goodbye. She headed for the car. Alone, she felt much less certain about her change of plan, but it was Norman himself who had insisted that Peter shouldn't miss school unnecessarily, as he had suggested she should agree to meet Diego again. Handing him over to the police was the inevitable solution; it was impossible to live like

308

this, in permanent fear of his next move, Diego tearing away scraps of their life bit by bit.

After a few minutes' drive she approached the motorway junction. 'Cambridge – Swanton' read the first sign she came to. She could go back. Frances was about to indicate, then she pressed the accelerator down again, and raced to the London turning.

Her hands clenched on the wheel, Frances focused on her driving, to keep any other thought out of her mind, but feeling in control of her car did not make up for the overwhelming sense of having lost control of her life; everything she had done over the last two weeks had been because of somebody else. Now she didn't know what she really wanted. She couldn't tell.

It was easier to decide what she didn't want. She didn't want to hurt Peter, and she didn't want to end her marriage. Whatever else it might be, it was real, as her marriage to Diego hadn't been. She didn't want Diego back in her life. She wanted him physically, but only if she could have him and forget him, until the next time. Frances wanted him as a creature of her imagination, fleshed out or not at her whim, a wish the more pressing because it was impossible.

Frances didn't want to start again. Every stage of her life had meant uprooting herself, giving up everything she knew and loved, either because it had turned to ashes or in hope of something better, something stable, something fine and good. Her marriage to Diego, her life in Argentina, had put paid to the promise of hope. She had settled instead for the certainty of contentment, and it had worked until Diego came back, showing her with just one magic trick, like a conjuror from hell, how shallow, how empty it all was.

There was a bridge ahead. Frances stared at its central pier, a looming mass of concrete in the middle of the road.

She was driving at eighty miles an hour; it would only take a slight turn of the wheel to hit it. It would be easy, quick, everything solved in a second. Frances had almost closed her eyes when she heard angry hooting behind her, lights flashing in her mirror. There was another car, a couple of yards behind her. Jolted from her trance, she swerved to the left without thinking; the car behind her zoomed past, its driver giving her an angry glance, two fingers in the air, and her hands relaxed on the wheel. I'm going mad, she thought as the memory of Peter, scrubbed clean in his fresh pyjamas, came back to her.

Frances took a deep breath and concentrated on the road again, moving into the slow lane at the first opportunity. She stayed there, cruising steadily, safely, until she reached London.

'You can take the rest of the week off, Miranda,' Frances said as soon as her secretary walked into the office the next morning. She had been sitting there since eight o'clock, waiting for Diego's call, her impatience building up.

'You might have told me on Friday,' Miranda complained. 'I could have stayed in the country, you know. You must think that I'm your slave.'

Frances jumped at the opportunity to let her rage loose.

'How dare you talk to me like that. You're fired!' she screamed. 'Get out, right now. I'll send you your cheque today. Get out, do you hear me?'

'I'm sorry, I shouldn't have said that,' Miranda apologized meekly. 'Piers dumped me on Saturday, that's why I'm a bit upset this morning.'

'Then go and be upset somewhere else, you stupid girl! I can do what I like in my own business. I can set it on fire if I want to!' Frances rose to her feet, but Miranda had already fled in shock; she locked the door, pacing up and down the room for a while, until she felt calmer, partly with relief that she had got rid of Miranda at last.

Maybe losing control was the only way to find out what she really wanted in life. And the only way to achieve it.

The phone rang at three o'clock.

'Did you have a good weekend?' Diego asked, and Frances could imagine the smirk on his face. Her fingers gripped the handset as if it was his throat.

'I'm not alone, so I can't tell you.' She didn't want Diego appearing here without notice. They had to meet at a pre-arranged place.

'Don't lie. Your secretary left this morning, and she hasn't been back.'

Frances sat down.

'You are a shit, Diego. A miserable shit,' she said.

'You *are* alone, you see? You'd never say anything so coarse otherwise. Although you look rather different than usual on the video. Not so elegant,' he chuckled.

'What are you talking about?'

'Come on, don't pretend.'

'I really don't know what you mean!' She waited for his reply.

'Your husband didn't tell you anything, then,' Diego said eventually. 'He must be very clever – or very weak. Not many men can put with the sight of his wife having a good time with someone else.'

'What have you done?' she cried.

'I sent him a video of you and me in bed. You always say that truth is best, so I thought he should have it.'

She hadn't been wrong in sensing a sting in Norman's remark about videos last evening. Shame and anger leapt at her like starving dogs.

'I told Norman about us anyway, but you are a bastard. A complete bastard. You are . . .' she ranted.

'I told you I'm not a gentleman. I'll go to any lengths to get you back,' Diego interrupted her. 'That's why you want me, and that's why you'll come with me in the end, because you want to. But you made such a big thing of my being a liar that I thought it was better to put the record straight. You lied to him, and he lied to you. Or at least you didn't tell each other everything, if there's a difference. Everybody lies, when it's convenient.'

'I lied at first, but only because I didn't want to hurt Norman,' she countered.

'You can say that about any lie, big or small. If that's your own excuse, why can't you extend it to me?'

'Because your lies cost us our marriage. You lied about something that costs lives. You and your parents killed people. Can't you see the difference?'

'I've never killed anyone myself. I just sold them something they wanted. I can't be responsible for anybody else's stupidity.'

It had been María's argument. Hearing it now from him enraged Frances to the point of silence.

'Is that your borderline, your point of no return?' Diego went on. 'Are you saying that you find me despicable because people died as a result of my business?'

Every word made Frances more determined to crush him, to hand him over to the police. Her impulse was to hang up, but then it would mean waiting for Diego to call again. Tomorrow. Or next week. Or next month.

'Where did you meet your husband?' he asked. His unexpected question disconcerted her.

'In Rio, while you were in New York. But only for a moment. We really met in Buenos Aires, after your death,' she said waspishly.

'What a charming coincidence,' he said. 'Did he ever tell you what he was doing in Buenos Aires?'

'Of course he did. Unlike you, he didn't keep anything from me,' Frances snapped.

'What was it?'

'Something to do with electronic exports.'

'That's a rather vague description.'

'What are you getting at?'

'Your great moral divide. Have you ever heard of John Fitzroy and Neil Campbell? Do the names mean anything to you?'

'No more than any of the other nonsense you've come out with so far.'

'You must have heard of the *General Belgrano*, though. The British always said that the *Belgrano* was part of a pincer movement against the task force, but the Argentines denied it, on the basis that the *Belgrano* was sailing towards home. The fact is that the Argentines found out that British nuclear submarines were in the area, so the game was up for their Navy, and they ordered their ships to return, but by then the British counter-attack was on its way. The submarine went after the *Belgrano*, while the Harriers tackled the Argentine ships to the north. Do you follow me so far?'

'Yes. But I can't see why you need to lecture me about the Falklands war,' Frances said.

'Among those Argentine ships were some frigates, ordered from England, and delivered in the early Seventies. Military hardware is a marvellous business, because whatever you sell becomes second-rate in no time at all. There's always something better coming along. The market never dries up. By the late Seventies, the ground-to-air missile systems on those ships were up for renewal, and new systems were commissioned from England. The change was completed in 1981. When the Harriers attacked, two of them were brought down, and the pilots died. They were the two guys I mentioned. It's rather ironic, don't you think? Englishmen killed by English missiles . . .'

Diego paused, and Frances waited.

'Don't you have anything to say?' he asked. 'You must be disgusted by this. People died because of others making a profit. That's exactly what you accused me of.'

Frances sat back. It *was* María's argument all over again, and she had expected Diego to come up with a worthier justification.

'I don't care. My brother died because of people like you, not because of arms dealers. They might be equally worthless as people, but you must be pretty desperate to use them as a justification for yourself,' she replied.

'I don't need to defend anything. I know what I am, and so do you, but I'm glad you find arms dealers so worthless, because the man who arranged the missile deals was your husband.'

'That's not true!'

'There's a loyal woman speaking,' Diego chuckled. 'What do you think he was doing in Brazil? And Argentina? And Chile? Your husband made a hell of a lot of money in the Seventies, selling whatever he could lay his hands on to whoever would buy it. The Generals all over South America were desperate for new toys, and he obliged them.'

'I don't believe you. You're making it all up, as usual. You invent whatever suits you. You have no proof.'

'I still have contacts in Argentina. I can get proof, if you want it, but you never know what can happen once a story starts coming out. "British soldiers killed by weapons sold by Minister" can't be the kind of headline he's after. Are you sure you want me to provide you with evidence?'

Frances didn't believe a word he had said.

'Why are you telling me this?' she asked. 'It doesn't make any difference about how I feel towards you.'

'I *know* how you feel about me. That's not the problem.

If it weren't for your silly moralizing, you'd be with me now, and everything would be as it was, as it should be. I love you, and Peter is my son, not his. Now that you have to choose between two shits, as you put it, you don't have to waste time on side issues. At least in my case, what you see is what you get. Unless you find not knowing – or pretending not to know – a better option. It matters so much to you, in my case, because you love me, not him. You know it. Don't . . .'

'I can't go on talking about this on the phone,' Frances interrupted him. 'We should meet and talk.' The prospect of Diego being sent to jail and rotting there for ever was irresistible.

'That's not easy,' he replied. 'I told you you're being followed. I have to be careful.'

'It shouldn't worry you. You can tell your men to leave me alone.' .

'My guys are better than the ones I'm talking about, otherwise I wouldn't have noticed them. I don't know who they are. They're not policemen, because they move out of the way if they see anyone official. Your husband must be having you watched.'

'He wouldn't do that.'

'How can you be so sure? By now you know he doesn't tell you everything.'

'Maybe they're following *you*,' Frances retorted, irritated by his last remark.

'They aren't, but it's risky to meet now. And there's no point, unless you've changed your mind. You know where we stand,' Diego said.

'That's for me to decide,' Frances replied. She tried to sound faintly teasing, hoping to weaken his reluctance. Diego remained silent for a while.

'Don't even think of bringing the police into this,' he said finally. 'I'll see if I can arrange something. I'll call you on Wednesday morning. Keep the afternoon free, just in case.'

'. . . And he said that you sold the missiles to the Argentines. I thought he was trying to use whatever threat he could come up with to force me to see him, but then he was very reluctant about it. He said he'll call again, on Wednesday. You could talk to the police in the meantime, and find out whom I should contact.'

Phone in hand, Frances waited for Norman's reply.

'Did he say if he has any proof?' he asked eventually, and his words reverberated in her ears. It was true, then.

'Why didn't you tell me?'

'Tell you what?'

'That you sold arms.'

'I haven't said I did, but I've made a lot of deals in my business life, Frances. You can't expect me to tell you about every single one of them. It was all before our marriage anyway. What you or I did or didn't do before we met shouldn't concern either of us.'

'That's neat,' she said. 'But I would have preferred to know. At least it would have given me the chance to decide if I liked what you did or not.'

'From what I saw on Saturday, I wouldn't have thought that mattered much to you,' Norman blurted out. The immediate silence at either end of the line confirmed to both that they knew what he really meant. 'I'm sorry, Frances, that was a stupid thing to say. Of course you're right, darling, but let's not lose sight of our immediate problem. He's trying to blackmail us. What does he want?'

'I told you. He wants me and Peter back with him. He wants his family,' she said, trampling over all the hedges laid around her marriage for years. Diego's reappearance had shown it up for what it was: a stage set carefully arranged, light and shadows falling on precisely the right areas, where the players moved with the ease of experience, leaving certain corners of the stage alone so as not to expose the illusion. Until Diego had burst in like a new director, exposing the flaws in the performance. Frances was tired of a simulation that had run its course.

'Why on earth would he want that?' Norman murmured, and she almost gasped; it would have been impossible for him to say something like that face to face.

'Peter's got nothing to do with him,' he insisted, and suddenly Frances understood. Over the years, the combination of good intentions, silence, and love, had turned the original lie into unquestionable fact for Norman. *If* he remembered them, the real facts made no difference. To spell them out now would either be pointless, or a stab to his heart. Frances couldn't do that.

'I know. I suppose it's just another threat,' she replied at last.

'He's a crook. Maybe what he really wants is money,' Norman said. He was trying to divert the issue, and they both knew it.

'He might, but I don't think so. By now I don't know what he wants.' Frances wished that the conversation would end. The closer they got to the truth, the more difficult it was for Norman and her to say what they really meant, to be honest with each other.

'It might be better to leave the police out of this, until we know more,' Norman said. 'Don't put yourself at any risk, of course, but perhaps you should meet him again, and try to find out what he's really after. There's always a solution.'

At last everything fell into place. Frances thought that what was always available was an arrangement, if not a solution, and she could understand Norman's reasons for needing one. In his own manner, he was trying to get what he wanted, minimize the risk, and disregard anything else.

As Diego had done years ago, and was doing again now. Only she had seen her choices as irreconcilable options, forcing her to sacrifice what she couldn't. It was time she tried to find her own compromise, as Norman was suggesting. They might be more alike than she had thought.

'Leave it with me. I'll see what I can do,' she said, taking refuge in platitudes.

'Thank you for calling. The office will be closed until Monday 13th April. If you have any queries, please leave your message, with your name and telephone number, and we will contact you as soon as possible. Please speak after the tone.' Frances ran the tape and checked the recording, then switched on the answering machine.

Ever since her conversation with Norman the day before, she had concentrated on completing tasks in hand, here or at home. She had given Eugenia the week off. The thought of having to face anybody else, to make conversation, was almost as unbearable as waiting for Diego to ring her. Frances dreaded her anticipation every time the phone rang, followed by disappointment if she heard any voice but his. He had said Wednesday, so he was unlikely to phone before then. Diego enjoyed the game, and games only made sense if there were rules. She was breaking them by leaving her office, but he could phone her at home. She preferred to wait on her own territory. It was time she laid down a few rules herself.

Frances glanced at her desk, at the unusually tidy room. Every paper had been filed, every letter answered, every outstanding bill paid. She didn't need to come back until Monday.

As she locked the door behind her, it felt like a farewell, as if she was saying goodbye to the place, a thought so absurd that she dismissed it in the time that it took her to turn the key. A minute later she joined the crowd on the

King's Road. Since her conversation with Diego, she had made a point of looking over her shoulder every now and then as she walked in the street, to see if she spotted the men he said were following her. This time Frances didn't bother. Whoever they were, it no longer mattered.

EIGHTEEN

'You weren't at your office,' Diego said. Even on the phone, Frances could detect a hint of annoyance in his voice.

'Maybe we're both unpredictable today,' she replied.

'You couldn't be unpredictable to me. Not in a thousand years.'

'You sound nervous. Anything wrong?' she asked politely.

'If there's somebody around and you can't talk, I'll call you later.' He *was* on edge.

'No, there's no problem at all. I'm on my own. Would you like to come over?' she offered.

'You must think I'm stupid. Have you got the police there?'

'I wouldn't want the police involved after what you told me about Norman.'

'So you know it's true then,' he said. 'How do you feel about it?' There was a crackle in the line.

'I hope you're not recording this conversation,' Frances said anxiously, as if it mattered to her.

'I don't need to,' Diego replied, sounding more relaxed. 'The bad line is because I'm phoning you from my car, just in case your friends try to track me down.'

'At some point we'll have to start trusting each other, you know. You'd better decide when. It's up to you,' Frances said.

'It wasn't like this last week.'

'A lot has changed since then. It shouldn't surprise you.'

'I'm glad you know what you want at last. I knew you would.'

'I don't know what I want, but I do know how I feel now,' Frances said.

'Do you still love me, then?' There was a note of pleading in his question, and the expectation in his voice almost erased everything else, almost made Frances forget.

'I don't know. Don't ask me now.'

'I'll ask you again this afternoon,' he said.

'You're assuming I can see you this afternoon. Or that I want to see you this afternoon. I haven't said that.' Frances enjoyed his silence.

'Don't play games with me,' Diego said eventually.

'Why not? That's what you've been doing all along, playing some kind of game.'

'I just made you see the facts. *You* said that you wanted the truth in everything.'

'Pity that you weren't so straight when it mattered.'

'Neither was your husband. What's the difference? Lies are lies.'

'There are different kinds. You know that. It matters in a different way.'

'Because you don't love him. Come with me, and everything will be as it was. We'll live wherever you choose, exactly as you want.'

'While you sell coke,' she said.

Diego chuckled. 'I'm respectable now. Well, almost respectable, but that can change. I don't need to do anything. I'd be whatever you want me to be.'

'You're crazy. I'll never leave Peter. The deal is me, on my terms. It doesn't include him.'

'We've discussed that. You wouldn't have to leave him. There's always a solution. It's up to you.'

'I know it's up to me, and I know what I want. You decide. Otherwise we can carry on like this.'

'Talking on the phone, you mean?' he sneered. 'That's not a life. I want you.'

'And I want you. At times, not always, you and I carrying on with our separate lives. That's the way I want it.'

'An affair with my own wife? That *is* romantic, but I thought you disapproved of lying,' Diego said.

'Sometimes it's all we can have,' she murmured. 'I want to see you today. We've wasted too much time,' she went on briskly. There was silence at the other end.

'I'm leaving tonight,' Diego said after a while.

'When are you coming back?'

'I don't know.'

'I want to see you, Diego.'

Another pause.

'Be ready at three o'clock. Somebody will collect you. And you must follow all my instructions,' he said at last. Whatever he meant, it suited her. It had become a game again, and there were no emotions in games.

Inhaling the rich scent of the mimosa oil that formed a sleek film on the water's surface, Frances lay in her bath. She'd had her shower that morning; this was sheer indulgence, and the more enjoyable for that.

The warm water spread over her shoulders in smooth ripples as she stretched her legs and reclined against the back of the tub. She would have Diego, on her terms, as she could have had him from the first day, if she had been prepared to accept that she wanted him. She had believed in his threats because they gave her an acceptable excuse to see him, a circle of self-deception leading nowhere. All it took not to be a fugitive was to stop running away, either from her fears or her feelings. She would have him now, and many other times.

Her eyes closed, Frances remembered the best time of her life, with the excitement of a dissident huddling against the radio to listen to a message of hope from beyond the borders. She saw herself and Diego in New York or Buenos Aires again, in different rooms, on different beds, fragments of images never forgotten, as vividly recollected as the reflection of her face in his eyes as he leaned towards her. The taste of his mouth, the heat of his skin, his whispering in her ear were also pieces of a mosaic she put together now, as lovingly as a restorer working on a fresco, far away from the ground, gingerly balancing herself on the scaffolding of her dreams, until the picture was as refulgent as new.

The water was cooling. Frances reached for the bowl on the bamboo stand next to her, and chose a fresh bar of soap from the heap inside. She rubbed it on her soft sponge, the thick, creamy lather filling its pores until she felt it slippery on her fingers. Water streamed down her body as she stood up. Cupped in her hand, the sponge glided over her skin, leaving long lines of foam, and then she turned on the shower, the clean smell of fern rising as the foam slid down her legs, gathering in a white, frothy ring on the surface of the bath.

At last, she stepped out of the tub and took a towel, rubbing herself dry with slow deliberation. Dipping her fingers into a jar of body cream, Frances spread it on her arms and shoulders first, then over the rest of her body, until the even coat gave her skin a smooth sheen. She inspected herself in the mirrored wall. Over the last few years, her glances at the bathroom mirror had become more anxious, reassuring rather than confirmatory. She would be forty soon, or at least sooner than she would have liked. Now she stared with pleasure at her reflection, as it used to be, because Frances saw herself as she imagined Diego would see her.

The clothes she had chosen earlier were laid out on her bed. She dressed slowly; unhappy about the shade of her tights, she changed them, then decided to do away with them altogether. Her legs looked too white, she thought, as she slipped on her dress and examined herself in the cheval glass. Frances went back to her dressing room and pulled out a dove grey trouser suit. It had been an impulse buy, totally wrong for her lifestyle, as she'd realized once she had taken it out of the bag. She hadn't worn it once.

Frances put the suit on, inspected the result, and was pleased with what she saw. Her hand slid under the lapel, to rearrange it, and her fingertips skimmed the lace of her bra. She shed the jacket, removed her bra, then put the jacket back on. The silky lining felt cool on her naked breasts.

By the time she added the final touches to her make-up and dabbed scent on her neck, it was nearly three o'clock. Frances was on her way downstairs when the doorbell rang. She slipped her coat on and picked up her shoulder bag before opening the door. A stocky man, wearing jeans and a bomber jacket, stood outside.

'Taxi for Melanie,' he said.

'Thank you. It's me,' she said after a second. The name didn't sound strange when Diego used it, but it was the first time in years that she had heard anyone else call her that.

'Any luggage?' the man asked. His question alarmed her, but to ask for clarification would trigger his curiosity, make him pay attention to this particular customer. He was a typical London cabbie, his leather-framed brass identification plate on a chain resting on the rounded ledge of his belly, his shining black cab purring by the kerb. Better to be just another passenger. Frances put on her sunglasses.

'No,' she said, stepping into the car, as the driver closed the door behind her. A few moments later, they joined the westbound traffic on Brompton Road, and Frances stretched out her legs, trying to make herself comfortable.

She was too excited to be relaxed, as she was too excited to feel guilty. Perhaps she felt a kind of guilt, a contradictory emotion, because it was only about feeling so guilt-free. It was impossible to feel guilty about something she wanted so much. She would feel guilty tomorrow. Or the next time.

There was always a solution, as Frances had realized after that morning's conversation. Norman feared exposure, Diego feared being caught, she feared for Peter. Norman wanted peace, Diego wanted her and Peter, and she wanted what she already had. Plus Diego, but on her terms. It had seemed impossible until now, until she saw it for what it was, an exercise in manipulation. Diego's threat was effective for as long as it remained unfulfilled. Once he destroyed Norman's career, there would be no reason for her to do what he wanted, unless Frances wanted it herself, in which case the threat would not have been necessary in the first place. Diego knew it, as he knew he couldn't get Peter back. All of them wanted whatever they could get, without destroying what they had. That was their common ground.

The car began the slow climb towards the Hammersmith flyover. Once they were on the far side, the driver turned left, following the 'M4' signs, and Frances felt a twinge of fear.

'Where are we going?' she asked. The driver gave her a surprised look.

'Heathrow Terminal Two, lady. That's what I was told you wanted.'

'Yes, sure. I don't know the route, that's why I was asking,' she said, stressing her American accent. Frances wondered if she should ask him to stop, so she could get out of the car. The possibility of Diego kidnapping her had not crossed her mind until now; after a moment's thought, she dismissed it. There would be hundreds of people around her, and she didn't have her passport. Diego had said he was leaving; now that he knew she wanted him, it would be just like him to see her at the airport before boarding his flight, to keep her waiting until the next time.

'Go faster,' she told the driver. Soon she saw the signs for Heathrow. It wouldn't be long now.

'That car behind us is driving me nuts,' the cabbie said suddenly. 'If I go fast, he goes fast, if I slow down, he slows down . . .' He shook his head.

Frances looked back. There was a blue car behind them, twenty or thirty yards away. The sun struck its windscreen, so she couldn't see inside. She tried not to look too often, but the car was there every time she checked. It was still behind them when they pulled in outside Terminal Two.

'How much is it?' Frances asked.

'It's all taken care of, lady.' Only then did she notice that the meter wasn't running. The driver handed her an envelope.

'The gentleman asked me to give you this when we arrived,' he said.

Frances put it in her pocket, and walked towards the doors. Out of the corner of her eye, she saw a man getting out of the blue car. He began to walk towards her. She rushed inside, then followed the yellow signs to the nearest ladies' lavatory. She locked herself in a cubicle, and opened the envelope. There was a small piece of paper inside, with a phone number. A central London number. Frances waited for five minutes, hoping that the man would have given up searching for her, before coming out. He wasn't there, as far as she could tell, although he could be anyone in the crowd. She hadn't got a good look at him.

The telephones were nearby. She dialled the number.

'Diego? I'm at Heathrow. There's someone following me . . .' she said as soon as she heard his voice.

'This is a recorded message. Go to the Iberia counter,

and ask for an envelope in your married name. The old one. It will tell you what to do next.' The message ended, and Frances put the phone down. Her first reaction was to take a taxi straight back home, followed by the realization that she couldn't stop now.

The girl at the counter gave her a charming, professional smile.

'My name is Melanie Santos. You have an envelope for me,' Frances said, and the girl looked under the desk top.

'Here it is, Mrs Santos.'

Melanie smiled back at her, and took the thick brown envelope. She thought of moving away, but then decided that she would be safer here, next to the girl and in full view. She tore the envelope open. There was an Iberia ticket inside: London–Madrid, M. Rivas. There was also a Spanish passport. She opened it, and saw her photograph, but the document was made out in the name of Marcela Rivas. Frances opened a folded sheet of paper slipped into the passport, and read the message typed on it.

> They must be following you. Check in with this ticket, and go through passport control. They won't follow you there. Once you are in the departure lounge, wait until they announce the flight, then tell a member of staff you've left your wallet at your hotel, and that you can't board the plane. They'll take you to Arrivals. Go through immigration with this passport, and come out. Somebody will be waiting for you at the Meeting Point.

Frances stood there. She read the message again. The exit doors were yards away. She could still leave. She turned to the girl.

'Where do I check in?' she asked.

*　　*　　*

The immigration officer looked at the passport, then stared at Frances. She smiled at him, hoping that it would conceal her nervousness, and prepared herself for another round of explanations, but the man gave the document back to her and turned to the next person in the line. Frances moved on, fighting her impulse to look back. At times she had wondered what life with Diego would be like, if only to strengthen her refusal to consider it as a option. Now she knew.

She reached Customs, and headed for the 'Nothing to Declare' area. A couple of Customs officers were chatting, while another one meticulously searched the luggage of a pony-tailed young man in jeans. Whatever they were looking for, it wasn't a mixture of excited anticipation, fear and guilt, because they paid no attention to Frances. The frosted glass doors opened in front of her, and she was out.

She knew Diego wouldn't be there, but somehow she had expected him. Frances scanned the waiting crowd, until she noticed a man holding up a board. 'Melanie' was written on it in bold letters.

'You're waiting for me,' she said. The man looked at her closely, then pulled out an envelope from his inside pocket.

'I was told to make sure you had green eyes,' he explained as he gave it to Frances, then walked away. 'Take a taxi to the Sheraton Skyline, on Bath Road. Room 547', read the slip of paper inside.

'Come in. Quickly,' Diego said. He checked the corridor outside before closing the door. 'They should have lost you at the airport, but you never know.' He saw her expression, and smiled.

'Relax. You're here now,' he said. Frances noticed his suitcase and briefcase on the luggage stand, his raincoat folded beside them.

'You *are* leaving then,' she said.

'I told you this morning. You should always believe me.' He led her to a sofa by the window, beyond the bed. Frances sat down. She liked the comfortable impersonality of the room, its anonymous intimacy. It wasn't a room made for memories.

'What would you like to drink?' he asked, and the innocuous social routine grated on Frances's nerves.

'Anything. I don't mind,' she replied. Diego opened the minibar.

'I hate these things. The idea is so cheap, don't you think? But maybe you like them.' There was a sting in his voice, and Frances looked up, but he seemed totally immersed in his task. Diego gave her a glass, and sat at the other end of the sofa.

'I hope you still like brandy. You used to,' he said.

'I still do. I haven't changed *that* much,' she replied.

He gave her a quizzical look.

'That's not what I thought this morning. Deceit didn't used to be your style.'

'I'm not deceiving you. Don't tell me that you are worried about anybody else,' Frances replied. Diego took a sip of his drink.

'You *are* cheating me, not to mention Mr Fellowes. And yourself, which is worse. Why did you come here?' he asked.

'What kind of question is that? You know why.'

'I want you to tell me yourself,' he insisted.

'Why?'

'Because you'll like your reasons even less than I do.' Frances jumped to her feet.

'I didn't come to be lectured on morals by you, that's for sure,' she said angrily. Diego stood up too, and came towards her.

'I leave that to your husband, but he won't mind you

329

being here, I imagine, if he gets what he wants. Is that the deal, that you fuck me to keep me quiet?' His hands ran down her back. 'Piece of ass for a piece of paper . . . that would be really good.' Diego pushed Frances away, then went to his briefcase and opened it. He pulled out a heavy brown envelope and threw it on the bed.

'There, that's what you want,' he said. Frances didn't move, so he picked up the envelope and brought it over to her.

'Come on, check it. You have to make sure you've got what you're after.' Diego pulled out some papers and held the photocopies up to her face. Frances half-glimpsed the Argentine crest, and the *Ministerio de Defensa* heading on them.

'It's all there. You can go now,' he said, walking to the coffee table and pushing the envelope into her shoulder bag. Diego opened the door.

'What are you waiting for?' he asked.

'I don't want to go,' Frances murmured, then she started to cry. She heard the door close, and then she felt his hands on her, his cheek against hers.

'I'm sorry,' he said. 'I couldn't bear the idea that you were pretending. I had to know.'

Her fingers gripped his hair. It felt silky to her touch, as did his lips when Frances kissed him. His hand undid the buttons of her jacket, and moved to her breasts.

'You weren't pretending,' Diego murmured, pulling her towards him. His fingertips ran along her spine, barely touching her, and Frances shivered. She wanted Diego to tear their clothes off, to feel him naked against her, but nothing happened. He just stood there, then moved away from her.

'It's no good. It won't work. You know it,' he said.

'This is crazy,' she said. '*You* came back. *You* said that you wanted me. *You* said that if I went to bed with you, you'd leave me alone. What do you want now?'

'I've told you. I want you to come away with me. Anything else would be a sham. You and I deserve better than that.'

'It's not possible!' Frances screamed. 'Can't you understand? I can't live with you, always worrying if you'll be there the next day. You shouldn't have gone. We can't change that.'

'Why would I leave you again? We'll be together, and we'll have Peter. That's all we need.'

'And you expect Peter to love you? You expect him to leave his father, everything he knows, and love you, a complete stranger? You know it can't work. You're chasing a dream.'

'It's not a dream, Melanie. We can make it happen again. I'm sure Peter would rather be with you than with Norman.'

Frances thought for a moment. It was crazy to be tempted, but it was tempting to be crazy.

'Maybe,' she said. 'But I don't know if I'd rather be with you than with him.' She saw his face, and wished she hadn't said it.

'You're lying,' Diego hissed. 'Or maybe you aren't. Maybe you enjoy this, having me around you, risking my life to see you. It makes you feel good, your little revenge, to keep me hoping that one day you'll change your mind, doesn't it? Then you can have everybody: me, your husband, your child, the way you want it. The trouble is *I* don't want it that way.'

He glared at her.

'It's funny. We want the same thing in the end, in different ways. We both want our lives as they used to be.'

Frances nodded.

'You want me out of your life then. Dead,' Diego said.

'That's not true.'

331

'Isn't it? Ever since I found you, didn't you wish that I hadn't come back? Not for a second?' He waited for her answer.

'There you are,' he said. 'The truth. But you can have your wish, and I can't have mine.' Diego walked to his briefcase, and opened it. He pulled out a gun from under the papers, then he fixed a silencer on to the barrel. He stared at the gun for a while before turning to Frances.

'You can have your wish,' he repeated, raising the gun to his head. 'You only have to ask. Nobody will hear a thing, nobody saw you come in. You can have your life back. Just ask.'

'Put that gun down. You're being ridiculous,' Frances snapped, using anger to stifle her panic. She had been mad to come here.

'Funny word, "ridiculous". I'm about to blow my brains out to prove my point, and you find it "ridiculous". You've changed, Melanie. You really have become very English.'

'Diego, put that fucking gun down!'

'Why? It will be so easy. Done in a second, and then you're free. That's your problem, you don't want something badly enough to give up your silly scruples and get it. Nobody is watching us, Melanie. I'll be gone for ever. Nobody will ever know. You only have to ask.'

She rushed to the door, but Diego blocked her way.

'You can't run away from what you want,' he said, pushing her back, walking towards her. She only saw his face, the skin of his temple dimpled where the barrel of the gun touched it, the slow, steady tightening of his finger. Frances closed her eyes and jumped forward, to grab the gun away from him. She thought she heard the trigger click as he pulled, but not the explosion, because her scream silenced everything else. When she opened her eyes again, Diego was standing there, smiling at her, unharmed.

'The catch is on,' he said, his finger stroking the small

332

lever on the side of the gun before dropping it on the bedside table. 'I just wanted to show you what you really want.' He took her in his arms and held her tight against him, stroking her head, gently wiping the tears from her face.

'I've got something for you,' he said, slipping a ring on her finger. 'Now everything is as it was before. As it should be.' Frances looked down, and saw the glow of Imperial jade on her hand.

'It came up for auction in Geneva last year. I knew I'd find you again one day,' he murmured.

They kissed unhurriedly, with the assurance of knowledge. Only their hands were impatient, until their clothes were a heap on the floor. The touch of his lips on her skin, the taste of his mouth, the slow dance of his fingertips, everything was as Frances remembered, as it had to be. Time made no difference. A pleasure so great, so desperate in its certainty, made time irrelevant; nothing mattered but this.

'I love you, Melanie,' Diego whispered in her ear, and the guilt and the doubt disappeared, leaving a dark precipice made for freefall; her fingers wrapped around his cock as she guided him inside her, and she waited for the crash, for the end that would set her free.

There was no end, only the fragile lull of contentment, a pause worth having only to break it, to start again, flesh touching flesh, lips touching lips, the smell of sex hanging over them like storm clouds. It was when her head rested on his chest, listening to his heartbeat, that Frances asked the question which mattered more than anything to her.

'When are you coming back?' She felt his hand stiffening its grip on her shoulder.

'I'm not coming back. You're coming with me,' he replied.

She sat up and looked at him.

'You know I can't do that. I can't.'

'You can. You only have to do it. You have your pass-port, I've got the tickets. Everything is arranged. We'll go together. You'll like Spain.' He said it as if they were discussing a holiday.

'I can't go. I've told you that I'd never leave Peter,' she said.

'What do you want? Explanations? You'll never do it, then. Go and get him. We'll take him with us.'

'You must be mad.'

'No, *you* are mad, if you think we can stay apart after this. I'm not going to spend the rest of my life sneaking back to London, to see you only when it suits you. I won't do it.'

Diego got out of bed, and went to the bathroom. Through the open door, Frances could see his beautiful body in profile as he leaned over the basin, framed by a rectangle of light spilling into the room. Night had fallen outside.

'That's not a life, that's a torture. You may want to live like that, but don't count on me,' he said, his voice raised over the sound of the running tap. Frances looked around her, at the hotel room dimly lit by borrowed light. Its anonymity had appealed to her at first, but now she saw it for what it was, a sordid little hiding place. She saw herself lying to Norman week after week, year after year – they would be conniving in mutual silence, choking them like slow poison. Diego was right, for then they would have nothing. Worse than nothing, because she would live with the regret of what could have been, in the uncertainty that she could have had him again, and the knowledge that she had not. It would be torture.

'I have a beautiful house in Mallorca,' he went on. 'It's an old stone farmhouse, on top of a hill, surrounded by olive trees, and you can see the sea from there. It's a great place for children. Lots of them. We're still young. You'd love it there.' Frances didn't need to look at Diego to know he was smiling, enjoying his certainty that she would do what he wanted, even if she had to leave Peter behind. And suddenly she hated him. She hated him for describing what could have been theirs if he hadn't destroyed it in the first place, if he hadn't betrayed her as he had betrayed everybody else, as he would probably betray her again, in time. He was holding up her dream in front of her eyes with the exaggerated vehemence of a market stall holder displaying flawed goods, a dream that was meaningless without Diego, but impossible if it included him.

'There's a small cove at the bottom of the cliff. I keep my boat there. Remember when we went sailing in Miami? It will be like that, day after day. You always wanted a place of our own . . .' His words scrambled in her ears as the memory of the past crushed the chance of an impossible future. There was no future.

Her mind became blank, like a newborn coping with sounds and images beyond its grasp. Slowly, calmly, Frances got out of bed and took the gun.

Diego was still describing his dream when she shot him.

NINETEEN

Peter gulped the last of his glass of milk, then stood up, his white-clad figure edged by the sunlight pouring through the windows behind him.

'I hope the weather will stay like this. I'll see you later,' he said, picking up his cricket bag and moving towards the door. As he walked past the head of the table, Frances reached for his arm and stopped him.

'Wait a minute,' she said. 'You're not quite old enough yet to give up on kissing your mother goodbye. Tough guys still kiss their mums, you know.'

'Don't be a bore,' Peter mumbled, reluctantly brushing his lips against her cheek. Norman raised his eyes from the *Sunday Times*.

'Good innings, sport,' he said. 'You can read about your Dad later.' He patted the thick pile of newspapers by his side.

'Sure. Later,' Peter said in a voice that held little enthusiasm, then he rushed out.

'Don't look so glum,' Frances said to Norman. 'Three weeks is a long time at his age.'

'I want him to be proud of me. Not everybody has a father in the Cabinet,' Norman replied, in a tone calling for her support in the matter.

'He *is* proud of you. We are all proud of you,' Frances said, knowing what was expected. Norman smiled, then carried on with his reading.

'There's something here about Aids research that might interest you,' he said, passing a page to Frances. Soon after

336

the election, once Norman's appointment was announced, a friend on the Committee of Aids Appeal had asked Frances to join them, and she had accepted.

Frances began to read. It was a piece about research for a vaccine in America, as vague in its promise as any other article on the subject. She guessed that Norman had given her the article to avoid being distracted by conversation while he finished his own reading. Her eye wandered over the page, and a small story caught her eye. 'Heathrow murder mystery still unsolved.' The information took only a couple of paragraphs. Almost a month after the crime, the police had made little progress. The original identification of the murdered man as Fernando Rivas, a Spanish citizen, had turned out to be a false lead, since his papers were forged. Aeroplane tickets to Madrid had been found in his hotel room, one of them in the name of a woman presumed to be his wife. The investigation was now focused on Spain, where the police were searching for her whereabouts, as well as clues about Señor Rivas's real identity.

Frances looked at Norman. She hadn't said anything to him, and they hadn't discussed Diego again. He couldn't know. It had to be a coincidence.

She stood up and cleared the breakfast things before moving to the old table under the window. The sun cast shadows on the thick oak surface, on the scars left by chopping knives over the years, giving the wood the texture of old hide. Frances peeled the potatoes already waiting in a bowl, laid them in an oiled roasting tray, and slipped them into the Aga, under the meat. Norman heard the solid thud of the oven door closing, and raised his head.

'What are we having for lunch?' he asked.

'Lamb,' replied Frances, and Norman went back to his reading, reassured by old certainties. She reached for the beans, soaking in a glass bowl, and picked up a vegetable knife from the block on the window ledge. Her eyes took in the still beauty of the sunny scene outside: the peace of her garden, the ducks on the pond, the grass of the village common beyond the hedge, the cricketers. Even in the distance, Frances could recognize Peter among them, and she smiled. Only the tiny figures in white, the blue sky and the golden-grey of the church spire broke the virtual monochrome of the landscape. Green was everywhere, the rich green of early May, still to be exhausted by the heat of summer.

The scene reassured her, like budding fruit on a young tree after a frosty winter. Peter had been the one that mattered, and he would have the life she wanted for him, the life she had never had as a child, the safety of his parents' love. She was prepared to live with her memories, until they faded over the years, old letters in a seldom-opened drawer. Diego himself was becoming a memory again, as he had been for so long, and Frances had learned to keep memories at bay. Only in her dreams his face appeared with frightening vividness, waking her like an alarm bell. Unlike memories, dreams were unruly rebels, but they could be ignored, and one day they might go away.

Frances began to slice the beans. Against the silver gleam of the blade, their deep, velvety hue would have seemed as vibrant as any of the greens outside, if it weren't for the sun turning the ring on her hand into a drop of liquid light, a green richer than any other.

She wore it every day, but Norman had never asked about it.

EPILOGUE

From the verandah, it was hard to say where the water ended and the land began. The grass around the house sloped towards the reeds swaying in the breeze, a rippling surface melting into the river beyond. The house was on stilts, high enough to give the old man in the rocking chair a commanding view of his land, but even from this vantage point he was unable to discern the other shore. Only at midday, in the full blast of sunshine, would he be able to see the fringe of jungle across the water, a fuzzy edge of green against the rusty red of the wide river, but now it was early morning and the sun was rising, tentative shafts of light piercing the swirling mist.

The old man stood up and walked to the balustrade, his hand reaching for the whistle he kept on a ribbon round his neck. He blew it, and waited. One after another, huge white dogs emerged from the surrounding forest and raced towards the house. In a second, the pack was gathered at his feet, leaping up at him, their wild barks shattering the silence. The old man smiled, slipped his hand into the large steel can on a table by his side, and hurled one large piece of raw meat to the dogs. There were other pieces in the tin, enough for all of them, but he held back, enjoying the sight of the animals fighting for their food, until he lost interest and tipped the bloody contents over the edge.

The verandah encircled the house. The man walked to the back and went slowly down the wooden steps that creaked like old bones under his weight. He didn't stay on the path, but moved to the thick grass instead, which glittered with dew; the smell of damp grass was one of the pleasures of his morning walk. Although he was wearing boots, he kept an eye open for snakes. They were unlikely to come near the house, but one never knew. The small ones were the worst, their fangs sharp enough to cut through leather.

He walked past the sheds, past the radio aerial taller than the palm trees, past the satellite dish, until he reached the razor-wire fence. By the gate two men armed with machine guns came to attention as he approached.

'Good morning, Don Amilcar,' they said in unison. Amilcar Santos merely nodded in reply and kept on walking, until he reached the radio cabin.

'Any news from the trucks, Américo?' he asked the operator.

'They left Bolivia at midnight, Don Amilcar. I should hear from Pedro in Santa Concha in half an hour.'

There was no need to tell the man to let him know immediately if there were any news. They all knew the rules. After his downfall in Argentina, Amilcar had spent years rebuilding his drug business here in Paraguay, and he had succeeded. He hadn't done it for the money. Even after Diego's betrayal, there had been more money in his other accounts than he could ever spend. Rebuilding his business was the first step towards rebuilding a life he had loved and lost.

Amilcar headed back towards the house again. He climbed up the rear stairs briskly, opened the mosquito screen and went inside, but he didn't slow down. There was a spring to his step now, because he was eager to get to the garden on the riverside, as he was at this time every morning. It was quicker to cut through the house; nevertheless he paused at the front room, as usual. The maid had opened the shutters, but the deep gallery prevented the sunshine from reaching the windows. Amilcar wasn't wearing his glasses; in the murky half-light, the gilded curlicues of the French furniture cramming the room glinted like the eyes of animals lying in ambush. Following his instructions, Amilcar's agents in Buenos Aires had bought María's favourite pieces when their house had been auctioned by the Government. Even the huge portrait of Aunt Meme, now presiding over this room as it had over María's salon. It looked cumbersome here, and its gold frame rested against raw timber planks, not ornate panelling, but those weren't the kind of details Amilcar bothered about, as he didn't notice the delicate furniture slowly coming apart in the hot, damp air. It would still be here when he died, and that was enough for him.

The light outside made him blink. He had to hurry now, and he pressed forward, towards the river, although his heartbeat echoed in his chest like the steps of a platoon about to break ranks. Amilcar only slowed down to catch his breath when he saw the outline of the statue by the shore, still in the shadow of the trees nearby. Over the years, he had timed his walk perfectly, to reach the sculpture precisely at the moment when the rising sun struck the white marble, and the stone came alive.

The full-size monument had been carved in Asunción, by someone who had been described to Amilcar as the best sculptor in Paraguay. He didn't know about that; María understood that kind of thing, not him. He had given the man the photographs, and paid reluctantly when the sculpture was delivered, because he had hoped for more. The details were right: the cut of the nose, the thin lips, the braid-edged suit, the pearls around the neck, but María was much more beautiful than that, or so it had seemed to Amilcar at first, until he stopped noticing the difference. Over the years, the statue and his memory of her became one and the same.

He came to see her every morning, and every evening.

There was no need to talk; María could always read his mind. Amilcar did everything as he thought she would have wanted, had she been with him. It cost him a lot of money to keep a fancy cook here, but he ate the kind of food she liked. He had forced himself to read every magazine she read, because his eyes were her eyes. *She* read them through him.

The news from London was good. Round-the-clock surveillance was in place; it would take time, but they wouldn't fail now. He had rushed things at first, in the joy of finding his grandson in *Hola!* The boy was a replica of Diego. Amilcar had noticed him instantly, as he had recognized the gringa. Whatever she called herself, whatever she did to her hair, it had to be her. She couldn't change her eyes.

María wouldn't have rushed, even to get her family back. She wouldn't have moved until everything was ready, until every action had been planned, and Amilcar had learned his lesson. *Her* lesson. There was no point in employing amateurs, small fry, as there was no point in getting the boy alone. The bungled kidnapping attempt had shown him that he had to use people who knew what they were doing, even if it cost a lot. The Colombians wanted ten million dollars plus expenses to deliver Melanie and the boy to him, but it would be money well spent. This boy was too precious for him to risk any mistakes, and he was very young; he needed his mother still. Then Amilcar would have a family around him again. He wanted that more than anything in the world.

They would like it here.

After a while.

Fortune's Child
William Gill

She had everything. She wanted more . . .

Marcus Ackerman is a gold-digger. Fabulously rich and powerful from prospecting in the mines of Chile, he cannot control the one love of his life – his daughter, Leonora. Creative, insecure, and all passion, Leonora adores her father. But nothing, not even his threats, can get in the way of her need to paint.

At art college in London, Leonora meets three men: David, Oliver and Nick. As diverse in character as in their skills, they are bonded by two desires: to succeed as world-class architects, and to win Leonora. For all three it is a question of balancing ambition with love – a combination only one can achieve . . .

'Intelligent, pacy and well written'   *Sunday Times*

'A brilliant storyteller'   Rosie Thomas

ISBN 0 586 21531 X